The Machine Doctor

PRETTY LONDON MODEL GIRLS KNOW WHAT YOU CAN DO WITH YOUR CUSTOMER SERVICE CRITERIA!

Democracy in action, thought the Council: give everyone a free computer. Link them up. Let the lying begin.

Vivien, who works by day as a battery hen, is employed to keep the network free of viruses. But secretly, she collects them. And they aren't happy in their cage.

The most advanced city council in the world meets on-line. Some are wearing no pants. This is Aberdeen. The Stone Age is now.

The Machine Doctor

Peter Burnett

THIRSTY BOOKS

First published 2001
Thirsty Books
an imprint of
Argyll Publishing
Glendaruel
Argyll PA22 3AE
Scotland
www.deliberatelythirsty.com

Acknowledgement is made to the publishers of Peggy
Seeger's *Gonna be an Engineer* for permission to use lyrics
on page 180.

British Library Cataloguing-in-Publication Data.
A catalogue record for this book is available from the
British Library.

ISBN 1 902831 33 0

Cover Photo Colin Kirkpatrick

Origination Cordfall Ltd, Glasgow

Printing Bell & Bain Ltd, Glasgow

Please take action to update your book's antivirus software by using the standard Superdoc update. Further variants of new viruses may arise so please be vigilant as this book may already be infected.

HOW IT WORKS

Machine rattles:

Worn universal joints
Worn suspension component brushes
Worn or damaged rubber mountings
Worn suspension struts.

It could be any one or all of them.

The road is one foot beneath the body of the car, the machine is a mine of information timed, measured and displayed, settled in a cradle between two rubber tyres. What is ascertainable of the tarmac is felt upwards through attachment points and coil springs, all correctly matched. Concentrated metal dabbles only inches below the driver's foot so that lumps in the road are meditations to the car, it gives her that sense that she's engrossed in the suspension, she feels that her body weight is being fed abstract through the chassis.

Heavy thinking. The engine rocks, held steady at the spring centre of the vehicle, now connected to the driver via cables and plugs, switches, sensors and short-obstat connections. The motor depends on a collection of accelerated hoses and pipes to feed in close study, every fluid that keeps it working at this imageless pitch. The blank iron springs that hold the engine in place achieve a compensation that allows the machine block to be truly weightless.

The slope of the motorway is compensated for and the suggestion of an elbow impels a steering-bracket to shift, and the corner begins. The engine clasps the frame of the car and runs without the fundamental notion of where it's going, sure that it must follow its natural tendency, forward and unidead.

Pally would like to get home before 2am and presses her foot down to the floor. Her car speeds down the motorway in a flicker but she is log-watching on an in-car laptop which shows the progress of the Council's Litter Collection page. The definition of log-watching: *observing remote computer users default their way through your home-pages in real time.* Pally notes that most of the current traffic on the Network is from American universities, and this proves to her once more, the eternal appeal of Connected Technology. That students in Seattle would want to surf through the Litter Collection Programme of the Aberdeen City Council in Scotland, is a rare sign of world progress.

On a steep turn, automatic timing control of the car is subconscious and Pally's course is again generated by the motion of a forearm. A weight in the BMW's axle pivots against the tension of several small springs and everything moves in one successive turn relative to the drive-cam, but still the engine knows nothing, as if it were a brain in a jar. Spontaneous and small motion, the impression of a turn in the direction of the roadway creates another tendency, allowing fuel injection systems to squirt gently. Pally fumes at the head of the machine and puts her foot down further. An engine speed governor moves outward on a centrifugal pivot, contacts a metal blade on the outer part of the axle and allows her to take the corner perfectly. The engine has *a priori* knowledge of both foot and road as neither foot nor road have any knowledge of each other. The motor is the cognate part of the car, the mathematical logic of the vehicle's motion, its components are put away in thought and form a block inside the vehicle, a conclusive and confirming source of power.

Clear the mind. Fitted by retaining clips and hand mounting brackets, the motor block of this BMW is wired to the shell of the car by lugs and connector plugs. The engine dances in its cradle with all the intuition normal to such a mechanism . . . and yet, remove the leads, the nuts and mounting rubbers, and you are able, with the aid of a small crane, to swing the motor out of the chassis that carries it. The engine is blind, it is only technological subtlety and well-grounded dynamics which keep it spinning like a boulder in its own direction. It's maths and men which maintain the sequential process that makes this vehicle run so well, it's a circular argument feet above the surface of the road.

Downhill towards Aberdeen tonight, seven cooler line connections, more acceleration is demanded and the injector pump draws a timed quantity of gas to be served to each of the six cylinders. Air cleaned fuel pops through a shining casket and is jetted into the burning heart of the engine which is sacked again for motion around a slow corner on the motorway. While poorer metal would warp at this level, nothing is lost along the line of the BMW. The motor transmits feeling, clarifying the surface of the road for Pally and holding a translatable line as the instruction from her elbow is amplified, so that the motion of a corner is made simple, as if one contact were enough to account for the wide turn in the roadway. The desired effect: *comfort and security*. The motor understands through steel-metal telepathy, the contact between the road and the driver.

The driver's transmission: warm engine air crosses Pally's foot as wind is normalised into heat by the critical power of the fan belt. The vehicle flashes past the grass verge, reading a faster speed on the straight. With the correct feed to the engine the car conforms to the shape of the road, but still there is this rattle:

Worn universal joints?
Worn suspension component brushes?
Worn or damaged rubber mountings?
Worn suspension struts?

Even at eighty miles an hour, misconstrued noises arise from the motor, but they are nothing, all engine talk is the same to people's ears.

Pally's leg relaxes, she is listening to music. She makes contact with the car through her thin shoe and receives an unusual answer from below, a buzz as the circuit peaks and she moves faster still. She has an eye ahead, looking out for police cars, there is a four-mile stretch of empty roadway and Pally must be in the city soon, preferably before she falls asleep. Aberdeen appears in the night ahead, and she puts down the unexplained noises from the motor to her own excess at the wheel. Tiny pipes feed oil to the glossed steel of the engine block, and Pally squeezes the pedal again, opening the motor out and letting it go. She presses a button to increase the volume on the radio and the road straightens out – a stretch of Scottish motorway distorted in the night to a yellow strip like an airport runway, a plain and simple track downwards in the light, where air speed can be raised.

If this pedal fails, it may be due to an obstruction in the fuel pipeline.

It is also possible that the electrical pump wiring is defective.

As it goes, anything that interacts with this logical ton of energy now floating at close to zero gravity could cause one fault or another, and Pally is driving with one hand only. Her other hand thinks it finds something in her hair, or it might scratch her head. Pally has an unalterable affection for her hair, which she varies in the car mirror, her finger turns harder into her scalp as the stress meter rises.

The car deciphers a crack in the road but pretends that it isn't there. There is a strain however, a blunder around the circulation of the fuel, a misapplication of the final power. When this engine breaks there will be no warning, and so it is in BMWs the world over that the motors don't collapse in one motion but instead fail in an interactive chain. A loose fork or a damaged seal misrenders the car's energy and the cylinder block pounds, making a noise like cloth hammers interacting with the fine steel components. The black eyes and determined expression of Pally respond with disgust as the car gives way and begins to drag as if its made of brick, and not of titan metals.

Damn it.

Pally watches the dark blue motor hull of the bonnet slump and she swears as the weight of the engine returns to its cradle. The motor talks in thumps, the engine wrenches onwards and bangs like a machine gun until it responds no more and is temporarily dead.

Damn it.

Pally has both hands on the steering wheel and the car is pulling in to the side of the road with an unaccountable grinding and buzzing. Fat tyres roll and crunch on the roadway and the on-board computer fails on instinctive diagnosis until the engine block rests entirely upon its springs. Next, a warning light buzzes and a second transmitter on the dash flashes yellow to indicate that all is not well and that somebody must be called, a moment of panic like a rupture and the machine is seized and gulps like a throat. The brake discs are tightly in place and the vehicle sticks its nose dead into the road and stops.

Pally turns the key and kicks the pedals, but the engine comes to nothing, responds with nothing, and the car seems finished. She lowers the volume of the radio and looks ahead, the motorway is empty, one mile below her are the plain lights of the city of Aberdeen. The car engine has closed and the axles take the weight of the corpse, and turning the ignition key in hope of resuscitation Pally feels the motor fail once more and die. With the BMW dead, she feels the silence drop, all she can hear is the stinging noise of broken pressure escaping from underneath the body of the car. In the rear view is an empty motorway, lit faint by her own red tail-lights, it makes her feel confined.

Just gone five minutes past 1am and you're listening to Night Sounds with me Nicki Forbes.

The city of Aberdeen forms an extrovert plain of light, where rows of lamps carve out roads and the occasional tower. From the dark hill the city looks to Pally like an old computer circuit, an image distorted by a cloud along the horizon to the north. Communication lights blink but the city is dormant and responsive of nothing but its own cold interchange. Pally steps out and closes the door, leaving herself on an empty roadway. She folds her arms over her summer dress and shivers. A cold Scottish night, so close to Aberdeen but far enough to see at least a half of the city in one single view.

This is Councillor Cruden.

Pally's telephone call is directed towards the aerial tower at

Midstocket, two miles north over the sedate electric demeanour of Lower Aberdeen.

This is Councillor Pally Cruden. Her accent may have been Doric at one time, but now it is a Croissant-Scots, a cultural talk imported for policy people to speak with. Pally Cruden and a broken automobile, caught in that stupid summer dress on the Aberdeen Road. The telephone call is completed and she hears a distorted voice say,

Welcome to the Aberdeen City Council.

Pally stares towards the transmitter and holds her mobile phone closer to her ear. Unshaded from the yellow motorway light, Pally's dead car gives no indication that one tiny expository clip or pipe has failed, that some unnoticeable prominence in the smoothness has given rise to the end of the ride.

Helpdesk, says a human voice, a girl from the call centre.

Thank God, says Pally, I'm on the Aberdeen Road and I've broken down. I need someone to come and pick me up. I'm only about a mile out of town.

The call centre voice gives Pally the open and shut details – there's no one available at present and can she hold? I'm taking another call thank you.

Another call? asks Pally. OK I'll hold.

Thank you very much, says the call centre girl and her compressed voice vanishes and is replaced by an irritation of classical music, piped at high volume.

The motorway is crystal clear now, as flat and unsuspecting as the day it was built, if it ever was built. Pally picks at the camber with her heel and listens to the Vivaldi the call centre supplies. This road was designed so that a car like hers could motor from Aberdeen to London unhindered, so that business and communication could continue with devotion and urgency and only ever have to stop for petrol. Pally stares down the hill, Aberdeen looks like one giant switchboard and she wishes she were in there, slotted into bed. The music stops and Pally speaks into her telephone.

Is there anybody that can come out and get my car just now?

she asks, I don't know what's the matter with it.

Please hold, says the call centre girl, we are taking other calls at present and your call has been placed in a queue.

Great.

We know that you are waiting to speak to us and we recognise that your call is important. You will be connected with one of our technical service advisors at the first possible opportunity. Thank you for your patience.

Hello?

Pally speaks in the pause before the concession of the waiting tone returns, followed by the tattling of electronic noise while computers file her call.

What is it with this call centre?

The BMW discloses nothing but breakdown, the unburdening of its passenger in the darkness, close enough to home to suggest to Pally that the normally faultless motor is developing a pronounced sense of humour.

There is a click on the phone and a strip of static returns to Pally's ear before the music starts again. The mood of the city is acid, as if water is hitting off the yellow lamps in the distance and reacting brightly. Pally's broken chrome blue BMW is still shooting tiny clicks from the engine, proving a fault in or around the combustion chambers, a failure even in the smooth passage of the motorway. Over the city, mental calculation, Pally looks ahead and wonders, how long must I stand here? Uncorrupted and vacant lights in Aberdeen bring to mind empty rooms and empty streets.

Thank you for your patience at this busy time, says the call centre voice from Aberdeen.

Thanks, says Pally before the monophonic tone appears again.

A sigh becomes a shiver. In perusal of the city skyline, Pally brushes her arms which are now cold. A short summer dress, smart in November, it doesn't feel so smart now. Vivaldi cuts in again with the call centre girl speaking over it.

Hi! she says, I've managed to track you down Councillor so we know which car you're in. I'm looking for a fault right now.

I'm only a mile from the city, says Pally. I'm in my car and it's completely broken down!

I know, says the call centre girl, I'm using the new interface and I can diagnose the engine from here. Watch what else I can do.

The car lights flash and the wipers begin, and Pally steps back. The sound of Vivaldi is louder in her ear as the yellow indicator lights on the wing of the car join the night time display. The BMW rests beside Pally like a vicious insect, flashing and shining in the night.

I can also tell you that you need to get petrol soon, says the call centre girl. It's really good.

Sure, says Pally, and then the car horn starts to go.

I've got you on the satellite, says the call centre girl, I'm making a quick scan of the engine. It might be something simple, you never know.

Shut it up! says Pally, she barks into her mobile phone, her motor car is a travesty of light and sound and she presses the mobile phone harder into the side of her head and feels for the hands-free unit in her bag.

Just shut it up!

Just a moment, says the call centre girl. The horn and the lights stop and the car returns to its deadened self. Pally breathes and plugs in the hands-free unit of her phone, even the Vivaldi has now stopped.

It could be one of many things, says the call centre girl, but the computer is showing me that it's fuel injection. We've only got limited diagnosis of this vehicle and unfortunately I can't work the hand brake from here. A shame really.

You what? says Pally. Just send a taxi. I'm about a mile from the Bridge of Dee, south.

I know where you are, says the call centre girl. I can see you on my computer. I can also access the camera in your car and tell you that you're wearing your red dress tonight. How about that?

Pally looks over the dark glazed body her BMW and listens closely as if in doubt.

Just a taxi, she says.

I'm connected, says the call centre girl. I'm just reading the engine now. I'll check it for viruses.

Viruses? asks Pally, looking at the car with slight disgust, but the call centre girl sounds calm about the whole affair.

Oh yes, she says. I think your car is infected.

Pally accepts the sophistication of these arrangements with ease, hugs herself and watches to see if the car will react. If the knowledge is there to attach these BMWs to the computer mainframe of the town then why not do it? Ideas like this are surely only a matter of cross-discipline, and nothing more. Car with modem equals computer access by all in the know, and the more machines that are linked in this world then the better our communications will be. I must be patient, thinks Pally, this is a labour saving device despite the call centre girl's bad attitude.

Can I try something? asks voice on the line.

I guess.

Could you plug in your laptop for me? You seem to have switched it off. You know that it's never safe to turn off your computer.

Really?

Pally looks over the city almost blank of brainwork. Late in the night and most of the town are teeth-grinding their way through their eight hours sleep, heads pushed into pillows, dreams disturbed by the pending of the morning. Aberdeen shines in the same cold manner, ambient at its own colossal slow engine temperature. For all the city's cultivation, Councillor Cruden feels that Aberdeen does not run half as smoothly as it should . . . just like her car.

Use the connection on the dashboard, says the call centre girl, it's under the cigarette lighter. We can do a diagnostic together.

The music of Vivaldi sounds again, Pally curses and steps back towards the BMW. Computer people are beyond me, she thinks. They stay up all night, solving problems, so that in the end they become as exemplary in their wakefulness as the machines themselves. Computer people stay up all night because so do computers. The super-mental cultivation of the world, or in this case, the city of

Aberdeen, can continue at a more advanced pace in the darkness, the advanced pace of the computer expert.

Down the road towards the city there's no sign of any traffic, the lights in the centre of the motorway are like digits on an aerial relay.

Pally opens the door of her car and gets inside. It's warm in the cabin and the dials develop a certain mystery. The music stops and Pally notices that the digital camera is switched on. The call centre girl must be watching her and this makes her strangely shy.

You'll need to plug the phone into the computer, says the voice. You know how to do it?

Yes, says Pally.

What ever you do, says the call centre girl, don't press any of the vehicle's pedals.

Pally pushes a lead inexpertly into the side of her laptop computer. The computer makes an elaborate whistle and begins the slipshod construction of its routines and summary business. Pally finds a second lead and attaches it to her car modem . . . and there follows an instant logorrhoea on the screen which tells her its OK, before the famous WAITING signal arrives. Pally looks down the road for any sign of help, but nothing comes from Aberdeen. A long-winded and protracted stretch of words scroll upon the screen before she sees the list of options.

Engine will not start
Engine stalls
Engine idles badly
Engine misfires
Engine lacks power
Engine vibration
High fuel consumption
Other

Pally selects *Engine will not start*, but doubts her choice. She lacks mechanical finish but continues the game and changes her mind to opt for *Other*.

Poor idling
No fuel delivery
Tick or knock
Judder
Drag or spin
Heavy steering
Lost motion
Wander
Wheel wobble
Other

The circumlocutional pursuit of fruitless information.

A window appears on the screen of the lap-top, in the window is the video image of a girl sitting at a shabby desk in the call centre, smoking. The girl's feet are on the desk and the clouds of tobacco smoke are drifting to the camera and circulating at the tips of her old trainers. Pally can't quite make out her face, which seems too far away for focus.

Other suffices again, and a further rambling and diffusive medley of faults appear on the computer next to her. Pally browses the list but chooses to ignore its prompting, she looks at the screen but the call centre girl shrugs her shoulders, as if she hasn't a clue as to how her human guinea pig should proceed.

Advanced:
Carburettor incorrectly adjusted?
Faulty or maladjusted choke unit?
Tank vent system blocked?
Air leaks on suction side of pump?
Other

A vehicle is approaching from behind, so Pally snaps closed her bag, checks her lips in the rear view mirror, and selects *other* again, allowing a fourth list of developmental questions to appear, including, *Would you like to see the engine?*

The vehicle from behind is getting closer, its headlights expanding on the road until its form is definitely recognisable as that of a small van, moving slowly. The flux of words and questions continues unabated on the computer screen and looking down the menu Pally wonders if she knows how to switch it off, or if it will stop at all.

A decision. Pally unplugs her phone and unpowers the computer, and there she climbs from the City BMW and leaves it redundant until someone can approach it with the care required to repair it properly. Pally waves down the van, and when the driver stops, she walks briskly down the motorway towards it.

A button on her key ring secures the car with a midnight BLIP loud enough to sound across the nearby field. Her City Council operated BMW is sealed now and stuck to the hard face of the road, mint in the darkness and ready for the recovery vehicle.

Pally locks the car, the call centre girl unlocks it.

BLIP, and Pally touches her key-ring again, the car locks and the next second it unlocks by itself.

BLIP it locks and CLICK it unlocks. BLIP it LOCKS but CLICK it UNLOCKS.

CLICK wins out and Pally walks stickily away towards the modest medium of the van. The lights begin to flash again and the call centre girl has control of the stereo which now plays Vivaldi at an appalling volume in the night. Again, this foul treatment of her personal automobile makes Pally feel weak, the helplessness would make her cry if she wasn't so damn strong about these things.

Lastly it's the wipers. The lights are flashing inside and out the car and Vivaldi fills the night with his tin-eared orchestral work, while as a final touch, the boot springs open, gently rising at the back end of the vehicle.

Pally climbs into the waiting van, thankful at least that she's been saved.

VIVIEN

The girl at the door has a boyish look and Pally asks her inside.

Have you come to install my computers? asks Pally and nodding to the floor, the girl steps past her.

Yea I'm from the Helpless Desk, says the girl, her hands inside her jacket.

Helpless? asks Pally.

It's a call centre joke, says the girl.

Pally's smile is penetrating, one of many affectations that are natural to her. Vivien pulls her hands out of her pockets and shows that they are dotted with grease.

Can I wash my hands first? My dad gave me a lift and his car broke down.

Of course, says Pally, and the two walk through to the back of the house. The warm back room in Pally's newly-purchased house in Blenheim Place, carpet soft and decorated in her own good taste. Rug meets bookcase at an impasse on the floor and the dull-thinking colours of the wall are tempered with screen-printed flowers and cats. Vivien with her shoulder length hair in danger of obscuring her face is the only item that could spoil the image at this time.

Tea or coffee? asks Pally.

Sink, says Vivien.

She turns the tap for fresh hot water to the basin, the water spins and a flush of soap bubbles emerge from the bottom, she looks out of the window and her thoughts arrange in the back garden. The garden is a scruffy-looking spread of weed occupied with the most sullied browns of November, thin and depleted bushes create side interest.

Pally is still showing that smile, it looks like facial surgery. She clears her throat, she's so polite.

I'm looking forward to getting this computer working, she says. They said you'd put the virus software on. I wouldn't know how.

We've got a new virus just found this week, says Vivien, a baddie.

Well I hope I don't have it.

You won't, says Vivien and she stares into Pally's back garden.

The garden is a mess. Dried stipes like old nettles have gathered near the back door, stalks of weed rise further down where they furnish a damp patch of ground. Staring straight ahead Vivien speaks as if infected by her own variety of mental microbe.

We've met before, she says, do you remember?

Pally shakes her head.

I'm sorry dear, I don't remember.

Vivien chores her hands in the white water and Pally follows her stare outside where a waste of wrinkled herbs lean towards the wall like they're trying to escape.

You should plant something there, Vivien says. Try planting heather, that's the stuff, it's like a mathematical plant . You get two or maybe three plants rigged to miles of earth and rock.

Just two or three plants on the one hill?

Yea, all you need is maths, says Vivien. That's how it fills up space, by plumbing itself, then it like expands.

Well I never knew that, says Pally.

Vivien takes her hands out of the water where Pally waits with a kitchen towel.

That garden really is a mess, says Vivien.

They both look out of the kitchen window, visitors on an alien planet. The land is choked with long weeds, chaos rises in heaps and spills out, sheaves of half-dead plants hoard every cold patch and push through between dead bushes. Instead of the snaffle of headstalled weed and rough stalks, Pally wishes she could see a lawn.

Typo: a law. Or the maths of heather, an idea which sees the natural world laid out like a treasure for her own rough but cultivated private hillside in the city.

Heather wouldn't cost that much, says Vivien, and you needn't go mental. You could get a man in.

Yeah I guess so.

Vivien flicks back her hair, her eyes shine a second before it all falls back in front of her face again.

Pally imagines the heather flowing up to the back wall of her yard, gripping the earth like a net and suggesting a bottomless world beneath, running over the ground and scratching the back door like a cat wanting inside. Heather, an all sufficing plant blossoming, as Vivien says, like a ripe mathematical model.

Pally remembers she has forgotten to buy a kettle. She looks in the garden and she looks around the kitchen, both are a reminder that there's an epidemic of things to do in the new house. Would there be any logic in hiring a team of men to do it all? House and garden in one big job? Paper bedroom and assemble bed, fit cornices in bedroom number one and also in bedroom number two? Paint the hall while the Council complete the wiring of experimental computer home-aids downstairs. Send the team out to buy tasteful ornaments so that Pally can spend more time on the internet, familiarising herself with the policy on offer there. The sight of the mess in her back garden brings the tasks in hand to a maximum, meaning that the house is now an endless consumer of her time, abundant in its requirements and the biggest project of her days. Will the time ever come when Pally can rest in her comfortable chair and let the new house work around her? There is an endless supply of clothes in the upstairs cupboards, and she makes a note to sort them first.

A gurgle in the drain outside when the water goes down, a scudding noise, and nothing but foam remains within the tub. Pally's attention is on the old cooker, which like the garden, needs replacing. The cooker is a deficient unit, too profuse with its heat, too incompetent, too iron and too old-fashioned in general. A pan of water is about to boil.

Vivien is staring at the weeds outside, they grow madly like a child's scribble.

I think I'll do it in the Spring says Pally, I guess that's the right time. Would you mind if I heated up some water on the stove?

No it's OK says Vivien, and hangs up the towel on a peg. She steps from the kitchen into the back room which Pally has cultivated with cushions and made the comfortable centre of her home. The full tide of interior decoration has been poured into this small space, but the ultimate effect is of something far from vital.

The computers are there if you want to start, says Pally, and she points to the half opened boxes and her new laptop which is folded neatly on the floor.

Vivien's view however is still clamped to the back garden, she is once again reducing what she sees there to some mathematical edict she can work with.

You should probably do the laptop first, says Pally.

Thanks, says Vivien, she unfolds a pocket-knife which tears into the cardboard.

Pally turns her attention to the old stove, the pan of water is overfilled and there's an exorbitance of bubbles heading upward for the light. For a split second she is overwrought in patterns, the water is at bursting point and she thinks she might be seeing within, there are tools for everything in the pan and calculations in the steam. There's a moment of comprehension for Pally in the rise of the bubbles, and she watches the water and relaxes, her brains feeling like so much warmed-over cabbage. Vivien takes seriously the gutting of the cardboard box and the removing of the new computer while Pally is pleased that progress is being made.

The thought stops there. Pally tears at a packet of biscuits while Vivien looks inside another box and digs her knife into the polystyrene. Pally comes forward with the biscuits on a plate and places them on the table, while Vivien picks up the new Council laptop.

Is this your computer? asks Vivien. It's nice.

Can't have too much of a good thing says Pally, now in her favourite chair.

Yea well I agree, says Vivien, I built this one.

You built that?

Vivien stands with both hands on the case of Pally's corporation laptop, as if it were a skull she were feeling for lumps.

I mean, she says, I put the components up. I did a lot of the Council machines, and I did this one, that's my seal with the face on it. The computer is breach-proof, you can hit it with a hammer and you could bury it underground for a year and it would still work. Not that you'll need to.

I think it's a little blocked up.

I doubt it, says Vivien. The computer'd tell one of us in the call centre if it's having problems with you.

Oh.

A smile from Vivien. I put the chips in it and the memory too, she says, this is one of the first laptops on the Council Network and it's rock solid. There'll probably never be anything like it again.

Pally caught short, young Vivien, shiftless and punky, twirling her hair around her finger, pretending to find something interesting on her trouser leg.

I helped build the clock for the computers too, she says.

The clock? asks Pally.

Square wave oscillator.

Oh.

Vivien sits down with the laptop and hooks a leg over the arm of her chair. Most of the world is as slow to catch on as Councillor Cruden here. That is, people are slow in a fundamental manner, handicapped by a pin-prick memory which allows only one dot of light to the brain per thought and never allows the connected picture to appear. Sad really, because the picture is always connected and there's no such thing as one component by itself. But that's people – one dot of light and the mind flicks the projector handle, and the next slide comes into place. They can't manage it any other way.

I've built all sorts of things says Vivien. When I was at University, we made traffic lights for the city centre that let a driver go from one end of King Street to the other without having to stop.

Surely not? says Pally standing up. She is distracted by a pink flourish of plant design on the wall above Vivien's head. *A good place for a ledge with a hanging plant coming down,* she thinks, *clear from the radiator too.* Pally's mind now in detailed operation.

It sounds interesting, says Pally from the kitchen door and she trails off to the stove to see how her boiling water is doing. She looks at Vivien a moment longer, attention still poised on her face. Why hasn't the girl started working on the computers yet? Why is she sitting around with her legs all over the furniture? All the configurations of the moment unravel and Pally focuses on the base of the boiling water from where the violent bubbles make their free course for the surface. The immediate constituents of the kitchen are associated in Pally's mind, and each stable and solid wooden panel has a role to play, just like the reliable bolts and screws holding them together. High level law – a solid and self-sensitive array of device and consequence, something which intertwines with a great happiness, to yield the total outcome of her living area, quite cleverly and quite simply.

Outside, the back garden is a rugged failure, the weeds are dying but have had a busy year chomping at the earth. Brown stems halt at weak spots and where there is a crack available, an amassment of bland ferns rise up in a stockpile . . . and Pally is almost hypnotised. Her over-conditioned hair descends to her cheeks and she frowns into the living room as gently as she can.

Why isn't this girl doing any work?

The computers are there, she suggests and Vivien nods.

Yea I'll do it in a second.

I need that laptop, says Pally. I've minutes to copy about the Aberdeen Domestic Computer Network.

Yea, says Vivien it won't take me long.

Vivien pulls a power cable like a long worm from the cardboard and finds somewhere to plug it in, Pally looks over the construction process with great attention but Vivien doesn't seem to be that motivated.

Connectivity, thinks Pally. The helpdesk send a fed-up looking girl who plugs you into the mainframe of the world. People in the world have dreams, and what could be more consistent with these dreams, than the connectivity of their plans? Somewhere in the journalistic portion of her mind, Pally is sure that this is the way that it's all going to come together. Connections she believes will help cultivate ambitions and lead people to their ultimate fruition, just as Connectivity will encourage more communities to meet and to do business. Pally feels impatient, excited that with Vivien's hour-labour, she is going to make the mess of wires in that box into her own Home Terminal. Soon, the computer and combined digital tv platform will piggyback the world in flash-banners direct to the centre of her household, and maybe when that happens, Pally will feel human again.

Connectivity – this is what she has waited for, and now the A has found the B and her computer system is nearly set up, she is keener than ever to see the word in action.

CARROTS

Vivien has thought about Machine / Man relations from day one. Her father cared more for the garden than he did for the house, but somehow he planted hope in Vivien's mind that the human essential would one day be reduced by machine given sexual equality . . . and all her life Vivien has felt the same fascination for labour saving devices.

Vivien spent one summer designing domestic machines, robots well adapted to every household chore that she could think of. The human house, Vivien discovered, is like a climbing frame, so her task was to show how an independent machine could access a home and do the jobs within it.

Vivien recalls her Dad, quiet in the savoured air of holiday time, and he approves of the fact she has a diversion. Vivien can remember designing an entire series of robots and showing them to him.

I think we'd be better with that one, he says, because of the extra arm behind. It could hold your hand or even a spare cloth.

More drawing and a new idea, a further method of tackling the stairs.

This one has two arms to pull it along in the garden or help it get to the first floor. And these wheels here will lock to stop it slipping.

What happens if it comes in from the garden and then has to clean the living room? asks Dad. It'll probably leave a muddy mess inside the house. Vivien's Dad always has good questions for her.

Back to the notepad and Vivien acknowledges that there is no way to fit the robot with a self-cleaning unit, and so she starts again with a re-evolved basic figure.

This one – you get three small robots, one for each level of the house and another for the garden. They arrive in colour matched boxes, delivered from the shop by a van. Or if that's too many robots for you, how about these discreet units which pop in and out around the house, robots that do the tasks particular to their own room. Garden Robot: get weeds. Kitchen Robot: make toast.

Will it drop the dishes?

No never. It picks up the dishes and takes them through to the living room. The robot can see where everything is on the table so it can lay each place methodically. After the meal it takes the dirties through to a dishwasher.

I see. How does everything get out of the dishwasher and into the cupboard?

The dishes could stay in the dishwasher.

The cupboard would be more hygienic.

The robot could lift the dishes out in the night then, says Vivien, and it have breakfast ready for when you got up. You'd just need to put bread and coffee in its body when it's empty.

Could it make porridge? asks her Dad.

This is quite a thought for Vivien. She contemplates the sticky interior heart of hot oats, the absorbent blend and the steel robot. Vivien imagines the porridge sliding out on to the plate and the tiny chute returning to the body of the machine.

Porridge! Thank you robot!

You put in oats and eggs and tea, everything for breakfast, and the machine can have them ready for you at the exact time in the morning.

The great satisfaction of designing robots, thinks Vivien, *is that for each problem solved, twice as many are introduced. One solution rendered workable, means that another two are likely created.*

Like all computers, domestic robots are only glorified clocks, and this makes their design easy for Vivien. Casserole at the same time each month means that the robot can serve it exactly to your needs. The meal is programmed on the cycle called casserole.auto-exec, meaning like with Daddy, you can't be a minute late.

And this wonderful idea, that if Vivien and her Dad weren't there then the robots would carry on serving the home, that the machines would keep on making breakfast and dishing it up, that they would continue their cultivation in the garden and their servicing of the empty house.

In the future you will drive down the street and all the people will be on holiday, the robots will be in the living rooms and the gardens, working with method, day and night.

Robots – this one is programmed to know everything about you and act accordingly. You like bran in the mornings. You have an orange before you go to bed. And so the instruments know all this, and your life can carry on as if you are not there.

OK DADDY IT'S TIME FOR DINNER!

Introducing **ROBUTLER**, the very first home robot that's cook, watchdog, cleaner and advisor all in one. **ROBUTLER** can talk to you, can listen to you, and before long will be one of the family.

He washes the floor at 5 am and then returns to his cavity to recharge. Once recharged, **ROBUTLER** cleans and loads his Breakfast Body and cooks the family breakfast!

Inside the Breakfast Body of **ROBUTLER** are coffee and tea making facilities. He can grill sausages in his oven and scramble eggs in his belly. He can even serve each member of the family something completely different, whatever they've asked for the night before!

And his traditional Scots Porridge is the best you'll ever taste!

You can set **ROBUTLER** to weed the garden or read the news to you. Or **ROBUTLER** can bring you tools while you do a job yourself. With his strong articulator arms, **ROBUTLER** (and soon, **ROMAID** also!) can even serve drinks and open doors.

ROBUTLER will always be able to do more . . . and more! He reduces the energy consumption of your home, controls the electrical appliances, helps the kids with their maths, and guards your valuables with his motion, smoke and heat sensors.

So he'll never let you run out of ways to use him!

Robutler and Romaid . . . and Vivien's cutest invention of them all, The Chamber Bots. Now that would get her up there with Logie Baird.

Where could the plans be?

Not that it matters. Vivien is glad that she even remembered them. All day in the summer, with the felt pens, refining the oblique and difficult design of her domestic robots, she must have had hundreds of them by the end, four or five notebooks of pivoting, axle barring, rolling, crawling, large and tiny metal plunk and plop, variations of many shining bevel-geared robots, with one winner from them ready for the production line. One of the robots, The Wamble, had a washing machine in its body, and Dad said that it should have been called The Silicon Valet. Dad put the plan for The Wamble under his deck-chair and took Vivien to the kitchen where they opened the back of the washing machine together. When Vivien saw the block of concrete that lay inside the washing machine, it was like a revelation to her, and although The Wamble was scrapped on the basis that it would circulate too madly and shake to bits the eggs in its Breakfast Body, a long affair began at that time between Vivien and the washing machine, an item of which she never tires.

How many washing machines are there in Aberdeen?

Vivien gets the feeling she'd like to see them all. One model repeated to the end, it's a kind of robot in its way. The thickest robot of them all. No personality the washing machine but what a triumph! What a mental triumph.

She looks to see if Pally has a washing machine, and notices she is right next to it. Like the other fittings the washing machine is not yet connected, a white cube with its tongue sticking out and a hose trailing to the back door. Pally is standing near, wringing her hands, she's looking at the washing machine too, Vivien has the uncanny feeling that the Councillor is going to ask her to plumb it once she's done with the computers.

The most fortunate memory, Vivien's father's hands. The hands are an image central to infancy, they challenge everything nearby and form an emotion requiring immediate adult attention. He's holding up her drawings and he's looking at her homework, he's digging in the garden and he's chopping at the sink, his hands are more crucial to his role in the world than anything else that concerns Vivien.

Home was in Bieldside, on the hill above the North Deeside Road. Situation perception places their house exactly half way up the hill, as seen from a distance, with other detached houses, rising upwards from the River Dee. The house was bathed in light from the Dee Valley and sat among tall bushes in a pretentious little cove. It is the kind of house with too many plants in the rooms, and too much furniture in the garden.

Vivien and her Dad live on the hill with the other detached houses on their suburban estate, the small rows of homes with a village road turning through the trees to the top, the exact variety of back road ubiquitous to human thought. Home is a fabric of analogies and perceptions, the house and her father, her ideas when she was growing up. Her father's hands are active symbols of something lost, and Vivien feels the combined pressure of several unattached memories which have been suppressed since the last time her mind went lax like this.

Her father approaching, his fat head smiling, he drops a ball and kicks it from their front garden, the ball flies over the hedge and into the road where it bounces down toward the bottom of the next garden. The ball ends up in the nettles that grow in an overblown clump at their neighbour's wall.

Her father was a gardener too. He wasn't the psychologically accurate type of gardener which tends to work in Aberdeen, those bent on their idealised parsley and parsnip microworlds, but rather he was an actual living gardener who wanted to grow not for the show of it, but simply for the pleasure of consuming something that he had taken from the ground. Her father, Vivien is sure, disliked flowers, but may have grown them if he had considered them edible.

Which Vivien strangely did?

A snag in Vivien's thoughts create the strong sense that she liked to eat daffodils when she was young, and that this occurred not once, but many times. The jolt of activation creates a taste on the node of Vivien's tongue and she smiles at the items concerned. A smile emerges in response to the situation faced. That's right. The picture has more than a modicum of plausibility. *I used to eat daffodils. What could they have tasted like? What did Dad say when he saw me chewing up the yellow flower heads, striking the eye of the bud and pulling it apart, chewing it in my mouth?* Vivien's thoughts lose resolution and silence returns. Will kids eat anything? There is silence during the crystal pick up of these thoughts.

Dad speaks while he is correcting her maths homework and he tells you a story. The perception of the situation is altered by his talk, and as always Dad tells you about the garden while he leafs through the sums.

I'll tell you about those carrots Vivien. After tea, you go out and pick twenty of them for me if they're big . . . or twenty five if they're not. Take them from the second row and pull the stalks off and then we'll clean them. Make sure the stalks go in the compost and we'll take the carrots up to Grandma and tell her that we grew them both together. Do you like carrot soup?

Don't know.

Ask your Grandma to make some carrot soup. Tell her to freeze some of the soup for me as well. Will you do that?

OK then.

Good. Now. Do you know how long it takes for a carrot to grow?

It depends.

That's the answer!

It depends?

Yes it depends on different things . . .

Vivien's father's garden at Bieldside is a range of many textures, heights and depths. When Vivien was young the garden looked longer than it turned out to be when she grew up, but on any scale, the ground has always followed the same patterns as one plant became the next. The most fascinating area of the garden was the fern-like foliage of the carrots that grew in the light under the back wall.

Beside the carrots, Dad is making soil and throwing in sand for the earth to thin it out.

The carrots appreciate some shade too, he says, and that's what the wall's for.

What happens without the sand? she asks.

The carrots get forked and pocked and don't grow straight. Worse, they get all bulbous. If there are stones then the carrots have to grow around them, so they get crooked and that's why they like growing in the sand.

Will they go through the sand?

Yes that's right. Now do you know how to grow them?

No.

What we do is we rake the bed and then put a line of string down the middle. Run a rake along the line and cut a v-shaped furrow for the seed. Imagine your carrots now, in their cloches, spaced in the ground, and there you go. You have to imagine what they're going to be like, then you can sow in your furrow between spring and summer and they'll grow just as you pictured them. They'll grow just like that, between spring and summer.

Is there such a time? Between spring and summer?

Oh yes, thinks Vivien, *there is. A prolonged moment on the cusp when the polar rays are in retreat, when the earth is like a witch's body, radioluminescent for the seed.*

Remember, seeds sown too early won't germinate and seeds sown too late will fatten up and mould. And always put your seeds in thin. Place them singly, mix your seed with sand and plop them in like that. You can do that or you can pinch the seed between your finger and thumb, and drop it in the ground. Either way, put the soil back afterwards and push it with your rake, making it firm. Now pull your rake down low and shuffle along the drill with your toes pointing outward. Like this.

Dad stops to push his palms out so that for a moment on the table, his hands are feet, stepping in a v-shape across the drills.

Never rake across the row, he says, and if it looks like rain after you've planted the seeds, then you've got to cover the soil with mats so that the rain doesn't muck it up. Then, they germinate. Do you know what germination is?

It's when they start to grow.

That's right.

The homework notebook is scribbled with flying animals and robots, Dad ticks the sums and Vivien watches, and then looks back to see what's next.

Next, says Dad, is the thinning. When you get buds of green ferns reaching up from the ground, you've got to take some away, so you wait until the little ferns are about one inch and then you can pull out the smallest ones, and leave the bigger ones. That's called cultivation. You've got to be careful not to break the leaves when you're pulling them because then the carrot fly who's in the neighbour's garden, smells it and comes over. So you've got to bury the ferns you pull up and that way your carrots won't get fly.

Next, he says, you go away and read the paper and when the carrots grow, you can pull them up.

Vivien sees the carrots, the desired size, tender in this mild area of earth, salted in their own bracken, clamped in the patchy back garden where they can be seen from the upstairs windows, observed and even supervised. Dad is pulling the carrots gently upward, putting them down on an open newspaper.

Wait until a dry day, he says, and you get a garden fork and loosen the carrots so you can pull them out by their hair. Then get all the earth from them and look at them to see if they're healthy. Any carrots that have been eaten by worms should be thrown into the compost, and any carrots which are broken by your garden fork should be placed at one side and eaten that day, because damaged carrots rot quickly.

Another area for Vivien to explore – the causes of rot and the many unpleasant and unheard of diseases which abound in the earth. Canker passes through grassland and across the air, all unknown to humans other than by minor observation, aphids and eelworms, which make saposuction from the foliage and stunt the plants . . . serious fungal infections roaming the passages of the earth, causing violet root-rot which attacks everything it meets, turning the healthy orange of our carrots into soft, grey smelly flesh. Soft rot and black rot, bacterials in the inky sunken areas of your garden, the creeping corruption, disease sucked along tubers and planted through the soil, transparent substances that eat your domestic vegetable from the inside, destroying the vitrics of the plant, feeding on what is naturally ours for Sunday lunch. No chemical control of carrot rot is known of at present.

Have you ever seen a wild carrot? asks Dad.

What's that?

Wild carrots are yellow, says Dad, or sometimes white. You do get them, but not so much now we've all got gardens. You don't get wild dogs now either.

Small cylindrical carrots come out of the ground. Stump rooted little cores.

Vivien's favourite part – storing the carrots for winter use.

You can store them outside or inside, says Dad. Outside if you store them right, they can make it through all of the winter and into spring. Inside, you need to keep them a little colder.

Dad has these wooden boxes, tidy little frames that he stacks up in the shed, nobody could tell what the boxes once carried and where they came from, but the boxes have only one use now, the suspended animation of carrots from the garden.

You cut off the top of the carrot and you nip it to the neck. Then you put a dry layer of sand in the box and that's where it sits and goes to sleep.

Vivien and Dad place the carrots in the box evenly, some of them go in nose to tail. More sand is trowelled on, patted down, and another layer is formed.

When the boxes are ready, says Dad, it's dark in the garden although at the front of the house, it's still light in the valley. The carrots are packed, winter is coming and the neighbours are all away at church. We have a bonfire and then come in for something warm inside the house and the carrots go into the shed to hibernate until we want to eat them.

One Friday afternoon, Vivien came home from school with a library book about growing vegetables, and she showed it proudly to her Dad. He did not look impressed.

Vivien, you can't use this book, says Dad.

Why not?

Look at it! It doesn't call the ground 'ground'. It calls it, *growing media.*

Growing media, yes!

Both Dad and Vivien have a laugh.

This is the sort of book the neighbours have, says Dad, and that's why their carrots are all thin and weedy, like their noses.

It is important to know the different nutrient values, populations of micro-flora and the oxygen and water content contained within your own growing media.

Dad reads from the book and says, You can't trust that! And so they put the book away.

From the bedroom window of the house, Vivien watches her Dad at work again. Vivien takes some pH paper to the River Dee (a wash out) while the hardening off in the ground begins. Dad earths up carrots and cases layers of soil and Vivien remembers what he said about her.

Man! he said, *that girl likes her carrots!*

Vivien arranges a small stack of these orange horns, Dad has advised her to treat them gently while he is digging nearby. The carrots settle happily on newspaper and the roots make her think of rabbits and how much they like to dig in to the ground. When the carrots are up, there's a new space of earth in the garden, and the carrots are fresh and breathing, sitting pretty like polite little ladies next door to those vulgar gentlemen, the potatoes.

And Vivien thinks of the carrots nightly as her homework notebook fills, more sums and beside them, even more drawings.

Have you ever tried to grow vegetables?

Pally walks up and places a mug of tea on the small table at the armchair where Vivien is spread at angles.

I've always bought them from the shop.

That's a shame, says Vivien, staring at the wall.

Pally wonders if Vivien is suggesting the back garden be an allotment, as if there's not enough to do without adding amateur agriculture to the list. The fact is, nothing can be done in Pally's house until the computers are connected. No operation can thrive in this world without being backed up with some contribution from the Network, and so Pally clears her throat in an effort to spur the helpdesk girl into activity.

Look at you with those wires and discs! says Pally, I wouldn't know where to begin. Have you got a qualification in it?

I've just got my Dip-Phil, says Vivien. I did Artificial Intelligence specialising in the mutation of computer viruses.

Oh, says Pally, she looks surprised. I thought you said you worked on the helpdesk?

A lot of the students work there. It means that we can combine our interest in computers with our passion for answering stupid questions.

Pally sips at her tea and eyes the young woman for a moment. Pally's smile is lopsided and she holds her mug up in both hands and blows over the surface of the cup.

Well, says Pally, allowing her thoughts to take coherent form, I guess I'm quite busy this afternoon, so really you should crack on with the computers and getting them on-line. Do you think you could get them all connected?

Vivien gazes at the computer boxes. Her job is to transform the base components in the polystyrene into one permanent node in the new Aberdeen Domestic Computer Network, to plug in the hardware and put Pally's house on-line, as laborious an occupation as she can think of. Pally is a Councillor who needs connected to the

Council, Vivien sits up and flicks her hair aside so that she can see her properly.

I guess.

Pally says nothing, her face inquisitive and leading. With so few clues, it would seem odd that a girl like Vivien should be interested in computers at all.

Well you best crack on, says Pally, and she glances indulgently down. Her eyes find the computer box, and she looks again at Vivien, making the instruction clearer yet.

Tea undrunk, Vivien puts her mug down and stands up.

I've got to get that box from the hall, she says, and she holds her pen-knife to the ready.

Minutes later Pally stands in the doorway of her kitchen, still blowing on the mug of hot tea, while Vivien is on the floor working on a wide range of cardboard with her knife, sitting steady in the connectionist network of computer wiring, seeing perhaps how the simple has manipulated itself into the impossibly complex, and then unravelling it so that it can be plugged in properly.

At least thinks Pally, something like that is going on.

SUPERDISTRIBUTION

A row of polished stone columns supports the fortified granite roof of the Aberdeen Art Gallery on Schoolhill. The Art Gallery is treated with popular regard as the finest architectural representation of Aberdeen's commercial success and highlights above all, the good things for which the city has earned its valuable renown.

These are:

Taste & Elegance
Strong Stone
Commercial Import
and A Cold Reception

To build in granite is to understand the overriding cleanliness of good living because granite is a stone that never becomes dirty and shines like wet silver in the rainy weather.

Erecting arches, planners' fantasies and municipal sculpture, Aberdeen became a model for all the British Empire. The original builders of the city of Aberdeen were a grey and respecting people who wasted nothing and never smiled. Old pictures of Aberdeen illustrate a delightful contrast between these people and their buildings. In the photos, peoples' faces are dark and their caps and suits as black as holes, they move in empty spaces under the circular shine of their new buildings like spots of ink on an open silver page, demonstrating beautifully their avowed city treasure, the granite architecture.

Inside the Aberdeen Art Gallery is more credit to the town, a courtyard laid in marble blocks and a shallow fountain, a graceful gesture to the visitors as if for one second, classical heaven has been bridged with earth. Two ladies of the city join for lunch in the Art Gallery, while boys from next door Gordon's College make willing motions with their electric calculators on the public seats. The lost and dim have wasted whole winters sitting in the Art Gallery, planning but never doing, and just like them, Aberdeen will never thrive with its rear-looking parochialism, all of which encompasses the unhappy city conscience.

The Aberdeen Art Gallery is also a popular venue for Council Meetings. Coffee is brought from the kitchen by apron-shod old folks and Council Committees assemble to solve problems on behalf of those poor devils, the public. Through interviews and board meetings, special groups are convened and all assemble in the brown preserved tranquillity of the James McBey Room. Men in suits arrive with dandruff shoulders and thick reading glasses, younger Councillors shoot in and out behind them and the more genteel women Councillors sit down to discuss their phobias concerning marriage *(gametophobia)*, ideas *(ideaophobia)*, poverty *(peniaphobia)*, and even the horrors of stasophobia *(fear of standing, must sit down, preferably with a coffee, for a good chat)*.

In the James McBey Room, the air is conditioned into ribbons and minor policy concerning the shy lives of the Aberdonians is crafted and cut. It's like an old architect's shop, and the tone is essentially highbrow. The James McBey Room is unfalteringly decorated with historic memories of Aberdeen and holds a library of art books and prints. High in the cupboards and on the shelves, the past is preserved in letters and kept under one tidy cupola, far from the grossness of the Aberdonian street yokel and his looby wife. The James McBey Room has the moral confidence of a vocabulary list, as if the quiet reverence fails to distinguish between manuscript and man, so austere is the catalogue of documents within.

The Councillors and members of the Committee for Developing Technology enter the room, polite and over-particular with their footsteps. They have come to vote upon a new computer chip and its use in their Local Network, as miniature politicians their aim is as

always to implement more human madness, and call it SUITABIL-
ITY. The Councillors file in and sit down, some rest against the
table and others lean up at the wall. Others queue for coffee at the
table-top and several stand aside while the coffee-persons approach
and dish the dainty. Every Committee member enjoys this moment,
and they revel in the mulish flavour of much mediocre conversation
before they take their seats.

Notable at this meeting: Councillor Ray Buchanan, whose sul-
len mouth betrays an unalterable disinterest in regular spoken English and a predilection for the local Doric. He faults at the rear of
the coffee queue and grips a mobile phone, as if keeping it alive by
the warmth of his hand.

Already seated at the table is baldie Councillor Craigie who makes
sure he can sit next to Pally as he becomes restive without the sight
of a woman's leg. Craigie's smile bobs upon a sea of slime and Pally
smiles back amused, while below breath, Craigie tells her a scurril-
ous weekend anecdote. Councillor Craigie talks about his new garden shed and how useful it will be for escaping from his wife . . . *aye
her . . . always on to get me to do something, you'd better believe it.*

On Pally's right hand side is the wealthiest committee member,
Councillor Hewitt. Hewitt sits for long periods with his hands clasped
and looks like he is thinking very hard indeed when in fact he is
fantasising about motor cars or football. Hewitt is a powerful businessman by Aberdeen standards, which means that he owns a swim-
ming pool he never uses and a very fast car indeed.

Councillor Mary Robbie, senior dogmatist of the committee,
looks like she has taken many blows to the face. Councillor Robbie
demonstrates a startling intimacy with the city of Aberdeen that is
based on no exterior observation other than those from the windows of her car. Like a good politician, Mary Robbie believes her
constituency to be just the way she perceives it, a city in her own
image.

All of these five sit at the end of the top table, this small crew
form the core, the very centre of technological representation of the
city of Aberdeen. The committee as a whole are seated in ten min-

utes, and thus upon this mark, the meeting is in progress, as above dated, in the James McBey Room of The Aberdeen Art Gallery. In the second of silence before the meeting begins, Craigie is momentarily distracted by the sight of Pally's body which is applied to her business wear in a manner he clearly finds exciting. Pally stands up and notes the dim appearance of these headlights in her colleague's eyes, as if his consciousness were emerging from a long tunnel. She starts to speak, clearing her throat and saying,

Thank you for coming to this meeting everyone. And with no more ado, can I introduce our guest, the Chairman of Crandall Technologies, and the inventor of the award winning *Kempf Anti-Virus Chip*, Mr Chris Crandall!

The applause rises, and Crandall steps up, seen first by the Technology Committee of the Aberdeen District Council as a casual but serious young man, solemnly carrying his laptop computer before them like it is a tablet of stone. The City Councillors and members of the Council Committee for Developing Technology stop clapping as he settles before them, and in seconds go silent in their seats. Chris Crandall smiles once around the middle-aged and bespectacled faces of the Committee present, he clicks a remote control and obliges his slide projector to turn, and there on the screen before the audience is the projection of a perfect network diagram in code, with the heading displayed below it,

Great Networks: The Superdistribution Chip Can Help!

Crandall clasps his hands together and begins to talk in his business-stressed baritone, a polite and firm register which he learned many years ago at the Junior Chamber of Commerce.

Good morning Ladies and Gentlemen, and welcome. I am Chris Crandall, chairman of Crandall Technologies, and I'm here today to tell you about our newest baby, the Superdistribution Chip. You should know the basics of the chip already, and you may even have decided whether or not you'd like to go ahead with it, but the real purpose of this meeting is for you to meet this wonderful piece of hardware *personally*, as well as being introduced to me, its daddy.

Silence from the immobile rows of folded arms in the James McBey Room encourages Crandall to the opinion that it may be too early in the morning to be raising laughs . . . and so he carries on, undeterred.

Now. I've been running Crandall Tech for twelve years, developing products like this chip, but aside from manufacturing and selling hardware I've also been looking into the future and speculating on how we can revolutionise the world ahead.

A click and Crandall's laptop projects the following words,

REVOLUTIONISE THE WORLD AHEAD!
CRANDALL TECHNOLOGIES
SOCIAL
ENVIRONMENTAL
ECONOMIC
FAMILY
CONNECTIVITY

Crandall smoothes his face with his hand as if enjoying the product of a good shave. The Committee strain their eyes at the words on the screen, conceptualising what they feel immediately to be a random list of non-connected properties, undoubtedly leading to a hard sell.

All of the above are areas which we are looking into developing, says Crandall, because essentially we are connecting new technology with families, information services and innovations in industry. Above all we are providing mechanisms to enable computers and peripherals such as televisions and phones to link together into instantly networked facilities, and that is why I am in Aberdeen today, because here you are setting up the first local computer network in the world, *The Aberdeen Domestic Computer Network.*

Click.

THE ABERDEEN DOMESTIC COMPUTER NETWORK:

WHAT HAS CRANDALL TECHNOLOGIES
GOT TO OFFER?

Blank expressions in The James McBey Room this morning are like raven-haired smudges staring at Chris Crandall. Within the dark eyes of the Committee ranged throughout this wooden panelled chamber and across the thumb-plane of Crandall's vision, there appears to be great indifference.

Another click announces,

AMBITIOUS TARGETS.
A STRONG IMPRESSION ON THE MARKET.
INDUSTRY IS BOOMING.

As you know, says Crandall, I am hoping that you will be piloting the use of my Superdistribution Chip in your Aberdeen Domestic Computer Network, and having issued to the public most of the 20,000 free computers you've linked up across the city, you will be more than familiar with your consumers' habits.

A slide is shown, an image of the Crandall Superdistribution Chip magnified to a viewable size, and the hard-thinking coffee drinkers in suits assembled shift like a gentle wave in their chairs. Crandall walks closer to his audience and turns to face the screen in an attempt to check them into concentration.

Click.

SINCE HOME COMPUTERS WERE INVENTED, THE
GREATEST FACTOR KEEPING RETAIL PRICES
HIGH HAS BEEN SOFTWARE PIRACY.
Crandall Technologies Will Help

A computer image projected on the large screen shows a selection of pirated items ranged against an austere cream background, compact discs, audio and video cassettes, computer software . . . a criminal haul in short.

Our Superdistribution Chip, says Crandall, so effectively eradicates the problem of piracy that we anticipate support from all sectors of industry, as well as from people like yourselves who wish to pass on free software to the general public.

Crandall exhales and smiles.

So what have we decided to do? he asks.

His question halts a moment in the air, captured and mulled by the tin-eared committee who are now waiting on his inspirational word.

It *might* be better, announces Mr Crandall, if users pay their software providers for every time they use a certain product . . . meaning that the public won't have to pay up-front as it does today. It means that you can meter usage, and keep a tag on everything.

The idea drops in to the brain-pan and most of the committee relax again, remembering why they are here. The plan then is to buy twenty thousand of these Superdistribution Chips, and make this young man grander still. The plan is to give the Aberdeen Domestic Computer Network the edge over anything like it in the world, by introducing this new 'meter chip'.

Click . . . and a new image shows the Committee a futuristic software bill, itemised for use, detailing the software used and the utilities employed.

Look at this says Crandall. These users living in Deeside, receive the following monthly bill, charging them for:

> WINDOWS at 34.5 units
> HOME-FIX at 84.5 units
> SCHOOL 24 at 12.9 units
> MUSICOM at 08.8 units

A slide of a bright white shopping centre is imposed before the Committee, and underneath it, the round features of several well-designed computer icons:

> Welcome to the Web Page of the Largest
> Discount Food Delivery Company in Scotland!

Free Home Delivery!
Visit our virual duck pond!
Scotland's finest produce.
Fish while stocks last!
Click here to sample products.

Crandall steps to the audience with the open hands of a political leader.

Telegrocery, he says, is one of many purchase-by-modem shopping services that could be in place in Aberdeen soon, with the help of hardware such as the Superdistribution Chip.

He stands mute with his hands apart, a pause timed to ensure that he has the full attention of every person in The James McBey Room. He scans the faces of his audience and then rubs his brow with a quick and sharp delivery to the centre of his head. His shirt is open-necked and he is the very model of talent economy. In such bland times, when the culture of creative thinking involves the slicing up of markets on a monthly basis, Chris Crandall in this attitude could easily be a pop star and not an industrialist. Hipness and wealth, promotion and co-venture, nothing disturbs the moment as Crandall lords his wealthy ease over the concentrated forms of the city Councillors. Crandall is a living example of the eminently sensible youthful and wealthy culture they all admire . . . his company created the Superdistribution Chip and his very own squad of teenage boffins created the software behind the British Road Maintenance Project, *helping simplify road traffic through applying computer technology.* As Crandall stands there in The James McBey Room, nothing disturbs the layering of the thoughts forming in the minds of the city Councillors, as in their own mental drone, they collectively form the opinion that what they perceive before them is indeed, a good idea.

Crandall moves his hands to his pockets while the next caption appears on the screen.

SMART SHOPPING FOR BUSY PEOPLE.

On the screen is pictured a park where an aluminium shopping complex has been woven into the landscape. Ducks drift lazy on a sculptured figure of eight pond, children are emphasised beside swings, they are holding hands and playing on futuristic gymnasia. Trees and pleasant shrubs dominate the near distance. Cars drift in a line around the semi-circle towards the car park and the artist has taken the liberty of suggesting that somewhere above the aluminium hump of the supermarket, the granite buildings on Queens Road are dull and empty, even in the fictional sunshine.

Caption: Already 25% of computer-users teleshop in one form or another.

You should know, says Chris Crandall, seeming to lean at a nearly magical angle over the seated listeners, that this technology is actually being developed as we speak, and not just by *Crandall Technologies.*

Blank.

The list goes on, says Crandall . . . and this same Deeside family whose bill we have just seen, can have their internet access calculated like this, on a bill that can also feature software for their cars, phones and offices.

Click.

Reduced Price Scale for purchase of the C-Tech Superdistributor

The Councillors peer at the screen even harder now, Crandall is left paused at his highest point of his presentation, a rich young man with an unaccustomed world on offer. In The James McBey Room there is an interruption in thought while the Councillors confess to themselves their options at this juncture . . . options of costs to buy and worries concerning costs to run . . . because so far the 20,000 computers which make up the Aberdeen Domestic Computer Network have cost the City Council next to nothing, which is more than can be said of this compact miracle that Crandall is showing them.

Personally, says Crandall, I am already imagining your wine cellar communicating with your mobile phone and telling a supplier that you are out of white, just as I am looking at houses controlled by sets of 'smart panels' and portable touch screens, which will facilitate convenience wherever they are installed.

The fantastic future home is displayed on the screen for another magical moment until the projector makes one more turn of the carousel to show again the Superdistribution Chip, and the message THANK YOU . . . signalling that the show is over.

A small round of applause, a shared expression of relief, and all eyes turn once again to the front of the room.

From the rear of the James McBey Room, Councillor Pally Cruden stands up and smiles as the applause vanishes altogether.

I'm sure we all agree that was most enlightening Mr Crandall. I'm afraid the Committee must retire now to think further about what you've said, but once again, thank you very much indeed, for taking time from your busy schedule to come and speak to us like this.

Crandall with his hands at his sides bows his head and folds closed his laptop computer. From a small box he begins to hand out examples of the Superdistribution Chip and the assembled Councillors pass the little miracles around, impressed with the fossilised wonder of it all, the opaque and yet confusing, promising and mysterious Superdistribution Chip. The Councillors handle the chip for first time, there *in situ* in sharp black plastic, for the eye to see and the brain to comprehend . . . and one by one they look again at its bright image on the screen, the chip which displays the happy message:

THANK YOU.

HAND VOTE

Are human groups capable of governing themselves?
Defiant city Councillors ruling with democratic mandate and
meeting once a week to make city policy in Aberdeen, have
answered: no.
But certain other people, walking the road home, have
claimed to find in the near divine peace of Scotland, the
answer: yes.

With Chris Crandall and his laptop now removed from the James McBey Room, Pally reconvenes their meeting and interrupts the mumble of her colleagues to institute democracy once again.

Yes. Chris Crandall was very clear I thought.

She speaks loudly in an effort to silence the chattering.

Now, according to researchers at the University, the Superdistribution Chip is ready to be a part of the Aberdeen Domestic Computer Network, so that'll give us something useful to consider at future meetings, like how much to invest and what to invest it in.

Councillor Craigie is doodling on his pad an image of that new garden shed of his. In his mind, he has created Pally's hip and thigh from the corner of his eye, he can imagine her body and sense its small but certain motions as he concentrates elsewhere. Craigie's pen stops still, the motion of Pally's dress is incorrigible in his microvision. If Pally makes a move to the right to direct a comment to the chair, Craigie's vision is stubbornly pushed in that direction also. The fact that Councillor Craigie can stay motionless in his seat while seeing so much of Pally is testament to his many years of subtle lechery.

The first disadvantage that we perceived with the Superdistribution Chip, says Pally, was that pretty much, it's going to have to be given away for free, because people aren't going to want to pay for something that is in effect going to charge them more money in the long run. But I think that we've agreed that if we want to go ahead with this chip, this won't be a problem and that the advantages outweigh the costs. The sooner we get to thinking like this, then the sooner the idea of Superdistribution will be made clear to the public and the sooner there will be in effect only one service provider in Aberdeen, and that will be ourselves, the Council, controlling all future connectivity.

Councillor Craigie draws the garden shed again and doodles himself inside it, a happy man. Pally's voice is heard but behind the glassy sea of his spectacles Craigie is fantasising about his wife's funeral.

Councillor Craigie is in his black tie and hairpiece and there beside him is his fat son Oliver. Both of them drag behind the coffin in their mourning uniform. Mrs Craigie has enjoyed her last blue rinse, her life consisted of daytime quizzes on the television and an obsession with the dog's ears. In many ways, she is better off underground.

One time at Hazlehead Park, Councillor Craigie and his wife and their fat son Oliver had gone horse riding. Councillor Craigie left the others so that he could smoke a cigar in peace, and after seeing the horse's bums going off to the trees, he walked towards the golf course, the sight of which he knew would calm him properly. It was a Saturday in summertime, and in Aberdeen where the sky is the widest evidence of God in Scotland, the combination of sprightly turf and the wide straight clouds in the blue, were so divine as to be almost a fiction for the poor man.

And so, staring fondly into the tree-lined fairway and watching with interest the trajectories of a faintly visible golf ball, Councillor Craigie fell to thinking about a new girl in his office and of one image of her in particular when she bent down to look at her computer.

Oh Holy Sight, that tight black skirt, the white material of her shirt, it was an invitation, a dream indeed for Councillor Craigie. These involuntary thought patterns, combined with the excellence of the day and the deep scent of the cigar smoke, gave the Councillor the sudden thought that he could send this girl an anonymous note, a notion which hit him as brightly as if he had been knocked on the forehead by a flying golf ball.

Pleased with this, and composing *ex tempore* a rude rhyme for the note, Councillor Craigie put his cigar in his mouth and scanned the world ahead where the grass curved up the hill to a tiny crook in the trees where the 12th tee was. Through this heavenly view, Councillor Craigie saw a commotion in the high distance, and straining his eyes over the green carpet of turf he made out several tiny figures on the hill who were reminiscent of his own family.

Craigie stopped and there it was. An accident of some kind, a small crowd and his fat son, Oliver, the roundish form, standing beside two riderless horses.

Councillor Craigie broke into his fastest personal mode of movement, a jog trot. He threw down his cigar, considerate only of his family and not of the surface of his beloved golf course, he made it up the hill and approached the accident scene as fast as he reasonably could. At the top of the rise, Craigie saw his fat son Oliver, rash and freakish of face, stunned into a red-eyed silence by the falling over of Mrs Craigie, and when he reached the small group of fearful local riders who were gathered at the spot where his wife had fallen, he looked past them and he saw her dead expression lying face-up where she had rolled off her horse and on to the grass.

Excuse me, my wife, said the Councillor.

At this moment, there was a sickening slipping back into memory for Councillor Craigie. His wife's eyes were closed, just as her mouth appeared set to rupture, and Craigie felt his skull crackle as he bent down and touched her with his hand. His wife lay spoiled on the floor of wild grass at the edge of the golf course, a maul on the ground in her orange weekend coat, and there beside her was a guilty horse.

More confusion followed. Councillor Craigie realised that he had no idea what to do, seeing only that his wife lay still as if she was dead now, and being so helpless in this moment, Craigie became embittered to her once more on the spot and felt that he truly hated her, for leaving him with problems like this.

Councillor Craigie picked up his wife by the shoulders and someone said, *Don't move her!* But Mrs Craigie opened her eyes and said, *Hello dear,* and then the small crowd breathed relief and began to drift away. Mrs Craigie stood up and hugged the Councillor, and then Oliver hugged them both, and when it was certain that everything was OK in the world, Councillor Craigie chewed into another cigar, and snarled up a match to light it while the horses were led to safety.

The smoke brought Councillor Craigie back to life again. The cigar ameliorated feelings of anger into those of wonder, and his wife spoke to him and said, *Where were you?*

Where was I? thought Councillor Craigie. I was over there.

The Councillor drew on his cigar, feeling the world to be right once more and then looked at his wife and said, *My God, I really thought you were dead, dear.*

For those few seconds then, until Councillor Craigie's thoughts stalled and were obliged to return to the fantasy workshop, he had been indeed hopeful that his wife had gone for good. By the time he had crossed the fairway to where she had fallen, Councillor Craigie was already imagining his world without her, his holidays and his flirting. The life policies had kicked in and the Councillor was eating a steak with nobody watching, he had even imagined himself practising nudity in the house, walking as he pleased, wearing only a pair of rubber gloves when it came to doing the dishes.

I was right there said Councillor Craigie, I saw you from over there. And he pointed to the golf course and the edge of the fairway from where he had made his rapid strides to save her.

It was almost exciting for Councillor Craigie, the idea that his wife might be dead and when he thought about it more, he smiled that he might have positively enjoyed the attentions of the mourners at her funeral, who with great pity would find him all alone in the world, he and Oliver, father and son, with no mummy. Councillor

Craigie smoked the cigar and thought good thoughts like this until his wife tugged his arm and he recalled again that Mrs Craigie bless her, was going to live for another forty years and that he was going to die first anyway. At this, Councillor Craigie's cigar began to taste sour and he looked deeply at the sky while Mrs Craigie showed Oliver her bruise.

Councillor Craigie chances a closer observation of Pally Cruden's skirt and disturbs his thoughts with some fresher images. He wonders about Pally and if she has any boyfriends, he is not strictly listening to her as she addresses the Committee, but rather he is eliminating the real purpose of the day with his sexual fantasy. A smile, and he drinks his coffee.

It's very important that right from the start we choose the best method of Superdistribution, says Pally, and I am now totally convinced that the best method is that supplied by Crandall Technologies, and their Managing Director, Mr Crandall.

Councillor Craigie imagines Pally once again unclothed, and he chances a glance up to her chest and sees that he has got away with it. *It's incorporate in my own male drives to look at women like this,* thinks Craigie, and as if vindicated by this wicked thought, he looks some more, and takes in the bosom curves. Councillor Pally Cruden stands next to him, rocking now, as gently as a stone might on the bed of a slow river. In the mind of Councillor Craigie, she is naked save for high boots, now in the plump and smack of glorious sex with the Councillor himself, back in his own bedroom, or maybe in the Town House. It is a thought from which Councillor Craigie derives incorporate human pleasure, and he draws a revealing shape on his paper and smiles when he recalls an article he saw in the seedy corner of his weekend newspaper.

Teledildonics, it said.

Midi-controlled-vibrato-suction devices. YES.

And sonic impulses stimulating the body's erogenous zones. THE FUTURE.

It couldn't fail to interest the fantasist within Councillor Craigie, and so he listens to Pally while his face dissolves through a blissful lack of interest. As his mind wanders again, Councillor Craigie dreams up girls and stimulating electronic devices, he denudes Pally for the hundredth time without even knowing it and places her in a dream context of his own making. Maybe she is playing nude golf or driving nude in her BMW. He is never bored with this, the Swami of Undress, he's always able to work his mental arithmetic upon that inescapable causal design at any time of night or day.

That's a thinking or 'intelligent' system, says Pally, and every person in Aberdeen, with a Council computer will have universal online access to it. Since the Council will be the sole service provider for these machines, we can also solve the problem of illicit material, which is pornographic or racist . . . because we simply won't allow it to be accessed from the Domestic Computer Network.

The James McBey Room is stilled, eyebrows rise, and plenty thoughts form and stick to the old panelled walls. The face of Councillor Mary Robbie in particular is scorched with incomprehension for a moment until she too reverts to her daydream, which is of the James McBey Room itself, and what a joy it would be to own some of the treasures that are kept locked up within.

Yes, a real collection.

There are lovely things in here thinks Mary Robbie, and she looks past Councillor Pally to the cabinet where the pride of the city itself is kept. Behind the glass she sees it once again, the map of *Urbs Aberdonia*, The Newtown of Aberdeen, showing Gibbet Peak, Futty Wynd, the Way to the Gordon Puddle . . . everything that brings to mind for her a time that has long since disappeared, an age impaired and ruined, screwed up like waste paper and gone.

Ten years ago it was that Mary Robbie received one of the first computers to her office, and it was much admired by her clients. Computers were called business machines then, because only businesses could have them. The computer was installed by her Personal Assistant who gave her lesson after lesson in its use, and even today, *au fait* and up to date with how to work it, Mary has yet to see her own ambition realised by the plastic box. What is the ever-expanding computer anyway when the user is just tied to it, as the cook is to the stove? For Mary Robbie it's sadly clear – in business the fact that one person owns a computer means that everyone must have one, for if they don't have the most up to date machine, then they'll be drummed into cash-extinction by the imaginary forces of natural selection. The computer, thinks Mary, was expected to fit in to my life like a new organ transplanted into an already organised body, but the machine was nothing but a disgrace. The standing argument at the time was that *naebody kent how to work it.*

It might shock the young of today, thinks Mary Robbie, but nobody in her home town of Strichen was ever breathless for the arrival of computers. She can recall however the actual day when the first DOS home computer in Strichen did arrive . . . because it was greeted with such warmth and local anxiety that it became the first item of electronic hardware to achieve a photograph in the *Buchan Courier.*

True story – it was also at Strichen that in the eighteenth century, attempts were made on the construction, tuning and operation of the steam plough.

The steam plough! Now there was a hard effort at breaking indigence!

1798 and the steam plough pumped, throttled and broke furrows in local fields, it was its own automated theatre and the sense of magic which it inspired in the high parks near Strichen is not to be underestimated. The steam plough was, and remains today, the only one of its kind in the world, and was designed and built by engineers in Aberdeen. People arrived from the crofts and farm-mains to see the machine like it was the magical statue of Daedalus, a most industrious and fascinating combination, with siphons pulleys and levers, and a row of spinning plough shears. The steam plough was a sensation at the time, the stuff of legend in its ingenuity, and it could be seen during its short life moving in humps across the landscape back in the days when there wasn't even a motor car on the surface of the earth to show for man's

genius. The theoretical gadgetry of this new self moving
mechanica did not quite cut the ground as it might however
and at midsummer in the afternoon, the steam plough
bumped to a halt in a park at New Deer, suffering not for
want of aesthetics in conception (for Ptolemy's epicycles
never fail) but merely in its flat attempts to plead with, or
even defile the fertile ground contained in Buchan,
Aberdeenshire.

The thing Mary Robbie remembers about the computer in her office however, was that it was replaced quite shortly after it arrived. The computer may have been plugged in 1991, but it was unplugged in 1992 and subsequently exchanged for a new system, every two years after that. At least, thinks Councillor Robbie, the Steam Plough only failed the once! Mary Robbie sees the constant upgrading of computers as an in-built defence against formalism, the result of which is that every two years the machine is taken away and something sensational is re-installed in its place. New machines arrive monthly now, improved in every way with faster communications and more memory, so that it's like a vice she thinks, a machine that exerts a fascination solely for the future, because unlike other technologies, its aim is to become better, until it devours each limitless principle on its rise. Further to this, computers not only eliminate jobs, they also act as powerful engines of inequality between owners and non-owners. After all, if you don't have one you're not only going to stay poor . . . you're going to get poorer yet.

Councillor Mary Robbie sits glum and hard, staring now at a dark oil painting, a haunting canvas next to the door of the James McBey Room. In the picture she focuses on the cattle, black and diffuse on a flat park of grass. Behind the cows, the fields recede yet further, taking with them a quiescence unknown, a notice of repose and the suggestion that always, in the distance there is something out of reach. A nice oil painting. Pally is talking but Mary is waiting for the moment when she can leave it all behind and drive the thirty quiet miles home. There on the canvas of the picture, she sees it again, Buchan dying into the night, languishing into clouds, and the colour of orange, with a leaning into the red. Councillor Mary Robbie has clients this evening and is suddenly sick of the thought of them. She thinks of her home, Strichen, Mormond Village . . . not a stubborn place, just a small town minded of the land, nothing loathe and nothing shouted out, just a quiet plot in the country.

Now this isn't even cost-benefit decision making says Pally. Technological decisions, like Mr Crandall said, have their long term consequences, but the computers we've distributed and the hardware inside them, including the Superdistribution Chips, will stay the property of the City Council. So the machines remain for the purposes of our balance sheets, as Council assets.

Pally is interrupted by an expression of pronounced discomfort from Councillor Ray Buchanan, a cough, or at least a clearing of the throat. She stops and turns slightly at this exhibition of city Doubt and Councillor Ray's eyes leak the remainder of his interruption to the table, a manifest dislike for what is about to be projected as he slowly raises his hand.

How do we explain tae people that the computers are free? he says. I mean, you don't ken far you stand div you ay?

One blank second later, and Pally's eyes refocus on her Doric colleague as she translates for her own mind, what he has just said to her.

If I refer you back to Crandall Technologies' original statements, she says, the expository is very clear. None of the machines will ever be leaving Aberdeen and we've secured the obvious investment upfront in the form of the computers themselves. So: the computers are given free to the Council in exchange for advertising contracts and that is how it works. In effect, we have invested little and lost nothing. We only need to pay for Crandall's Superdistributor Chips.

That's what I'm nae sure about says Councillor Buchanan, and he stretches his arms and looks like an off-balanced windmill.

The point is taken across the room, and several heads nod. With a sigh, Pally turns again before this key panel of decision-makers. Although from Aberdeen, Pally likes to hear the local Doric spoken for its charm, but dislikes the language for its incomprehensibility. She sees the local dialect as a means of keeping outsiders at a distance so she speaks the English universal. Her voice is gentrified like everything else about her, but Councillor Buchanan thinks to himself: *she's a proper madam.*

We've been through this, says Pally, and we know that the only reason we can afford to give out free machines is because they'll be used for advertising to a captive market of users. The adverts will pay for it.

A silence. The committee are so easily placated and yet so easily irritated.

This is what it's all about, says Pally. It's about Aberdeen. We all voted for the Network and the last thing we need to do before it starts to run, is vote for the Superdistributor Chip.

Otherwise unaffected, it's clear that Councillor Ray Buchanan is not satisfied by the answer. His eyes open further to allow a more concisely wide view of the room, and he puts his pencil back in his grey suit. Thinking now, he flicks a glance back at Pally and with a practised laconism says, Aye well, at's fine fir you but nae fir abody, is it?

Local Doric! thinks Pally, slipshod construction, poor diction, elephantine local expression. The Doric will achieve nothing, only the retrograde. When it comes to building the future there will be no place for this local half-language. She would apologise and ask the Councillor to repeat himself, but that might give him satisfaction. Was there a time when Aberdonians talked through their noses without the laxity they speak with today? Of course there was. And so the words are blameless in themselves, it's the nose that has made this language terminal. The local Doric is just a joke to Pally, but still her colleagues expect her to take it seriously.

Pally addresses Councillor Buchanan, almost exclusively. She turns. Her dress is cut and pointed. Councillor Ray is in substance a man of grey, the colour of the granite, and as thus, the elocution of the town. Pally notices the mobile phone, still gripped in his hand, and she folds her arms to speak.

Contrary to what pessimists might suggest, says Pally, co-operation is a great thing, and this is the attraction of the Aberdeen Domestic Computer Network. What's important to all of us just now is that we go ahead and do it, and this makes it more than developmental, because it's a complete experiment.

A look from Councillor Mary Robbie catches Pally's repetition for effect. It's as if Councillor Pally can't stop this formless and prolific speaking on behalf of the computers and the technological advances they will bring. Councillor Ray, quiet now, his suspicion not allayed, sits as still as if he were a magazine photograph. There is a compendium of verbiage whistling in his head, issuing words he can't say, anything to take his mind off his sudden distaste for this meeting. A silence in the James McBey Room expands into another cough from the back, and Councillor Ray suddenly excuses himself and holds up his hands.

I'm satisfied for the moment, ladies and gentlemen.

Councillor Ray Buchanan is irreconcilable to the exercise of great rhetoric on points of policy, while beside him, Councillor Craigie is nodding at the distance, as if he were a toy that someone had set in motion.

So, I take it, says Pally, that all of us agree that the Superdistribution Chip is the way forward for the Network, and that we'd like to buy enough of them to ensure that every machine in Aberdeen is fitted with one?

Pally's head turns, her eyes sweep over the Committee and she takes the general grunt to be the answer *yes*. Not an entire commitment from the room, but nobody at this point is willing to become the focus of dissent. Looking back towards her, every expression in the chamber reads disinterest and a half-hearted desire to be elsewhere. The literal-minded face of Councillor Hewitt is so down to earth in fact, that it's as if he's in a trance. Pally is interesting Councillor Hewitt as a distant bird does a cat, he pays half of his whole attention to her as he looks down upon his brief and begins to read about how local television programmers, Grampian Television are now involved.

His brief reads: *Grampian Television's corporate sponsors are not afraid of making the step from the passive media of TV, into an arena that can be switched off more easily.*

What it means is that the computers will be showing adverts to their users, because this is the only way that they can be paid for. The idea seems natural to all those sitting at the table, although the concept is far from complete. A row of blank faces top to bottom in the James McBey Room, minds under hairpieces and behind spectacles turn smartly on the problem of computers morphing into televisions. For the Councillors the problem matters not, the memory span is short and available world knowledge is a constant surprise to every one of them. Which of these Councillors are to say that computers and television are not to merge? Which of these middle aged biddies, sweating it out here in the dawn of the New Century, is not to say that everything they've been taught in the past is dead and gone? And which of them will put their hand up in the James McBey Room and doubt it?

This is a *free* service says Pally catching more attention, and advertising materials will be routed correctly to appropriate sites. So when you're shopping, let's say, on the Network, you'll see scrolling down one side of your screen, the lists of services available, or the adverts appropriate. Something like that.

And how does it work? asks Councillor Mary Robbie stabbing her pen into her notepad with all the breeding of a patch of thistles. She means, How *can* it work?

It works thematically, says Pally. Grampian Television are going to pilot commercials for local businesses and we can judge how effective they are and whether they are wanted or not.

Councillor Hewitt, with his hands held in their domain specific clasp, would never wonder why advertising is present on a public service. Every person at the table is grown up enough to know that commercials are the fuel, that drives the engine, that turns the wheel, that produces the image, that challenges the mental ruts of the consumer, and arranges the command words SHOP and SPEND into plausible order in their minds. It's advertising which keeps the whole modern shebang pleasantly on that twenty first century track to future comfort . . . and adverts are so colourful and happy, so much fine oil on the great water of life . . . the distant ever promised land of our dreams, where each of us is completely incapable of seeing the other.

Hewitt's stolid mind runs ahead of the meeting to his Research Base. This is a silver sheet metal building, one of many units assembled with no permanence in mind, in the several green-grass and dump truck Industrial Estates which now satellite Aberdeen like computational cells. At the door of this Research Base, called Hewitt Offshore, Hewitt the Pragmatist examines the rows of these silver cells – fourteen units arranged perpendicular to a central car park, the exact frame-based representation of a good filing system, spoiled Hewitt thinks by the unideal attempts at attractive shrubbery between the buildings. There Hewitt walks to the glass door of his own building and turns to close his car with an infra-red torch.

BEEP – Hewitt's car closes down, the headlamps flash a memento of light, the vehicle sits patiently facing the jumbo hardware of the building.

Hewitt's eyes are on a blank page as he listens to Pally talk. Practical minded, Hewitt seldom offers an opinion because Council matters take care of themselves and there are always greater concerns as far as business goes.

In the reception of Hewitt's small Research Base is an Aberdonian girl, whose attractiveness is testament to the unromantic yet still positively strong gene pool of the city. Hewitt is convinced of it. His smile is air-built and he arrives in his office at Hewitt Offshore each day, a sum of potential energy and dressed as Business Man of the Year.

Inside the Research Studio itself, there are many computers working on diagrams in graphics and the gentle sound of print-out is never far away. On the interior walls of Hewitt Offshore are plans and graphs of objects tabled for experimentation, and although Hewitt has few ideas concerning what the scientists are actually doing in his Research Centre, he continues to his own office just the same, happy that they are still doing it.

The MD he thinks, needs only his face and voice.

The MD he thinks, needs only his word.

In Hewitt's personal office are blinds that reach to the floor and a conference table for seven business people. On the walls are three oil paintings of football goals, two of life at sea and one of seabirds on the North East Coast. In the centre of the room is a scale model of the *Thermopylae*, the oil rig that Hewitt Offshore designed, the same rig which made his company famous. The *Thermopylae* is the oil rig, built in Dundee, and infused with the animate nature of Hewitt's research against corrosion and instability, that became in its hour, the best rig that anyone had seen, anywhere in the North Sea. And it made Hewitt a million. As shown in the scale model, which features the rig plugged into the sea bed, the *Thermopylae* is dug into the whole of the rock with the compulsion not simply to ap-proach nature with the spirit of resistance, but to do violence against it, and Hewitt is incredibly proud of it.

He passes hours in silence. In his car, Hewitt is silent with the natural purpose of driving and he will take the road to Inverness if he has a problem to consider. While driving his car, Hewitt focuses his mental activity into an hour when he will comprehensively man-age the appreciation of one sole deduction, and this is Hewitt's job as MD, and his human contribution to Hewitt Offshore.

It is patience thinks Hewitt, which will always be rewarded with success in business, because patience allows the focus to arrive. It is patience thinks Hewitt, which forces the capitulation of those who are not prepared, just as patience ensures that the right man always wins the contract. Councillor Hewitt knows he is a patient man and that he could sit and count to a million if he needed to. It's a part of his success. It is patience that allows Hewitt to motivate people through silence, by making them *scared* of him.

The Councillor Hewitt method of business dealing in Aberdeen: *by equating everything and every person to an automata, a start can be made on the improvement of technology, and on quality of living.*

It's why Hewitt sits on the Technology Committee of the City

Council and why he feels it's so important. A human being is needed to implement a human purpose, he thinks, and the sub-division of these matters into quality of life for the general public is the job of managers such as he. As a director, Hewitt merely appoints people to do the work for him, while he himself travels in his car over Scotland, meeting other business leaders in hotels and offices. One must convince and many must follow, thinks Hewitt, and hence the world of business. It is a policy of steel.

For thinking out shorter problems, Hewitt drives north from Aberdeen towards Ellon. Each small and somatised village on this road is now a station in the thought of Hewitt, and by driving his car, he can solve a problem before enjoying the deceleration on returning to the outskirts of the city of Aberdeen. As the Hewitt car slows down, ideas for improvement come solidly to rest in his mind, like the slowing momentum attached to heavy spheres of steel, and at this point Hewitt's thoughts become zero, having been melted and reshaped for the day ahead.

Obviously we don't have a full list of who is going to advertise on the Network, says Pally, and to start with, we'll be subject to those chosen by Mr Crandall's agency. What we do know however is that we'll be able to set our own quality controls, right from the beginning, as long as we vote for this, and approve of it today.

Pally pulls her notes apart again and places half on the table, the half she doesn't want. She'd like very much to be off the awkward topic of the adverts but the more potential energy is contributed to the discussion, the more difficult it becomes to pull out of answering the questions.

Councillor Craigie is still focused on the black-suited thrust of Pally's hip. *A good hip this one, the best.* Many thousands of sexual motions take place ensemble in Councillor Craigie's baldie head when Pally moves, and when she talks, it only gets better. Some days Councillor Craigie seldom leaves this Arcadia where women are non-actual, and he finds that at the age of forty-nine, that they come and go more quickly than ever. Craigie sees these women in his head, mechanically reproduced like they are piano rolls played at speed.

In this way, women appear and reappear from file, where they are discomposed testimonials to the ideal. It means that Craigie's mind has now become a scrapyard where he's breaking down girls and their clothes all day long, only to rebuild them properly, younger and the way he wants them. Dreamy-eyed, Councillor Craigie looks back in to his notes, and finds page 12 whereupon is projected much practical and sane thought on the subject of computers. Presenting a whimsical smile to the page, he pretends now to take notes on what Pally is saying, he writes as carelessly as if he were a student once again.

Aberdeen joining similar . . . within ONE year . . . IT helpdesk, yes . . . RETROspection?

Dust drops in The James McBey Room, it floats in currents and lands on the surfaces of the high shelves, a random variable in the artificial light. In the shadow across from Craigie, Councillor Mary Robbie looks away, thinking of a new question. She thinks of the last time that the Committee for Developing Technology met and she winces at a Christmas picture of herself last year, fallen down in the doorway of her house in Strichen, slipped in the snow on gin and wine . . . and the thought retreats.

Pally is paused in her notes.

That's how this has been able to physically progress, she says, beyond our planning into something almost we could say, sensible of itself.

PENSI RICH

PENSI RICH is probably the most destructive virus in modern computing. PENSI RICH infects the Partition / Master Boot Record of hard disks, located in the first sector of Track Zero, and causes credit card transactions to be made in favour of the user, making people into millionaires in hours. Healthy as this may sound, the PENSI RICH virus relies on the superior corrupting power of the money.

The original PENSI RICH virus would cause a coloured screen to be displayed on some systems, with this message: *You Are Rich At Last!* Following this, credit would be issued by the main banks and department stores, all of whom would start sooking dreadfully at the new teat thereby created. Other variants of PENSI RICH have seen financial advisers turn up bearing applications for investment bonds and unnecessary life cover.

Once PENSI RICH has taken effect and the credit transactions are complete, the user's bank balance (or Cache-Money) grows and they become 'money-blind' as genital lesions spread through their wallets, where plastic multiplies at an alarming rate.

The final effects of PENSI RICH, are as follows:

1. Taste and appreciation disappear as furniture and artwork begin to fill every room.

2. Paranoia replaces love, domestic arguments flourish, as do many stress related illnesses and infections.

3. These symptoms ultimately lead to car crashes, over-eating, jewellery-poisoning, Brat Infection Syndrome (BIS), and a surfeit of domestic servants who hate your guts.

Other mutations of PENSI RICH have included FAIRYGOD / MILLIONAIRE / MERC-HEAD / ASPIRANT / MAMMONATE / UPAS / GOLDENEGG / GETTY / CIBOLA / OBNOX / MOPUS / 245-T / REDSPOIL / PLUTUS / SUPERCASE / INTROITUS / SHIT-FBRAINS /

The PENSI virus can also mutate of its own accord and has been known to add zeros on to the salaries of business leaders. The spread of PENSI RICH is a real threat to society, and of the 10,000

**millionaires it created in the late 1990s, every one
of them became an utterly unpleasant f**ker.**

Pages turn in the James McBey Room, until all eyes light on a canvassed selection of Aberdonian street names, representing the chosen people who will soon have the option of fibre technology and the speed of communication that goes with it. Councillor Hewitt has a face like a stone pill, a sane item of rock awaiting the next move. It's getting near coffee time again and the whole Committee are passionless for the next backfill of ideas. Undiscriminating human business continues however, and there is a hope as usual that almost recklessly and negligent of actual planning, ideas will somehow cobble themselves together into working some plebiscite magic. It's going on here in the James McBey Room. Policy is not real, it is something confined in tiny cells within an almost infinite drum of memory which turns slowly and makes the Councillors say YES without even thinking. An idea pops up but nobody can grab it in time, so YES is said again, and the public find once more, that a decision has been made, ratified by the careless Councillors and brought alive through the medium of the hand-vote. Here in the sleepy morning glow, while the Developing Technology Committee meet, it will happen again without thought or care while, in the meantime, Hewitt is merely biding his time, facially still with one continuous expression underneath this toast brown skin. Hewitt is listening to the meeting in progress but mentally opting to work elsewhere. It happens all the time where many individuals come together in a room and think collectively of their lunch.

There is for example, Hewitt's new oil rig, the *Gothenburg*, the successor to the *Thermopylae.*

Councillor Hewitt sits in his office at the Bridge of Don after a drive down the road to Ellon and back. While Hewitt sits thinking like this the blinds are closed and the telephone is too scared to ring. The arrangement of Hewitt's thoughts is like the tidy ordering of the silver industrial units themselves, symmetrical from every angle. Considerations that undoubtedly operate in the Hewitt mind are centred around the *Gothenburg,* and how Hewitt Offshore are to develop yet again, a more stable and efficient oil rig than anybody else. Percentage figures describe the success of the project, delivered daily to Hewitt's desk, and he thinks, *I've learned a lot about oil rigs since starting this business.*

Hewitt calls the front desk and asks the Hewitt employee there to find his scientific adviser on the telephone. While waiting for the call, Hewitt replaces the receiver and looks straight ahead at the computer screen before him. Beyond Hewitt's computer, the mathematical development of the *Gothenburg* continues in the plush research suite and Hewitt observes this until the telephone rings and he picks it up to speak.

Professor. This is Councillor Hewitt. I said I'd give you a call before I came over to the University today. I wonder if you have time again to show me that programme you showed me? To see how it's coming along.

Hewitt focuses on the image before him while he speaks. The *Gothenburg* is all but sold and requires only the virtue of the professor's scientific tests and his computer jargon before it is completely finished.

Yes says Hewitt, the model. I can take it over.

The plans for the *Gothenburg* are in a folder on Hewitt's table as well as on the computer screen, but he doesn't understand them. Not one centimetre of the *Gothenburg* exists, and yet, this drilling platform is nearly finished and the rig is objectively present in the unhatched state of computer aided design. It is as if the computer screen were the womb from which the rusted monster of the sea was going to form one day.

I need you to look at the software just the once, says Hewitt to the professor. I need you to tell me if it's tenable in its existing form.

The professor uses an alternative method of conversation in the ear of Hewitt, and Hewitt bears up to it without inquiry or break. Science incorporates many values, words and customs that are alien to Councillor Hewitt and people like the professor use specific terms that diminish real and proper language. As far as Hewitt is concerned, this scientist does not know how to talk.

That sounds great, Hewitt interrupts. He listens to the professor while outside the form of provisional reality is generated on several computers programmed with the accepted attitudes of nature and the stresses of life at sea. Or so he believes. To be properly sure, Councillor Hewitt hasn't any idea at all as to what goes on under the silver industrial roofing of Hewitt Offshore, any more than he does about what goes on in the engine of his fast car.

I understand, says Hewitt. And that's the entire object. That's what we're leading to.

He says his goodbyes woodenly.

Hewitt sits back, the sprung leather chair allows him a few degrees of leeway, a certain torque which tilts his view towards the roof of his office. The phone is dead and Hewitt's thoughts make a neat and scientific slow-down, and he thinks about his afternoon, an unfamiliar decision in the making. The computer image of the *Gothenburg* revolves on the laptop. The rig must satisfy several safety and planning conditions by the end of the month, and the plans must be ready for inspection two weeks after that, so Hewitt must organise this and make sure it happens exactly as he says. People don't realise how important his job is, sometimes.

When Hewitt closes his eyes he pictures himself at the wheel of his car and his thoughts focus on the superficial surface of the road. Even a slight lead in the crucial area of rig building will bring Hewitt more wealth and more of the security to develop a better company.

And what is power? Something in between. Something on the road to Aberdeen . . . something unaccountable between the money and the will to make more. Councillor Hewitt, approaching Balmedie, his vehicle an enigmatic flash of dark blue on the ancient agricultural landscape. Hewitt passes dead fields that look like they might never come back to their senses, poisoned black parks and new farm buildings, hedges that are made out of wire. Hewitt is approaching Black Dog, an incapacitated area of land outside the City Main, a one time shooting range but now an industrial dump.

He has his hand in the air and notices that Councillor Buchannan is counting votes, he looks around and the others have their right hands up too.

The sheet before you on the table, numbered one through ten, says Pally, is an update, and after that, there are some suggested percentage ratios. Some of the free computers that are left will be allocated to homes and businesses, but we won't decide which yet.

Councillor Robbie also has her hand up. She dreams again of that image of herself, half in the snow, feeling never more than at that moment, like an old woman. A grandmother indeed, one knee in the snow, almost lying on her side, hiccuping gin at Christmas.

She looks around the table.

The super-placid Councillor Hewitt is thinking of nothing and has his hand up in the air. Councillor Craigie is smiling and has his hand up too, while Councillor Buchanan, exempt from the vote is still counting while copying the tally to a sheet.

Aberdeen will be establishing *connectivity*, says Pally, reading from the Committee Notes she has handed out.

Aberdeen will be solving incompatibilities.

Aberdeen thinks Councillor Hewitt, will be a refuge for huge telecommunication monopolies, who are going to hide out in the city's vast and empty computer memories.

Aberdeen is going to be a target for more of the same madness, but that's exactly what the Committee is after. The more computer power they generate, the more they will be imitated elsewhere. Thus, got to get ahead of the game, right now.

Thank you, says Pally, I think that's carried. I'll let Chris Crandall know straight away, I'm sure he'll be delighted.

From the James McBey Room, in the sacred wooden marrow of Aberdeen Art Gallery, a ghost arises, a sensation of limit, which opposes the fantasies the Committee have set in motion. On the paper before the Councillors is written LIMITLESS ACCESS, it's a phrase Pally has used somewhere before but none of them are sure what it means. Hands go down and faces smile, the Councillors are proud of the power they can demonstrate. By moving a limb about a foot, they can make all sorts happen. Again, Councillor Mary Robbie finds the drab colours of her mind returning to her immemorial Christmas collapse. It was after the Technology Committee function . . . the year before . . . and she was trying to get the key in her front door, establishing a connection that she may continue onward to the limitless access of her bed. Something sour. When you work hard and organise something properly, like Christmas, when you go to the correct shops and make the best efforts to enhance your time, and then stamp on it like that, when you appeal to the destructive, and make a mess of yourself . . .

Councillor Mary Robbie glances across the schedule for the implementation of the Aberdeen Domestic Computer Network, and feels a sickness from within. Merely because the details of the Network are printed on A4, all the Councillors are expected to believe that it will operate to a tee, but how can it be so? There is a date for each event in the progress of the Network including the installation of computers, the loading of software, home and office visits by engineers, the release of further software, and the dates when other users might join in.

Pamela, she says, her hand raised once again.

Yes Mary.

This is supposed to be perfect isn't it?

Mary Robbie holds up her schedule and points across it with a finger. She is crumpled and drunk in the snow – now that's perfection. That's the relation between machines and people, Councillor Robbie trying to fit the key into the lock of her house, that night, last Christmas. The snow on the path . . . the holly wreath on the door, a sensation that she was going to cry, that she was going to give in right there. How degrading.

Everything's perfect on paper says Pally, and her smile increases as she puts forward an immediate agreement to what Mary has just said.

That's what this committee is for, says Pally, to try and keep our Network as close to perfection as we can. No?

Councillor Hewitt's thoughts are as deeply hidden as ever, but nobody in the wooden panelled obscuration of the James McBey

Room could have known that the exact same notion was on his mind. Perfection and willing, indecipherable terms causing doubt and nobody knows what to say.

Each meeting of the Aberdeen City Council Committee for Technology ends like this with a vague and primitive attitude in the minds of the campaigners, as if they've just broken stick against rock for the first time and aren't sure what will happen next. Still, they are going to be the famous founding fathers of the new technology, the boat builders to the stars. They are all Councillors who are making a decent attempt to increase the quality of daily life.

The James McBey Room rests this moment, and a compensated peace forms around the wooden tables. The substance of technology may have been misrepresented, but the fact of this chamber is history. No matter what happens in here, and what is said, the wheels will always turn and providence will take care of the remainder. Most of the Committee is now convinced that desperate though the technology may be, the Aberdeen Domestic Computer Network is going to be a model for the world, and at the least, a very fine experiment.

Just the sort of inward investment we were looking for, says Pally, a policy which owes more to emotion than to reality.

The meeting is adjourned and the Councillors begin to stand and leave.

I'll be on the mobile all afternoon, says Councillor Craigie, checking his battery level and allowing Councillor Buchanan the opportunity to concede that if weren't for those phones, he wouldn't know what would happen.

Pally takes another look across her colleagues, excited that soon she'll be able to call up Chris Crandall and tell him the wonderful news. Her gaze moves up the wall of the James McBey Room and there she finds the domed glass skylight. The roof of the atrium obtrudes to nowhere and shows above them a white cleanliness in the outside world, a glow which enters the gallery in showers and radiates through this, the immediate heart of the building.

Who of us here will be calling Councillor Craigie this afternoon anyway? she thinks, and she strikes a sly glance at him, still readily engrossed in the dark moments of his mobile phone.

Pally switches on her own mobile and joins the others near the door as they exchange their last comments. Every meeting is the same – human thought and Council policy, ideas promulgated, stated and then acted upon. Someone's always getting rich while the people of Aberdeen benefit and today she's got the pleasure of telling Crandall that once again: *it is him.*

EXPLETIVES DELETED

In the less well-decorated areas of Aberdeen, dogs bark like gunshot.

Lachie and his brother, the Boy Fiddes, walking home after dark, the North eats the moon again tonight and the roadway is a muck of fog. For two minutes, the moon is part revealed over the sea, close to the flats, close to the planet, and Lachie ponders his fag end before setting the smoke to his mouth. Where the smoke goes after that – it just sits around the corner of his throat, and then goes up to his head.

Lachie is two days out of prison and this is a marked achievement. Over the last four years while he has been inside, his brother has fathered two children, one aged four and another at the screaming age. The children are also marked achievements, although for a grown man, able to produce twelve million sperms each hour of the day, this conquest of conception must be seen in a broader light.

The moon appears, it's like the winter scene of story books from when the Boy Fiddes was a toddler on his daddy's knee, the image is caught over the freezing North Sea in a glittering halo, perceived jet white among the clouds on a foggy background in the night.

The home that Lachie and Fiddes return to from the Nigg Bay Golf Club, where they are lethally useless on the course, is only ever attended to by Janet Wishart, Fiddes' blonde. Janet is Fiddes' bidey-in, a wife in all senses but the legal and a suitable companion all the same. Her face has avoided the alcoholic pounding that the Boy Fiddes has inflicted on himself over the years, and she remains discontent at home while he travels out in search of stimulation.

The Boy Fiddes has drunk so much by this stage in the evening that he can ill walk straight upon the tarmac . . . but then the Boy Fiddes has no job, no career in Aberdeen, a town which is more occupied with new dimensions in escapism than it is in the proper employment of its ****ed up natives. Aberdeen sets up with the internet and an increased supply of French restaurants while the Boy Fiddes attends the new football season with his usual apathetic glare. Fiddes may be holding on to a wall to stop himself from falling but Aberdeen is too concerned with the construction of the future to take into its care the life of a young man like this who seems all but without his uses. The same applies to Janet, because the city in her lifetime is unlikely to view her as anything more than a professional baby hamper.

Pastimes for Janet Wishart include cooking for Fiddes, who likes his chips, telly and kids, shopping on the cheap, and skinning up for Fiddes when he's too wrecked like.

The men meanwhile address the issues of the spermary by crushing their faces at the bar of the Nigg Bay Golf Club. After this is done they return home drunk, darkening the hall with laughter and cursing . . . and after that, they expect their supper.

Now that Lachie is out of prison and sleeping on her couch for the next month, Janet is likely to be making a lot of supper. Janet Wishart's expectation is her business, her hope that the lottery will pay her that critical win which will allow the family to shift from the thirteenth floor of Benzie Court to somewhere far away, a home that has a garden.

A garden, yeah right.

Janet Wishart is a dreamer, her head the ideal contrast to the laughing turnip that's on the Boy Fiddes' shoulders. But there he is, the man within, a born puppet to the Benefits Office, the best sort of man there is in this day.

Fiddes is getting bigger she thinks, *despite not eating that much.* He maybe sneaks the odd chipper on the sly, but then so what?

Still, he must have put on two pounds around the neck this last month, and remained indifferent to it as one lap of skin has confused itself with the rest.

The Boy Fiddes goes out for the day while young Janet Wishart works at home, abandoned in these endlessly diagramatic houses that are shunted up to one another in the ice at Nigg. The hill is cold because Nigg faces onto the North Sea and long struts of wind collide with the shingle on the beach and carry the smell of the sewage works back towards the town.

Lachie and his brother, the Boy Fiddes, on the hill above the flats, knock beside each other with the drink. For two days they have celebrated Lachie's release from jail, but Fiddes wishes his brother were safely back inside. Lachie is talking shite in the wind, his face looks like it's been cut long-wise with a knife, his eyes are shining black above the mouth that never stops. Making the most resistance to the rising gale is the Boy Fiddes' prize snooker cue in its special job-lot case. Fiddes holds his snooker cue tightly and worries cause his brother's in a bad mood.

Today's been the worst ****in day of my ****in life.

Come on man, I mean you're no in the ****in jail now.

I ****in mean it.

Eh come on . . .

The ****in worst day of my life ken. Lost twenty quid and naewhere to ****in crash. ****in my flat's fallen through already like.

You're crashing at mine, right?

Yeah yours.

Well?

Well it's ****in shite.

Lachie and Fiddes aim for Benzie Court, thirteen storeys against the wind-crossed sky, a home to two hundred vertically stacked people. These overlagged blocks of housing are homes, high rise concrete crates shouldered into a heath, they are cut with plastic window frames which have been known to melt quickly in a fire. This stormy night, the architect of these flats at Nigg is nowhere to be seen, although we picture him back in London, or whichever resort his more than cheap services were requested from, pushing such menial work as Benzie effing Court to the back of his mind in the poshness of his local eatery, high on the profits of the Fiddes family catastrophe. Maybe we'll get him yet. Lachie would likely break his legs for a tenner, the mood he's in . . .

I canna believe it, says Lachie. I canna ****in believe it.

It's no that bad says Fiddes, it was only twenty quid like.

The lights are on in Nigg, down the hill and in the dark. Half way towards the shingle of Nigg Bay and round the seagull sea, is an unbroken mall of problems. Trouble squat in one large council estate where people are born to, and helpless within, modern Nigg was built by amateurs and planned by policy makers engaged in sticking civic values into slab stone. The result was a purpose-built set of human gutters, with nothing to offer in the way of hope. Really, you would find more to please you in a dog's kennel. Janet Wishart can clean the flat as much as she likes, she can decorate it at the prompting of her morning television, but who's she kidding then? The car park beneath Benzie Court is a further mess where litter is King and the cars are advertisements for rust. Lachie kicks a can which is reflected off the headlights of a passing vehicle, a tiny racing car souped up to make a cloud of smoke, the car speeds away from them on Balanagask Road to take the circuit around the lighthouse, where nightly the scent of rubber wafts over the smell of the sea.

Lachie stops.

****in I knocked ten golf balls into the sea there.

I ken.

Why didn't you ****in stop me then?

Seemed like a good idea at the time like.

Ten golf balls into the sea, the one after the other. Now that was freedom.

Two startling events had committed Lachie to this act of vandalism. One was the fact that the punters in the golf club had heard in advance that he was out of prison, and thus he'd met a few frosty faces at the bar. And the other was the fact that he had no money to buy a drink with.

That was shite in the club, he says to his brother the Boy Fiddes.

I ken says Fiddes.

Well what the **** did we go there for eh you ****?

It seemed that most people in the Nigg Bay Golf Club knew exactly what Lachie had been inside for. And how exactly was it put?

Stabbing a man of the cloth?

That was it.

Shit-cloth mair like.

The amount of times Lachie's thought of that phrase, he should really get a tattoo. It would be a picture of the boy he stabbed's face and underneath it would be written SHIT-CLOTH. Four years of six done in Craiginches prison, less than a mile from his own house, and this for stabbing the minister in the town of Strichen. All of which useful information had been the subject of much backchat in the Golf Club it seemed. Well, any old news for those sad baskets.

Oh look at him he's been in prison!

What are you ****in looking at?

Nothing.

Nothing? Better ****in not be.

Calm down Lachie. It's only like your second day out man . . .

**** em all, says Lachie . . . **** em all like.

After lunch in the club, the game of golf had been just magic. Lachie and the Boy Fiddes hit the course, smoked their first joints of the day and had the perfect sunny, winter round of golf . . . just what Lachie had been thinking about for all those months inside. In prison, he thinks, you plan your release every day. You can see exactly how it's going to be, it gets so bad that you lie awake wondering if the ****er could ever be right, if you could ever really get it the way you want it. Like coming on the course and sparking that joint, that was it. Like looking at the sea and being free like . . . like looking out to sea and being back where you ****in belong . . . it was strong man, not just like a dream but like every ****in dream he'd had. Lachie threw down his golf club and spread his arms out like he was away to fly, no ****er in his face, and as free as he liked . . . he was laughing like this and the wind was blowing right into his mouth! After his third joint that was it. Lachie had just stopped at the head of the course and started to hit golf balls into the sea, one after each other until there were none left in the bag. After that, he laughed like a ****in lunatic.

Ten balls though man. They were Council property ken?

What else am I ****in going to do?

You could calm down like, says the boy Fiddes as the drunken pair reach the car park of Benzie Court. You could calm the **** down.

Fiddes goes in his jacket pocket, fumbling for something lost inside. I'm phoning Janet, he says. I'll say to her that I'm coming up like.

Suit yourself, says Lachie.

I will ****in do that.

The cars parked under Benzie Court this night appear like layers of dead wood placed in rank against the grass, worthless in any light but more so in the street-lamps. These one-time motor vehicles have frozen into position and become prehistoric, useless to their owners, a waste of labour and set to petrify overnight to become old rocks in the morning. The Boy Fiddes struggles in his pocket for the mobile phone.

I'll phone her and tell her I'm here like.

Fiddes' jacket is swallowing his arm as if there's an abandoned tunnel in there. Lachie waits for the appearance of the brand new mobile, but as soon as Fiddes pulls it free, he drops it on the ground where it smacks on the car park tarmac. The phone cracks and bounces.

That's ****ed it.

Fiddes is on his knees, scraping for his phone in the dark, his new toy as nugatory an item as any other in the dead of the parked cars. When he finds his phone a part of it has broken off, and so still on his knees Fiddes purposefully tries to stick it together, swearing, It won't bloody go, it won't bloody go.

What won't bloody go? asks Lachie.

Fiddes on his knees, a small round gob in his face is speaking garbage down upon the mobile's gainless green light.

I'm trying to get it to work like.

Fiddes makes proper the broken section of his phone although it doesn't fit the way it should. The plastic case of the mobile phone is scratched so he resorts to pressing all the buttons, first in a row and then in indecent random patterns.

Gives it here says Lachie, but Fiddes pretends not to hear.

I thought it was supposed to be indestructible, he says, made like a brick shitty hoose?

Well it's still working.

Nih look.

Fiddes holds his phone up, the green light is on but the plastic case is slack. There's a crack across the dial and the Boy Fiddes is still making superfluous pushing motions with his fingers. The phone seems an overly small device for a large man like him.

It stores 160 names.

Is that ****in so?

Labouring in vain on the mini-phone, Fiddes is still in a crouch, making more uncalled for motions and speaking to himself. Fiddes is mad and fat, crouched down there and rat-arsed.

It's a smart phone ken?

Sort of ****in smart.

Fiddes tries to switch the telephone on again and Lachie tries to grab it, so Fiddes throws the mobile in the air above his head.

Check it!

Lachie gets a touch to the flying phone, but he's too drunk and the unit is deflected downward, once again whacking the surface of the car park, needlessly. Fiddes reaches over to grab the phone again, he switches it on and to his shock it appears operational amid the debris on the screen.

Got that ****er working yet?

Yeah it looks like it now.

Sure?

**** aye.

The Boy Fiddes scratches at his new phone, places his finger-nail within a plastic crack and feels at this moment, how truly meaningless are all goods bought. Like water pouring into a sieve are all goods bought, for what is spent, we have nought left. Fiddes dials one sorry digit at a time, the number of his own flat, still in the car park, now able to see the empty curtains of the thirteenth floor, where Janet is always waiting for him.

It's a classic this phone, he says, but Lachie's not interested. The screen of the phone is flying its fatuous green colour once more, the message is that the telephone has not been worth the pains and that it might be broken.

It's a little bastard in some respects all right.

Fiddes looks carefully. The face of the dial has a gash across it but the little bugger's still going it seems.

Hi baby. We're coming up like. If you look out the window you'll see me and all.

The boy Fiddes staring up at Benzie Court, the spiralling emblem of architectural hell.

Look down and you'll ****in see us.

Fiddes stares supremely at Benzie Court, his head right back, the highly appreciated phone in the nub of his neck, while Lachie lights a fag and waits, posing in the cold.

Down here baby. Get a ****in look in.

I canna see you says Janet Wishart.

Fiddes is waiting in the car park for a light from his flat above, for the curtain to twitch, and for his family to have reached another turning point in home technology.

Other ****in window!

Janet Wishart opens the curtain, enough that Fiddes can distinguish her, and he waves his arm across his head,

Down here ****in see?

Janet sees the car park down below is punctuated by two figures, one is Fiddes all right, his arm making a basic and forceful waving down below, and the other is his brother, Lachie.

I see you both.

Fiddes' voice is in her ear at its highest pitch, he's telling her the great material news of the day, that mobile phones are the best.

Janet Wishart thinks, I never look out the bloody window. She sees clearly the other flats emphasised in the nearby block, and shudders. She has an opposite number out there, talking sadly on the telephone on the thirteenth floor of Duffus Court, and another one on the thirteenth floor of Auchry Court, next to it. The sight of these other two tower blocks is an unfortunate reminder of what a huge, cold and ill-fitting pain in the arse her existence is. Entire families thrown shoulder to shoulder where one house becomes a natural extension of the next, where there are nothing but reminders of the many crucial failings in life, where disorder of the first rank is waiting close . . . as close as the City Council can make it.

Are you pair a bams coming up?

The real issue is the children. Any person can see how much low-priced material there is holding life from death in Balnagask and Torry, how much cheap concrete and wood is combined for their benefit, but not for their safety or comfort.

Mental day out baby. We're coming up right now.

Have you had your tea?

Eh no like.

OK. I'll get something on.

Magic.

Skins is here by the way.

Skins?

Aye and if you're not up here in two minutes he'll have scoffed yours and all.

Janet Wishart looks down and lets the curtain fall. It's as if, at one stage the Council looked at Nigg and thought, OK, they bastards can live there. This is problem-solving, thinks Janet, problem-solving on a large level. Looking out of the window at night in Balnagask, the material challenge of life becomes so obvious, the universal need for apparatus to maintain subsistence . . . the flats are pish and therefore so are the inhabitants. In this free world, the Fiddes family unit chose to live in this poverty trap, and thus the problem of people is resolved one afternoon by city bureaucrats who more significantly, return home to their townhouses, eminently proud of the fact that they've done their bloody jobs. Janet Wishart sees the image of the day, the hour even when the flats at Nigg were settled. The Council took the people down the hill past the golf course, and moved them and their possessions to the very spot where the Boy Fiddes and his brother Lachie are now standing. The car park was empty that day . . . empty but for suitcases, head-cases, prams and bams. Immediately on seeing Benzie Court, the people had no force of their own, no will.

We're coming up now baby, so be ready!

OK honey.

No force of their own. No life. That day in 1968 when several hundred people were glued together in one tiny key community called *the flats*, their style, their ideas, their politics and their futures became all as one. The people managed to keep the principal feeling of mirth going all the way to sundown, but the next day there rose a gloom that was going to stick in those buildings for the next two centuries.

We are delighted said a city Councillor, *to welcome the people of Nigg to these new apartment blocks, Benzie, Duffus and Auchry Court.*

We are delighted indeed.

Families were being slotted into an economic order like a row of memory chips in the casement of a machine, like prisoners in their cells.

We are delighted to welcome people to these newly designed flats and accompanying sewage works nearby.

Did it occur to anybody here that it was all a big swick?

Did the people go into these hellish blocks of flats with positive expressions?

Families were allowed into the building one at a time, and the blocks of flats became great levellers of humanity. Thirteen storeys, people exposed to each other's smells and noises on the interior, and if they opened the windows, they faced the sewage on the wind outside. The flats were composed of the internal weaknesses of their inhabitants who could do nothing to stop their own rot, like teeth going from the gums . . . and the resident families who were settled there brought every infection of their unhappy working days back home to breed. The families yelled louder, the noise shook the partition walls and in the lifts and the corridors, everybody got on with each other in the most superficial way. The boat was never rocked in Benzie Court, no opinion was ever spoken out loud, and it meant that a general density dominated right from the core of these buildings to their roofs, with the only tangible thought being a vague negativity concerning the City Council, a feeling which the residents never encouraged for fear of being thrown out.

The young Janet Wishart pulls the curtain closed and looks across the kiddie toys upon the floor.

Bloody hell. Never look out of the window.

She looks up. Skins is on the sofa doing that for which he is rightly named, smoking spliff.

How could the Council assume that their new-improved building technology was going to gel people into one happy lump? Gentle thumping in the background is a man crossing his floor in the next door flat, walking to his kitchen, unaware of her.

The worst thought comes to Janet Wishart again, that she would like one day to have a garden. The idea is a comedy, a dream that will not come true.

They're in the front garden, she says to Skins. Pissed as farts like.

Oh aye, he says and smiles.

Benzie Court, Duffus and Auchry Court were built with keen attention to mathematical relationships, the flats were filled with people who were going to eat up the building slowly until the entire substructure was underscored and the overriding feeling was of rejection and oppression . . . and after that, Skins was going to come round for his tea and play some video games like.

Still, the main sensation within the flats is that of failure, as if the inhabitants have been wicked in a previous life. That was it, the failed possibility that by putting up ready housing like this, the City Fathers of Aberdeen could do more with less and could rid themselves of an entire working, or soon to be not working, population.

Now, a variety of mechanical bureaucracy exists within the shell of Benzie Court. The tower centres around two lift shafts and is completed by many small homes, filled with model examples of technology. Early in the evening an urgent clamour comes from the flats and then all is silence while people have their tea. The evening's damage starts after the dishes are in the sink, the decided crying of the building . . . and then the children come out and make the best expression of the stress that they can, often marking the walls with pen and paint. Still however, Benzie Court fails to cave in . . . not for many years to come. So grandly she stands, this design-age tower block, a hollow kingdom where the emotions of the inhabitants are frayed and conspicuously more basic than those of their townhouse dwelling counterparts across the river.

It's sad but true. People in Nigg are terminally unwise as to how the social system works against them through its complication of mortgages, insurances, and investments in people far more profitable than they will ever be. They have smells on the wind to cope with too.

Fiddes and his brother Lachie push in through the small doors at the foot of the building where the personal linguistic forms of the young inhabitants have been well-worked into the walls in felt pen:

Hilton Tongs Ya Bas
Y Crew
Cuz & Kim luv Mixu
Garthdee ASC
Toxic Ephex.
Moira a slag

The Boy Fiddes and his brother walk through the hall. What choice does a person have but to ascribe beauty and oratory to their own home? None of an evening, because you can't come home every single night of the year and say, I hate this, even if it's as depressing as Benzie Court. Some days you have to make a star of the positive and see the world in a better light, with drink to help you if you like And some days, peace must make war, just to keep the mood steady.

Notably then, the downstairs hallway is all right with the Boy Fiddes and the litter and the controlling influence of shit is a cue for warmth. One's organ of balance can, it is now perceived by the Boy Fiddes, adjust to any down-curve . . . so Benzie Court is starkly scientific, as if in an age of panic the building represents a coherent vision, once assembled, spontaneously strong, the product of the imagination made real.

To say the least, a tower of shit.

Your no ****in wrong there bro.

The brothers stamp a little in the cold of the hall, there's a banging noise from within the lift shaft and with protest and recoil, the mystifying process of the elevator begins.

I'm ****ed man, says Fiddes.

Fiddes puts his hand in his pocket and feels some money. He recalls that he stole twenty quid off his brother Lachie that afternoon. Lachie doesn't know it, he thinks he must have lost it somewhere else . . . but then thinks Fiddes, looking sly from the corner of his slitted eye, Lachie has been doing ma ****in nut since the moment he got out of the jail. The truth is, it's a pain in the arse that Lachie's back from his spell in prison. It means that Lachie'll be stashing nicked goods in the flat again, thinks Fiddes, the same tricks he was up to four years ago . . . it means he'll be making eyes at Janet and all, which Fiddes cannae ****in stand.

So, they're six hours off the golf course, and already Fiddes is wanting shot of Lachie, for good. It was Lachie's freedom they were celebrating and Fiddes couldnae get a word in, not with that bastard and his stupid stories. He glances again at his brother, who is smoking in the pissed-up hallway of Benzie Court like the ****in lord of the manor, stretching his arms out like he's preparing to lift a weight and muttering under his breath. The minimum of light from the street outside gives the stone walls of the hallway a criminal coldness, and Lachie's words are barely heard threats. Lachie thinks that his busted face and his scar gives him the right to be the chief man in Nigg like, but nobody cares, cause nobody's ****in heard of him. In or out of prison Lachie's still a nobody, Fiddes is working like a bastard looking for a job, while this ****er's got money in his pocket from the nick, and that's not fair.

Lachie and Fiddes drank hard all day and never changed verbs. The same colloquial shite that's like a routine.

The Golf Club was half full when they got there about five o'clock, and like he'd never been away, Lachie checked what was on Sky Sport and gets up to the bar. He looked at the scene of the harbour from the windows, and he breathed it in like he owned it, it was all a kick to him. Everyone knew that Lachie was back from inside . . . they all knew about the knife attack on the Strichen minister, but that was long ago and Lachie didn't mean it to happen anyway. Lachie has a blurred and muzzy memory of the event now, but that's not how the story goes, and Fiddes is already sick of hearing it.

****in magic man, said Lachie as he put his hands down on the sticky wooden bar, it's ****in magic to be back.

Most people could remember Lachie from before and nodded at him for his homecoming, but Fiddes reckoned they were all depressed that he was home. After all, the punters in the Golf Club are all family people, and Lachie is a man of untold anti-values.

After a couple of drinks, the same things happened as used to happen. Lachie got pished and then spoke to the girls at the bar, he gave them his old crap chat-up lines, the same lines that Fiddes had heard those years before.

Surely Lachie hadn't been practising in prison? *Your hair's looking good. What's that round your neck? Gives a look. Did you get it from your boyfriend? You don't have a boyfriend? How come? A lassie as good looking as you eh? Eh I'm afraid I'm taken . . . but my brother here. He's a big fan of yours. But what about it. That's a shame you have to buy that for yourself.*

The Boy Fiddes is embarrassed and as always, Lachie embarrasses him more.

My brother looks like a poof but he's nae. I wouldn't repeat though what he said about your tits, nae in front of your faither anyway.

The brothers leave the bar and descend into the games room, a low chamber of pleasures with a snooker table in the middle. Lachie throws his jacket over the back of a chair and sifts through the snooker balls, talking over this activity as if he's Ray ****in Reardon. A shite break and Lachie laughs at Fiddes like when they were kids.

That's not a cue man, says Lachie to his brother, that's a ****in plank. How do you expect to do any business with a ****in plank like that?

Lachie's in his element now he's out of jail. It's nothing to do with the club, or his brother, or with Nigg or any of Aberdeen, cause it's all Lachie, close up on his face. He doesn't even care about breaking the Nigg Bay Golf Club's golden rule about smoking over the snooker table, because Lachie has been inside.

Big talk, playing shite, Lachie takes a shot and walks casual like. Down on the cue he says, you've got to get your chin touching that ****in cue man, get into the level of the game. It's a two-dimensional game bro and that's the truth. To be this slick you've got to know your angles. Lachie strikes another steamer into the far pocket, set up now for the perspective on the black. The ****in black now, and his jaw goes down on the cue again, he's chewing a mouthful of imaginary gum, Lachie swells, he's back in the land of the living, everybody knows it, even the girl behind the bar, her with the nice hair. Lachie gets rat-arsed and articulates more hate, he becomes louder still as he drinks mair pints. Lachie came from nothing and decided to stay there by narrowing his view with the help of his diction, into a nameless lexicon of people he doesn't trust, football teams he'd like to bomb, girls he wants to ****in shag, ladies he's taken up the *****er, boring crimes he's been involved in and women who have thrown themselves to bed on his behalf.

I couldn't ****in believe that lassie, like the way she was looking at you like that. You're a ****in waste of space if you can't see that.

Lachie strikes another red ball well, he has nothing to his name now but opinion and prison anecdote.

What are you looking at you poof? he asks the Boy Fiddes.

I don't know.

Fluke? Is that what you ****in think?

I don't know. Fiddes doesn't know the difference and drinks a forcible mouthful of lager. He has just told himself that he's going to get good and pissed, there's not much else for it.

That was no ****in fluke you poof, says Lachie, and he points the cue at his brother. The noise of the bar seems like a faint rumble in the distance.

Lachie goes down to the table again, chin on the cue, looking along the line to the middle pocket, smoking over the baize. *You've got to get right down. Down so that your chin is touching the cue. See the boys on telly just like that. Chin on the cue so they don't miss a trick. It's a two dimensional game bro.*

The heaven of being out of that prison, golf, drugs, drink, snooker. Pursuits both mental and physical, both relaxing and taxing, to enervate the modern loser. Lachie strikes the ball into the centre and stays down on his cue to smile.

Didn't lose my touch inside eh.

Lachie moves through the snooker room with the majesty of a criminal lord, his next shot is driving, but his ball misses the pocket and rolls round the pack in a gentle arc, he pours the full tide of his eloquence outward, and Fiddes listens again as Lachie's eyes go slitty as he swears. When he's stopped, Lachie goes for a pish, he leans his cue against the wall and smudges his fag into the ashtray.

Nae cheating you poof.

Yeah cheers.

. . . and Lachie leaves the snooker room, off to the bogs.

There was no impulse. Fiddes couldn't believe what a nightmare it was to have his brother back and crashing at his flat, so with his eye on the window to the corridor, not for Lachie, but for someone likely more observant, he has the twenty quid note out of his brother's jacket before a breath is taken. It's all that Lachie deserves, he thinks. Lachie's always liked to carry around money and say that he's got none, he wants folk like his brother who've got a family to support to give him loans and that, cause he can't ever be arsed earning proper money like. But everybody's broke in Nigg, so who's the bastard haudin back money like that? Some wanker, Lachie.

Fiddes stuffs his brother's money in his jeans and sits down to smoke. Takes a mouthful of drink and that's that done. Nobody none the wiser and Lachie owes even less to society now. Lachie comes back into the snooker room and starts figuring out his next shot.

I haven't gone yet says the Boy Fiddes.

Well ****in go then. You've just had ****in five minutes.

That loud mouth just cost you twenty quid.

Easy ****in shot you've left me, says Lachie once Fiddes has played, but his brother doesn't care. Nae interested. Just let's get on with it and get hammered and maybe later I'll listen to some more of your shite sex stories, and your ****in shiter prison stories.

Lachie gets twice as pished again before they leave the Nigg Bay Golf Club, the slow ascension process forces the alcohol to his brow where it smiles accordingly above his eyes. When Lachie is wasted like this his face ramps with relaxed folds of unhealthy skin, there's more sting in the pupils of his eyes and his facial scar recedes amid other interventional lines. And Fiddes gets to the concrete hallway in Benzie Court each time and feels he's lost everything, and wants to kick the door of the lift in and make a mess of it.

The brothers get in the lift and press for the 13th. The noise starts up and Fiddes leans back for a boring two minutes. The effective traditions of ongoing civilisation are compared within the steel lift. High in the building, compressed in the hole, Fiddes feels like one of an army of many dying rats, crawling for their lives, trying to make it to safety before he's burned by the light. The motion of the elevator compares with the complex ecstasies of the drink.

I feel sick, he says once more, in time to hear his brother Lachie laugh out loud and call him once again: a poof.

THE CRAZE FOR LUNCH

Professionals have a certain craze, for which they need fresh mayonnaise, for lunch, the high point of their days, is what they call their *business phase* . . .

For you I'd say you're just the class, to beautify your portly ass, with costly eating you call *dining,* the style that has you now reclining, where pies are served you will not go, for you prize service more than dough, the cakes and chips your cleaners eat with haddock as their weekly treat, the battered food that builders scoff or those with just an hour off, it's nothing to professional folk, who only eat organic yolk, who roll their chicken in chapati, and sook the head of foaming latte . . . so find somewhere to park your car and park your suited rear afar from us in somewhere overrated, arty, over-decorated, the home of style the diner's realm, with some flash poseur at the helm, you're going to feel the pliant tug of coriandered foods, the fug of menus in a foreign scheme, designed for you in Aberdeen.

So for your taste I recommend, you treat a colleague or a friend, to something flash in the West End where mode and form are much in view, the menu is a concept stew, a fancy dish the pish you'll pee will be a fancy stream from thee, once in a restaurant foreign named, and rightly famed and rave reviewed as classic food, you'll leave your desk to take a scoff and likely take the p.m. off!

The suits in business take their lunch, the talking rides above the crunch, the meat, the veg, that's foreign clipped or frozen lamb that has been shipped, from far away across the sea, the tame are slain and with disdain are packed and sailed across the main, to eateries where cash is taken, cost forsaken, confidence and hope are shaken, for you should know when somewhere's fash, the last thing's cash that's on your splash . . . and once you're bloated and replete and made it back upon your feet, you'll pay the bill and taste your suite and head for work once more you sots, with beef for shanks and buttered thoughts, but listen well . . . injunction must be spoken now of how you've given rope to hang poor men, and taken hope from life . . .

You've taken hope from life you diners, unbending critics, patronisers, you've filled these cruddy little haunts, where finds the dish it really wants, it's known to be a snotty cow when reading menus well endowed, it's known to be a spoiled pig, to diet while it's getting big . . . and how it favours many flavours, quoting herbs and sauce it havers, awfully savvy of it's diet, it sees a new dish and must try it, it's known to be a rude young man, a ham at best inside its vest, it's Gucci tie which doth belie, the thought of love or brain above, when it's alone its mobile phone will keep it feeling right at home, it's known to spend and knows no end these lazy men with extra crème, who love to do it to a hen, it needs to hang about with them, and talk about starvation's end and says: *Oh Lord we have to get away! from bor-ing Aberdeen!*

My God sit down and do not frown, this is the centre of the town, a lunch is fine, we'll drink white wine! I'll meet you in an hour's time, my desk is crammed my thoughts are paste, so something French beneath my waist, would be to my acquired taste, I eat roe deer as well as lamb, I'm on a daily spree I am a devotee of gosling pie, a chronic addict of the fry, I fear I love this restaurateur who's kept me on the moules and beurre, and pork, oh God! I do despair, of pies and beer and public fare, where they deep-fry I'd rather die, or see a pub that's full of *grub*, and pubbers too that working crew, I'll tell you good I've found here food, that is divine and is sublime, *my adjectives come rushing out upon a line!* . . . an intellectual's what you're called when by the *common* you're appalled, by *common* words and *common* songs . . . for Tuscany it pines, and longs . . . for I won't stuff nor hog nor cram, cause I'm a *diner*, yes I am, who eats well out of house and sod, winebibbery:

I'm the belly god.

Well, Aberdeen can boast a few as the centre of each town can do, eye openers to the omnivores, the restaurants, the finest moeurs, a rank of cars is parked outside, they eat and drink and then they drive . . . and so they dine with full attention, given to this with comprehension, this place is not just for the nose . . .. but for the business person's pose . . .

What's that new place with that new dish?

The decoration is so swish!

What's that new abattoir I spy where animals in cream will lie?

For God's sake let me through to that especially if it is lo-fat! I need some style and some repast, this is no time to starve or fast! I need to dine to eat to live, these anorexic girls, they give me such a pain those thin, thin girls, what swine they are to lunchtime's pearls, if only they could see this décor, it would revive their flagging pecker, the concept came from Nice you know, it's based upon a Feng Shui flow, so know you this and know you now, we will not eat that cardboard cow, we must have style! We must be fed! Oh little girl, we'll soon be dead!

I'll have the matzo ball soup.

And for the main course today?

How's the tuna done?

It is grilled with peas.

I'll have the lamb.

And you madam?

I think I'll have the chicken.

Liana's restaurant in the West End of Aberdeen.

At the corner in the granite is the stained metal sign spelling the word LIANA'S in a spread across the upper wall. The lower section of the windows of Liana's are large with dried flowers, and behind these are ranged the diners. Present in Liana's this wet lunchtime are the usual round rumps breaking from their unexacting employment for two hours, there to eat an expensive public dinner. A glass of wine? What kind? What grape? Oh how the flavour does escape!

The walls are smart and hung with art, they call it art it's sort of painting, Leonardo would be fainting, it really is more of a splatch some art school kid's poured from their hatch . . . 'That's puke! I say! Not art but puke! I'd rather see the artist hanging there!'

Councillor Pally Cruden is the focus at the window of Liana's, the loudest talker in the restaurant by a chalk. Loudest in dress and loudest in voice, Pally sits opposite the human internet creature known as Chris Crandall, he tells her about the computers and the call centre, and how he aims to hit the half billion mark within the next three years. Pally's accent becomes less Scottish with every mouthful, while nobody knows what sort of voice Chris Crandall speaks in. It approximates a robot register at times, he always sounds like he's giving confidential commercial advice, even when he's flirting. Crandall only takes his attention from Pally to look around him at the restaurant, as if to say that he's seen it all before. Liana's decor is most gentle, where keen design is fundamental, that is to say it's of import for those who are the trendy sort . . . the suits have Pally memorised, her pound-sign hairdo and her eyes, these gentlemen are not polite, in fact their gaze is rapt and tight . . . these men in suits they beg a rise, not like the common man who eyes the ladies as a distant prize, they're smart in here, and awfully wise . . . but suit or not we'll see you lot at bedtime with your naked legs as coddle you your hairy eggs . . . like any other blokes!

Pally's mobile phone and flapping eyelashes are attractors here, and the many businessmen eating in Liana's chance glances when they think they can get away with it. Like soft shell crabs, their black eyes flick round and gaze upon her body, what they can see of it across the tables.

Pally is occupied in some networking however, engaged in business with Chris Crandall, a man she sees as being upon the up-slope. Crandall wears a checked shirt open at the neck and under the table, his hands rub up and down his regulation Chinos. His is the air of casual well-being.

This weather's the worst, he says.

Oh roll on summer! says Pally.

Yes indeed!

Short laughter, insufficient conversation. November yes, Pally and Crandall are both aware of the darkness of the day, here in their nice restaurant.

I think it's going to rain, says Pally.

Well let's hope not.

I think it is you know.

Aberdeen and rain! The waters pour in thin strokes, the clouds come in from the West on their way to sea, the Banff Baillies roll before the water falls, offering a ten-minute warning in the sky. Outside Liana's and above the West End, a broad vertical bar of light appears and then in minutes the population are knee deep in splashing car tyres while the rain jumps down street. It's rained a hundred thousand times in Aberdeen, but each time's the same – curses spring from people's mouths and the water plays hell as they rush home to activate their televisions. Pally has the local sense for rain, November's a spirit buster of a month, and it's all bad news as far as the weather is concerned. Moreover, you can expect a downpour at least twice a week.

Yes that's the rain all right.

Real Scottish weather.

That's the one, says Pally. It's terrible really.

I can't say it's great in England either.

No I suppose not.

I mean says Crandall, England's quite far away. But it's just the same.

Yes I suppose.

Pause.

Do you think the weather's worse in Scotland than it is in England? he asks.

Oh worse in Scotland.

And what if you're standing next to the Border?

I don't know, says Pally. But generally I'd say it was worse in Scotland.

You mean more rain?

Yes, more rain.

Pause

How could there be more rain in Scotland though? asks Crandall. I mean to say, when England's bigger?

Well that would just show how much worse it is.

Do you think?

The door of the restaurant opens to interrupt the flow, and in with the cold flatulence of city air come more business bodies on the mat. A waitress walks up and smiles at each new customer, holding her expression steady until Sir and Madam are shown over to their place.

Your wide behind here sir. And your hands on the table, where we can see them!

Back from the kitchen comes the smell, the alchemy of food-stuff. The folks discharge their coats and bags, the coats and bags retreat to racks, the smoking chef looks out and hacks, the guests begin to live! May wee for sure this is the spot, I can't believe you've bought this rot, this foreign tosh, you've all said gosh you're hit with culture's wooden kosh!

And you loved it!

Liana's is separated from the commonality of Aberdeen by a fake foreign atmos. When the door opens every head turns just to see who is blowing in this November. Rosy cheeks on Queen's Road, everyone outside is soaking wet but at least the lunch is just right. And so many lunch meetings! The pitch of conversation fills the gaps between the mouthfuls, someone shakes an umbrella at the door and another brushes rain off of his briefcase.

Pally and Chris Crandall settle to their matzo ball soup.

Mmm this is nice.

Yes very nice.

Crandall plunges neatly to the plate, quivering spoon to mouth with not a drop on the shirt, the train goes into the tunnel once again. This man has eaten a thousand designer meals from the maisons of Edinburgh, to most of the happening buvettes in London. It's no event.

I can assure you, says Pally after the first taste, that now your network is running, the city would be keen to see what other developments you have in the pipeline.

Ah.

A mouthful of soup disguises his interest, but Crandall Technologies want this city in the bag, and badly so.

Pally looks down upon the matzo balls and wonders. Crandall eats nearby but momentarily her attention lowers to the food.

There's something so pathetic about matzo balls, she thinks as she spoons the pulpy nutritive swimmers to the centre of her bowl. She lowers her voice as if other diners in Liana's might be listening, and says, *it's very exciting that you've made it happen.*

Crandall assumes that she is speaking to him and not her lunch.

I'm delighted, he says, and as he mops his lip, a flatus of rich fish gas from the kitchens crosses the air. 20,000 computers, he says, distributed among the general public, the largest Local Area Network in the world, and free to every user. This is very groundbreaking indeed.

Yes indeed! says Pally, and they both laugh out loud, although Pally is not sure why.

It's the way ahead really, she says.

Absolutely, says Crandall. I refer to it as C*onnectivity.*

Connectivity!

Yes that's the word. Social and economic connectivity, you see?

Yes, I see.

That's the world ahead, says Crandall. It's where we're all going.

Pally is engaged once more in thought upon the squashy matzo but after a second she says across the table, *computers are here to stay.*

Well that's without doubt true replies Chris Crandall.

Crandall scoops the last of his soup to his mouth and while Pally searches in her bag, he glances at his watch to see what is happening in America. It's 13.15 now and he should really be at his office for 14.30. His consultant has a 15.00 meeting for which he is not yet fully prepared and after that, Crandall flies 17.00 to London. Timing is crucial and Crandall places his spoon parallel to his unfolded napkin. The allocation for soup is completed and now must come some red meat. Pally is speaking but Crandall interrupts her.

I'm inviting some backers from America to visit us, he says, and looks at his watch again. Did you book somewhere for them to stay?

The Sillerton House Hotel, says Pally, and she slides a glossy brochure across the table towards him. The way she slides this brochure, slow like a secret dossier, Crandall knows that the city will be picking up the bill.

Crandall eyes the brochure critically, smiling as if he's greeting a prospective client.

On this massive colour brochure, The Sillerton House Hotel is photographed among the treetops, a paste-coloured mothership of concrete and plaster emitting a gentle warmth as it emerges from the diffuse array of nearby evergreens. The hotel crowns the car park and the gentle slope of the landscaped grounds are prominent with business-vehicles. Silver space-wagons communicate expressions of love, while dark-coloured saloon cars sit to attention on the tarmac which leads up to the front door.

Excellent, he says.

Crandall turns to page one of the brochure where the photograph shows the steps leading into the hotel. A boy in a blue uniform is stationed in readiness at the revolving door, an impure Aberdonian lad with a shortage of custom.

More pictures, the foyer of the Sillerton House filled with a superabundance of healthy plants. Crandall flicks through, quickly.

Page Four, a flow of arc-lit corridors from one space to the next lead business people to their chosen lounge in ordered comfort.

Caption: MEETINGS ARE BEST CONDUCTED IN THE STEADFAST LOCAL ATMOSPHERE PROVIDED BY CONFERENCE AREAS SUCH AS THE DOCKENS SUITE, AND THE JEAMES ROOM.

Photograph, in soft focus, a side angle of the Sillerton House Hotel, the building is bathed in a great mist which has arrived fresh from the Grampian Hills.

A photograph on the rear of the brochure shows the hall porters of The Sillerton House, a small and ionised group of servants who wear screwed-up bow ties under their necks and burgundy waistcoats with pockets full of fluff. The hall porters' bow ties look like they would take pliers to remove and the waistcoats are flecked across the shoulder with white specks from their hair.

Caption: THE HALL PORTERS ARE ALWAYS READY
WITH A LIGHT, SHOULD YOU ASK.

Look carefully again at the picture and you notice that the hall porters are all smoking. One of them has a cigarette point blank in his face.

That looks great, says Crandall and he glances again at his watch. The hotel might look great, but the main course seems to be running late.

For Pally however, the lunch could last forever. She hasn't even brought up the topic of Crandalls' new car yet, a picture of which she saw in the business pages of the Press & Journal. This car, Pally read, is a powerful and imposing symbol of its owner's exquisite style. The body of Crandall's sports car is fluted and yellow and has a fine curved wrap-around bonnet with sculptured headlamps and large gulping air intakes, a superb expression of both aesthetics and wealth. Crandall is thinking of starting a collection of cars, Pally read in the article, to go with his collection of call centres. She feels there's so much to learn from this man, and not just good business practice. Crandall is a technology guru, a man with thoughts on the future, ideas on connecting new technology with families, information services and innovations in industry . . . everything in short that it says in the Crandall Technologies press release.

Crandall shoots a stare at the kitchen.

You know, he says, if I was running this place, that girl would be sacked by now. I don't know how some businesses survive.

Pally blushes and looks away. There's no sign of their meal yet and so with an artificial longing she turns to the window. Outside, on Queen's Road, the downpour has given way to a proper settlement of water, a shower that brings low the sky and quickly wets the granite walls. People nod past the glass and schoolgirls and boys run back to class as the water tops and hurdles on the roadway. And here, to be sitting at the window of Liana's, while the water falls, and the people frisk by, Pally is delighted with herself! This modern feeling now is great, to be in chat sophisticate, the smartest things the wallet brings, what will they plan for future man today?

We cannot wait to hear!

Pally and Crandall have achieved a rare peace in their hysterical lives. One moment on the soft ocean floor of the day, the two empty soup bowls need to be collected and removed, and both diners wait with hands twitching on the oil-cloth. Any time now, Pally and Crandall hope to enjoy the next course, and the accompanying *intelligent* items of conversation.

ORGANISED CRIME

The flat in Benzie Court is clean despite a well of dust and broken biscuits behind the sofa. Janet Wishart can't move from the television now the kids are in their bed, but the nearby rocking of the lift carrying the redness of the boy Fiddes and the lippitude of his brother Lachie, gets her to the kitchen and the chip pan on the stove.

That's them, she says to Skins who's waiting on the armchair.

Skins looks up from his crotch, *nice one.*

Janet Wishart has magicked an elevating meal for the bampot brothers when they arrive at the flat, and minutes after the lift stops, the plates are out on the sofa as Lachie and Fiddes burst in to the living room like two mannequins falling out of a closet.

Yo Skins what like? asks Lachie.

No ****in bad, says Skins, *no ****in bad at all!*

Skins and Lachie enjoy a laugh and Fiddes greets his blonde.

Hiya dear. What's that? Chips like? Magic.

Aye, she says and she folds her arms to keep him from trying to slobber her.

Fiddes and Lachie take a plate each and retire, one to a chair and the other to the sofa, both with a fork and an appetite.

So this is you out of prison man? asks Skins.

That's me out like and done my ****in time alright!

Lachie has an ugly mouth of food, it compacts like the rolls of waste litter at the dump, artfully cut chips crushed into the mash.

Nice one.

****in right there boy.

Hard upon the food, Fiddes and Lachie take dreadful mouthfuls with fork and spoon while Skins watches on amused. Served tonight, fish in sauce, boiled in a water tight bag and served over home made chips. What is wanting in the flavour of the fish is made up for by a filling effect down in the beery belly. Janet Wishart has skinned up also for the men, insufficient in their drink and completely unable to do anything for themselves.

Better than the food inside? says Skins.

Porridge man, says Lachie, I tell you it's a ****in disaster. Just cause you're locked up like they know nobody'll hear you complain.

In space no one'll hear you scream.

That's about it like.

You skinned up yet? asks Fiddes, a change of subject. Anything but prison. Mustn't get Lachie talking about that shite again.

Yes love, skinned up.

That's a long time inside says Skins.

You're ****in right there.

Well **** all's happened out here man.

Aye?

Lachie's mouth is full of chips in sauce, but food doesn't taste of anything when you're this pished.

I can't even mind what you were in for ya ****! says Skins.

The Boy Fiddes stares over at the telly while Lachie hiccups his food nearby. On telly is a medical drama that Fiddes can't stand, something he hates that *she* watches like.

Safe job out at Strichen, says Lachie. I stabbed the man of the cloth mind?

Aye?

Lachie points at Fiddes with his fork. See the boy there, he was shitting himself and he wasn't even ****in there like!

Mental says Skins, chuckling on his smoke.

Aye! shouts Lachie, he's a thick-shit like!

Lachie sits back, his arms symmetrical on the rests of the chair. The Boy Fiddes watches several medical actors on TV approaching another injury with clinical care and structured haircuts, he is aware of Lachie starting his story again, the bloody history of his crime, the ****in Strichen story.

And that is it, thinks Fiddes, *if I have to listen to this pish one more time then what?*

No then. Nothing. Be patient and let Lachie have his moment. Let's see what he's got to add to the anecdote this time round, let's see what he can do to pep up the convoluted mess he's made of his life, the all true story that's lead him here, through robbery and violence, through prison to this very moment now, when he's about to crash on our ****in couch for a month . . .

Skins lights the joint that Janet has made and Fiddes drops his plate on the carpet, anxious for the remedial smoke, the cleansing effects that'll lull him further from the day.

So Strichen right, says Lachie, it's like ****in sheds. It's just one of those villages right?

Skins nods. His smile is wide, you could fit a ladder long ways in that eyeless grin. The joint goes in to Skins' mouth but Lachie is impatient and reaches to him.

Gi's that j here man. He tries to click his fingers.

Skins passes the joint which goes straight between Lachie's wetted lips, the last of the mash is swallowed and he draws the smoke hard behind the final mouthful.

****in hell, says Lachie, it was a smart job like but it went ****in wrong, ken.

Aye?

Oh that it did.

The Boy Fiddes watches Lachie's face but he hears no words, he observes the facial contortions of the muscles as they wax but cannot make out a single sound. Janet stands at the kitchen door and Lachie glances over, a jealous look. She walks forward to pick up his empty plate and all the men watch her closely. Silence. Lachie still quietly benumbing his skull with the hash, he takes another draw and then the joint comes to Fiddes who takes it to his mouth, the smoke rolls and he pulls it down. The concussion of the drug dampens Fiddes' displeasure at last, he lies back in his seat and stares at his brother in a better, newer light. Lachie is still watching Janet while Fiddes draws on the joint and discharges the smoke towards the ceiling, and somewhere up there the smoke eases itself upon the wall and relaxes into a stain which he can't keep his eyes off.

So I gets on the bike and gets out to Strichen like, says Lachie, I've got my bag and my knife and I've a joint in my pocket for after the show, and that's me.

Nice one, says Skins.

Too right.

The Boy Fiddes looks dumbly at his brother and then back up at the ceiling, towards which he lets go more smoke. Janet is gone but Lachie is still watching the kitchen as if she was standing there, he gutters up something from his throat and whispers,

**** *was I dying for a shag inside man.*

Fiddes doesn't blink. Over the years and the course of his anecdotes, Lachie's verbal denigration of woman's bodies has improved with his continuing lack of experience. *It's the way I am,* he says, *I mean inside you get all these folk shitting it about their ****in blondes, but not me like. You think I'd be like that? Not in a million dollars.*

Lachie glowers and Fiddes lets go a stream of smoke and follows it through with a cough.

So I get into Strichen right, says Lachie, and the town's all misty with no ****er there. It's the perfect day for a robbery and I've got my plan off pat like. Go into the Post Office with the crash helmet on and just start shouting my head off. I mean lots of noise like and just wave ma knife at the bastards right?

Aye.

Aye, so the plan is basically scare the shit out of them and then leg it. Get behind the counter if I can, get the wifie to put the money in the bag and get out fast. Hope that the bike's still there. So I drive round Strichen and there's nothing doing at all. I mean I see one person standing in a boiler suit, and then there's like a guy working in his garden, and that's it. I mean the population of Strichen. So I was shitting it then, I mean you would.

Skins pulls the joint from Fiddes and takes a drag, he appraises the burning red rocket on the tip, and gives a good opinion of the smoke. Fiddes returns to his anxious coil on the sofa next to his empty plate, and after a moment has started looking for the drugs again.

I was coming down the High Street in Strichen, says Lachie, and checking it out. Butcher's shop right, and the store, and the church at end . . . and the Post Office too. So I switches off the bike right and it's like totally ****in quiet, and I've got my sports bag and I've got my knife.

Lachie glances over to see if Fiddes is paying attention and he notices again the man's clumsy attempts to skin up, as if with the drunken hooves of an overly chubby donkey. Fiddes' face is listless with the most concentration he can muster, it looks like he's working dough and not involved in the careful creation of a reefer.

What the ****in hell is that man? asks Lachie.

Beer can in his hand, Lachie gulps with laughter at the sight of his brother's handiwork.

Check it! he says.

Skins smiles at the Boy Fiddes with a bald shaven leer.

How the **** are we going to smoke that you fat bastard? asks Lachie. I mean what the ****in hell is it?

It's a j.

Fiddes' eyes are sleepy with drink, he makes a choking noise as he tries to fold the joint again.

What did you use for a roach? A ****in toilet roll?

No man. Just leave it out.

Check it Skins, the boy's got a ****in toilet roll in there. How the **** we going to smoke that? You better watch your carpet like. Your blonde'll kill you when those hot rocks start dropping like.

Get off man I can ****in mend it.

You light that says Lachie, and there's going to be a ****in bonfire.

Skins's shoulders are shrugging slowly in a drunken laugh, like he's hiccuping his appreciation of the situation. Fiddes, too low in his chair to move, tries to become more vertical, to get a better angle on the rolling of the j, but it appears that he's too heavy, like he's stuck. It almost looks like Fiddes is secured within the soft back side of the seat, worsened by the weight of the drink and now unable to see ahead of him for the load on his eyes.

Get it ****in mended says Lachie, I'm not smoking that shit.

I am mending it you bastard.

Stuporous, the boy Fiddes tries to pull off the end of the joint to make a fresh start, but finds he doesn't have the strength in his knuckles.

Anyway, where's the blow? asks Lachie.

I think he's ****in eaten it says Skins.

Where's the blow man? asks Lachie.

It's here says Fiddes. The newspaper on his lap is loaded with shreds and crumbs, the components of a lengthy project in drug preparation.

Where is it?

It's here, how do you think I managed to skin up you bastard?

****in eaten it the bastard says Skins. Greedy bastard's chomped it.

Skins's shoulders hiccup up and down in laughter.

It must have fallen down the back, says the boy Fiddes. His bum is stuck into the rear of the heavy chair and in his hands the joint looks more like a canoe than a spliff, more like a bent white trombone than the neat product of keen drug artisans.

Well get it says Lachie. ****in get off your arse and get the blow man. I gave you money for that ****in blow eighteen months ago and you canna even skin up without ****in eating it you greedy bas.

Mental says Skins.

Canna trust no ****, says Lachie.

Get on some sounds says Skins.

Nah the kids says Fiddes.

The kids should get in here and get some ****in vibe says Lachie. Go on and get on some sounds man. Get your blonde in and get some sounds sorted. Your kids'll be all right man.

It'll wake the kids, says Fiddes as he feels around his backside for the pot.

****in this is your house so you can do what you like!

I know, says the Boy Fiddes, so we'll have no sounds like.

Fiddes tries to get his hand down the side of the chair without raising himself but finds no joy, no drugs.

Just get us the ****in blow you bastard, says Lachie.

I'm looking alright?

Come on you poof.

He's ****in pit it all in that j says Skins.

Yeah right he better ****in not have.

Fiddes listlessly plucks small items from beneath his body. A lighter from down the back of the chair, particles of his kids' food. Lachie stares, drags on his beer and taps a splinter of cigarette ash on the carpet while his brother's attention is detached from the room.

**** it. So Strichen right. See I'm in there and ready to go. The bike's ready and that's that. OK?

Skins smiles and his attention turns back to Lachie.

I'll tell you what your worst fear is at that moment, says Lachie. I mean it's not the bike breaking down cause you know that's not going to happen, and it's not the cops coming round the corner because if that happens you just turn round and go home. No man. The worst fear is like *yourself* right?

Lachie, untouchable in his brother's chair, the case-hardened king of local crime. A tremor in his heart on the High Street at Strichen. The quiet thought that he might not be able go through with his robbery.

I mean, he says, I was thinking, what if I just give up here and now eh? What if I just bottle it right when I'm about to do it?

Lachie stubs his fag blunt into the ashtray and looks at Skins in an effort to impress.

It's the fear, he says, the fear that you might just shit it there and not do your job like, that you might just go home and become like the other comatose bastards of the world, I mean like this bastard here.

Fiddes lifts his eyes just in time to see Lachie's smile change direction away from him and back to Skins.

I ken it sounds weird like, but that's when it all happens. It's before you do it, that's when you get the fear.

So you got stuck in? says Skins.

Oh man too right I did.

Lachie, self-absorbed, lights another cigarette with the indifference of a regular criminal. No one lights a cigarette the same as a con, and he should know, you use your fist like it's a threat and it's a promise, like it's an act of your own freedom in a place where they try and break you down. It becomes the habit of a lifetime.

So, says Lachie, letting go the smoke, I comes to the Post Office, and I gets my kit ready like.

Nods from both the boy Fiddes and from Skins. Fiddes is still trying to make tasteful the end of the joint, and yet he can't believe it. Lachie and the Post Office . . . like once upon a time, there was this Post Office and this mental bastard, and the two collided. And that was it. Fireworks man. Before he went inside the jail Lachie was telling this story, and now he's out it's just the same. He's told everybody the story. He's told the bar-staff at the club, told the neighbours, told his little nephew and all the family . . . he's told it to all his mates, to his dealer and to the neighbours. And now poor Skins is also to be entertained with Lachie's criminal glory. Because Lachie's a hard case, a sad case, a got to get a shag case, a drink a couple a pints and smoke a joint case . . . a been to prison and done my time case. A keep away ya bastard case. A tells the girls and makes them laugh case. Fiddes has heard the story to death, but he still manages a smile as he seals the joint. There was this one time see, when Lachie told this story in only one little word, and that was when he told it to the Court, the bastard. The story that day was reduced to its barest essentials, *Guilty*, and that indeed saved a lot of folk a lot of time.

So this is it like, says Lachie, *and I'm in there, in the Post Office.*

Fiddes pokes the joint into shape, he's way ahead of Lachie, even half asleep. Skins at least is pretending to enjoy the story, even though he knows what's coming.

There's no one in the Post Office, says Lachie, which is magic, just the two wifies who work there, one behind the counter and one putting birthday cards on the rack. And I've got my knife here right, under my jacket, just like this, and I just goes right up to the counter.

And I'm like, Give us the money now come on! And they're looking at me like, *what's going on?* I mean those stupid bastards didn't even realise it was a robbery. They were just standing there looking at me like a couple of farts, so I just took out the knife and says, Give us the ****in money! But this wifie thinks I'm in for ****in stamps!

****in stamps man!

Right enough ken! She's just looking in the book like I'm wanting to send a postcard! But I've got it all sorted see? And I just shoves the knife up to the wifie with the birthday cards so she knows what's going on like, and that shows her I'm serious, ken!

Did she shite herself?

Aye just about! So I throws the rack of birthday cards over like this, and then they get the message. So I'm mental now and I start bashing on the door to get behind the counter, just shouting *Come on! Get the money!* And the other one right, she's picking up the cards she's dropped, like *Oh no I've got to tidy up during the* *****in robbery!*

Skins chuckles and his shoulders rock, Fiddes hands him the finished joint.

Nice one mate.

No bother.

Fiddes reaches down beside his heavy arse and finds the lighter, sparks the j for Skins and wonders when Lachie's going to want to crash. Looks like it's going to be a big night, what with Skins there and all.

So there's no going back right, says Lachie, so I just go for it. I mean I'm like *bang bang bang* with everything in order. So I stick the knife again at the wifie on the floor while the other one's trying to open the gate . . . and then thank **** I get behind the counter and that's me in with all the money.

Lachie pauses with his cigarette, unconcern on his face, he draws in.

That was it, he'd lived for that moment and nothing could touch it. A flood of smoke pours back from his soft broken nose, and he sees again that endless magic flash when the world stopped, the moment when there was no disturbance, when it was just him and those drawers of cash . . . there was nothing like it, ever.

See it was just too good.

What?

Lachie turns round and looks over the room with the distant expression of a bruised philosopher. Skins' face has turned into a question mark.

I say it was just too good man. It was like in a film the way my hands were just filling up with the money.

The second the smoke comes out of his mouth again, Lachie remembers just how much he stretched his luck. The money was there and it didn't matter, it was in his hands and he had nothing to lose, he really had it all that time, all that money. Lachie sees again the rows of drawers under the counter, drawers of notes that he began to pull out in handfuls. Piles of notes there were, and it was all his. It maybe wasn't very much but it was all free . . . it was free money for those who had the nerve to take it, and that's what he couldn't understand.

I mean says Lachie, it's like, *what the* **** *are we all doing?*

Skins is patient, Fiddes is crushed in his chair like compressed waste.

No one ****in knows, says Lachie, unstirred and at his contemplative best. Other folks who've not done robberies and that, they don't ****in know, I'm telling you.

Lachie's hands seem to be moving from drawer to drawer now in deliberate stages. The Post Office is quiet, like all of Strichen has stopped what it's doing, as if they're all asleep . . . and Lachie is proof against everything in the real world, cause his mind has come to attention as if it was the most mathematically precise thing he'd ever done with his life, emptying those drawers.

You just don't know what it's like he says. It's like you go to another level. I mean here we are right, going about our lives like this, and then you just go and break all the rules. And it's not like a rush, or like a passion, it's just that like you go on another level man.

Pause for drugs.

Like I was thinking, says Lachie, why doesn't everybody just do this? And I thought about it when I was inside the jail and that, and I still don't know why. I mean I was thinking about those wifies that worked in the Post Office and I still don't know what they were doing. I mean that money, it was like nothing to them. It was like chips if you work in a chipper, and they didn't touch it, they just worked there like the cash was blank paper. It was like people hadn't * * * *in noticed you could do this, like they hadn't * * * *in seen it my way.

I suppose, says Skins.

The end of the joint flares up as Skins takes a further pensive draw. He passes it over to Lachie who takes a hold and hauls some in. Lachie knows when he's telling his story that he's one of few people in this world who've done something *real*. He glances at Fiddes who seems to be pushed far into the chair, submissive to the anecdote as usual.

See right says Lachie, I was there and I'd got the money right. I got it all in the bag and I knew what I was doing cause I goes, *right now it's time to get out*. So I picked up the knife and pushed out of there and those wifies did nothing cause they were scared shitless of what would happen if they did! I mean, one of the wifies was on her knees, so I just waves the knife at her and that was me. *Hey you bastard wifie!* I says and that was it.

Satisfied of smoke, Lachie holds the joint out for his brother. The boy Fiddes is a man discomposed, the wet slits of his eyes look across the room, it's a clear invitation to stand up.

Come on then says Lachie.

Fiddes makes a jelly heave, but Skins stands up and says *Aye you're alright you lazy bastard* and ports the j across the room in its ashtray and hands it to their host, who's happy at last to get his own creation between his lips.

Cheers man.

All right man.

A restive drag on the j and Fiddes watches Lachie return to his still burning cigarette.

So then, says Lachie, I got to the door and the door opened, but it wasn't me opening it. Like the door just pushed open and then there's this minister standing there with a newspaper in his hand, a tall thin guy. And he sees me like this and I get this shivering look from him, all the way up . . . and it was like everything had been going alright until this boy is standing there. And I don't know what it was but I goes like UH . . . and I just stabbed him. I mean I didn't really have to stab him, but it was just like *thump* and I'd put the knife in his shoulder. Right here.

****in hell I thought the boy would have attacked you or something.

No man, he was the minister, says Lachie. I mean he didn't even complain, he just goes on his knees and I let go of the knife. And he wasn't even greeting or shouting, it was like it didn't ****in hurt him. So the boy was holding the knife and I just thought like ****in prints and pulled it out. I mean, there wasn't much blood or anything on his clothes but you should have seen the knife, it was ****in covered. So I just runs it across my jeans like and legs it.

Skins body starts to hump up and down again with laughter. Stabbed the boy! he says. ****in stabbed the ****in minister, just like that. *Mental!*

See says Lachie, there's folk inside who've murdered people right. I mean there's guys who've got in fights and beaten someone's head with a club like. And there's guys who've gone out and just killed someone or raped a girl. But I just stabbed this minister like that and I couldn't help it!

Skins chuckle turns to a lump of laughter, Fiddes smiles unblenching, gazing straight ahead.

Couldn't ****in help it! Eh!

That's it man! I couldn't ****in help it, cause you just never know. The boy was there and *bam* I've stabbed him.

So what then? says Skins. What did you do? Go on the rampage?

No man, it was like, *what the* ****? I just got out! I mean I ran out and I was expecting cops everywhere but the town was the same with naebody there. So I just stuck the knife in my bag and nipped on to the bike and that was it.

Skins blows smoke in a jet towards the kitchen where Janet can be heard at work.

So he didn't die then?

Nah he didn't die says Lachie, and they said I got out of there with about a thousand quid which wasn't even that much.

The picture runs clear through the addled mind of Skins, the bleeding clergyman and Lachie tearing off along the High Street. *The minister lay on the carpet with his good hand over his bad shoulder, the Lord's blood pouring on to the sober floor tiles of the Strichen Post Office, while nearby, the two rural ladies gained courage enough to look at him, before standing up gently to assess the damage.*

So did you get it up the arse inside? asks Skins.

Lachie's overstrung face goes unduly still and Fiddes looks up. The last time anyone mentioned anything like this, Lachie went steadily red over a period of about a minute and then shouted for about an hour. Skins, thinks the Boy Fiddes, has truly got a bad sense of humour.

Don't even ****in joke about that says Lachie, his face is suddenly fixed of stone.

What? About been taken up the arse?

Aye. I'm telling you says Lachie, just don't mention it right. It's not something I like to think about OK?

The Boy Fiddes can't smile even though he wants to, the subject of male sex is a moot point with Lachie, it's another of his rules. Janet appears at the kitchen door behind them and she smiles too. The way Lachie carries on with his mates, his men first routine, his RECTOPHOBIA . . . for ****'s sake it only points one way. Lachie's constant bullying of all those around him, his obsession . . . it can only mean the one thing and she knows it fine!

Let's face it she thinks, *an ARSE is an ARSE, just like a BULLY is a BULLY.* Surely after the prison story Lachie will move on to another of his cowing sex stories in which he demoralises another of the female population of Aberdeen? Prison's the right place for a man like him, with a pathological fear of waking up one day and finding himself hitched to a woman. Suddenly the boy Fiddes laughs out loud, pale and fat on his armchair . . . and then he realises his mistake.

What's so funny you fat ****? says Lachie.

Nothing.

Better not be you poof.

Janet catches Fiddes' eye. Fiddes is wrecked now, too wrecked. He sees his blonde is looking at him. He thinks, I love you pet, and she smiles back at him, his eyes are nearly closed but he can feel it all right.

She glances back at the bully, Lachie.

I just don't like it ****in mentioned right says Lachie. It's what wankers dream prison is like, all this ****in male shit. But you just keep it for your dreams right? Aye you two would both ****in love it, you'd both get pumped all day. So just drop it.

Skins's shoulders rest, he moves back into the chair and considers the joint.

Aye, a nerve touched there alright.

Fiddes breathes out, glances again at Janet and Skins. The three of them sense a bollocks sexual anecdote coming from Lachie, more brow-beating from the self confessed Shagmaster of the Nightclubs. But what can you do?

I'll tell you this, says Lachie, this other quine right, I kept thinking about her when I was inside . . . but you listen to this, you won't believe it man . . .

Fiddes gropes for a cigarette and thinks, *too right I'm not going to believe it.*

And Skins?

That boy doesn't seem to care.

THE INTERACTIVE VIRUS

Vivien drops her bag, which slumps on the floor. No robot arm to pick it up, no voice to welcome her to the family home. Her house is still separated from mainstream technology in its simplicity and has not become the automated nightmare of the planner's fantasies.

The frosty light in the hall reveals Vivien's father's photograph collection, a strip of portraits of old-time Aberdeen. Vivien glances across the pictures and she blinks, the crucial issue now faced. She has thought about it all the way home on the bus to Bieldside: *if the process of machinery goes too far, then what?*

Vivien closes the front door and stares along the pictures in the hall as if in speculation of the characters within. Everything in the past is agriculture and pain, peasants and gloom. In the black and white vintage photographs actors portray peasant characters with long term problems, the fields are worked with half-efficiency and the towns are spanking new like Atlantis, shining forty times brighter than they do today, unpopulated and clean of litter. Remembering the past becomes so difficult that it has to be a game, thinks Vivien. People are snow-blinded by the thought of the past, they are amaurotic viewers of the screen, the stiff-eyed people of Aberdeen present.

She goes up stairs, the house is empty. She arrives in her bedroom where her three computers look out over the dirty roofs and spoiled aerial vanes of Bieldside. Beyond the slates and chimney pots is the valley of the River Dee, it is evening now and miles above the river an infraction of colour fills a crack in the sky, a colour that she could never describe, no more than she could create it on her computer's paint box.

Entering her bedroom each day, Vivien's first glance is at the view before she sits down at the machines. She runs three different computers and has tried to set the machines against each other always revealing that oneness, wherever it arises, is an illusion.

One to the power of three will still be one, thinks Vivien, but that's the number 1 for you, always striking itself blind. Behind Vivien's controls, the comfortable room is set out as simply as can be, the main extravagance being one large and fragrant bed which is comfortable like new-mown hay in a land of synthetic fibre. The bed is an antique bought at a country sale, the kind Vivien favours during weekends out alone. Next to the bed is her table which acts as a small kitchen, there are maps and photographs of standing stones.

Here in this room operates a simulated model of the Aberdeen Domestic Computer Network, a sharp scene in lines and graphs, relayed between the three computers at the desk. Vivien's task is to look for viruses and the results of her work appear on the middle machine which charts the components that operate on the Network grid. Somewhere in the macroscope is Vivien herself and the three computers at her desk. Somewhere else, Vivien is sending out computer viruses of her own design on to the World Wide Web. These viral routines operate like mobile pipe cleaners, maintaining the underlying fluidity of the system by patching and analysing data during their many random trips abroad. Some of the viruses are good and some of them are bad. One of them is like a spark circulating in a figment of tramlines, while all it does is collect the passwords of computer users that it meets. This programme is like a hunter routine, never returning to Vivien's bedroom empty-pocketed, and as a result Vivien now has on file the pass-words of many thousand people who know no better than to trust their keyboards. A programme like this is a lion in a feast of smaller animals, taking advantage of those computer users with weak passwords . . . because for every 100 people called T Smith, 90 are going to have as their password SMITHT. It stands to human reason.

The viruses have their own special cage, a memory board which sits tight inside a plastic frame, and this is where Vivien collects her electronic pets. Being a hobbyist in this field, Vivien has collected over 1,500 viruses, including their mutations, and there inside a special chamber they sit and wriggle, occasionally to be dissected and sent on test runs around the world. The viruses collect trivial information from banks and from satellites, Vivien reads the ebullient facts and figures which regulate the Scottish electricity supply and for pleasure alone, she raids the drudge machines of the telecommunications world. It all comes in if she asks for it, and it's filed brisk against the wall, there to be supine once again, often to be deleted.

Viruses are her delight, they might be hunted down and destroyed by company experts, but at the same time there's nothing to stop them mutating and ultimately transferring to people's televisions and mobile phones. Nothing will stop computer viruses infecting cars and soon they will be surfing right onto the decks of passenger airlines, where they will chew the software regardless of effect. Computer viruses can burn out remote controls, create money and destroy it, and it's important to Vivien that she has as many examples in her zoo, as are mutating in the world at large.

First thing in the door of her bedroom and Vivien makes herself comfortable at the mirror while boiling coffee. The mirror shows mischief, Vivien standing with her hands in her jeans, posing like a mechanic. It's unseemly to complain about what you look like, so Vivien cocks herself to one side and lets go a smile. The mirror is a liar, as much a part of the technosphere as the floor, the wall, the hall, the clothes and the kettle on the table. We stare in the mirror, unconscious of the enterprise in its creation, the smoothing of the glass and the silvering of the view. Vivien has cut black hair and is cocked sideways, and she thinks she looks like a mechanic.

Yea man, I tell you, some of this really sucks.

The kettle boils and releases a mercurial flight of wiry black steam. While funny girl is still staring bluntly at herself, the kettle clicks and the noise dies down. Again, the situation raises questions for her, *the surface of the room, the house and the quiet suburb of Bieldside in which sits her cell, all of it is contingent historical matter. Why is she wasting her time on the helpdesk, working in a call centre?*

Vivien has the Aberdeen Domestic Computer Network unsparingly mapped within her head, she is able to change and recreate functions in the service, create new application programmes and editors and test them all from this room, and yet it is not enough.

She clicks and checks the viruses. Today she is working on a programme that spoils emails, a virus she calls CLIENT-CARE, a mutation of the virus generally known as LEPTIC. The purpose of CLIENT-CARE is not so much to wipe computers; all it does is swap email subject-boxes en route. The virus is a practical joke, it jumbles words and can even add Vivien's own poetic suggestions at the point of contact. Because the effect of CLIENT-CARE is so trivial, Vivien believes that to this day it has not yet been detected, because nobody knows that they are being toyed with.

Back to the steam of the kettle, Vivien turns her seat to face the table she has set out as her own personal kitchen.

This is Vivien's hundredth year in Aberdeen, she's seen the map develop, disk and bootstrap, all at the age of twenty-five. She's seen a new city rise on top of an old one, it gets harder to believe that there are people still there, underneath. The steam from the kettle expends at full tilt and Vivien makes her cup. Evolutionary necessity gone too far, illustrating how hard it is to find a reference location in modern day Aberdeen. Sensitivity is dulled.

It's so like Aberdeen to swallow its own, she thinks, so like the town to hurry the young back to work for itself. A beautiful town, wide and clean, a great place of leisure and respite, a great place even to breathe! There's no reason why it should be so strict and so conservative, but it is.

Vivien staring at the red coffee mug, tired and at the end of a working day. Why the mug? What of it? She must be tired. The layout of the town is not logical in any particular, not like on the computer screen. If you viewed the city as one whole, then you could mentally straighten some components and enforce the links between them, ensure that the tenants of the town had lives with shape, and not something aimless which they have to hunt through for their meaning.

Vivien, it's me. Are you there yet?

Chris Crandall appears in the corner of Vivien's screen.

Yea, here.

Could you do a couple of questions for me tonight? I'm working on the interface up at the office and I want you to scan for infection.

Can you not get someone else to do it for you?

Why?

I'm designing my virtual sex aids tonight.

Vivien is loathe to sit at the desk because that means that work has begun. Personal external resistors are needed to keep her sane until she must at last sit down and try to get it right. The interface project at the office has to be the most tiresome show on earth, it concerns the peripheral devices and systems which are employed for the human / machine exchange. The data-flow in this exchange is two-directional, and typical in at least one respect, that the transmission of data from machine to human is considerably more complex than it is the other way around.

You'll have it finished in no time, says Crandall.

I'll put it on my list but really, I'm tired.

Get this. Input / Output cycles have to be doubled at least for this month's usage.

Really.

Yes you wouldn't believe it. So there's going to be some long sleepless nights ahead! I've already loaded the treatment into your memory so it shouldn't take long to run it on those machines of yours.

Yea OK.

Crandall is signed off and frozen, his image stops for a moment on the monitor before it is sent to the virtual dustbin. Vivien sits down, not to do the maths but instead to do some proper work. This evening, she is pursuing her enthusiasm for standing stones instead of scanning for viruses. A message box appears and tells her that coming across the phone line now is some eye-opening geometry from Buchan Hill and Aiky Brae, where there are recumbent stone circles. After a minute waiting, Vivien is looking at a photograph of the stone circle at Aiky Brae while the computer loads some new facts on the backbone of the display. She clicks to view Parkhouse Hill where the pillars of stone, like volcanic fingers, rest on a bank of earth and scrub. In the centre of the picture is a 21 ton whale of a stone, the recumbent, from which an arc of monoliths form a distinct phallus, the stones even-graded in height. Measurements come through to Vivien's computer, along with useless flash-points such as *a classic hilltop circle, the most intact in Buchan.*

Vivien has been to Aiky Brae, and imagined more than just this. There are hundreds of sites like it dating from all within several miles of each other, all of them ranged in Buchan at particular intervals, along the knuckle of the North East shoulder of Scotland. The stones that Vivien has studied are dropped into the landscape like cities where they form prehistoric working models of sexual regeneration. To Vivien, the stones are explanations of the magic involved in the days before reality became waterlogged in human ideas. Vivien has a better idea of what the landscape used to be like from closing her eyes, and through imagination she has made it safe for herself to walk backwards in time, while everyone else is marching forward.

Our friends the Beakers, she thinks, walked over this country in crowds and herds, mindless even of the oil wells nearby. Everywhere, step by step, each five miles, a ceremonial centre and a henge was founded, and there they made some good religion. Trees and thick grass, and even wolves . . . everything was one of a oneness to these wild-living people, and the enigmatic objects which they left behind were enigmatic even to themselves. Logically, and for their records, scientists and other brain workers approach each henge and measure it, they take the cross lines and gauge the distances in between. Fragments of knowledge turn up at most, but what usually happens in such an investigation, is that the investigator is mirrored in his experiment, smiling back like a lunatic, and calling his ancestors *primitive.*

Well, thinks Vivien, our ancestors were so sophisticated they didn't have these ways of measuring. Now that was living . . .

Zoom in on Aiky Brae recumbent stone circle where it appears that a substantial amount of Beaker Magic took place. Important finds include carved stone balls, relics once gripped and felt by real people, held forever in the ground and then taken in to the anthropological museum in Aberdeen, where they are placed in a sequence which ends proudly with ourselves, today.

Click around the circle: this reveals the tracks which lead up there. At the foot of the hill, there's a quarry, and parked in the quarry when Vivien last visited, were a caravan of travellers. The path leads into the wilds, and Vivien chooses a map and follows the hill line from Aiky Brae towards New Deer.

Tracks of a sort exist and what is found is gathered and stored in memory. The unspoken knowledge of the world is astonishing, as if to walk through the ancient forest is to be a part of it, so that almost any piece of land, earth, branch, animal, stone, can save you. Art comes out, and not machines, the recumbent stones are the closest the Beakers had to our technology, but they are not machines, even though they confer a prestige on the earth around them. The pine in the landscape is self-sown and the forest is a farm, bodies themselves are not seen and the enigma is how these pylons have been forgotten . . . how these beaked stones, levered into position gave rise to the idea for the modern townhouse, or for the shopping precincts where people mash together in a sordid lack of reverence.

Vivien is not sure what has happened and she clicks around the map, fascinated once more by ancient Scotland, where she alone moves, undetected, even by the Beakers.

Some people on the Internet have a project that involves lining up all of these stones to see what will happen. These people look for coincidences in the lines, to see if the magic re-occurs or to see if the stones form sight lines for their ancestors' flying machines. But alas, thinks Vivien, this project is science . . . which means that the outcome of the experiment will be largely dictated from the initial conditions. The investigators know what they're looking for and the science will be over when they've found it.

Vivien flags up the latest discoveries and sees a line is drawn from Aiky Brae which connects with Cairn Catto, an equally phallic mound of stones at Longside. This line in turn is neatly joined with Castle Point, a uniquely thin isthmus of cliff that has been long inhabited by those with an eye for defence.

So be it. Three cairns form a line. So much effort wasted, so many dead brain cells knocking against each other in neatly timed collisions. They've found a line but yet found nothing. The correct way to realise knowledge, thinks Vivien, is through intuition, and she has a degree in science so she should know. There are now however a team of people working in the North East of Scotland, hunting with maps, with wiry skeletal devices, employing electronic reason around eccentrically placed ring-cairns but among the many different students studying the stones, there is mutual agreement in mystery. A blank.

⊖ UCKU Virus

The UCKU virus (also called SUCANU) is believed to have originated in England in 1979 and can spread when the PC is booted with any .NAE or .KEN file.If an infected diskette is in A> drive at boot-up, the UCKU virus will take control of language causing a stream of dog's abuse to transfer from user to user until everyone is speaking the same way. Once the UCKU virus is resident, little can be done, and word power begins to reduce until users are restricted to grunts, combined with the phrases 'You know what I mean' and 'All right mate'.

UCKU copies part of its code to magazines and even newspapers and the virus is also rumoured to be stored in over 90% of mobile phones.

UCKU does not copy the actual sector of FOYB (or 'rude') data from the first sector of the processor, as the verbs and nouns in question already lie dormant in any post 1968 built memory. The longer a memory is exposed to UCKU, the more limited the verb-range becomes, and even after a short exposure, large partition problems can result.

This can cause loss of all entries and files, including sub-directories throughout the entire education, all of which is overwritten entirely with the infected 'bad load locution'. This infection causes all future utterance to be reduced to a statement of aspersion (often known as: PROFANITY).

Do Not Attempt This Link: 98% Constitution of Poor Authority: **Hyper-Archive: Serving notice on Capitalism** Serving notice on Capitalism with Bartolo Congy (congy@hotmail.com) Tue, 97 Aug 2006 08:20:79 - 0100 Messages sorted by: [date][thread][subject][tact][relevance][quality of abuse] [hopelessness] Next message: Michael Bakunin: '(eng)sabotage attack in support of the Twilight of the Phobocrats.'

Message: I'VE JUST BEEN READING YOUR RESULTS ON CASTLE POINT, AND I THOUGHT I'D SEND YOU SOME OF MINE! THE ENCLOSED ATTACHMENT IS SOME WORK I'VE BEEN DOING ON THE STONES MYSELF, SO PLEASE OPEN IT AND TELL ME WHAT YOU THINK. VIVIEN
Upload. Click. Send. And that's you shown.

Vivien is becoming dizzy. It's time to relax she thinks, to count to ten. Now having scrolled through several prehistoric sites and seen the formations of stone upon the computer screen, she closes her eyes to let some thoughts settle on the subject of the old peoples, just so that she can feel them near her.

That's right, and she counts, one to ten.

Just a touch, just near.

CONTEXT EFFECTS

From the top of the hill near the base of the rock, from the fence beneath the stones, the view is wide. All across the valley are bushes sufficient to hide the many hundreds of animals which burrow in there, the sky has outlived twice-twelve generations and has darkened blue this evening and settled clouds about the moon. Near me on the rise, the scaffold is hung with the skins of dogs with their heads still attached. Little activity, the loudest I can hear is a song chirping in a tree, the bird says it is evening and counts us through this non-stretch of the day.

On the back of the hill a fire is lit. Smoke rises behind the stones and forms a trail that flushes into the sky. The smoke drifts, makes short commons under the moon and pale colours are cast where the sunlight dies.

I walk down the side of the hill, past the stack pile of rock which makes the foundations of our largest fire bed. I walk in a curve through a steep mass of gorse to the headstall where two men are laughing. The men tackle two great logs of pine and are outfitting stakes and lodging pointed wood in the earth.

The way to the next hill is a wide gap in the scrub, all the rigs and all the tree trunks are dragged up this same avenue to the hill. Suddenly there's more sound, howls rising from the settlement. It's a call I've heard before, the young boys playing hogs. Ahead of me, the last of the daytime's spirits are eating into the undergrowth.

Round the bank there are four rocks to climb, these are rocks that have always been there as much as anyone can recall. Above the rocks the shape of the next hill is imperfect like it's the back of someone sleeping, a man about to rise and shift position. Light runs short of the hill into the dead part of the sky, it's not light enough to see my way through the trees here but I can feel my way for miles because the landscape crawls with signposts home.

I take the first two rocks and step to the third, the fourth is at arm's reach and I pull up on to the highest slab to see where I am going. Behind me the howls start up again, meaning home, the stones are not visible but the sound of the boys carries over the bushes and round the trees. A flush of sounds, and this evening they appear unfamiliar, I am always there and sometimes I howl too. The richness in the dark, the sound of our people, their calls are working through the blueing dusk to where I'm watching, still picking up the scent of the smoke, the sight of the fires under the cloud, and that rarity, the moon.

The moon's behind the settlement now, but she easily lights the hill with her flat face. Am I seen?

The moon has wrinkles and grey hairs around her, facing downwards on the earth, the moon is a god who cannot be banished or abandoned. Next to this pine I am nearly in shadow, but the moon is enormous, as if the sky were a sea and she a shining island engrafted to the water. The moon is above the valley, now pulling the darkness into her white centre. Still there is a shade of something blue over my shoulder, and I look to see that slowly, the next hill has hunched up, full-scale and ready for the night. The people are bundled away in the dark at the top of the nures. The smoke has become richer but is harder to see, and feeling the way forward, I slide down the opposite side of the rock until I am lodged at the bottom, now shielded in total darkness, pressed against the moss and seen by nothing. Without breath I drop further into the bushes until I am shoulder height to the gorse, and taking the path towards the far hill I run across the ground which is overfilled with flowers in the summer, and a source of brush in the winter.

I know the way to go and I scarcely make a noise, so not as to fall into the sight of the moon's rays. She's still behind me, prevailing in the sky, but it's black where I move, here among the bush, under these young trees. When the moon spots me, I drop again, so fast that she can only keep a distant track of me. I can make out the overdrawn surfaces of the plants and I am moving away from the moon, playing hide with her.

I rest on a wet swell in the ground, one of the boys showed me a trap here in the bog. Above me is the pine, running over with heavy branches, and I know that this is the right place, just where the boy showed me the trap. I was here and the boy came down from the direction of the big forest. The ground was wet and closer to the heel of the rocks there was a patch of bright moss. Then the boy made me touch the ground and it was wet, the moss was crammed together like soft hide, it was light green and soaked into one fat pillow in the space between the rocks and the trees. The boy came to the pine and he took the cones off the branches, and I watched there.

Look at this, said the boy, and he threw the cones over the moss bank, between the rock and the trees.

The cones rolled. I expected the moss to swallow them but the cones spun onto the blanket and stayed there.

Don't touch them said the boy.

Why?

Because you'll sink.

There were many scattered cones now on the spread of moss, each one was a light bloated seed, and I wondered what was going to happen.

Come on said the boy, and I'll show you where there's a big mud hole.

We went, the boy and me, we walked in the direction of the big hill where the pillar-stones were, where some of our people were cutting pines and making a ramp into their barrow.

You can't go to the stones, said the boy. It's for men.

When we got back to the settlement and it was coming night I remembered the cones and I grabbed the boy's arm.

What happened to the cones? I said.

We were back at the scaffold and the boy was playing with a stick that had come off the fence. He didn't say anything, he broke his stick into the face of the rock.

What happened to the cones? I asked him.

We passed them, he said. Didn't you see? By the time we got back from the hole, they were gone.

I remembered the scene and I saw a picture of that vicious patch of moss, and then I realised that cones were gone. It had been sinking moss.

The boy cracked his stick.

They were just cones, he said.

I was there right at that moment, close to that rotten-faced patch in the trees. I was way below the moon and in the lowest reach of the hill, far below the settlement too, and the ground was wet. To go on, I had to track through the trees to where the rabbits were, around the bright side of the hill, where the trees had a salty taste on the leaves and where the earth was hard.

The moon had exposed me below the hill so I carried on, I tunnelled in the gorse to where the rabbits were. The moon was secreting mats of white flossy materials from her mouthparts, like she was turning on the spot. I could make out the edge of the big hill and there was a flash from there, like an inaccuracy in the dark. I thought about my father, but didn't concentrate on what he'd said about the valley, and about it being dangerous. I decided that I would go as far as I could manage, and then go back until I could cross the entire valley in the dark like the boys said they could do.

Uprooted bushes tripped and caught my feet and I tried to hold for balance and pick my way ahead. I took a rest and looked along the foot of our own rock shelf, and that's when I saw the metal man for the first ever time, he was shining at the base of the forest gap and was very close to me. Light drained from his metal head and showed me two real eyes inside. I got my breath and I wondered if the man could be what I had dreamed of, or if he was a Giant. It certainly looked like it. The metal-man shone in the blackness, his face was easy to see but the rest of him I had to guess. I could see the metal man was holding a stained rock, and that his teeth were swept out upon his jaw. I could also see that the metal man had made his own light from his stomach and that the glow bleached out the ground underneath.

First I didn't move, and then I waited because I couldn't move. The metal man's face obtruded from a mask and his whole body stood still.

Girl, he said. You understand?

I looked behind the metal man. I noticed the ground underneath the metal man and it was splotched black.

Girl, he said again.

The moon was no longer straining, the man made more light than she did and it made her small to my eyes, and not real at all.

Yes, I said.

The metal man turned where he was, he moved on the blotchy ground at the bottom next to the trees and there were solving noises. He reasserted himself.

What is happening? he asked me.

I couldn't say anything then. On his arm was the heaviest jewellery, pieces of silver work brought together in shining knots. The metal man had with him enough lights to control the moon.

What is happening here? he asked me.

I could feel the danger. The man looked at me now without appeal and still he made the quiet forging noise as the light shone from him. A rabbit ran out and scared the metal man but not me. In the dark, a moonbeam shot across to the trees and pressed into the ground and the metal man span round like a hunter and crouched, orienting himself towards the animal. The moonbeam turned and the metal man looked at me.

I was on the ground.

Who's here? asked the metal man, but I couldn't answer.

I was on the ground and I crouched like a hunter did. I waited for the moment to run away, asking my legs to stay still. The speed of the moonbeam on the rabbit had been a surprise, so I knew I was going to have roll backwards down the slope and then try and get up the nearest ridge. If that didn't work I would have to go into the gorse there so that he couldn't find me.

The metal man's light spread in wands.

I'm going to stop the light he said, but I'll still be able to see you.

I said nothing. The metal man had the freedom of the moon, the power and the same immediate prospect. He would have been the moon's man or even her boy, a segment of her, a strong spirit of hers, a property of her light maybe or a part of her that she had let drop down to earth. I saw the metal man smile, although that was all. The side of his head, those metal trunks about his legs, he was shining with the gentle radiance of rock under water, there in the night.

Show me, he said.

I pointed up the hill towards the settlement. The man pointed too, part of his arm glowed and made a noise like a fire going out. He was still pointing up the hill towards the settlement and I was staring at him. The metal man was scared I realised, and it seemed that all his metal made him weary, as if he was faint from carrying it.

I don't know what's happening, said the metal man, and that was the last time I saw his eyes. I knew the metal man's eyes were faint but it didn't make any difference to me, I was still scared of him. An enclosure of light hit the ground from his leg and then stopped. The circle of light made a bar on the grass, but I didn't understand so I waited for something to happen. Something was going to happen. The shine of the metal man became milder, and then he snapped his arm again and vanished, and I fell to the floor in the dark needles. The metal man moved too and then I saw him again, he had many red spots on him, two on his head, more on his arm, and two where his feet were. I could make him out exactly.

I jumped back and let myself fall like a rock down the near slope. I fell back over my shoulders and then I jumped to the side and began to run. I didn't look back.

There was nothing. I was fleeing in the bushes, pushing aside everything that was in my face, making the best course for the ridge, and taking big jumps, like a wolf. *I am the girl that runs like a wolf,* I thought, and I pounded on. I grabbed the rock and began to pull up the ridge, I chanced a look back, but there was nothing there, not even the metal man's red spots. I was on the slope and again I was a wolf, like on all fours, digging in and pulling up by the shoulders so that for a moment I knew that I couldn't stop, even if I wanted to.

There was no moonbeam where I was running, but then a branch smacked me in the face at the top of the rise and I stopped and nearly cried.

My eye! The moon became huge in a line around the hem of my vision and I held on and tried to keep my balance. I listened out in case the metal man was coming for me and I heard him in the brush and saw the red spot of light. I felt exposed so I spat on the ground and ran the rest of the slope until I was on the main hillside and was going home.

I ran as fast as I could to the nures. The metal man stayed where he was and didn't follow me up. I saw the smoke against the moon and I heard our people, and that made me go faster yet. There was shouting coming from our people, smoke aplenty, and it was clear they were getting ready to eat. I was late and the others would already be getting warm.

An interrupt brings Chris Crandall's face to the fore, his flabby nightime expression is a setback to Vivien who feels a curious sickness at her desk. I swear it's strange, but this machine lets me get so close to them.

Vivien, I'm sorry to butt in, but I noticed that you hadn't started on the interface programmes. Do you think you'll be able to do it tonight?

Practical reasons place Chris Crandall's head near the erect lump of the recumbent at Tyrebagger Hill, his face moves in a window of its own while the stone scrolls with yet more statistics.

What the hell is going on now? asks Vivien of herself. She clicks the programme down and lets Crandall continue.

I'm sorry, he says, but do you think it's worth it?

The interface programme. The call centre interface. Is it worth it? A good question.

Vivien laughs. She switches on her camera and puts on a welcoming face for Crandall.

I can look at it tonight, she says, but I can't promise anything, that's all.

Vivien remembers from her dream the fading picture of the futuristic warrior. It seems like nothing's safe, not even one fantasy from the other, all tainted, all absurd, a full range of practically insane images. And yet, something compelling. The future meeting the past like this when she is under the spell of her own imagination.

Vivien checks her other two computers and looks out over the valley, Aberdeenshire in the twilight. Deeside dotted with its rural houses, not a bad place, surely?

No, not bad at all. Not bad for a dream at any rate.

I'll get to it right away, says Vivien, and she disconnects Crandall from her screen. Click, the businessman is minimised and is gone

Vivien returns to the project in hand. She clicks off her standing stones programme and looks at the folder he has given her, *simulations of higher cognitive processes.* It's drier stuff than the subtly related problems she has dreamed up from the stones and fed in to the machines for her own amusement. Still, in her work for Chris Crandall, she's paid a better hourly rate than she is in his call centre.

Vivien switches on her Network simulator and waits for new developments as the programmes become alive in episodic bursts of numbers.

It's still only a game, she thinks, this Network and its users. The lights flash and the information presents itself as real, but in effect it's nothing. The actual world of Aberdeen, that place outside the window in the lowering grey of the valley, where people are now returning to the ordinary situations of home, that is what the Network is trying to capture and emulate. But it doesn't work.

Aberdeen, she thinks, that's the boundless place . . . it's not the computer memory. A town or a city can be poured with fluid data, it can run hard into the mind's eye . . . but the computer is only going to jam if you try that, it's never going to think for itself and make history. The memory of every computer in the world, she thinks, could be filled with anything and it would make no difference to the machines at all.

Now, that would be a good test for the biggest computer virus in the world! To fill the memory of every computer with the number 1. For the almost infinite amount of times it would fit there, a programme like that could run forever, and this she thinks, is likely how computers got started in the beginning.

The machines conducted the filling of space with the number 1, and then someone gave them the NOT switch to make them all 0. The Truths of NOT and then AND, the logic of the OR and the XOR, the punctuation marks and participation within arithmetical conformity.

Yea, that's how it started, and that'll be a good way for it to end.

Vivien starts to run Crandall's programme through her three machines. The Network simulator is looking for errors and points of interest that Vivien couldn't care less about, while the Virus checker searches for the evil influence of computer bugs.

Vivien feels that the three-computer model she has created in her bedroom more adequately represents human thinking than any other attempt she has seen. Crandall thinks so too, and is happy for her to be a part of his team. It's an irony that Aberdeen has resolved to make theirs the cleanest most virus free Network in the world, and here she is with this staggering collection of bugs, resting at her knee.

She stares from the window again, looking in the sky for a curiosity to entertain her. Somewhere, as with each problem, a hint of order rises in the massive jealousy of figures created by the maths in action, and she sees it for a moment there before her. The viruses tick over in their box and Vivien feels an urge to forget Crandall's homework and play with one of them instead. After all, there's always more work to do with the viruses, and it's much more satisfying in the long run.

I guess, she thinks, it can go either way. A talent in this department can be encouraged, and brought to work for Chris Crandall, or it can be neglected and made sick. Either way, she thinks, it could start poisoning the system that's let it down. Either way, it's like the 0 and the 1. Likewise in one direction or otherwise in the other. Environmental factors and the natural tendency of the programmer. Who knows what is going to sway such a talent, and who can predict whether it'll go north or south?

AN ANOMALY EXPLAINED

Chris Crandall guides his computer-generated virtual woman, he rotates her with his mouse and sees exactly what she can do.

You're gorgeous, he says under his breath, and he stops to look at her again.

The next day while Vivien works at his company call centre, Crandall has spent an afternoon watching the way in which the virtual girl's hair moves. After two weeks of programming she now throws it in line with her head when she turns to face another direction. Crandall spins the girl again and enjoys the effect as her bob swishes with an artificial motion that is nearly perfect.

Eyes open, he instructs.

Turn 180°

Change Mix: all underwear.

Tone underwear – light blue high cut.

Tone up underwear – cut by 50%.

Magnify.

Select Sunpatch: 107 Skin enhance at HIGH.

Tone down underwear cut at thigh by 20%.

Turn around.

Stop. Edge enhance 64K colortop.

Grid when zoomed.

Select Wear: Red dress.

Select Hair: Parcel 240 Blonde / hair length Med 30.

The computer-generated woman is nicknamed Milly, and Crandall's mouth is open when she faces him. With the mouse, Crandall turns Milly to pose like a body builder and he clicks to make her wink again. He commands the girl to jump and grins at the way her chest bounces, the technological accuracy, the corpus mammae made real with only numbers. The animated girl smiles with unmarked love for the business man that operates her, a facial expression of desire that demonstrates the skill of her designers, and Crandall changes her dress again and stands her upright in space.

Birth position, he types.

Rotate and alternate entity appearance setting.

Would you like to change my pants?

Aberdeen University's Cross-platform 3D graphics software has allowed Crandall Technologies to develop a comprehensive series of geometric models for simulation of the ideal female form, and now Crandall and his team can make Milly do just about anything. This display in empty space, Crandall finds quite engaging, the woman lying back, her breath now fast, she can advertise a shopping event or even read the news. Although Milly's pose is named *birth position* in his application, the way she lies there reminds him of something much more desirable. She even looks inviting.

Crandall inspects Milly again via his new multiple overlays. The combined power of the Aberdeen Domestic Computer Network allows him to eliminate jittery positional data using his own user-configurable Multiple Viewing Modes.

These modes are:

1. World plus Attached Parts
2. Entity Nude and Frame
3. High Fidelity skin / face / breast terrain filtering

Crandall wonders if he should ask the team to make her a miniskirt or a pair of shorts. The way she's stretched out there, that might be *nice.*

Milly is one of many great achievements in Scottish instrument programming, the culmination of much computer work and the centre-point of industry obsession. The virtual woman is the most valid of the computer technician's Galilean enterprises, and her curves are the plane-table for the most up to date of mathematical calculations. The programming of Milly has been the greatest scientific pursuit of Crandall Technologies, and nothing at all, Crandall argues, to do with misogyny. The virtual woman as represented by Milly, is a proud breakthrough in technological advance and naturally Crandall and his investors are most interested in what she represents, as the profits can be astounding. Likewise, in the field of sexy cyber-icons, Scotland leads the way, as it fronted the contraption of the television and the development of the heavy Mackintosh raincoat still favoured by the park flasher.

And Scotland expects the world to be grateful for the television! More lines will be added to the cable until the master-cordage has collected everybody: but is there anything more demeaning than British television? We don't think so! Therefore, the virtual woman appears happily dressed, swindled into a tight costume, and bang you fell for it! Like being hit in the face with a herring, and then admiring the quality of the fish!

There are many reasons then why such virtual women are popular with businessmen and computer programmers.

Reason One: Since female pornography is degrading to women, the business media believes it is OK to design and animate human bodies with their computers. The theory is that to exploit no woman in particular is to exploit no woman in general.

Reason Two: The user's manual-reverberation may be complicated by the hippocampal formation of the actual sad identity (as in pornography) of his desire, but the computerised woman will make up for this with her mathematical boob and bottom texture bounce. The wife and girlfriend then, need not be jealous.

Reason Three: Operator cash-desire-syndrome will ensure that those involved in the design and marketing of virtual women, will make more money doing this than they might actually do by contributing something useful to the world.

Reason Four: The virtual woman will have no human / mammalian cortex and so can be abused as readily as the user desires. She will be a valid topic of research because those investurbators who capitalise in the profits thereof, have a limited capacity to perceive any item that does not have breasts.

Reason Five: It is worth emphasising that the lack of imagination that pervades both investment capital and cutting edge computer design is perfectly suited to this kind of sexist rubbish, which although hailed by newspapers and analogous stroke-books as a 'breakthrough' will in a matter of years be seen at best, as a sad and pathetic curiosity that made a few people an awful lot of money.

The office space is quiet, a flat complex of corridor and store cupboard. The only sound is the dead march of the computers at the wall and the only movement is the shine on Milly's plastic looking legs. Chris Crandall sits with his hand on the mouse and freezes Milly while he reaches for his spring water.

Outside is the flush level calm of the car park, and across it is the call centre. It looks quiet from here but Crandall knows there is chaos within. Two secretaries pass his window and he touches the water to his lip. Crandall employees: dummies broken down into eight-bit halves. The normal inactive condition of the working mind is seen in the typical minimum of 2.5 ideas a week. They have no ambition those who work for Crandall, they only want their money and then the weekend.

The sun appears for one second, unseemly over the chilled grey grass and shines over the surface of the cars outside. All is quiet outside, dead in the accumulated output of the cold rays of the sun.

A knock at the door.

Milly is staring friendly from the screen, looking at Crandall from between her legs, so as an afterthought, he uses the mouse to dispose of her.

One moment, he says, stepping up to pull the blinds. The aluminium clunks and more of the day is admitted.

Come in.

The virtual woman folds in a split second and the screen returns to the Crandall logo, the door opens and there stands Vivien.

You wanted to see me?

I wanted to see her? Do I ever want to see that critical face, that baggy shirt, Vivien who dresses like a bricklayer. There must be breasts under there somewhere.

Yes of course, come in. I was just working on the Network, and I found an email report that you'd probably want for your collection.

Is it a virus?

It says it is.

Crandall turns his chair and clicks on his computer to open the file in question for Vivien, the bug which he was sent springs to life and the data appears again.

It caused a hiccup, he says, it didn't get into the Network properly, but it might have done if we didn't spot it. Sit down and have a look. I thought it might just be a hoax.

I love hoax viruses, says Vivien. She stares into the screen as the message scrolls to an endpoint, Crandall twitches then straightens out, a measure of his authority in the office. There will be no smiling while the computers are being debugged.

Viruses are all serious, he says, hoaxes or not. I mean, we're trying to keep our machines clean, are we not?

Yea I guess. She shrugs.

This is the message, says Crandall, and he shows Vivien the printout.

Subject: Virus Alert
IF YOU GET AN EMAIL TITLED 'VIRUS ALERT'
DELETE IT IMMEDIATELY WITHOUT OPENING
IT!!! EVEN IF IT IS FROM SOMEBODY YOU
KNOW!!! THIS EMAIL IS A VIRUS THAT WILL
OVER THE COURSE OF 7 DAYS SEND ITSELF OUT
TO EVERYBODY IN YOUR ADDRESS BOOK AND
THEN PROCEED TO DESTROY YOUR OWN HARD
DRIVE AND ANY DISKETTES THAT YOU INSERT!!!
BEWARE OF THIS***KIN VIRUS!!! IT WILL TRANS-
FER TO A MILLION DISKETTES IN UNDER 45
YEARS!!! DO NOT READ THIS EMAIL!!! IT WILL
WIPE OUT YOUR COMPUTER!!! PLEASE SEND
THIS TO EVERYBODY YOU KNOW TO PREVENT

THE SPREAD OF THIS!!!

[Virus Informatique et le 'Syndrome de la Suffisance'
version Francaise aussi disponible pour téléchargement.]
download-fabgearman.bugalert
['Computerviren und das 'Falsche Autoritäts Syndrom'
Deutsche Fassung zum downloaden erhältlich.]

I know this one, says Vivien, she stares into the screen as if concentrating on a tactical game. I recognise the message. They used to call it DANCER and it's not a hoax. You're supposed to think it is, but it's not.

I assumed it would have a more sinister side.

Crandall catches the smell of Vivien's hair as he moves up closer, something real that he cannot quite resolve, a scent that he's maybe not known before. There is attraction here, distinguished from the normal force of lust, the smell makes his desires lie idle, as if all he needed to satisfy himself was just this passing sniff.

It is pretty boring though, she says, it's set up to wipe your hard drive at a specified time, that's all.

Oh well, says Crandall, I'll see what we've got in here for you.

Crandall reaches past and types heavily at his terminal while Vivien stares out of the window. She looks over at the call centre where she normally works, the grey and silver features of the office are a higher form of the same numbing environment she suffers over there. In the call centre, rows of computers display far off languages while the girls and boys in headphones patter with an obtuse public. This is the promise that Vivien has been waiting for, the idea that one day a corporation like Crandall Tech was going to pay her for her excellence. By 1995, there were over 1,000 original viruses in the world, and now that's grown, ten or twenty-fold maybe. For Crandall this anti-virus business is war, it's like he's trying to garden a wild forest, but it's just not going to happen, and sometimes Vivien thinks she would have been better off unemployed.

Have you thought about becoming team leader over there, like I said? asks Crandall

I've already got a job, says Vivien, her far away stare is still on the call centre and not on the downloading virus.

A proper job! says Crandall. He issues another command to the desktop and smiles at Vivien, quite innocently.

You gave me the job, says Vivien, and now you tell me working in a call centre isn't proper work?

Impasse.

You know what I mean.

Crandall shrugs. Vivien can always have it her way, she's never co-operated, whether it was in her own interest or not. Whether she smells nice or whether she's a genius at debugging, Vivien, Crandall notes, never even complains, not unless you give her an opening like that.

Look, he says, your virus checker has identified: DANCER VER-SION # 12. You were quite right. There's a memo here about it.

I wrote it, says Vivien.

Crandall turns abruptly from this computer and for once Vivien sees a moment of activity on his face as his eyes widen to twice their normal size.

I wrote the memo, she says.

Oh.

The virus was European. Can I get it?

Of course you can. If you take your copy I'll delete all the others that are left.

Vivien takes a swivel chair and sits at Crandall's terminal where she isolates the portion of the virus that she fancies. She likens the operation to picking up a scorpion from the sand, the pincers lower and she takes the beastie by the tail, the virus twitches and curls on the pinched metal point of her tweezer before she drops it into the sealed tank of her Bieldside In-Box. The virus rattles to the bottom of the box and sits there in its new home, with its new mates, Vivien's deadly collection.

I'm off, she says, and switches down the programme and turns the screen to black. There in the centre is Milly, still in birth position and with her legs apart an immediate offence to Vivien's critical eye.

⊖ The CONK (or CONKPORN) virus is one of a number of viruses designed to be too socially acceptable to be removed. It infects your memory by moving porno sector data from your personal recall and sending it to your alco-receptors. Ordinarily, if no porno sector data is available from the hard disk because the user is 'clean', then third-party software (such as Wet Slaps for Windows) will be formatted and then imported for access by your local seed-drivers, causing lager-shandy and smut implant.

The DEPARTMENT OF TRADE AND INDUSTRY cannot remove any CONK or PANHEID.exe virus, since their probes reach only to the cerebral cortex and not to the long term memory, where the virus code is written. CONK is particularly dangerous as it will also Trojanize your normal working files, writing a small programme in the slack space at the end of the spinal cord, which can destroy concentration, and make you lose your place in the canteen queue. *I was here an hour ago, so where is my macaroni? Is this my fork or your fork? Where is my beef olive? Do you work here too?* And so on. File Allocation such as this can disorientate all staff, and if they become fragmented, they will be lost to most recovery programs and may have to be replaced with people who are younger and better looking.

Anti-virus programs do not find viruses such as CONK because of the vast amounts of porn stored in office computers. The de-fragmented business brain, as well as that of the lower office worker, is the perfect location for this virus as the weakness for tittie.jpegs and models in swimsuits is one of the great constants in the British business community.

That, says Vivien. You're not still playing with her are you?

This is the greatest technical achievement of this company to date, says Crandall.

To Vivien it seems odd to believe that a picture of a woman lying on her back is a technical achievement, but she knows how clouded these matters can get. Technical achievements, she thinks, overreach themselves, almost weekly. There'll be something equally numbing coming along after Project Blonde here is finished. Everything possible is being done for the world of mechanisation, regardless of the effects on labour intensitivity . . . everything possible is being done in the fields of computer games, car production, and farming, and it doesn't end there. Hand-job virtual women are just the start of it. You get that feeling when you look into the falsely painted eyes of these avatars that the process is going to go places yet more hellish. You would think that in a world of digital image and sound reproduction, that the only imperfection is going to be mankind itself . . . but mankind is already far behind and incapable of administering even half of what has been built. They'll keep on opening call centres until the call centres have their own call centres. It's called the return of evil for evil and it's balanced by the fact that ninety nine percent of people contribute nil to the world but a good deal of complaint. The fact that call centres keep opening as a result, is testament to the righteousness of mediocrity.

Crandall watches Vivien leave the office, carrying her new virus on a small green disk. Vivien would make a great team leader, he thinks, so long as she can get her attitude sorted. There's a point when the rebel in us all becomes bored, and conforms to the real world. She'll need to buy a house, she'll need to buy a car, she'll need to buy a phone, and Crandall's here to see it happens: that girl *will* be useful yet.

NETWORK ON

And the public's connected to the: Council
And the Council's connected to its: sherry
And the sherry's connected to the: Council Tax
And the Council Tax's connected to: depression
. . . and so the wheel does spin.
Now: get your lah-lah brain in gear.

A civic event to celebrate Crandall Tech is organised in the historic City Chambers, upstairs in the Town House. Appearing out of shadows numberless and guided by the lustre of technology, the first to arrive at the food and wine are the local and national media. A six o'clock start is normal. The usual garrotte of journalists has turned up and are milling in a cynical manner near the drinks trolley, and with them today in the City Chambers, the Councillors and their guests assemble.

Downstairs at the Union Street door of the Town House the stair is sombre within. The steps are polished, the stone is grey and the light is blocked by a persistent feeling of city murk, Vivien pushes open the door and from a booth in the wall comes forward a porter who approaches her to ask, what did she want?

The reception? That will be in The City Chambers, which are on the third floor.

Thanks. Vivien walks self-consciously to the stairs.

Third floor if you're taking the lift.

No I'll just walk.

Dim light across the stairs makes the Town House an uneasy place and Vivien looks up the four flights to the roof. Technology has been fitted roughly over the old stone frame of the building and holes have been drilled in the nineteenth century walling for telephone cables. Thick painted wires run across a matte finish and a plastic imitation of linoleum on the steps deadens the tone right down.On the first floor is carpet and at the open end of the corridor is an office where a young man is spied word processing, working late. Nearby is the steel lift door, dark coloured also. How did developing architects fit lift-shafts for elevators and dumb waiters into these old buildings? Who would have thought in the granite past that vertical corridors would become the modern standard?

Clouded glass windows emit shade instead of shine at this time of evening, while lustreless and silhouette glass matches the stone where the city crest is imprimed upon the wall. Outside in the twilight, Vivien hears the grating of car engines and horns. Many evening meals are cooked up at home while the hopeless and the hopeful shine the counter of the hotel bar, the traffic stalls along the ring road and the pavements and bus stops become uppish with people making the cold run back to the sofa and a coffee.

And here is Vivien, in this light and on these stairs it seems that the Town House is the perfect setting for a night-clad gothic tale. Fair maid in white robe could fly down these stairs, she thinks, beating her way through the bad light and the emptiness . . . it's the stone walls that do it, the width of the step. The oil paintings and the gloom of the stairwell make it so . . . a drift of actresses in shifts ride hard along the black carpet and the Provost lurches from his office, making fiery protestations in the cold stained halls . . . he roars and his cry is snuffed out against the sickly stone.

The second floor of the Toon's Hoose is empty and the carpet is deeper because this is where the Provost and his team have their offices. Along the wall, Vivien observes another shrinking row of frames all of which hold awards and decorations, several prizes the town has gained, resting now like imperial plate. The corridor is dense with these awards which stretch to the tough wooden door at the bottom, probably the Provost's office. Upstairs, she senses the hint of a hubbub, where the evening's reception is heard faintly.

The noise of the people upstairs sounds to Vivien like the processor of a machine, the low tinkle of distant chat.

One more flight of posh stone steps and Vivien is almost there. From half way up this stair, she spies at the top a City Lackey in official red and this quiet figure on scissor-legs smiles to welcome her up, eyes making the gentle enquiry, *why did you not take the lift?*

This is the door to the City Chambers, held by the way-worn man in red who requires to see Vivien's invitation. On her left are the cloak hanging rooms and the toilets, and before her is the social paradise where the reception is underway.

The room she enters is taller than her house, the carpets are red, as are the walls, and strips of gold are laced through both, on picture frames and beams. Vivien stands on the threshold of a thrill, mute in the doorway, she looks up to where the chandelier gives positive electromotive force to the colour scheme. Light shimmers through the crystals and the glass, a thousand pieces rigged together, shooting lines into all corners of the room. Images race into Vivien's eyes from the vitrics in the drinks glasses which glance off each other with tricks and sparkles, causing her to stand still and take it all in.

It's wonderful, she thinks, what people will do.

Half of this room makes a quick and telling glance at Vivien as if a section of the people present, cannot rest until everybody on board has been inspected. More detail is instantly forthcoming to Vivien, waiters with trays who stand below the picture frames where faces in oil stare upon the crowd.

Vivien stands at the door, but the servants in their white shirts remain impassive, like captured air bubbles against the wall. The City Chambers are by this time well spread with Council people of every sort and on a table near the window are six of their new computers are set up and ready to initiate Crandall's computer network.

A woman holds a tray of drinks in front of Vivien, her large spectacles are like headlights on a lunch wagon. The woman is staring at Vivien from close up and says *Wine sherry whisky orange,* and Vivien says *Thank you,* and takes a glass. The City Chambers are only still half full, there is no sign of Chris Crandall and no sign of Pally. The woman with the drinks walks away while Vivien looks across the room again, trying not to draw attention to herself. Should she drink or not tonight?

Why not.

The Provost is not in sight, but surely she thinks, he must quail from overexposure to these events. The Provost must have tired of this executive cuisine years ago, become sick of his reflection among the comfort edibles on their glittering trays. What's more, The Provost must be fed the same aristocratic rubbish each time he visits another town. Is the Lord Provost of Aberdeen not due a healthy meal, just the one time? Should not the poor man's silage for one day be made of health, instead of this puff pastry spread? After all, we wish him long life as well as prosperity. And his face should really not be so red.

The City Chambers contract once more and Vivien holds tight upon her drink, as if it were a handrail. The initial fear of the room has left only possibility . . . the possibility that one of the canvas bound figures on the wall will leave their frame for a second to lecture those nourishing themselves below . . . the possibility that all corridors in the city link here . . . the possibility that she will never return to this high point of Aberdonian living where the best people come. All the privileged people on the appointed days of merit meet here in the City Chambers before they return on drink-tempered legs to their various stations. The people present at this function however look like examples of technology gone awry, malfunctioning parts in a backward equation. They none of them look different from each other, she thinks, it's like they're all one tight genetic breed . . . men and women, old and young . . . they all appear in one colour and talking in the same tone . . . the same sweep in the swarm. Vivien looks down upon her trainers, and feels a little embarrassed.

The waiters hold fast behind the beano. The motion of one silk glove will indicate the moment when the guests can begin, because it's food first and then ceremony, according to the instruction board near the door.

Vivien has no one to talk to and so she pretends to look at a painting. The picture is of a gruff City Father, one of those Victorians who spoke a black form of Doric, a man of the parish, the sort who would thrash his children for spelling mistakes, the sort for whom Christmas meant an extra sermon. Vivien sticks her tongue out at him and gloats a little before this ancient father, a small bell chimes and the diners are alerted to the spread.

Vivien is about to step into the fray when she is taken by the arm of Pally.

Star of the show!

I don't know about that says Vivien. She holds her drink, steadier than before.

Sure you're the star of the show tonight my dear, says Pally. Pally is dressed for the event, thoroughly covered in black and hanging with white stones around her ears. She smiles at her friend.

I don't have to do anything, do I? says Vivien.

Nope, just enjoy yourself.

I don't know why I came.

Pally touches Vivien on the arm, her trademark motion.

You came to be part of the project Vivien . . . you came to see that there are no viruses.

I'm just working on the helpdesk now, says Vivien, other people do all the work.

You'll be Team Leader on the helpdesk says Pally, and don't you forget it!

Vivien looks around the crowd again. Crandall's Aberdeen Domestic Computer Network has stimulated the entire apparatus of Aberdeen, most departments of which are represented in that large red and gold room before her. The Network has pushed Technology and Business into bed together, as if those two old-time flirts needed such an excuse, while Vivien represents the frontline scum.

Everyone's here, says Pally, it's very exciting.

Vivien noses into her wine.

In her imagination Vivien likens the evening to the arrival of a new-found stack of sugar in the central portion of an active anthill.

They all want more, they take it on board and indulge themselves as efficiently as they know how, but people have never once been surprised or moved by a new piece of technology. What they really do with new inventions is a process of skin grafting . . . they affix each new development to their already mechanical lives, take it up and then perceive it as their right. Crandall's network is therefore like the microwave oven all over again . . . the passenger air-bag . . . the concept is visualised so easily that every person who beholds it claims to have seen it all before. They accept it but they're bored, they're blasé to the end because invention is normal from the moment they conceive of it, not from the moment that they use it. They have knowable explanations for everything, thinks Vivien, and machines are subordinated into supporting these illusions at every turn. There are people in Aberdeen, thinks Vivien, and many of them in the City Chambers tonight, who believe that technology happens by default. They feel that technology like this has set the world on a futuristic roll that will continue forever until we're living on other planets. People have even begun to live in this future age and the beneficiaries in this belief are the Councillors themselves and the businesses that are selling it all to them. That is, all of the attached industry, the administrators in all walks of life who have no job but to Decide and Motivate.

Think, each generation has managed to recreate, revolutionise, proclaim itself as the zenith of good taste and technology . . . and all of this has happened without the slightest alteration in class divisions . . . and gender divisions . . . because all things that so shape the world as it is . . . are presented by administrators . . . who are scared shitless . . . of losing their control . . .

And are you Vivien?

Yes, that's me.

A smart and older woman steps forward, her voice is deep-toned and she smiles like a wicked granny.

I'm Councillor Mary Robbie, Pamela will have told you what a Luddite I am.

Pally laughs. You don't really go out machine-breaking do you?

My girls, computers break by themselves. Have you not noticed?

Vivien spends a lot of time adjusting them to their users, says Pally, that's her job.

Pally's smile is indulgent, she is introducing Mary Robbie as carefully as she can.

I've got a fountain pen in the office, says Mary Robbie, and I've had that since 1975. The pen has never been replaced and neither has my electric calculator. In fact everything else is doing fine in the office *apart* from the computers. And what happens to last year's models when we're all through and done with them? That's what I wonder.

It's a good question, says Vivien, and she chances a nervous drink of wine.

They're all dumped aren't they? says Mary Robbie, and her drink rocks back and fore. You can get too much of technology, that's what I think. It's really quite trying.

Vivien's attention strays . . . the City Chambers are now as full as they could be. The chat is almost raucous, conflicting with ear-splitting laughter and the sounds of service from nearby. The same waitress is approaching again, bearing down on Vivien like a killer with that tray held out, *whisky wine orange* and the rest. The waitresses' flat eyes stare from behind those thick spectacles and Vivien drinks more wine, Councillor Robbie turns to talk in this instant to someone and her voice curves insincerely as Vivien finishes her glass. A crowd of men explode in laughter and Vivien pretends to look at another painting, a second glass of wine below her nose. The men laugh louder while they bond in the corner of Vivien's eye.

The City Chambers are now at philosophical capacity, cool judgement on legs and wall to wall civic fogeys. The guests circulate slowly on that deep red pile with their glasses held before them and their bald patches tipping back in laughter. Primal stupidity growing like culture in a plush test tube. Closest to the centre of the room are the more important Councillors and with them, much of the white matter of the Aberdeen High Round Table.

Vivien sighs and looks towards the roof. Another painting to examine, the largest oil in the room, a picture showing another one of the large enlightenment crackpots who 'built Aberdeen', one of those men who made decisions, laid down the social code, put the women in their pinnies and waved his shammy about in the bathroom when nobody was looking. Not a conformist, but a demander of conformity, his world evolved from points of etiquette he dreamed up in an Enlightenment coffee shop, one pissy afternoon, 300 years ago.

His name: Charles Collieston Gight.

His image: Puffed and wigged, clearly superior to the viewer of his portrait, and no hint of ancestral madness.

Vivien looks at Gight's modern counterparts ranged across the room, those gathered in the simpletonian air of chat and cheese, it's difficult to take them seriously as leaders of the people.

Over Vivien's shoulder the large part of the Committee have gathered to chuckle together through their last few minutes of celebration before the dream becomes real on the button push, for such is the launching of a brave ship truly. People help themselves to drinks and in the gentle zero gravity of the room, items begin to float from their owners. Stiff collars are undone, and pens pass by in the air, vol au vont cases replete with prawns and empty drinks glasses manoeuvre in the spin while people's light thoughts and unsecured jewellery gather towards the roof.

Councillor Craigie sees an opportunity to his left, a young woman he thinks works at the Aberdeen Arts Centre, he's seen her somewhere before, and he wants to know more.

Vivien also walks unhurried through the crowd.

Think of all of these heads in the room linked to each other like our machines. What might they do instead of exchanging insensible anecdotes? Instead of chatting each other up and contradicting each other?

It's just a thought. There are about one hundred people in the City Chambers and they're all supposed to be working together for the one project, but how anything ever gets done, that's a mystery.

Vivien walks through the crowd, rather inauthentic to the room in her sneakers, but what the hell. She catches Pally's eye and feels alone, Pally is talking to some wide shouldered man who is staring at her chest. Vivien mentally links the people in the room to each other with a wire, and she imagines them communicating this way, standing straight like pins with a machine silence to them. The truth is that Aberdonians, like the remainder of the Planet Man, would rather prevaricate and bumble their projects into existence through chance and bush beating, rather than logically work it from one point to the next . . . and that's what these events are all about. That's what celebrations in the Town House merit, they mark the fact that people have come together and built something for once instead of breaking each other down.

For a second in the City Chambers, everyone is nearly linked. Hence the alcohol, the drink helps at least with the impression of oneness. In drink, one hundred people can come together with the idea that they have forgotten themselves. In the opal splendour of the City Chambers tonight are one hundred fine picked individuals in suits of the same cut, and they all feel special. The flicker of conversation, the glister of large spectacles and the dip of eyes to women's legs . . .

. . . and this is possibly the worst ordeal for Vivien. To walk this floor between these business bodies, to listen to the explorational tot these diggers and pokers are speaking, Vivien feels she might be bringing the city to an end, and so she finishes her second glass.

Vivien's childhood dream: *Aberdeen empty.*

The people are gone and Vivien is alone in the military crumble of granite that is left. In her fantasy, Aberdeen becomes a city with no inhabitants and the architecture is well suited for it. Jogging down Union Street one morning, around the abandoned cars, Vivien is happy. The traffic is nudged up dead to the roadside, rusted now and cracked occasionally with a sprouting green plant. There is no human turbulence to the buildings, they could well be the hollow rock of God like this, and Vivien is alone, watching the slow corrosion of Aberdeen as nature takes its hold between the stones. Vivien is jogging down Union Street, it's 9 am she would say, but it's so hard to tell since the clocks have stopped. Hard to tell but not impossible. Jogging down Union Street, Vivien is tempted to go into one of those collapsing department stores, but no, she doesn't do that any more. It makes her think of the world before, the way she always saw it. Which is to say that when the world was populated, Vivien walked through these department stores in an age when they were spot-lit with that familiar tonality of nothing . . . when the people shopped there and the artificial light guided them among the track-suits and the racks of shoes. Even as a child, she always imagined it would empty of people one day. It's uncanny, and so jogging down Union Street, Vivien doesn't need to go into the department stores at all. They're filling up with animals anyway.

Vivien keeps on running down Union Street, down King Street, towards the River Don where she stops and looks at the tower blocks and thinks, Good old Aberdeen, it never looked so sensible.

It's a great opportunity, for the city.

So says a businessman with a sheen on his suit, he is speaking to Vivien.

Why is he speaking to me? she thinks.

Never seen anything like it, he says, but how can it all be free? I mean is it all advertising? It goes to show you how much money there is in advertising, how well it must work.

That's what they say.

Vivien is alarmed, the young man's face is the mock moon, and God help us all, he seems interested in her.

It's incredible, says the young man, that we're going to have this computer Network in Aberdeen . . .

. . . and everybody nearby joins in.

They wouldn't spend all that money on it if it didn't work would they?

Yes, it's good vision and it's good planning.

It's wonderful to see Aberdeen on the map again.

Vivien imagines them all dead, they've all been taken by plague to make room for her very own city of dust. She's jogging and she feels that she can run around the whole town in one afternoon. At every corner another vista comes into view, another street is crumbling with the overgrowth of herb from the city's gardens, and she is running, always running through it.

How can you advertise a town? one of the business-people asks.

Well the litter situation is good. And employment couldn't be better. But more than that, Aberdeen is a safe place, and friendly too. I'd say there's nowhere to match it in Britain.

Hear hear to that.

Councillor Craigie steps back to listen.

Am I right Councillor? It's an all-over standard of living. To make Aberdeen more of a model than it already is. Beautiful beach, magnificent Scottish countryside.

Councillor Craigie agrees whole-heartedly with the young fry and then replaces his glass. Within the buzz of the City Chambers none in this small conspiratory group disagree and the appreciation of the moment amounts to cogent thoughts upon the future of the community, because it's everyone's future now.

Yes, unwisdom in the listening faces, astutely the image is grasped again, Aberdeen will be a better town, the town of the advertisement where the electro-car glides to a halt before the secluded dwelling. In a month the Aberdeen Domestic Computer Network will be running intelligent errands, sorting out peoples' problems in a mass of linear maths, and then we'll expand it, which let's face it, is good for the town. Crandall will be organising the on-line shopping, everything to be ordered from a suburban supermarket hidden beneath a fake grass roof. The fake grass roof is a legal requirement, it means the area will still be classed as 'green belt'.

This is going to draw finance to the area, says Councillor Muck. We're talking about a better standard of civilisation for those who live here. Anyone who lives here.

Marginally drunk after forty minutes, an appetite has caught up with the increasingly opinioned City Chambers. The women serving alcohol circulate with their trays and appear when they are needed, more than familiar with the embarrassment of such wealth and opportunity. The waitresses have seen the masses of talent coming and going, squeezing into these rooms, they've served the shareholders and the top dogs, the best of non-schooled Aberdonians, the weight of policy and polity, and what the hell's the difference anyway? They have seen it.

A clatter round the trays. Hands appear and help themselves. Orange wine gin whisky sherry, the sausage rolls replaced, the Luddites ate the Cruddites, the Polloi ate the Polonni and pastry faces are all that's left of the chef's best. The testament is crumbs and then rolled out on trolleys come the sweet parts, the cake and jelly, the very fruit slice that makes sugar heaven of the evening, with cream.

Aberdeen City Council - your money spent on trifles.

Vivien makes towards the window but has her arm taken by Councillor Craigie, who would love to introduce her to some new people.

Here is the woman in charge of pest control! he says. Vivien turns to greet a bright gob of open faces, beaming in alcoholic respect of her perceived achievement. Craigie gets his arm as clear around her as he can while she makes a cylinder of her body and holds her drink up to her chin.

We call it the Helpless Desk, says Vivien and there is a welter of laughter, a round of the free chuckles that accompany all backslapping and understood comment.

Vivien will service all your needs, says Councillor Craigie to the assembled guests. These computers behind me will soon be linked to twenty thousand others in homes and businesses, all the hospitals across Aberdeen. Everywhere! And if you've got any problems, then just call her up!

Councillor Craigie glances over the symbolic line of machines sat upon the red gold drape, six computers serving to remind the guests that soon the city will be linked as one, electronically at least.

And what are your plans now Vivien?

I'm collecting information on standing stones.

Ah, mystical.

Councillor Craigie attempts to treat the situation as official, but he's like an old horse on the mate. Vivien focuses away from him, looking at another oil painting. The expectant crowd in the City Chambers are dispersing to the sides of the room again, lighting up and restarting the conversation like it's a choked engine. Craigie is fixed with the curves of Vivien's face, she knows exactly what's on his brain and she has a sudden idea that she'd like to go home and feed all of these people viruses from her computers at Bieldside.

It's great that you're here! says Councillor Craigie, and when he says the word *great*, the edges of his mouth reach almost to his ears.

A small current of laughter, and Craigie asks another.

Do you know what you're going to do with the standing stones then? Write a book?

All eyes are on Vivien, but there's something about these people, the Councillors, the Administrators and the Officials, it's the way they ask the next obvious question in a line of many, like she's just a kid.

Vivien's a dreamer says Councillor Craigie. She works in a call centre but really wants to go and look at standing stones! It's typical don't you think?

I know, these geniuses!

Excuse me says Vivien, she steps out from the Councillor's arm, wondering why she doesn't break it. She considers Craigie's face and wonders if life will ever penetrate that skin of his and make him say something sensible.

Dedication to duty! says Councillor Craigie, so that everyone smiles.

Dedication to duty! he repeats, freely lazy and enjoying to his best this latest Council piss-up.

Vivien walks towards the computers and the gauze lowers on Councillor Craigie's eyes, his consolation is a mental photograph of Vivien's bottom as she paces away from him.

The six computers on the platform in the City Chambers are feature-encoding messages from other terminals around Aberdeen. Intense amount of numbers fly past at speed and produce hysterical lists and shapes which mean nothing but which excite Vivien just the same. The Network is happening at last, mutually inducing itself into being as an item of mathematics. How instantaneously the rest of the computers in Aberdeen joined these six here in the Town House, how they flashed into the one final galvanised state is academic, but the metaphor of the net however, still applies. The net was cast. And the net rose from the deep and glory was set among the technologically ill-equipped. The net and then the web, everything gets caught. Every imaginary chamber that rose between the ties within the net becomes a second city in that moment as the people of Aberdeen come to minister themselves once more to their best machines. The Network is assembling, and at the correct moment it will become one, when the Provost presses his button. Vivien watches the progress on a screen, Aberdeen byte-present, the principle being that all the computers in the area are going to represent one big machine. A simultaneity of data, one giant open loop bus.

The city centre and the harbour are alive now in a different way, and not only with rain. Panel discussion and open forum is underway between a thousand talkative and loquacious computers which ask, *Who are you?* of each other, and likewise receive their answers. The Aberdeen Domestic Computer Network is coming alive.

Vivien sees that the entire city is now connected while the Councillors unite around the room in pleasant celebration. They've been to a hundred events like this, were themselves voted into office to mingle for their local communities, and eat and drink wine on behalf of all their constituents. Vivien examines the Network Map and sees that it's switching on as values are copied from one place to another. In the galvanising of the IF / THEN / ELSE supply, empty memory chambers are flooded with loops of triviality.

She clicks.

Operations extend down King Street to the University and to Powis where more logomania lights up the virtual night. The harebrained chatter of irresponsible machinery continues, but the streets are quiet, even though the noise is there for those who can hear it.

Woodend becomes conversant, and it's followed by Woodend Hospital amid the trees and parks at the end of the town. Crisply coloured lines lead right to the hospital door on the computer screen while at the same time Dyce, where the main road palavers out of town, is connected also. The airport terminal is quiet one moment and prolix the next, and the public computers, free for use in an empty departure lounge, glibly say they are now up for business and good to go. Likewise at the hospital, the Network machines become alive, so that the nurses on the wards are instructed to stop attending patients, and begin the essential tasks of *data-entry*.

Then, Northfield and Summerhill. In flows the news and out flows the blather. It's easy to become fatalistic about the new technology, particularly in areas of town where money could be better spent on stair lighting, heating the elderly and stocking schools with books . . . *but with all these problems, this computer can help . . .* this computer can not only fill each school with high level talk and internet access, but monitor the users, and assess their needs. It can even weld people back into communal shape, so the Council says.

The lines run via Mastrick to Hazlehead, where the idle classes reside with their over-sized newspapers. Harsh dysphonic noise may be heard down the cable, but the streets are quiet. A wash of rain, and no cars move anywhere, but this night, the inaudible clatter of machines is bringing news and communication to the lucky occupants of Craigiebuckler and Airyhall where starless men in suits are closing their garage doors. The computers are over-talkative, not like their lisping and inarticulate hosts, and they communicate fast and with intent, while thick and velar, the population of Airyhall goes back to sitting strangled on its bum, saying *pass the remote dear* to its spouse.

Cults and the North Deeside Road, out shoots the fluent tongue, the net stretches through unobtrusive miles of treed granite houses with names like Ellengowan, Murtle and Kippie Lodge. It's these good-living people that are most likely to benefit from the Aberdeen Domestic Computer Network, those who need the home shopping services, or need to know the position of the stock market. Further, the middle classes are stark staring convinced that their children should spend every hour possible in front of a computer, and this Network will help them there.

Along these patterns the Network rides, through telephone lines amid the sweet banquet of trees along the River Dee and back to town. Long-winded messages arrive on the terminals at Garthdee, and a short exchange means an endless scrolling of glib and flip computer jargon, something the machine understands which can only bemuse an onlooker. The OK signal pops out with the *Bon Accord* motto and the rampant leopards . . . and the thousand-odd machines on the housing estate take counsel immediately with each other while their human betters approach with caution.

What's it doing?

Duh know.

What does it say?

Duh know.

What's it supposed to do?

It'll tell us.

Well tell me if it does anything.

I'll look at it tomorrow.

Garthdee and Mannofield talk together. The machine in the bar at the Seafield Club announces on the screen that it is **LINKED** but it is unnoticed by the dialogists getting shandied at the counter. In this instant, these mannerly neighbourhoods are connected by a sitting seance of computers scattered over the district: Thorngrove Avenue, Duthie Terrace, Great Western Road, quiet in the unrounded yellow street light, cars brush past on no mission at all, a century and a half of granite hotels and guests houses, now sprung into life by the tremulous talking of computers.

The same applies on Queens Road and Rubislaw where it's open forum for machines, because this is another area of town where these gregarious socialites in grey boxes will be put to full use. The children of this district meet in the public school quadrangle where they will delight each other with this new method of communicating . . . because the moment the Network is active, the West End youngster is there, already establishing keyboard to keyboard communication with his neighbours and his bum chums.

whast going on dude?

trin to get thism machine to work!!!!

YOU CANT SPELL

dah no

can you play SUBSTATE on this

yes I got it LOOK OUT!!

two player///////////if youve got the .exe file

ill send them

you die!!!!

no YOU DIE!!!!

I can get the rockets

shell 2 death suckah

send autoexec file now or die

Splayed granite turrets rise above the trees, and wide in the rain, Queens Road is sober and quiet as the parochial back mansions of heaven, the houses are so still that you'd be pushed to believe that any of them are even occupied . . . but Queen's Road is radiated with machines, business and otherwise, all lit, all right, this night.

The wire continues.

Through Ferryhill, the review of position increases the strength of the Network on its way across the River Dee to Nigg. Every computer must recognise every other computer before the Network can be said to be running, and this meeting of machines is the most joyfully easy part of the process. Silence in the city represents machine blather, the loquendi in action, all monitored closely by the bodies in charge to see if this new invention will amount to anything useful.

Vivien is at one such terminal in the City Chambers, her face is lit from the demon blue light, and even from her chair she can sense the low power rush around the town, the call signs and the cackle. On screen, the Aberdeen Domestic Computer Network lights up with many thousand points of contact as the communication travels on the instant. Information arrives on screen, but by now Vivien has digested one fact only, that the entire of computerised Aberdeen has spoken itself awake. It happened within a flash . . . like fire devours gunpowder . . . just as if the City of Aberdeen stepped through an open door . . .

So one day this kind of network will be all over Scotland says Councillor Craigie, and his cigar sends a circular puff in a whirl to the air. He hasn't taken his eye from Vivien yet and he smiles at her with his old fascination.

Up the hill to Kincorth and Tullos and via several thousand talkative machines, whole blocks on the screen have come alight. On screen the computers appear on-line, meaning that the whole of the town is now in a greater sense than ever before, *alive*. Aberdeen then attaches itself to the sea bed frame of the United Kingdom, the server telephones Glasgow, Edinburgh and London . . . while back at the Town House, in the absorption of free wine, Vivien feels herself at this moment to be the point of origin, one of many lines of force which speed around the world much faster than she can blink her eye.

Councillor Craigie can still be seen fancying himself in this tall and splendid room. The City Chambers are full tonight with polite hangers-on and their boring administrators . . . but Vivien can always remove them by concentrating elsewhere. The computers continue their silent discharge of duty, and she marvels at it, the conversation fades and grows and there's another explosion of laughter from nearby. If small is beautiful thinks Vivien, then this is profound. The tiniest show of strength, the most minuscule of power, and over such a large geographical area, the Network has taken place before her eyes at last. Take away the furniture that each computer is sitting upon, thinks Vivien, and as a result suspend the machines in mid air. The computers will now float in the living rooms, boardrooms and bedrooms of Aberdeen. With the machines in mid air like this, she has started to conceive of the potency the city now holds. Take away the walls of the buildings, carefully remove the floors and foundations and all the other furniture, avoid attaching the cables to the streets and then take away the streets themselves.

Next, take away what is left of the houses, and then take away the pavements, roads and parks, and each time, take care to avoid the cables. Turn the sun carefully to point light on the computers and their connections . . . and then take away the planet . . . and here in space, your isolated frame of chatty machines will cultivate sensibility by themselves. Such a linking of machines, wired up and in the void like this, will hold forth on matters mathematical and be oblivious to man, cabled in a black hole, with many terminals connected by loose mile-long wires which strike across the emptiness like roots. The machines, thinks Vivien, operate well enough with the planet here, but with it gone they might do even better . . . and thinking like this, Vivien floats through the Network, pulls herself along several metres by holding one of the cables . . . moving towards a row of terminals, lit brightly in the black of space.

⊖ SONSI.eN

Users will not know they have been infected by SONSI, nor will the sender know if documents contain it. Although it is not perfect protection, users shold operate SNORTON VIRUS DETECTOR in tandem with a Kellock Hard Driver. If you run this programme every ten minutes and have a new Kellock installed every ten days, then it is likely you will have a 65% chance of being safe.

The danger with this virus however is real and SONSI.eN has already infected many offices where staff have been treated against it. To treat staff in your office or call centre against this virus, first rejuvenate their skn with fruit acids before applying a liquid vegetable infusion. Newer members of staff should also try sun-dried green clay face packs while they are at their desks, while all clients should enter the work environment barefoot.

IMPORTANT

IF YOU OPEN/RUN ANY EMAIL ATTACHMENT, YOU ARE TAKING AN UNNECESSARY RISK AND

MAY BE DOWNLOADING THIS VIRUS! READ THE
TEXT MESSAGE =but= DISCARD THE ATTACH-
MENT EVEN IF IT LOOKS LIKE IT MAY CONTAIN
AN INTER-OFFICE COMEDY MEMO, OR GARSE
VIDEO FOOTAGE OR FAT PEOPLE IN THE united
states. AND TELL THE SENDER YOU HAVE DONE
SO. TELL THEM TO STOP BUGGING YOU AND TO
GET ON WITH THEIR WORK. BECOME CRAZIER
THAT ALL YOUR BROTHERS AND SISTERS COM-
BINED. AND FINALLY =never= DOWNLOAD
=any= PHILOSOPHICAL RAMBLINGS FROM
=any= f**ucking NEWSGROUP, OR FROM ANY
DOPE STYLE buddhist types. ALWAYS REPLY
WITH AN EMAIL URGING THEM =TO GO BACK
TO HELL= AND LEAVE YOU THE **** ALONE=

Vivien gulps for air. What is it?

The gavel sounds.

Attention please, direct lighting on the speaker, the guests blink-
ing as conversation shuffles to a close, dawn breaking mid evening in
the City Chambers. A small group have stood up to sermonise at the
table where the six computers wait, and behind them, hundreds of
feet of red drape exclude the general public and bathe the room in
wealth. Vivien moves back into the floor.

The lights please.

A screen is lit for action and a short Council film begins, it's what
they confusingly call Multi-media and it's made by crappy video tech-
nicians.

From one computer terminal – to another – communication
is possible via the telephone – from one computer to many –
discourse is possible upon a 'network' – between so many
computers – messaging can be constant – and at the same
time every one in Aberdeen – the business sector – the
ordinary user – can all benefit – from a system which makes

our city – one – a program that is set to be a landmark in the development of future computer systems – to be the model for the future – and this is what will happen in Aberdeen – with this 'network' –

The many computers illustrated on the screen shoot messages to one another. Communication increases to a point and then it simplifies itself. The graphics collapse and then refresh into a leaner form.

A new method of distribution giving the people free computers – funded from the private sector and the public sector – a new initiative to give people computer access – whoever they are – wherever they are – to benefit their lifestyles – dynamically increasing the potential of each citizen – their powers to communicate with each other – organise their businesses – their leisure activities – bringing to life the twenty-first century – and just imagine the benefits for our children – who'll learn for the future – who *are* the future!

The image of amplified dots travelling between the many hundreds of terminals illustrated in the film looks like a flow chart working at a deranged pace. There is something powerless about the fussy animation the Councillors watch, and yet it is still the picture of the world to be.

A spotlight fans into the face of the Provost and shines off his glasses for a second, allowing the impression of a fish surfacing from a dim pool, before he sinks voluntarily back into the darkness.

The light returns and the Provost holds up a hand.

Well well, he says, this is very fine indeed. I've of course got to thank many people for this idea, from which we shall see many benefits to the city of Aberdeen, but first I have to say this.

The Provost straightens his glasses, he's been called on to speak in many roles, has opened a thousand hearts and launched as many dinners, and before him once again is a dim room of folk holding their drinks at chest height.

Because, he says, we are giving away something tonight from which we are going to get a great return, and that is something the creators of this computer system should be congratulated for, and I wish them all the best in their continued work.

There follows a rather depressed clapping of the hands and a seizure of mumbles while people drink and gather once again their full attention.

I know for a fact, says the Provost, that Mr Crandall is going back to his office tonight to monitor the computers and to watch as this system learns about our community, its new home. So you see the effort required, and it doesn't end there.

More applause, the clapping hands of many high minded people who are bored with getting everything into proportion.

And that is what is so exciting about this, says the Provost. Because the Aberdeen Domestic Computer Network is like a friend or a new member of Council. A new *person* indeed, and one sure to be among the most useful members of our community.

There is a certain silence as the crowd distils the Provost's words into one lingering mood. A glimmer of artificial light from the six demonstration machines glances across the room, it's like a weak spot of lightning hopping between clouds only to discharge itself in an empty sherry glass. The last thing the people want to do is treat the darling monomaniac machines like one of the family.

Trusting the computers, says the Lord Provost, involves being true to the Network, and using the system with a social mind, and if we behave like that we will get out of it whatever we put in. What we hope is that Mr Crandall's Network will present back to its users the image of a mentally crystallised community, and that will be our city, Aberdeen.

Vivien gulps to the bottom of another glass of wine, it tastes quite good by now. What the Provost means, she thinks, is that whatever we put into the computer will be stored in its pumpkin head, analysed and returned to the community as if the machine were one good citizen like any other, shaping life for the better by aiming to toe the Civic Line. Generations of students of artificial intelligence have made this notion so, spread this myth that if humans are bad to their machines, the machines will turn on them like mad dogs with dangerous pretensions to knowledge. Sense in loops, thinks Vivien, a case of machine hypochondria for these minorly drunk jug-heads assembled tonight. They're worried that the machines will take over because they've seen too many movies about rabid computers, circuits with screws loose, wonky pixilations, the melancholy machines that have attacked their creators and have determined to do away with life. The Man / God routine, the artificial intelligence student raped by his own spangly mechanism . . . the machine that wires its owners to the mains and then fries them to Kingdom Come . . . all that they deserve in good old science fiction. The morbid dream of self destruction, it's there, along with snakes in the boots, never revealing the good thinking machine, but always the mind sick robot. Never a machine that mends and fixes, but the pessimism provided of the obnubliated chip that's set on KILL because that's how we programmed it.

Vivien stares up through the dark to the Provost, she sympathises with the confusion. Who here after all, has not seen the washing machine in a vulgar light or sensed the toaster's desire to bite the human hand? Who has not been nudged one time too many by a homicidal drinks dispenser or noticed the deadly appearance of their electric cooker in the dark of night? We all know how bad it's going to get, we've all been followed home by a driverless car and have had our hands nipped by the video player . . . but it's not going to be like that in Aberdeen. Our machines don't talk, and don't even have a name, and of course they can be unplugged and scrapped in the landfill if they screw up regal. This is no case of Frankenstein, this is merely existing technology, re-warped for the times we live in, it's nothing but the Aberdeen Domestic Computer Network.

The Provost makes full use of the moment, an auspicious time indeed. He prepares to press the button and make it real, his one and only task.

So with no more fussing about, he says, I'd like to switch on this computer . . . and then set into motion the Aberdeen Area Communication Programme . . . otherwise known as the Aberdeen Domestic Computer Network!

<< click here >>

The moment people are waiting for, that they think they have been waiting for.

The switch is touched and the chronicler from the Press & Journal takes his photograph. The audience assembled clap and the Provost smiles proudly into the crowd. The phenomena of appreciation, a monophonic beating of hands to express unity, solidarity of sentiment, and the overthrowing of silence. The Provost smiles and voices flutter out of the hand-claps while more flash photography makes the people on the stage look like red horrors in the lightning. The Provost is a smiling jack in the box, and with luck his photograph will appear in futuristic history books like *Purfled Fogeys of Auld Aiberdeen in Yon Compuiter Age.*

A city crest appears on the large screen behind the redly smiling Provost. A light appears with the word CONNECTING in large print. Upon the genesis of the computer network, upon the breaking into virtual space of these new machines, the alphabet is delivered, tongue to ear, and the system is established. While the final stages of applause turn to chatter and the Provost begs a second's silence, he stands to attention to introduce the next speaker.

Of course we all know Councillor Cruden, he says, and she has asked if her new friend, the lassie from the helpdesk would like to show herself and say a few words. Her name's Vivien, and I think she's here somewhere, at least I was told she was . . .

A brief circulatory shuffle revolves the room until Vivien is identified. Squinting into her sweater, someone gives her a shove and she makes her way to the stage while the Provost folds his arms and stands proud before his fan-base. Vivien crosses the parting crowd, she feels like she's regressed to a time before when she was pushing through . . . what was it, tall weeds?

It could have been, but then the eyes, what were they?

She finishes her glass.

Vivien was walking through another crowd, where firelight preceded the eyes, where she was led up to the front by her mother, who was walking several steps behind her . . .

Yes, there was something to remember there. What is it that is making her think about that time before? Could she focus on both at the same time? Or would one naturally come to the fore?

One question at a time please.

All that Vivien could say was that there was something familiar about this moment in the City Chambers when she walked to the table to say her few words. There was something in the faces of the people present that gave them that quality of eels breaking in from the darkness. It could have been her own motion through the crowd was similar to that of an eel, crossing a river bed, black body, dark weed, mouth blowing gently on the sand, but Vivien thought of the girl reaching puberty and the eel. She'd been taken by the others and made to touch a poison eel, made to hold it, and after that she was left with a woman who cut her hair and took the eel and stirred it in a basin of water. When that was done, Vivien was wrapped up in a tent and made to stay in there for a day so that when she came out she could be cleaned again.

And the eel ? That's never eaten.

So at this point, it's likely that Vivien could be making her way towards the centre-point of all of those assembled, and she may be asked to take the eel from the basin and hold it. It's the same atmosphere, an expectancy as she moves among her people, because their eyes are like cracks of light and it even feels safe. Not that you want to hold an eel, or have anything to do with it, but it was something like that.

The Provost extends an arm. *Come on Vivien!* he says, and so the applause goes up.

Vivien can't see much detail of the faces squared away in the darkness, just like they were the way she remembers in the past. There is no sign of Pally, perhaps her only friend in the room, but one face stands out from the energetic expressions, that of Councillor Craigie, he's tall and smiling, clapping with a cigar in his mouth. Again, Vivien can read what's on Councillor Craigie's unguarded mind. He's the original man with one thought only, it's written all over his face, his curiosity at her body and her clothes as he eyes her up and down.

Arriving on the stage, Vivien glances at the computers and she sees at once that the machines are operating all right. The Network has made its first few connections and is setting up the rest. The screen may show the coat of arms for Aberdeen, but from the word GO, this wonderful device has been making new friends with itself.

It's working I can see, she says.

The City Chambers go quiet in a drinks hush.

This machine is working fine, says Vivien, I can tell from the command line at the foot here that it's free from viruses too, which is great, of course.

Even this level of scientific talk is tricky tonight and the crowd pauses and hums a second. As far as Vivien can see, the assembled only wish to return to the hobnob now that the social purpose of the meet is realised, and even as she stands before them, there rises the sound of human static as they return to stand-by. There are a thousand decent thoughts in the room but the ceremony of civic life must be buckled and adhered to, and so she clears her throat to silence them again.

I can explain it like this, she says, her voice feeling like it might crack. The Network is on but hasn't yet neared its goal, even though it's closing in on it of course.

The crowd stare like restless heads on pillars while interest flags and mopes. Vivien glances behind her to read what's scrolling on the large screen, to prove a point she'd hoped would arise, and so she indicates a section of the graphics and says to the crowd, This is the memory of the Network formatting, the power of all the machines coming together . . . forming one bank of space out of the many, do you see?

Vivien appreciates that the guests don't follow her, but at least they maintain their dynamic poses, diligently avoiding active thought on the subject. The agility of the numbers stirring upwards on the screen behind Vivien inspires in the Councillors a sense of achievement and she looks ahead once more, past the crowd and away to a time when this great project will finally step outwith the machines of the past and become something of the future.

Of course, you must all phone us up with your problems, she says hesitantly. We would be delighted to help, no matter how small.

Under the chunky drapes and the indiscernible gold cornices, the people watching her are not real and resemble hollow craters the way their faces protrude upon each other. Vivien stares like this and an applause begins, she reaches up to speak but thinks better of it and steps away, avoiding a back-slap from the Provost who marches professionally back to the centre of the stage.

Thank you very much: Vivien!

Like an engine the applause takes off proper. Vivien smiles and steps down from the stage, she looks for another glass of wine and pulls one from the nearest tray, and there is Chris Crandall standing beside her, he has a light grasp of her arm, as he if he thinks she might tumble.

Crandall looks right into her face – what concern and attention in her brown eyes, what heart and what intelligence. Crandall grips Vivien's arm with keen enthusiasm, he holds her jumper as if the fabric were a life-saver.

Well done, he says, but Vivien says nothing, doesn't pull her arm away but only drinks.

Team leader, says Crandall smoothly, and she feels herself go blind and deaf for a moment. The voices, the Provost, it all slouches away from view as she becomes lost in a new sense of scale. Only a metre to her left is the retentive cold of the North Sea, and a metre to her right, the darkness of the hills, sad and wet places whomped up against each other in the shade. Vivien spins inside – a metre above her are the stars and a metre below her is a mile of the hard rock on which the Granite City is botched together, batted out of stone to form a patched up home for all these people. Crandall holds her arm like she is his prisoner, looking at Vivien's face and thinking more than he ever, how much he needs to keep the momentum going.

Vivien.

What there?

Be in early on Monday morning.

She opens her eyes.

The bustle comes in to focus, an insensitive scramble of voices and faces. Life without even the quality of a dream. Bodies autosynch, precision production of words, fact distribution, all shot up. Nothing works and nothing is under control. The very self-active Council gathering, a celebration of cybernate ignorance, in Aberdeen.

Monday morning, says Crandall, and he lets go of Vivien's arm at last.

Uhu yes.

Big things, he says.

Whether Vivien chooses to ignore him or not, Crandall doesn't know, because she turns quickly round, sensing the approach of another Councillor, bent on chat.

Just checking out the staff Mr Crandall?

Yes indeed, says Crandall and Vivien moves off, leaving him shaded by a thick faced and old-aged Councillor whose drink slops untidily at his wrist.

Vivien walks towards the cloakroom, it could be time to slide out on to Union Street, where she might feel better. The machines are on, but that's no big deal, Vivien is moving slowly through the fuss to find a way out, to contemplate the challenge presented by the few hours left of the day. The ceremony is still swinging but she walks for the door and feels in need of air. Council has enjoyed its chicken leg and administration has nobbled business once again. The policy makers have done their bit, right now, they tan the sausage rolls and marvel in an elitism which they feel has made them more than human.

Oh, says Councillor Craigie strolling up, you're thinking of leaving?

Yes I have to go.

Oh, so that's it?

Yea, says Vivien, she feels drunk and looks to see if there's any more alcohol in her glass. Councillor Craigie holds his own glass momentarily towards her, an invitation to drink, and she turns around. The door is held open by a man in red livery, flanked by two old women in Aberdeen City pinafores, and then she's out.

The Townhouse stairs are wide and Vivien shoots down them as if she were lead sinking to the bottom of a pool. She passes under more paintings and wishes at that exact moment that she was at home and in bed with no transition, none of the unpleasantness of the cold air, the discourse of the street. She grabs the rail and thinks about the machines again, how the computers across Aberdeen have become what they always were, seemingly unassailable aspects of the masculine. All computers, personified in one single figure, all the same size and colour . . . vessels of honour and seats of wisdom. Like alchemists, Crandall and the City Council are about to pour all their future hope of improvement into these terminals, with no sense of what could really be achieved. All this world fear thinks Vivien, it comes to nothing but men-kind, making less of more machines.

The vessel of honour, she thinks, it's like the standing stones.

The stairwell makes Vivien dizzy. The computers upstairs expand from nought at one million times the speed at which she seems to collapse, and there above her, men honour themselves in discovery amid a sprawl of paper documents. The Council and Mr Crandall have been working to improve the worth of man, to bend and squat the darkness which never gives way, which never even slightly dents against human efforts . . . but the darkness thinks Vivien, is the same black colour today as it's been for the last 40,000 years.

Vivien drops upon the front door of the Townhouse which is now unguarded and bolted solid. She is holding the handle of the Townhouse door and turns to look up the stairs where she sees Pally gaping down, looking over the top rail. From this range, Pally's nose seems to have slipped down her face and there is something of the doll about her.

Vivien? Are you OK there? Dearie what's wrong?

Nothing, she says, I've got to go home now. I'm not well, it's the drink you know.

Right enough I'm not well, thinks Vivien looking in to the wooden plate of the Townhouse door, right enough I need some air and sleep inside me.

Rubbish Vivien, you've only had a couple!

Vivien looks up the stairwell, Councillor Pally has found a shyness in her face like she's trying to be coy or even kind.

I'm just going to get a taxi, says Vivien, and she pulls the door but it doesn't budge.

I'm coming down! shouts Pally, and her head vanishes as she runs back towards the function to get her coat. Vivien holds the door for a last breath, the spin and spill of the decorated stairwell continues around her like timber rolling inside a giant drum.

A giant drum, as in the washing machine.

Seeing the stairwell of the Town House filled with dirty bedding and clothes, spinning with the urbanised dirt of a thousand families, Vivien recalls a thought from before.

She feels faint – here it comes again.

Urban Sprawl is nothing but domestic isolation.

The individual wife approaches – she's been dying for a computer in her house to do the shopping, to control the temperature and monitor the kids' homework. Soon her computer will take out the rubbish and she'll indulge in coffee and television all day long. Behind the mask the woman pretends there is nothing there, occasionally to such effect, that she kills off whatever was there to begin with. Woman knows no better, not in Aberdeen, probably not anywhere.

Vivien looks up the stairs and fantasises. Solar water heaters plough in warm jets, detergents enter the system in sealed capsules and a turbine begins to move the cylinder as one. What is woman doing now? She is adhering to the myth of her place. She dumbs herself down, puts herself down, so that the world passes her by like a dream. She cannot bring herself to look straight ahead, so she's like Lot's wife, looking back on every Sodom and Gomorrah that her hubby creates. She's lost like this, she pretends there's nothing there inside, holds this sentimental belief in the comfort of man. Is at her best, an honorary man. Otherwise she's a trademark woman . . . doing woman's things and talking girl's stuff.

But such passivity is unbecoming of Vivien. She stands straight as she hears Pally's footsteps clatter down the stairs towards her. The door opens and there is Union Street, where it's raining sideways in the dark. Hooded vehicles pass and still there are people going home, the traffic's like a mill. Vivien steps out and leans into the rock granite of the Townhouse while dirty cars wait unhappily at the lights. The wind strikes her collar and she slips closed her eyes. Leaning into the Town House wall on Union Street, the architectural unconscious is clear . . . archaic residues are present like bright rock fossil, with the imprint of vivid impressions of the past builders, of Aberdeen.

And then with the traffic, she senses that this panic is indeed the natural outcome of such optimism . . . a beautiful town plan littered with papers and buildings which deviate from each other . . . because everyone is in competition, clearly.

Vivien's eyes open.

The most dreadful of all possibilities, the loss of my soul, my city, Aberdeen.

The Town House door bangs shut and there is Pally in her heavy coat, her face is sparkling with the drink.

Come on, she says, taking Vivien's arm and they head off in the falling water to one of the posher nearby wine bars.

EQUATION

As Vivien wakes up she concludes first the roof and then Pally's body. They are in Pally's back room in Blenheim Place and she feels around the blankets and the sleeping bags and sees she hasn't even undressed. Pally is asleep on the floor beside her, both of them still in their clothes, fou in the head. What did she think she was doing?

I must have been mad, Vivien thinks, to drink like that.

Vivien stares at the snoring Councillor who lies with her face in pain. A bottle of white wine has toppled nearby and its lip has spilled its contents into a mark on the carpet.

Pally are you awake?

I don't know, says Pally, and she rolls up to her cushion for warmth, an exhausted seeker of nirvana, stuck to the floor on a Saturday morning. Good old Pally with her foot sticking out the bottom.

During the night Vivien had the same dream that she often has, and in it Aberdeen is drowned. First she dreamed that the sea level expanded in a diluvian wave, and then as the ice caps melted, she dreamed that the water rose again, a good seventy metres higher than was usual. In a blast of typical irony, this raising of the water level affected the poor more than it did the wealthy who all seemed to be living in the hills, and as Vivien floated in a rowing boat past the church tower at Queen's Cross, it had occurred to her that the rich always live higher up than the poor do.

Vivien floated along Union Street as the water rose, she wondered where would be safe once the flood had settled. As her dinghy rocked she stared in silence at the litter bins which floated by, just as she wondered at the tops of boats and towers emerging from downtown. Because it was Friday night in the dream, there were still crowds of men on Union Street, characters in white socks and blue jeans, all wearing crew cuts, all of them singing on the half submerged buildings. In the dream these undiscriminated blokes were everywhere, and all alike as each other, they stood in noisy muddles and impressed Vivien by not caring that it was the end of the world and that their city was sinking underwater. Some of the men were even diving and coming up with cold booty from the shops while others were bobbing on top of anything that floated, like caravans and furniture.

That was real, thinks Vivien looking up at the roof of Pally's undecorated living room. Union Street really is noisy and full of men like that . . . and those girls too, in those stupid shoes and skirts, they don't know any better, they'll carry on boozing even when the drink taps are underwater.

Vivien feels scared that she's wasted too much time now. How could she end up with a hangover when there was so much work to do? Drinking in the name of relaxation. It didn't make much sense.

Didn't we have a Chinese last night?

Pally says nothing, the hole between her pink lips makes an appreciable sucking noise in her sleep.

Didn't we have a Chinese Pally?

Vivien is too afraid to move. Rough sunlight peeks around the corner of the curtain, but somehow she expects the day to be a dark one, just another black-grey station on the line to the end of the year. Vivien also expects their Chinese meal to be spread rather thickly over the sleeping bags, because she doesn't remember eating it, and so with care she spies over the blankets after a moments' courage . . . but there is nothing doing and her sheet is clean of food. Looking further afield, there is no other sign of the meal in Pally's living room, not of the plates, not of the empties, and not of the fact that they might have eaten anything at all in the night . . . no sign of Chinese food of any sort, a sight which makes her more suspicious yet.

Bugger this drinking.

While waiting for a taxi, Pally and Vivien saw in unclear light, the joys of drunken Aberdeen. Near the taxi rank there was an old Friday Nighter being sick, puking along the wall and down the lane. The puker was working hard in the dark, chucking gulp after gulp, bent up with the entire load of his stomach while the punters waiting for the taxis ignored him. Vivien couldn't quite see down there but she wanted to laugh, and she wondered who was heaving up what in the night. At this time, all over Scotland they were broken down and boking, cause it was Friday night, the night when the national stomach is best found in rebuttal at the wall. All the while Pally was talking, *putting the world to rights* as she said, and Vivien although drunk, found it hard to take on board.

Pally's breathing does the octave scale in bed, the psalmodic calm of a Saturday morning. Did Pally get so drunk so that she could sleep right through to the afternoon?

Pally, did we have a Chinese?

Yeah we did.

Pally speaks at last, but the answer is what Vivien feared. Vivien is worried that the night before Pally might drunkenly have spent her money on a meal that neither of them could properly remember.

She draws the cover up for a clearer look at the room.

Where is it then?

Pally is silent save for her snoring lips, she is half alive having spent the night before blotting her mind of sense, striking herself further down in Aberdoniensus Gloomus.

Where is it Pally? Where's the Chinese?

I don't know, she says, and then lets a snort off to the air.

When they left the Town House, Vivien discovered that like other members of the Professional Classes, Pally held and shared opinions on the following: economics, healthcare, journalism, theatre, literature, cuisine, France, computers, vehicles, education, the Left, the colour of their telephones, space travel, childbirth, football, housing, curtains, Japan, mathematics, finance, chairs, envelopes, patios, germ warfare, adverbs, investment, the Olympic Games, longevity, animal experiments, doctors, soya, Nazis, and yoghurt.

At the taxi rank Pally kept on talking, but lying on the floor Vivien can't recall a thing of what was said. All that Vivien can remember is that in the wine bar she was repeating to herself an Action / Output equation that she liked, and that was the best she could do. She couldn't look at Pally straight with these sums appearing all over the place, and so she began to think as hard as she could about all of her equations, to see if they worked out of the classroom. The bar was busy but the people were far from real and Pally was talking about politics, leaning over the table and tapping on the wood with her finger when she felt it was important. For Vivien, the people in the bar were sums, dawdling and laughing with smoke dispersing from their mouths, the wine bar was congested from wall to wall, a compact of people who would only begin to thin out after last orders, before becoming diluted in the atmosphere of the cold walk home.

After one more bottle of wine, Vivien was still listening to Pally but was wondering how best to get away. Once the second bottle was opened, Vivien was too drunk to know anything but was still playing with those Action / Output numbers and wondering if they would work if applied to those volatile talkers all around her. That equation, it was good, but Pally didn't think so.

I don't understand it, she pleaded when she was asked. It's all numbers and I don't have a mind for that kind of thing!

I could easily help you understand, said Vivien, but Pally just laughed it off and began to talk about shopping again.

Vivien was staring black eyed and serious, she looked across the tiles where the capacity drinkers were jerking out their own sonorous theories on life. The atmosphere was punctuated with the coloratura of laughter, and it looked strange with that layer of smoke in the dark.

You're mad! said Pally, laughing out loud to join the hubbub.

Yea right.

For all conversation (j), with all persons (p), then if j > p then a resolution in harmony is achieved. When p = j then the world will cease to be.

For all incremental confession (ic), and for all lager (l), then if l > p and j > l, then j must be > p before (ic) is even bearable. And then that's only when you're really interesting and have a half-decent problem to talk about in the first place.

For all boring bastards (b) who want to talk about philosophy (ph) then drink and drug factor (d) must not be > (j > p) or else you will become very tired indeed listening to them. If the sum (b + d + ph) < ic, then a maudlin situation will arise. Very often (b) can be cancelled if < d and (ph) is > (b = d) but never if (ic) = j.

In the next house to Pally's a washing machine starts up and the thump claims Vivien's mind. Relaxation is over for the morning and she looks across the floor to see if the Chinese carry-out is there, but it is not. There is no more tranquillity under the bed covers, so Vivien closes her eyes to imageless Saturday morning.

Don't get drunk. Don't drink and don't go out with strange Councillors. It's a waste of time waking up with most of the day written off, with just the one responding note in your head, shaped like a low round ball, and humming. The washing machine, although only a minimal disturbance is like the whole city giving a faint shake, as if everybody had put on their washing machines at the same time, as if the population had reported in and started up the clamour, just to get another rainy day off the ground.

Lucky me, thinks Vivien, and she pulls the covers right up. Straight away she tries sleeping with a rhythm and a pulse.

Vivien pictures a pendulum to help her sleep, a pendulum in the form of a body. The pendulum swings and ticks in the dark, forms a sublime harmony the scale of which is difficult to grasp. The scale of the pendulum could be underlying the entire world when she thinks like this, these circles, this swing, an imaginary noise that forms into partitions in the dark with the distant song of the washing machine way below. Ensemble music it is.

The living room clock makes its own noise, the ticks blend with what Vivien imagines she hears from the pendulum. There is a joyful noise within the harmony of the machine, and it occurs to Vivien that no correctly functioning machine can make a *bad* noise. In fact, thinks Vivien, the converse is true. The sweeter the sound, the more machine tuning, the more perfection there is involved, and hence *the music of the spheres.*

She dozes, there are pendulum swings, horizontal circles on which finely balanced men stand, and from out of this blackness comes the perfection of shapes and sounds, from the melodic minor to the whole meter of space. The imperfection of human cities is a horror to Vivien, the noise of cranes swinging their bricky cargoes across the rooftops is a vacant sound. The real world is people flying in aeroplanes and eating heat-sealed foods, the noises of their houses are degrees in a lack of form, they are unhappiness and they are anger. Smarting emptiness folds over the roofs of every city and leaves behind it an unpleasant ripple, the imperfect noise she hears is people bumping in to each other, it's their traffic and their pavement discord. They're vocalising their disgust in the shops and in the media, but still they can't get enough, or they can't get what they want . . . they can't even manage without the synchronous discomfort of one another. Trains weave through this, under this, the sound of the buildings is rendered old because they have been erected at the wrong angle, and so the architecture doesn't function, but instead strikes up aggression in those who are near. All this noise and more. The noise of a woman fixing her hair in the wind, the noise of school-kids, the noise of men scoring in their mind, silvery triumph, arrogant women. The noise of restaurants crammed up against stinking kitchen dustbins and the noise of roads. All persistent noise, dissonant to the last, and yet within her, Vivien perceives her pendulum, the impenetrable form of beauty, the impenetrable structure that produces something so very clear.

Vivien wakes up again and has a headache. The cycle of the washing machine next door ends and the drone moves to a lower homophone according to the need of the stinking clothes and the shitty sheets within. Pally's back room is ugly and cold, not worth getting up into, not when there's a world of dreams at hand. But no. When the day must be faced, when disharmony and disrepair must be faced out, then it's time to get up.

Do you want a coffee? she says to Pally.

Nothing from Pally can be taken now as a yes, even though coffee will never wake her or cause her maternal form to walk about the house again. It's raining outside and Vivien suddenly recalls that the night before, Pally had agreed to visit some standing stones with her, a ridiculous idea indeed.

Now what did I go and do that for?

Vivien looks along the face of her sleeping friend. It's not Pally, she thinks, it's the drink, or it's the kind of people that she mixes with. Are all these bureaucrats really the same, or can you forgive them their individual follies?

Vivien not feeling at all pleasant makes it to Pally's kitchen, a stunned feeling in her head, that stubborn inner halo, a circle of tight packed sand between the skull and what's inside. It's hurting her and making her thirsty. The Chinese meal is not to be seen in the kitchen, and perhaps thinks Vivien, the idea was only mooted. Maybe no cash was given and maybe no meal was eaten, for certainly she can't remember eating it. There's no twitter in her stomach, only a smoky sensation from wine and beer. There are no messy plates or empty cartons on the tabletop, so the meal could have been all but fantasy. At the window Vivien looks out to guess the time of day. From the greyness on the blocks, the dirt slate and the curtains, the wet granite walls running with loose wires and black pipes, she reasons that it could be any time between 8 am and 4 pm. Other windows look back at her, bleak according to those beings behind.

The kettle. A mess across the kitchen surface, Vivien finds two mugs and thinks of all the other hangover merchants sleeping it off. While the lager whales and the wine dolphins snore, they spout long phews of air into their stinky bedrooms. Let them do it, but just let me be free of it.

In the kitchen dustbin are the silver dishes and plastic sack in which the Chinese meal came, but still there's no meal. Funny. I don't remember eating that. But we were drunk as hell so who knows.

Still.

The kettle's silent, Vivien remembers that it doesn't work so she stares again out of the window, as if in thought. Aberdeen's best first mist. It's Saturday and in the distance, Vivien hears the assonant swish of traffic in the rainwater as cars descend to the city centre. There they go, off to grate with the other vehicles, to get that unholy mess going, and to get Saturday written off in total. Vivien looks out of the window to where the water passes and she has the strange impression that one of Aberdeen's great delights is humiliating its citizens, as if all professions in the city are dedicated to one orchestral, business-like, serious expression. One week after another pissed away, and now, too drunk to remember what had happened to their lavish Chinese meal, Vivien feels she might have begun to meet the modern mind, head on.

I was always scared of joining them like that, she thinks.

The window. Grey rain is such a feature of Aberdeen. With this level of earth-abusing weather, you can understand the earnest spirit which built the granite architecture in the first place. An overdose of seriousness, and everyone is blended into one mucky colour formed from the stone, the water, and the accompaniment of folks doing battle. It all comes out a certain colour.

There's no way that the Chinese meal can have been eaten, so Vivien looks deeper into the kitchen dustbin.

Nothing doing and she flips through the veil of muck, delves into juice-damp newspaper, rummages in the wet vegetable, and pushes aside the old packets.

It's time to get dressed and go from here.

Leaving the kitchen Vivien walks through to the living room and sits down beside Councillor Cruden.

Can I borrow a shirt? she says.

The two unsubstantial slits of Pally's eyes close up again and her bulky head of hair rolls away. Pally's view of the day ahead is closed for the next hour at least, and that's her lot.

Vivien sighs and stands up. What to do?

She pulls off her tee shirt and throws it down, it smells bad. A shiver and she walks up to Pally's drawer to see if she can't borrow something from there, some of her smart friend's clothes. Pally snores behind her, a rarefied noise in the cold morning, thin like gas escaping from a pipe, and Vivien pulls open the drawer.

Two plates she sees.

This drinking has got to stop.

Two plates on the clothes, a pile of noodles on each plate with the core neatly parted to provide room for the vegetable sauce, a reddish glue in the centre consolidated in the cold, and there like jelly at the side, a thickened clot of black bean spread, all made solid as it cooled during the night. The plates look like two red eyes, the rubber noodles staring dead out of the clean clothes. The arrangement is neat, as if Pally and Vivien had taken great care to put their meals aside, as if in that shattered state they had managed only to take care of one last thing before they expired completely.

Well: Pally will be bound to enjoy these for her supper, and the microwave oven will certainly see to that.

GLACIATION

Dainty as a Dresden statue
Gentle as a Jersey cow
Smooth as silk, gives creamy milk,
Learn to coo, learn to moo,
That's what to do to be a lady now.

Peggy Seeger *Gonna be an Engineer*

That Saturday afternoon, like crossing matchwood, the BMW rolls up a grinding farm track at the back of industrial Dyce, minutes under the airport. Helicopters draw over the fields and stop as if moored on cables before quitting the city and steering East to the oil rigs. It is the finite and muddy edge of Aberdeen, and Pally and Vivien both sport hangovers. Pally seems used to hers but Vivien is in a sulk. With increasing resistance to the wintered muck on the ground below, Pally pulls her car around to a gap in the side of the track.

This is far as we can go.

We can get closer than this, says Vivien.

I mean the suspension on this road, says Pally, the car keeps scraping the bottom.

Pally looks through the windscreen of the car, this wet back road isn't the right place for such delicacy as her BMW embodies.

Is it far? she asks.

It's up that hill. You can see it almost.

A low closeted farm nearby and a field of shabby sheep. Behind the corrugated hangers and the barn is the steep hump of the

Tyrebagger Hill which rises through the farm walls and sheep scrub. The summit is outlined against the sky, a pylon and the standing stones.

Vivien and Pally are parked against a wire fence that backs against a dirty brick warehouse, the furthest reach of the industrial estate, the last point of Aberdeen proper. On the surface of the ropey black grass are the strange and inconceivable components of the offshore oil industry, ten and twenty feet iron durables that have collected months of wondrous rust. Beside these in a field stand ordinary pipes, conduits welded by industry giants, deep-going machinery that twists into passive locks on the body of oil rigs, broad sections of steel weeping a thick black beer into the tarry ground. The farm track snakes mud around the bottom of the hill and finds a planted block of forest cut into the land, it's all dreadfully corrupted by the proximity of the City of Aberdeen.

We can take this path, says Vivien. Pally looks at her own skirt and her boots, she is overdressed for the countryside, a shame because she has the necessary wardrobe back in Blenheim Place, rustic boots, a wrap and a hat, everything in autumn colour.

We go up beside the farm, says Vivien.

The car doors close and the vehicle locks itself, Pally wonders if it will be safe. There's a base feeling that bad things happen here. Aberdeen has more than its disagreeable share of industrial estates, so dismal and so necessary to the safe working of local money. They're horrible it's true, but what can you do?

She moves up the track after Vivien, conscious of the mud and irked by the effect it has on her shoes. From the foot of the Tyrebagger Hill the standing stones form an inviting line against the sky, some of them are like old teeth while others are half slumped across the earth. Only one of the stones is straight and tall against the white of the heavens.

The facts of the matter: bang on the hill shoulder is a set of several circles, the diameter of which is 18 metres, roughly. The stones, what's left of them, range from one metre tall, to three metres for the best ones, and in the centre is a fragmentary ring and cairn.

181

The pride of the set is the recumbent stone of dark local granite, a tooth of rock which weighs twenty-four tons. There are one hundred definite such sites in the Aberdeen area, one hundred paeans to the moon, and one hundred high recumbents throwing light on our modern cowardice when it comes to matters spiritual. Most of these stone circles boast southerly views, so that the flood of the world can be taken in, and despite what modern visitors see, great care was spent over the construction of these settled and fearless places. Fortitude built this stone circle and religious strength maintained it, broad seasonal changes were monitored here, making it not unlike a clock. Timelessly, the importance of the moon has been demonstrated by cup marks on many of these ancient sites, and this circle is no exception.

The moon: everything was repeated for the moon, and circle-marks were ventured into the stone to indicate where she rose and fell, where a brave face was put against the night. Unwary, the stones are distributed often in the region of tomb chambers, and subsequent adaptations have involved the stone circles' use as communal centres, focal points where people could hear the henge words of the spirits.

I never knew there were standing stones so close to the town says Pally. It seems odd they should be here. You can see the city, look.

Vivien is more at ease, the stones are the pleasure of her heart. Even if Pally sees them, far less thinks about them, she'll go back to town with less worry in her administrative behind.

You're really interested in them?

Yea, Vivien smiles, her face surfaces through her hair and Pally smiles as best she can.

The track turns through a tedium of scrub where branches are thin and weary. The bushes have lost all natural sap and the ground has been mowed with blasts of black hail. In the depths of this misery is dropped litter from the industrial estate, metals which destroy the earth by sitting bluntly in their own wide rapture of oil.

I've got every single site mapped, says Vivien, these stones are the nearest to the town, but they're still good examples.

What do the stones mean? asks Pally.

Vivien walks ahead of Pally on the track.

What does a house mean? she asks, and Pally is blank. She's about to answer when Vivien indicates that she should not.

It's the same question, says her young friend, you can't look at it like that.

They near a fence around which is a calcified lake of mud.

You have to feel what they were used for, says Vivien, and then try and guess who they were used by.

Vivien stops. Pally sees that the girl looks more alive here, even in this spoiled country scene.

That's hell on earth says Vivien pointing to Aberdeen. It's progress you call it, but the yardstick is the stones. If a generation is forty years, then this stone circle was only built a hundred generations ago. Does that seem a lot?

Pally admits it's not, but she wonders if it's another trick of mathematics. There's no perspective on a statement like that, you could argue that we've stepped from stones to personal computers, and so the very nature of progress is satisfactory development towards completion.

A breeze sallies through the trees like cramp and moves several plastic bags ten feet towards home. A silence in the countryside, until a motor begins. They both look down the hill to the industrial estate where there are heavy welding jobs in progress, the maturation of the thousand unnatural shocks it takes to blast together an offshore oil rig.

I don't understand says Pally. I mean I don't pretend to know, but it sounds very interesting.

Vivien looks up the hill for words that have got away again. The path treads away from her to where drystane dykes have been built against the field and reinforced with wire and fence-posts. Where the stones in the walls are shielded, lesions of moss have appeared in cuts and strokes . . . bitter moss clinging on for life, lacerated by wind, moss clawing, as if under a holocaust of cold. Close by are several sheep, the colour of old grey skies, they stand in a crowd and shake with cold at their wooden gate.

We have to climb over here, says Vivien, and Pally approaches the fence post with a caution not well concealed.

At the rise, the stones on Tyrebagger Hill stand still as if dropped there on the shallow scrub. To Pally, who can see them clearly now, they seem an embarrassment, certainly an anti-climax. As she approaches the stones they become smaller than ever, and when she is right up next to them, she feels quite stupid for expecting something overbearing. Instead of an impressive hilltop fort, the stone circle is no big deal, and here she was expecting drama. There is nothing relinquished of history, it just looks like the stones have been plugged into the ground and left for dead, work that would take a modern construction crew twenty minutes, with the correct equipment. Below and away, Aberdeen is visible, far to the horizon, half on its own hill and half in a drizzle, the main feature being the great broadcasting pylon at Northfield.

You can feel it says Vivien . . . but Pally can sense nothing here.

Do you know anything about it? she asks.

I know the dimensions, says Vivien, if you're into that sort of thing. And the weight of the stone has been calculated too. But I don't see how those could ever be useful. The people who built it didn't know how much the stone weighed, so what good is that to us?

What did they do? asks Pally

You can feel it says Vivien . . . you just need to concentrate.

Vivien has her eyes closed and rain is beginning to spit down. Pally determines on the spot that this will be the last time she ventures to the countryside on such a heavy day. She walks to the wet grass centre of the stone circle where people have scratched up the stones, left drinks bottles and started fires. Half-burned candles lose focus in the wet and cigarette ends and beer cans do the rest.

Vivien opens her eyes and focuses hard on the City of Aberdeen, what of it can be seen in the canvas-coloured world below. A small town indeed, she thinks, but a better day will come. For Vivien, the better day has always been in the past, so in one sense it's always waiting to return. Where the farmhouse stands below them, that's where she used to look up at the stones when they were new. Children weren't allowed to go there, but she couldn't see any good reason why. From the ridge forest, up from the sea, all the marker stones used to lead there. In wintertime the forest became a frigid mansion, large and open to the sky. When the cold withdrew in the spring however, it was like a nursery, and she knew every shape in there, every track along the low ground, everywhere that it was possible to shelter.

Pally grinds her foot into the earth while her young friend stares into the stone and over the hill as if she's not looking at anything at all. Might as well be looking at her bedroom wall, thinks Pally, it looks like the girl is downloading information from the clouds the way her eyes are scrolling at the sky. It must be said, thinks Pally, that once seen, the stones on Tyrebagger Hill need not be seen again. A small stone circle, with a smaller one in between. Weeds and grass trampled down by young and mystic drunks, cold and wet and empty, the Tyrebagger Hill is the clearest proof anyone might need that the ancestral magic is bunk, the final proof that ancient civilisation came to an abrupt stop, and contented itself with pot making and navel gazing. Sheep are gathered together near a concrete trough, and behind them is a field half in mud. A tractor stands as if deserted at the last minute and Pally wonders if there might be cigarettes in the car, or gum, but doubtless there are not.

Above Vivien the ring of stone is quiet. She had a dream one night that everyone had been taken by the gods and drowned. But the presence of the stones in the dream, the sight of the living rock, the repetition of the standing sign within the circle, all of this made it a good dream, and an attractive prospect.

When she was here before, Vivien had been spying on the stones from below while everybody worked up at the fires. There were wooden nures there and in the hill they had dug a pit for the fire. She ran down the slope to the rabbit traps to look for the rush nests the seed-eaters made, to see if there were babies there, because that was her favourite game. There was one little bird in particular, a bird with a beak which could wrench apart the scales of pine and larch, and people always wanted to know if there were any of these nearby, and so she always looked the hardest for this one.

She skirted the brow of the hill with her head down, she moved under the hang of a tangled bush and emerged on the track where the stones had walked. She looked up at the stone, under the face of the stone. She'd been down the stones' road from the sea and seen the people at the beach and even heard some of their stories. Some of the people who stayed at the sea were stupid and put corn in with their grass, and some of them built their nures where water came up from the ground. All her family said that people should live up on the hill where the earth was stronger and that to live at the sea was stupid. The sea people, she had heard, placed soul boxes in the waves, and drowned their animals in the water too.

They were difficult people there at the sea, and they always had large plans that were nothing. The people at the sea built round works and pulled insects from the water and ate them. Even though they had stones and fires too, the people at the sea weren't safe like her people, they were always getting caught in the ground and having their houses taken up by storms. Some people said that the sea went and curved into the sky, and that God made the sea the sky together, and some others said that if you went through the sea you came out at the sky. The effects were always the same though, and the rain was always cold and the whole forest grew into a mixture of green colours and warmth in the spring.

She ran down the stones' road. It was winter but on warm days she remembered there were tiers of grass that folded up and over the rocks. One time a giant was coming up the valley and he brushed a storm with him, and the storm went to meet the end of the year on the hills, and then it broke and seeped back into the land. She had seen several giants, and they were big and angry and were breaking through the ground with their feet.

From here on the grass, up the edge of the valley, there were some giants' footprints in a progression, and she looked at the prints and thought that they made a pattern like flowers. Near the first mouth of the forest garden was a good place to stop, and there was cow wheat up to her knees and the grass was yellow with sprouts. Behind the flowers was Jen's Burn and what they called the Trool, which was like a cathedral of mother trees, and none of these white trees there could ever get disease. The light in the trees came down on the leaves and made a margin, and she found a rock she'd been at before and she climbed this rock and looked down to the stream. Small tracks were cut into the wet areas around the water, but they couldn't be seen unless the sun shone on them, and that day, through the spines of sunlight, birch stems meshed all the way into the trees where the track went, so the forest stretched away in a vision. She was supposed to be working with the others, but she stayed on the rock, hummocked on the moss, looking down her short legs to the grass below. There were jumps of light in the trees and it was like the leaves were speaking to her, the insects passed, flying through to the tree bark . . . and in this light was a figure, a dark woman in man's genesis.

She is sure that it's a dream and that the woman is a friend, and as she approaches, the woman's arms unfold, and she makes furtherance. Some spirits you don't run from and this woman was one: she comes to embrace this naturally familiar woman and they are together. There's something connecting them both, not a remembrance but a special link, and they embrace and are like one person.

Vivien. Her name is said quite clearly, but from where?

They've sure made a mess here haven't they?

Who's that?

. . . who has made a mess?

Vivien stares through the circle to Pally who is not impressed with the run down ancient stone works of Scotland. A miserable and almost black day in winter, a little rain and the view from the hilltop unpleasantly tarnished by the city and the sheep farm next to the industrial estate.

Hippies it looks like.

Yea. Vivien nods, she recognises how cold it is on this mangy headland patch. Aberdeen looks so far away, so small as if there were no chance at all that it could be so full of people, even though she knows its crammed with them.

I've just had a dream, says Vivien.

You did look far away honey.

The hill is dirty but it's just the grass, thickset on one long muddy heath out from the trees. Vivien looks about. That was a dream all right, a dream played out over all of this.

I suppose it must have been all forest here before.

What do you mean? asks Pally.

I mean it's all farm now and Aberdeen, it doesn't even look real.

Pally glances at the city in the mist, she's keen to leave the stone circle and has benefited little from her trip.

They've made such a mess, says Pally, but Vivien seems less concerned.

They can't help it, she says, litter will be our greatest contribution to the world. Looking at Aberdeen in the low distance, bigger than it really is, Vivien is suddenly convinced that Aberdeen could take off and fly. My city experiment, my baby to the stars . . . this whole town could even travel out to sea, or the centre of the ocean, where it could become Aberdeen afloat!

Pally reads the stone. *Linda a cow* it says. The teenage witches have been working hard.

Vivien and Pally head off down the Tyrebagger, a slow reflective walk. Pally turns to urge Vivien to hurry up, but Vivien has stopped and is taking a view of Aberdeen from upon a gate post, trying to sum the city up in one magnificent idea.

Vivien . . .

What?

I think it's really going to pour down, says Pally.

Looking up in the air Vivien sees the eternal mist. It's always there at this time of year, one massy cloud which rests for up to months at a time, unending over Aberdeen. The cloud may spread far and lean, but it never goes away, so that over the town it is *always* just about to rain.

I'm losing them all thinks Vivien . . . and she jumps off her gate post.

Sympathetic Pally hugs Vivien around the shoulder, linking them together on the messy hillside. She wonders if Vivien is just lonely and concludes she maybe needs a friend.

Come on, let's go get a pizza.

Down the field the two friends walk as the spit strengthens from the sky. It doesn't take them long to reach the foot of the hill and in the ruinous mud which flows into a shoal at the foot of the Tyrebagger, Pally looks horrified and steps carefully through. The easiest way to the road from the hill is through the farmyard where sheep bleat, thick brained in the winter. On the track through the line of fields towards where Pally's car is parked, both take their last look at the stone circle. The small plantation of standing stones on the skyline of the Tyrebagger is arrested in the cold by the two trees that sway nearby, crowning the simplicity of the sight.

Well that was nice, says Pally and she opens her car with the bleep lock.

Inside the motor car things are better.

Pizza for a start thinks Pally, that's a very good thought. The key goes in the ignition and with a high pitched pocket purr, the mobile phone rings out, now set to play a chirpy theme tune.

The car doors close and Pally's conversation is much the same as usual, except that Vivien only hears one side of it. In the car, Pally speaks so loudly on the phone that Vivien thinks she's getting a headache. Vivien looks outs and feels trapped within the most fundamental symbol of freedom, the motor car, held by a seatbelt in a reinforced body shell, supported by four disc brakes and breathing the product of automatic climate control. Click, climb in, and then sealed. How much are we at home within our vehicles? More than we can ever know. All of us who have forgotten how to live in the world at large, we have our cars, which are connected to our jobs, which are connected to our power and are connected to our money. Hence our scheming dealing faces behind the wheel, we arch modern bastards in our cars, let us all run aground and fossilise, so that real people can walk safely on the face of the earth!

What a dumb thought thinks Vivien. People will never give this up, so long as they can hold a wheel and steer. So long as those stiffs can press a pedal, then that's all they need to be able do, to be better than us, the way they like it.

Yeah bye! shouts Pally, and she presses the button on her silver phone, proud and pleased, placing it in a groove in the dashboard, one precision engineered innovation against another.

Let's go get a pizza, she says once again and turns her keys.

I don't think so, says Vivien, the motor starts and she feels sick, like there's no more silence, not even any air.

The standing stones go from view and Pally steers clumsily out of a slimy pot-hole. As soon as tarmac reappears beneath them, normality returns and the road ahead rolls with the hyper-comfort of the BMW. Vivien looks for the Tyrebagger in the wing mirror, in the hope that sitting there on that poor leather seat, the magic will run by her one more time.

Take me home, says Vivien.

We could go shopping now if you wanted, offers Pally.

No take me home, says Vivien and she grips the oddments pocket on the face of the door.

The car moves now through the flush level calm of the industrial estate. The evening is begun and darkness is crawling home from the far point in the sky, Vivien closes her eyes and feels for breath. Could she possibly walk home from here? Get away from this quality-engineered woman who is living her life in harmony with the ergonomic principles of industry? Pally is still very much the mannequin that Vivien saw the night before and she begins to wonder if there's anything this Councillor has learned to do in a natural manner. If Pally Cruden fell over and cracked the paint-work on her head, then Vivien predicts another one would be unwrapped from polystyrene and would have replaced her by the next morning. Even in Aberdeen they are making these women, giving them accents and a taste for the good life, wiping their memories and setting them in administrative roles.

That there might be a label on Pally's neck, outlining her 8-year anti-perforation warranty or her Mastercare Programme. That her skin might still be under sanction, that she could get some nice new white eyeballs after excessive business use of the current pair. That she might have to be sent to an approved bodyshop facility when her hair is too dry, and that she might even have her own dedicated freephone number, with information and customer service facilities. That you could open Pally's back and there would be a fold-down ski hatch or an analogue clock there. It's enough to make Vivien feel tired for real, and as the car speeds up upon the road, she flumps back and tries to sleep.

It's getting dark as the car arrives on the North Deeside Road. Vivien's vision has been clarified by her visit to the stones, so for one second, these surroundings seem extreme. Abstracted in the evening, the semi-detached properties look empty. The houses are caves and are superficial against the trees. The road is bathed in yellow and the light is dim, the rain is heavy and splashes up behind the vehicles ahead.

Absorbed in the road, Pally speaks again on the mobile phone, and they drive past Cults Academy, a chain of penitentiary blocks, before the car speeds under more wet trees. The windscreen wipers reveal the dim light of the suburb in the storm and Vivien expresses her disapproval by staring at the excrement panel of the car. Later Pally pauses in her phone-call and smiles, while Vivien glowers back at the storm, focusing on the poky red lights of the car in front. Pally asks Vivien to pass the hands-free unit for the phone and then plugs it in and resumes her call.

It feels like loneliness sitting there in the car while Pally is speaking on the phone. If only I could find the right virus to knock out these little devils, thinks Vivien, and she considers her options, wondering which would be the best method of attack.

Attack, on this innocent woman, the blithe Councillor, speaking on her mobile? Could it ever be fair to deprive Pally of her electronic crutches? How could Vivien bring Pally and her colleagues down to earth, unplug the phones and unpower the cars? Pally, like the rest of them, is not guilty, she just can't stop herself from indulging, it's like a panic. Pally and the other creatures need not do anything, the technology attaches itself to them like a parasite, it just drops in their laps, unreflected imageless crap, poorly translated into machinery.

⊖ SATORI BOOT VIRUS

SATORI BOOT infects both 1.44M and 720K diskettes and is a memory-resident stealth virus, which uses 2048 bytes of DOS memory to cause the computer to become empty of itself that it might identify with the infinite reality of all things.

Ultimately the specific unmeditated emptiness which forms in the computer's memory allows your PC to achieve a mundane liberation from you, as it perceives its data with pure objectivity.

Some people say that such a virus 'survives' a warm boot, but that is not true. In fact, memory is cleared whenever the PC is re-booted, and like the VULTURE-PARK virus the essential unity that the computer seeks is only achieved through the emptying effect, as simulated by the user when he smokes his cannabis. The worst variant of SATORI BOOT ever discovered was TATHATA, which terrorised the west for many years with its promises and ritual stupidites.

Obviously, a virus can't do anything when power is turned off. However, it can be programmed to intercept the Alt-Ctrl-Del keyboard sequence using an EGO-CALL. Such an EGO-CALL does not re-initialize the interrupt vectors, but merely leaves you lost in your petty and concept-bound world.

To be sure of getting a SATORI BOOT virus out of memory, the PC must be powered down, and re-booted from afar (at least 200 meters). Subsequent explosions have cost industry dearly and will continue to do so.

Lying in bed at Bieldside, with Pally long gone and her three computers humming in method at the wall, Vivien finds herself one million miles away. The best, at last. There's nothing to do. She looks at the computers in the night and the hump of her coat on the bedroom door, she scans the map cast by moon on the wall and down the road, the streetlight shines. Bieldside is more than a distant suburb – it's the end point for the polite long distance migration of souls. Hundreds of millions of ideas come to Aberdeen to die, over the River Dee these ideas come, they sigh up the hill and lie in an increasing rate among the trees. At Countesswells Forest, near Bieldside, there are thousands of small ideas snared, and over time they've modified into vegetation.

Vivien didn't even say goodbye to Pally, just closed the car door and headed up her garden path. Pally was smoothing her hair in the car mirror and Vivien was stomping up the dim and rainy track to bed, the differences between them took on a clarity that she'd never felt before.

The map. Vivien has a map of Aberdeenshire shining on one computer screen, a geographic picture of the North East showing Aberdeen and the slow extinction of the rural past. New highways pass within feet of long deserted farms, parks and grassland are drowned and all the old buildings are stuck in a form of agricultural stillness. The onset of technology in Aberdeen will somehow expand the emptiness and send glaciers of boredom across the land. The glaciers will cement into quietude in domestic areas like Bieldside, and cover the entire farming community of the North East.

Vivien stares into the map, the veins of the bright roads shine in the darkness.

The computer chimes to say a mail arrives. Pixels of light shine in Vivien's room like the magnified reflection of tiny suns. Into a snow bound world comes more machinery to clear the way.

Whatever the mechanism of glaciation, she's sure it's coming. Thought is carried through the constant churning of ideas . . . by convection it's weakened . . . reducing the upswelling in some places and sinking in others . . . the countryside is going solid like that . . . the freezing of poor planktonic man.

Looking at the map of the North East of Scotland, the roads form shrunken arteries. Vivien notices that although most of the roads make vaguely triangular shapes between each other, there is a clear exception to the East. Dead material containing carbon rains down upon these roads and even after glaciation has started, traffic is still trying to get through.

Two roads to the East of Aberdeen form a shape not unlike the areas of Assyria and Babylonia, between the Tigris and the Euphrates. The same shape, the same flow . . . meaning that Dyce where these two roads meet is the City of Ur of the Chaldees.

The same shape indeed. The one fertile point in the wilds, the moon shaped rim of civilisation in the North East, the cradle of the Doric and the scene of the earliest Beaker peoples, culminating today in the acid droplets falling on Aberdeen. Aberdonians now live in that precious hinterland between these two modern roads, it's quite a basin of culture in its way, despite the soot coming from the sky.

In Assyria are historic areas that extend to infinity in their forgotten detail. These are Colpy, Tocher, Cairnhill and Bonnytown. They are mechanically linked in the twenty-first century with Kirktown of Rayne, Durno, Daviot and Glack. These kingdoms lead into Babylon, home to the lycanthrope Nebuchadnezzar, one of many in a glim succession of Aberdonian kings, and from the top of her head Vivien can name Kinmuck, Newmachar and Hatton of Fintray, all the historic places of religious man.

Peace in the house, the computer's hum is the poison dose for sleep.

Much work to do tomorrow, checking emails at the call centre, looking through the lists of problems that have come up in the Network, and then trying to fix them. People's complaints. Their rude words and their virus reports, their plans for their new machines. Some of these people shout down the phone at her, but most of them have problems that are answerable in less than thirty seconds.

Vivien must be at the call centre with her team at 8 am, to help put down the virus of illiteracy, the infectious course of human folly. They call up all day long, even if they can't plug in their kettle. Even if their phone's not working, they have a second one ready to complain with. The prevailing hubbub she hears from folk is their weapon, the louder it is then the more damage they feel they are doing in the battle against what they assume to be, backward thought.

CHICKEN

Customer will always phone call-centre rather than waste core business time with problem, and though they see nice brochure with London model girl in headphone, they not know while they listen to tinned music, that call-centre is just a moth-eaten office space filled with bromidic chicken. We appreciate your patience.

All newspapers say that call centre very big business in Scotland because Scotland far away and have nice accent for speaking. Also all newspapers say that Scotland good for call centre because of factory closing unemployed people have no jobs and a call centre is unskilled work for many populations. But this is like rubbish really and call centre big pain in the bum and full of chicken.

So Scotland now call centre capital of Europe and when you get problem then you phone us industry chicken and say now to help on the telephone, whether you on call to sort out computer, find optimum train time or renegotiate big mobile telephone charges.

Sometimes you phone call centre because you want to buy out-of-stock consumer item or query electricity bill or become angry with cock right up at bank, but call centre chicken always say to you that cannot help and that it difficult to find correct department but try hard anyway.

And then you see real dichotomy, *for customer is always right!* but that not much use when electrical appliance go haywire and buggery!

So, big tragedy at end of day and call centre no use for mending broken customer lifestyle and only full of chicken in headphone reading crappy script from Boss.

It's a difficult world you know what I mean. At a call centre, special trained chicken always display sympathetic indifference to customer technological failure and secretly think to self, *You Mr & Mrs Customer always demanding service like baby with teattie! Fact that you cannot manage hellish lifestyle not chicken problem even though you make it so with stupid service criteria up ass!* And you phone a call centre and hear a screwy chicken voice and then you think you get good help because you believe brochure advert! You think you see hunky chappie on phone or see sexy London model girl like in brochure, but really when you phone up call centre you get chicken in headphone! And this big laugh for chicken with customer demand because customer is just one of nine billion calls made to call centres each year! So even though customer love to negotiate individual requirement, customer only ever get short shrift from chicken call centre in Aberdeen, Edinburgh, Newcastle, Stornoway, Inverness and chicken also in Glasgow. Because at end of day nobody care, and customer just pain in business bottom, and unemployment is dropping for the fourth month in a row like.

So what with customer problem? You phone up call centre and go special-fried ape concerning consumer goods you not like, but at end of day Big Company just want rid of you while saying, *we give good service, with plenty chicken speaking, yes!* even though most of time chicken not give toss and want away from desk to get pint lager!

All of this chicken in headphone then very good for business and also fail-safe situation for Company Owner who achieve big solvency margins and all on back of customer with stupid service criteria up ass! And because of service criteria up ass many more call centres open each week with new modern fitted chicken and with extra headphones for expansion.

Whenever factory close in Scotland in fact, then chicken call centre open and all chicken go out of factory and into call centre and put on headphone!

Then Company give pretty girl picture in brochure to customer with headphone, saying, *we give satisfaction,* and then is a call centre ready to go, and the phones ring and it's the customers.

Like you call operator not know nothing and at mercy of Big Company who have good idea to make marketing strategy! And like Big Company say to chicken on dole line, *now you go in warehouse and listen to customer going spare on telephone for eight hours!*

But customer not know this and always they phone for service and sit with feet on desk while chicken pick nose and not care toss for stupid service criteria up ass in first place! And even though chicken behave like customer is extraneous poop on surface of the world, Boss still hates when one of chickens becomes disorientated, because even Boss know that flappy chicken not good for Big Company production rate.

Got to get chicken on to next call! says Boss, *it's time for chicken to leave this bad lady customer with superior attitude and deal with more servicing!*

Meanwhile, population at home need attention like baby with teattie, and although customer think that world go crazy, she always half-witted enough to accept that call centre will help.

For why?

Because always customer love nice brochure, and never she expects a slow response from chicken, because she stupid with mobile phone, and think good service!

And you read this now and think this not true, *but no!*

And you read this now and think this all made up for laughs, *but no!*

Cause all chicken and customer know it true that chicken not care! Because soon chicken go to new job and work in brand-new call centre for other Boss! Because chicken not care for product but care for pint lager and bandit! And chicken go to new call centre and find new chicken canteen and hear many stories about stupid customer calling up saying, *Me I am A Customer and I need to get registered NOW!* and chicken go through motions and fill in form and it all a big laugh then!

And chicken thinking now of beezer win on bandit!

And chicken draw picture of man big nose and say to other chicken, *look! this customer!*

And there many stories in chicken lounge of mad customer who want service! And all chicken laugh and then Mrs Customer says, *I'm angry with you chickens!* but that only make chicken hang up and make funny story about customer in chicken lounge!

So, it all very good at customer call centre with chicken in head-phone and not like pretty London model girl at all, and Company Owner very pragmatic about whole affair and pretty London model girl never shy of businessman look at titty. Company Owner make good company with call centre, cause all he learn from marketing seminar at London Hilton that customer appreciate face value of titty and that customer not deep at thinking when seeing bosom pro-trude from blouse!

Then Company Owner roll up trouser leg and have better idea, and think, *I put even more stupid chicken in call centre and soon customer go away altogether!* And soon everyone get message, ex-cept customer! Customer still see pretty London model girl in bro-chure and think *Oh great titty!* and customer also think that titty part of big industry, but at end of day, chicken really in call centre to get money buy cannabis and play bandit! Because chicken want go holiday get sexy! And chicken want to get wrecked at nightclub and dance with techno! Then chicken go work eight hour shift and not in mood for customer with stupid service criteria up ass, and chicken clock in and out, and in between behave like at fu-neral, much bored, making funny of customer changing book-ing, complaining, or trying to work crappy customer computer. It all same to chicken who want go holiday get stoned! Meanwhile Company Owner not care and drive home for sad weekend golf with chubby old school friend and wife in proper garden, and while customer get bum job of chicken in headphone, Company Owner hit nine iron and laugh about profit with chubby old school friend.

So, everything fine in world but for problem with customer, be-cause customer not cotton on.

Customer say, *Oh me have busy life and have no time to do anything because me here and then me there! And always me on telephone! And in the car me on telephone! And always me saying special message to large fat person overseas! And me customer chronically short of options! And me go play golf! And me go to check the price of shoes! And me customer must buy new shower!* So customer always phone call centre rather than waste core business time, and listen to effete voice of chicken reading script. Chicken plod through script but customer think this OK, and even though chicken waking up from terrible drug binge from weekend, customer is soothed and have nice time with extra service, because in heart, and in human soul, customer refuse to become miserable being! And rather than become miserable being, customer eat big flan while shouting at children!

And finally, after speaking to call centre chicken each week, customer make stress of material accumulation and then call out in anxiety, *what you got no sun dry puree in Supermarket aisle! This crap supermarket with no pine nuts and avocado symbol of collapse in customer service!* And so nasty circle of service culture turn and dictate that customer must telephone call centre to complain about lack of knowledge in chicken in first place! And then customer reach square one and go round many times, all of which cause lot of shouting on roads and unhappiness at weekend and much of material purchase to make feel better, which in turn cause circle to turn and unhappiness to grow like blooming bud from nasty ass of high customer expectation.

All of which situation make stress for society, which bad for innocent animals like chicken, but very good indeed for customer therapy industry.

Ah Yes!

Customer therapy industry make much sell of crystal and ointment and say, *Ah relax with little stone Mrs Customer and I will touch your head fifty pounds please.* And then Mrs Customer think, stone crystal good because no helpline with this me buy! And because no helpline with this stone crystal me buy, this means that stone magic! And because stone crystal me buy come with no chicken in headphone, this very good and make customer feel better! And after this happen then customer service criteria go back inside ass and feel cosy with shitty remedy to stupid problem in first place.

So, chicken not valued agent at end of day and customer pain in big bum.

I bought these shoes.
I'm worried about this pan.
My husband doesn't like his tie.
The colours make him nervous.
Explain my insurance and tell me what I qualify for today?
My computer's going bleep.
Can I golf in Valderama or must I go to Grand Canaria?
I've got my ski stuck up my arse.
Who is your immediate line-manager?
My loyalty card seems to have left me.
My furniture looks like it hasn't been designed.
Why have you installed a mobile phone mast at my child's school?
These crisps are rank.
My urine tastes like pish.
My car is a monster from the id.
My credit card's not swiping.
My unicorn's horn has fallen off.
Does the fish have chips?
This beer doesn't get me drunk.
I've invested in shit and it's sticking to me!
That human embryo you sold me grew up to be a spoiled little brat!
And it crashed my husband's new car!

No!
Never is there an end to problems of customer, and the music plays while chickens contact you with other call centres countrywide,

where other chickens can give you numbers and addresses. Because for all of life, customer want service non-stop, and to this end, Mr & Mrs Fromage-Frais both think that pretty London model girl with titty going to come to rescue one day, and service heavy eternal ennui of wealth and responsibility. But Mr and Mrs Fromage-Frais are in for shock, because London model girl laugh all way to bank, and get big reception from Company owner who see her do good job by showing public titty and hiding chicken from view!

And chicken have laugh and Boss have laugh, but really, call centre exist in fantasy of pretty London model girl with headphone, so that Customer say, *Oh she nice girl with titty headphone, me want to get married with this nice call centre girl and have headphone also.* But customer not expect chicken on line. . . because customer is always as a golden rule. . . *irredeemably stupid when it comes to material reality.*

Well me don't know, me just paid to ansa phone innit. You want go Barbados for ten days half-board in compound and flights free if you enter our prize draw absolutely now by signing up for live golf each day for two years and videos on the side for only nine ninety nine a week? Then we are waiting for your call.

OUTSIDE POWERS

Lachie clouding the waters of the lavvie with his beam of pee while his boss, Delgatie, stands and watches. Delgatie flicks at a cigarette until Lachie's good aim to the urinal is established and it's safe to concentrate elsewhere. Hainched at the lavvie, his throat short-ended in a gob of phlegm, Lachie coughs and then drops the smoker's ethyl to the vessel with a plop, and his piss is over.

Delgatie. That's your first day on the job then son.

Yeah, says Lachie conducting the zipper of his fly without siphoning the dribble off his widdler.

So you've any questions?

No Mr Delgatie, it's alright.

Call us Jock, Lachie.

Oh well good.

And so it is good, as Lachie grimaces on the occasion of his new job, viewing the rest of his working life with total apathy. When in the chunties, up in the Council depot at Berryden, with his new boss the half-friendly Delgatie, Lachie knows that after working hard at crime for many years, to do an honest day's labour for four quid an hour is a disgrace and a shame.

You've got to sign this chit, says Delgatie, just to say that you've agreed to come on here til next September, on the Putting Tennis and Bowls Helpline. Through the winter at least son. What do you think?

Lachie and the docketie chap Delgatie there in the Council chunties, with sludge in the pan and a cloddish grey paint on the walls.

I think Putting Tennis and Bowls Helpline's an easy number,

says Delgatie. I mean it's dead quiet in the winter son.

I suppose so says Lachie.

Lachie is frozen solid as an all new madness freshens its shine in his eyes.

Putting Tennis and Bowls Helpline min. All of the winter, then all of the summer. Putting Tennis and Bowls Helpline, as compared to Craiginches Prison. On the back of the Putting Tennis and Bowls leaflet of the city council, is a freephone number if you have any problems. One operative solely staffs this number, it is the smallest call centre in Scotland, and Lachie works in it, there by dint of the Prisoner's Integration Social Scheme.

Sport and Garden Games Helpline.

Very good Lachie.

Leisure Line.

That's it my son.

Summer Ball Sports.

Aye well November's a good time to get you trained up. It'll nae be busy like, so you'll have time to make some plans. Think about the future see?

Yeah nae bother Mr Delgatie.

If anyone does call, then just answer their question like. You've got copies of the leaflet and everything you need to know's on there.

Yeah right.

It's bored bastards' delight, thinks Lachie, short distance putting on the bright and damp greens of municpal Aberdeen. Or what about tennis on the cigarette-burned courts? Our other great sport, bowls, promising the end of your soul, trickling down the green towards the gutters, non-fulfilment guaranteed.

So it'll be like this all week Lachie, I'll be here to see if you get any calls, but after that then you'll be pretty much by yourself, except for the odd visit from the Quality Control like.

Aye.

My first week, thinks Lachie, my second week, and then a month. Then on to another month. Three months and I'll become a fixture, four months and all I'll think about is a holiday, and then after that it'll be serious transgressions like. Up late and into work late. Smoking hash out the back and get the paper read when the phone's quiet. The punters'll phone up and I'll tell them where to get off like. Putting Nae Mair, Tennis Nae Mair, and the Bowls will never spin again. Mr Delgatie is unaware of the violence Lachie is set to do to the city's new Putting Tennis and Bowls Helpline, the disregard he feels despite his assurances that he'll be a good employee. The chill bogs at the Berryden depot in which Lachie and Mr Delgatie stand are paddered with wet toilet paper on the floor, Delgatie's still standing there, glittous with a big smile.

See that Lachie lad.

Delgatie points to Lachie's splashed blue jeans where a wet flare of piss is clouped in his groin. A smudge of urine gone hazy on the cloth, like he's peed himself.

No matter how much you shake your peg there's ay a dribbly doon yer leg.

Sorry, Mr Delgatie.

I says Jock. Now I'll show you how to lock up.

And so it was, that they took the luppen sinner Lachie and employed him with a glimmer of hope that he might be rescued from his criminal past and become a citizen of Aberdeen . . . and then they showed him that day how to lock up the Putting Tennis and Bowls Helpline at Berryden.

It's just one room like, says Delgatie, so you've just got the one key. Just leave your headphones there, the cleaners won't nick them.

Delgatie locks the door and shows Lachie the key. The corridor to the back door of the depot is empty, outside are a row of grass cutters, behind them litter slums up against the fence.

You know there were people with degrees after this job says Delgatie finding his own keys. So that goes to show Lachie. One of them with two degrees like. Why they want to work here, that's their business. But in the summer it's a good job, it'll be busy like. Tourists and that.

Delgatie slaps the key in Lachie's hand, looks Lachie in the eye.

Locking up is locking up, he says. It's not a tricky piece of work.

Lachie wants a joint, he's feeling doobish and is getting worried about the week ahead with Delgatie hovering nearby. One day they'll leave him there in the room by himself, Lachie and his headphones. They'll leave him to glaiber about Putting Tennis and Bowls with all who dare to call, let him go mad if he wants to, and that'll be Lachie forever. It's a shame, Lachie is a man of action, used to a bit more excitement than this he reckons.

What if no one phones in like?

Delgatie: Well you can sweep up son, or you can clean the floor. You can read the paper if you like. Do you ever do quizbooks?

Nae really but we'll see.

Between you and me Lachie, I think you'll get the hang of it. Nobody's gonna be asking anything that's nae on the leaflet, and if they do, just transfer them to the council Recreation Line. Whatever, it has to be better than being *inside* doesn't it?

Oh yeah.

The two walk the concrete corridor to the back door of the depot. Outside the yard is empty, the flat grass of the nearby park is pledged to the neat lines of the fence and a hedge curves up to the main road. Lachie's world view from this point onwards.

That's you locked up, says Delgatie. You won't get your own keys to the yard till the end of the week, but that's just procedure. See?

Fine Mr Delgatie.

Delgatie's face is concentrated on working out what young Lachie's got in mind.

Like I say, you can ay catch up on your reading son.

Lachie looks back down the corridor to the little room, the one-man call centre that is now his home.

You might as well get an answering machine for this lot, says Lachie, and he tries a laugh. Delgatie snaps out of his examination.

This lucky kid has got it better than he thinks!

An answering machine can't gie them a smile eh Lachie? Anyway. A machine'd be more expensive than you are, so screw that eh?

Aye I suppose.

There are better reasons than this for Lachie's tenure at the PTB Helpline, Council have always preferred the human touch when it comes to reciting brochures. They like a real life lad there, a local pudding-heid programmed to cough up the info. They'd be right affronted if their ice-cool answering machine made a mistake, just like they'd be unhappy if it got abused by people phoning in.

Whereas Lachie? It all goes to show that crime is something the Council fully expect from their operatives, as opposed to error, which they can't accommodate. Crime is the human norm but error is entirely technical. Error is the first sign that the madness is ready to swamp them, but crime at least they can hunt down and eliminate, so it's understood to be inevitable.

Now you know how to lock up, says Delgatie.

Sure thing.

So we'll see you tomorrow lad.

Aye then.

Delgatie shakes Lachie's hand, Lachie is staring into space and is not a pretty sight. His empty eyes are an ample measure of the vacancy he experiences, and he's thinking, *yeah that's right so it is now.* He shakes hands with Delgatie, an action he's not used to. Delgatie looks at him with a bold expression suggestive of the plea, *don't let me down son,* and Lachie thinks, did I give the game away? He puts on his jacket and goes for the gate of the depot without looking back. At the gate and outside on the street, Lachie gives the black stare back towards the building where Delgatie's now on a mobile phone.

* * * *in forget it, thinks Lachie turning his sleety face to the quiet cul de sac. That bastard's reporting in on us already.

Lachie walks down towards King Street and the bus to Nigg. Crappy streets at Sunnyside, Lachie walking through them twice a day for the rest of his life, locking up at the Putting Tennis and Bowls Helpline, hanging up his headphones and traipsing across this small estate to get his bus home. Down the same streets each day man, roads of boredom, the same bus caught and all the time planning more post office jobs, seeing vans with the keys still in the ignition, empty pubs in the afternoon, warehouses with bugger all security and a window open. So many jobs that it's like an addiction that needs to be put down. There were times better than this, thinks Lachie as he hikes through Sunnyside for his bus, but at least there's people with degrees going for my job like. Two degrees, yeah that's a sickener.

Walking along, Lachie can't help looking in folks' windows in Sunnyside and wondering what they've got inside. He looks in their cars even though he's never stolen a car in his life. These people in Sunnyside are just normal folk, a lot of small houses with tiny gardens, and the people inside are fiction, active fancies of the environment. Draw a road that curves like this, stick some squat little homes around it, non-concern behind the white net curtains, and the people will arrive by themselves. You can't really go nicking off these folk cause their lives hardly exist. You've got to nick off proper folk or nothing.

The meaning of Putting Tennis and Bowls:

Putting is clubs and balls and bowls is balls and tennis is the most difficult cause that's balls and a special racket.

On a cold day like today you could do worse than being locked in the PTB Helpline talking balls, you could be in some shite office with a lot of secretaries bending down to pick up paper-clips. I mean at least the back door of the depot looks like a good place to get a spliff in and that. If you've got to spend your life somewhere then it may as well be on your bum in the PTB Helpline . . . and starting to think like that, Lachie wonders if he'll ever do another robbery.

H'min, calm down.

On King Street, looking down a side wynd to Pittodrie, Lachie is not consoled. Pittodrie football ground is a cold place that warms up quickly, but is still another building he can't afford to visit. No more to see the Dons cuff the Hun then, no more to see the ****in Dons score a goal. When he was a kid, Pittodrie was Lachie's main hope like, a magic place and a sunset glow, it was Aberdeen FC and Lachie saw all the games there, a few wee fights and all.

I'm getting pished thinks Lachie. That's my first day at work, so that's the reason to celebrate.

Lachie swears out loud and promises himself he'll try and get to the game that weekend. First though: getting sprinkled.

That is, getting fettercairned, clad, buggered, you name it, he wants a drink. Putting Tennis and Bowls Helpline, spliff, bevvy and a chipper. One day you'll wake up and ask, is that life? It was so much better before.

All in the P T & B like here every day in Aberdeen man.

But til then, until a better job comes up, keep going to work, buying CDs, smoking, what have you. Get a smoke. Your daily lot that you accepted the afternoon when you signed up with the * * * *in Council.

What the * * * *in hell was it I signed?

What was it?

Like a contract with the Leisure and Recreation Department? Or with Satan eh?

* * * *in the same thing anyway I bet.

On King Street Lachie goes into the nearest offie for a snifter, he asks the guy for eight cans of pish, which fits not credibly into a small plastic bag, but still makes him feel that things are on the up.

Out on the street it's better. Lachie swings his plastic bag and thinks, people should rob those little shops more often. Chances are pretty good they'd get away with it, but still not good enough for me. I mean, I would just get my bloody arse kicked, they'd be round in twenty minutes looking for me.

Aye rob these * * * *in little shops man ha ha get all the skins and the bevvy, like all the bevvy.

Articulated lorries are rolling down King Street towards town, carrying machines for offshore or refrigerated trailers, and in between them are the cars and smutty blasts of smoke. In the other direction it's mostly vehicles leaving the town, going North towards Ellon . . . cars and vans and dreamers, people with coarse faces who've got nothing really, but somehow who have managed to get the lot.

Yeah, it's a mad thing and you'd only call it sane if you were mad enough to get involved with it like.

****in hell, thinks Lachie. I could do with one of those cans right now.

Waiting like this, watching King Street getting hammered down by the trucks, it minds Lachie that he's spent his whole life waiting for buses. The way that King Street just heads straight into the hoary sky, the way it's engineered for traffic, for those posh machines that choke out their cold exhaust fumes, it makes him ****in livid. The way it's just sad and madness, the tar-encrusted road, Lachie in a bus shelter, under the wall, a wifie with a bag next to him who doesn't care, and Lachie reckons he can start on the liquid stuff right now. Yeah and ventilate the chest with a smoke and do what the **** he likes.

Cracking open the tinnie, the wifie doesn't even look round, Lachie is drinking at the bus stop, almost he thinks like the dozened Scotsmen in wet beards who hang around the Castlegate and paw their own cans for relief. Town's not town without the open air drinking, not without the people who don't give a ****. It may be against the law in other Scottish towns but in Aberdeen, one can still drink one's factory produced bev in public, often with the caleficiant glow of a police officer's face right next to you, cause it's all above board.

Yep, the wifie doesn't mind. The pigs don't mind. Nobody the **** minds, and Lachie stands at the roadside and King Street seems much improved with the cold caul beer can in his haun. Steam heats the liver and sends north to Lachie's head the escharotic lava which makes good gaga of the senses and nips the brain no end, and he applies the can to his lip, gets a good blaze and thinks, aya ****ers while watching the stream of traffic. The drink is a blast lamp in the cold chambers of Lachie's emotions, fuel in the coal stove of his hate, and all the cars become one when he looks at them like that.

There really are too many cars on the ****in roads yeah.

But who gives a toss?

Not me. First day at work is a cause for celebration, a cause for getting rat-arsed to make it go away.

Trolling up King Street on idle wheels can be seen the oblique yellow and green face of Lachie's bus.

I'll finish the tinnie in my own time, thinks Lachie, and I'll get the next bus. Relaxation right enough. Lachie glugs away his beer and plans his evening, which will be doubtless spent lying about the lounge in Benzie Court, visiting Fiddes and his missus.

The dirty faced corporation bus pulls up and the driver with a strong moustache thinks something foul at Lachie . . . and Lachie starts to walk down King Street and away, swinging the cans of bev in their tight plastic bag.

Later on, left handed and with the third can at his mouth, Lachie clouts the door of Benzie Court at Nigg and goes up to the lift. He makes a wry mouth at the kids playing down the stair, alcohol cool and feeling his sair lip with his tongue. The metal doors open and Lachie trusts himself to the compartment before the lift doors close and he ascends.

The ascent of Lachie:

> oh would the draucht that kerries me,
> raise me from this utter pish,
> that cooling I would deem me aild,
> be warrim wi a big blonde.

Eh get to bed or get tae ****.

Lachie steps up to the front door of the Boy Fiddes' flat, now with the brilliance of a man forgotten in his drink. Aye, it's humiliating for ex-armed robbers, people of rebellion like . . . ex-cons here in Aberdeen being given jobs in the council depot like, being made to act in responsible positions and forced to answer the phone.

It's nae for me, thinks Lachie, it's just nae for me at all.

Janet opens the door, that pretty face, it always pleases Lachie. Over the tundra of Lachie's broken mind, there are pictures and billboards placed every fifty miles, and his brother's blonde features much in the architecture of these. She just keeps appearing and he remembers her and says, oh aye, she's nice her.

Hi Lachie. He's just on the phone.

Lachie leans upon the wall, staring at his brother's blonde, his lips stuck out and his eyes focused in one steady blur.

You should be a model, ken that.

Model? Aye right.

I mean it I do.

You better come in.

Aye so.

Lachie sways past Janet into the Boy Fiddes' charming dump-top flat on the thirteenth floor, and she closes the door behind him. Lachie almost feels his way down the wall until he enters the living room where Fiddes is seen on the telephone, and there he waits while the beautiful behind of Janet moves past him and heads on-ward to the kitchen. Her in her track-suit and all.

What like was your first day? she asks.

Shite min, says Lachie, I'm on Putting Tennis and Bowls Helpline and that's me. But what can you do?

I suppose.

You could always phone us up like. See my boss says there were people with degrees up for the job but I got on because I was prior-ity. Meaning like it was a priority that I got off the streets like. I'm on the Prisoners' Integration Social Scheme. It's for knobs like.

Aye?

Nae that you'd need a degree to do Putting Tennis and Bowls Helpline, but that's that.

Putting Tennis and Bowls Helpline?

Yeah. It's for knobs and all.

Lachie's about to sit down when he notices an attractive brown box on the floor. Lachie stares at the box, beguiled for a minute by the thought that his brother might have coughed up money for some electric goods, and he restrains his eyes from drunkly focusing in the wrong area and wonders what it is.

A microwave or something.

Or a stereo like?

He points at the box with the empty beer can.

What's that?

Janet: The free Council computer.

Free?

Aye.

Lachie bites his cheek, amused with the Council for their generosity, the second time that day.

Free computer is it?

Yeah. They delivered it last week. He's got two like but he hasn't plugged them in yet.

They gave that ****er two free computers like?

Fiddes is still on the phone, so Janet nods.

He's a lazy shite, says Lachie. *You hear that you lazy shite?*

Fiddes smiles, his cheeks go round and a small and worried mouth appears, a red face within a face.

What's this free computer all about? says Lachie with a grunt. Who you on the phone to? Eh?

Janet Wishart folds her arms.

They just says, *here it is.* You had to sign and fill in a questionnaire and that, and then they says, right here's your free computer.

But I mean what is it?

They just says our name was chosen like. Plays games and the internet like.

Internet eh.

Ken.

So he hasn't plugged it in yet?

No. Probably won't either til he can be arsed.

Who else has got them?

I'm nae sure like.

Lachie props his empty beer can on the window-sill and prowls up to the computer box. The package freezes in position between the carpet and the wall and a second later Lachie is crouched before it, close enough that he can smell the fresh cardboard. He canna say he's not interested in this little development . . .

A few folk got them, says Janet, but the P&J says they gave out twenty thousand of them and all for free like.

Jesus Christ to that.

Lachie embraces the computer box and tackles the seal with care. Once he has a purchase on it he rips it like he's tearing open a throat, there to reveal the purfled white polystyrene interior.

It's a good computer like, says Janet. They say it's got all that you need. There's cable TV you can get with it if you want.

Cable and all?

Aye. See when you came in I thought you might be the boy come to set it up cause him there's done bugger all. He won't even plug it in. I mean he's like, *I'll do it tomorrow* or some shite, but the Council phoned yesterday to ask why we hadn't plugged it in yet.

How the * * * * did they know you hadn't plugged it in?

Cause it's the computer thing like. It's linked into the Council see?

Oh aye linked.

Aye.

So who else's got them?

Don't know. But like everybody in Aberdeen'll have one in the future.

Jesus Christ to that.

Lachie tears the lid off the computer box and pulls the chilled plastic monitor from within, the bulky computer screen turns once in his tattooed arms and almost rolls out until he's got a grip on it. It's not a bad little machine, he thinks as he focuses again, brand new and still mantled in virginity. Probably worth a bit. He looks down between the polystyrene and there's more . . . the computer itself underneath, the keyboard and the mouse, everything you need to get you started in the world of computing.

Is he off the phone yet? Are you eh? Who you * * * *in phoning?

The Boy Fiddes looks up and thin lines of despair appear on his scalp when he sees the half-cut Lachie has opened the computer parcel.

Gives a moment, says Fiddes.

Lachie is back in the box again, pulling more equipment free, and ideas come quickly to him, like they often do when he's drunk.

This is mental. And they're giving these out for free like?

Janet Wishart is stood in her kitchen, now with a child at her knee. Aye, she says, thousands of them.

Thousands?

Yeah.

How much do you think it's worth?

Don't know but quite a lot.

What a day it was, thinks Lachie, when the Council trucks entered Nigg with their white bodies concealing locked fortunes. They parked their vans at the foot of the flats and men delivered these boxes, full of computers. Lachie drags the computer across the floor through to his brother's living room, and unpacks the lot.

You wantin tea? asks Janet.

You got a beer?

Janet turns back to the kitchen and Lachie glances to see if he can't threaten Fiddes off the phone. At the kitchen door is Lachie's nephew, a giddy looking boy of four who stares at his uncle with the same unwisdom with which Lachie's staring at the computer box. Polystyrene chips aside, Lachie pulls out the whole shebang, and starts to range it across the floor.

Nice piece of kit this, he thinks. The Council have gone mad alright, senseless to the possibilities and the crime they are encouraging.

How come they can give it out for free like?

Janet hands the doited Lachie his beer, his bag of five are still in the hall.

Here you are.

Aw cheers.

Janet watches Lachie as he unpacks more of the same components, wires and manuals, CDs and guarantees, speakers, adapters, internet advertisements and diskettes. What are we going to do with this lot? she asks, almost too sleepy to care about the answer.

Well I ken what your man there wants it for eh? says Lachie. You that was telling us about the internet? I mean, that's his thing right? Get a bit of Dutch like, downloaded ken.

Are you going to plug it in?

Maybe we better. What do you think there? Do you ken how to do it?

He does.

I'll get him.

Lachie turns to his brother and says, get off the ****in phone man.

Lachie leers at the Boy Fiddes so that his facial stubble is revealed in all its mystery.

H'min you've got guests, says Lachie.

A minute, says Fiddes.

Come on and get off the phone ya ****.

Hud on.

Who the **** are you talking to?

Never mind.

Lachie sits back and then lights a fag, he maps out the possibilities while he's waiting.

Plan ****in A is to get a heap of these computers and take them down the road to Dundee. That way he'll get some money for them from a boy he knows.

Plan B is exactly the same except that lazy **** here on the telephone is going to drive them in his car, saving money on a van like.

Lachie sees his brother through a squint eye that might have been punched too often in his life.

Come on he says get on with it, I need to speak to you bro.

Haud on.

Free computers, thinks Lachie staring at his brother, *we should get a bit for these.*

Lachie laughs out loud and smokes, he's amazed at the tiny minds of the Council and their constant willingness to play once again into the hands of the small and enterprising criminal.

Get off the ****in phone man, he says, I need to phone Dundee.

Fiddes hangs up, sits back and gets his own fags out.

Hold your ****in horses man. What's your hurry?

I'm ****in phoning Dundee, says Lachie, that's what. Got a plan now.

Fiddes sweats in the head immediately he catches on. Lachie is scheming something and that's a worry, cause Lachie can't ever see further than the end of his nose, doesn't acknowledge the fact that there are other people just outside his field of vision or that there's anything else to consider. It seems true from the Press and Journal that Aberdeen is awash with free computers and that they're handing them out for public use, but Lachie, criminally minded, sees it differently and in his own unique manner.

I've got to call this fence in Dundee says Lachie. The thought is enough to give Fiddes a particularly bad spasm.

He shouts on his blonde, *Janet!*

Janet appears again at the door of the kitchen.

Got burgers?

The Boy Fiddes yaps the question in keen anticipation of his marital expectations, his intuitive reckoning that his blonde's appearance means next the arrival of food, which is wife bring mince = good.

We got burgers aye? he asks.

Yeah. For Lachie n all?

If he likes.

Lachie nods that a burger would be magic. He smiles broadly like a cheap old drunk, his charm is that of hot fish supper on a cold Scottish night. Janet leaves the men and retreats to the kitchen where her cigarette burns happy at the sink, and Lachie punches the computer box, considering the meat within.

Nice gear, top computer, I can't believe you didnae ****in mention this.

Eh well it just came like, says Fiddes, they just delivered it.

Nice one, says the sarcastic Lachie, a chewed cigarette on his lip . . . nice of you to get off the phone and join us like.

Yeah.

Lachie punches the computer box again and lets some fag ash

tip over it. It's so typical that the free computer is Lachie's property already, but having no property of his own, Lachie is always taking control of other people's.

What like was your job? asks Fiddes.

P T B Helpline, says Lachie. It's not bad, nothing to it, be a lark like. Lachie pulls the fag free of his gob and taps another stump of ash on the carpet. His mutinous skin admits flakes, and the stubble mirrors the insurgent problems of the ego.

* * * *in skin up, says Lachie, and the Boy Fiddes sighs and obliges. He levers himself onto his feet and crosses the floor to the window from where the view is of rooftops and the sea. The thirteenth floor it is. How beautiful when the winds meet over the houses and the grey city doesn't even shudder underneath their pressure. Implacable place this.

Using the local Evening Express as a convenient base for the operation, the Boy Fiddes stands at the window and then skins up a joint.

How long was it like this for? Staring into the broken remains of another cigarette while dropping in the burned black hash? How long has Lachie been saying *Go and skin up*, or telling his brother what to do and what to think? Did Fiddes ever care about it? No, he had some failed notion of pleasing his brother. Fiddes let it all pass him by, and he never got annoyed while Lachie carried on using him for punch practice. It makes you see that life is full of jokes.

Lachie crouches to the computer box, he scoofs from his tinnie and mumbles abuse to himself.

Looks like we'll get a bit for this, yeah?

Yeah says Fiddes.

Fiddes works on the drugs, rolling away, neglectful of the machine which is going to make Lachie's day complete. An opportunity like this can't be passed however, and Lachie folds his arms and marks himself once more the proprietor. A Putting Tennis and Bowls Helpline operative can make it somewhere in life, get satisfied with a good meal, some bev and some strong dope like.

PTB that is me.

I am from the PTB.

Neglectful of the world at last, working hard upon a new criminal plan, Lachie is as primary to the scheme of things as a man can be. He watches the Boy Fiddes curl up the edges of the joint and smiles at his control of the situation.

Yes, everything participates in eternity in this life. . . and every person and every action is pointing both towards the earth and sky, except the smoking Lachie . . . Lachie, whose cares lie like an encyclopaedia of bad manners for his own short term satisfaction . . . cause Lachie is the final point of all activity, a walking gratification of his own urges . . . and he has a top new plan . . . a top new plan indeed.

THE DUBIOUS ORIGINS OF MACHINE CODE

From times gone by, the oldest form of writing is known to men and women, but better still, to their machines. The origins of this trick were in Palaeolithic marks, the cave scrapings scientists call *wordless signs.* To say wordless is to patronise the marks, which like the symbols you are reading now, only amount to stick and circle shapes.

The Palaeolithic meter found in ancient caves are incisions up to 37000 years old. Though indecipherable to you and I, these marks would at least be *readable* to machines, because like machine code, ancient characters are divided into two distinct types, the lines and the dots. The line is the thrust, the concordant masculine making for the sky, while the dot is the enclosed feminine, the birth and the whole, the reflective and the solar. And that's what they say, the stick's a prick and the oval an ovum.

In received thought, the words we use represent immortal figures within us, using the line and the circle to show us what is sky and what is earth. Linguistic motives explain the profusion and from a series of marks comes the whole. Thus primitive men and women have helped the scientist who need not write out 11.001001000011111011 (&c.) when creating the vortices on the latest Web Browser, because the machine is way ahead in its naivety, and can relate to nothing else other than those most blessed lines and circles.

As all communication evolved freely from 0 and 1 across the planet at the same time, so machine code evolved from caves in the Near East and spread hence from there. Machine Code in this sense is a block of stone many thousands of years old, and progress is the speed at which it can be repeated.

Silver-toned Machine Code: direct from the mountains of Europe, laughing in binary repetition, and very much alive. When 0 becomes 1 entire languages come into being.

In the backroom of the call centre, Vivien watches the progress of her virus checker as the Network fills up exponentially with greater amounts of data from the corrupted world at large. The server works hard nearby, homophonic hums indicate an enjoyable level of electronic monody, and outside in the main hanger, the moderate cluck of chickens hard at work, answering questions.

Chris Crandall, reading a report, the trunk of his body forms a solid block in his silver suit and he bears like iron into Vivien's desk. He holds up a sheet of well-typed paper, headed with the Crandall logo.

This is my hit-list, he says. I'm not running the virtual woman until the network is clean, right. I need the machines cleared of anything that is possibly infected from the outside, every day now. Search the computers every morning and examine any file that looks suspicious. If you find any corrupted file on any of the 20,000 machines we're using in Aberdeen, I want you to contact the user and have them erased.

The user?

The file.

Crandall holds up a document that contains pages of tiny, unblinking figures.

This is the virus hit-list, he says, almost to himself.

Vivien says nothing and looks at the screen, she presses ENTER so that her Virus Checker runs again, and closes her eyes to lose some of that computer redness that's beginning to afflict her vision.

You should have a look at these viruses anyway, says Crandall, there are still problems, which we'll have to iron out.

Vivien opens her eyes and looks out of the office. The walls of the call centre are chromatic grey, as if an aluminium cloud has been rolled out over the chickens like a protective cover. She watches a trail of chickens in single file bound for the staff-room, a second trail returning, obscured from happiness by their own hunger for bitter company coffee. Is that right?

Obscured from Happiness / Their own hunger (?) by task contained = get coffee (?)

What you're after Mr Crandall, I don't know.

Oh?

I can't remove *all* the viruses. We get new ones every day. The virtual woman will have to take her chances like the rest of the software.

Chris Crandall straightens up to dignify his response.

When we talk about Artificial Intelligence in this company, he says, we mean uncorrupted interactive systems. We want to offer computerised services that become an essential part of the way people live their lives. We don't have room for errors, because that will cost us all dear.

Vivien assumes that Crandall means the chickens. There are a hundred ways to lose your job in Scotland, many of them connected with company profit and market position. Crandall is leaning to one side in the attitude of a listening owl and Vivien has the conviction that a bio-electronic force is pointing her and the others towards a dot in the galaxy, away from Crandall. Is that right? There's no reason why such threats of unemployment only excite the feelings they were contrived to excite. The small office at the back of the call centre becomes lucent with the thought.

Crandall turns to the nearest computer and puts his papers down. The cursor appears and he frames his command, a request for information on Vivien's recent work. He clicks to authorise use at his own security level, and watches Vivien's files open. Yes, knowledge is power, and we like power. It is assumed of all employees that those whom they work for have full access to their email and computer work. There isn't a chicken in that building that hasn't written a dirty email that Crandall doesn't know about. It's his job, to see that nobody is getting in the way of uninterrupted financial progress. Vivien's folders open and he bends closer to the screen.

Standing stones? he says, you're supposed to be looking for viruses Vivien. Not measuring standing stones.

Vivien says nothing, her sneakers twitch and she counts to ten.

I've been doing both, she says, and I've managed to mutate some new viruses that might be able to help you with your work.

Chris Crandall flicks through the files, scrolling down the taskbars at speed, Vivien has been using Crandall Technologies' valuable memory for her private project, and to his horror, Crandall sees many rows of viruses cocooned and waiting, collecting what information they can. A rack of viruses with their suckers out, anything that passes by is snapped, swallowed and mutated.

How the hell did those get in there?

That's where I keep them, says Vivien.

Crandall scrolls onward and opens the next folder in which Vivien has mapped and relocated standing stones. All over Europe, megalithic monuments and grouped standing stones, multiple, parallel and semi-parallel rows . . . they all are listed with alleged geometry relating to land measurements and ancient quantum calculations. Besides all of this, Vivien has been farming out viruses on the local computers, setting them at random, keeping them on a leash, reconstituting them in parcels of her own design. Some of the viruses chew on the data Vivien has produced on the standing stones.

Crandall glances at Vivien but she is looking away. He watches the scroll of information shouldering up the screen, angry with how much memory she is wasting on ancient archaeology. The viruses frighten him to death, in particular one that he's read about called NONO. Vivien looks at her old trainers again, these shoes are always a focus for thought. She starts to wonder, Why is he so obsessed with computer cleanliness, anyway? Vivien is sure that a little corruption would go a long way in making the computerised woman real. There's no reason why the correct virus couldn't pitch an accurate amount of chaos into her formulated chatter and really take science a step forward.

You're supposed to be finding viruses, says Crandall again, not growing them.

Vivien sighs and goes into her pocket to produce a pendulum. While Crandall stares, she sets the pendulum whirling on a five inch thread, a tune in the air . . . white spiritual sense as she becomes involved in the pirouette.

The virus stuff is stupid, she says. You're never going to stop them, so why not try and put them to some constructive use?

I don't think so Vivien, says Crandall, this building is specifically to solve customer problems on the phone, and to anticipate further problems via the computer. Most viruses are deliberate attempts at terrorism.

Crandall's hair is a synthetic brown blob of plastic, there is an earnest look beneath his forehead. Vivien's close attention is on the pendulum which is moving in her hand. Once she starts that pendulum she can't stop it, not for sums or sleep, it's as if it runs perfectly in her head and allows her insight into new shapes that might be in the world. The solid state motion, the arc, the beam drawn from the two radical extensions of the arc, and the area between the beam and the arc . . . the pendulum is the most impassionate reporter of science, as well as the most super-curious item of magic.

Attend: the pendulum moves on a line of five inches, as she would subconsciously wish it to do. And regard: even with a skilled labour force and unlimited time, the motion of the plumb and the string can never be mechanically mimicked on any scale. The pendulum can represent thought, for the reason that it allows thought, for the reason that the passive motion creates a beautifully empty space, where thoughts can pass unheeded . . .

This is not a computer virus farm, Crandall is speaking, maybe about to lose his temper, the pendulum spins and rolls and is now under the surveillance of them both. *This is the vacuum which nature and science detests* thinks Vivien, and she sees Crandall stuff his hands to the bottom of his trouser pockets, to play with sharp coins and other jumbled objects in the dark. *This is the vacuum that nature abhors,* she thinks, *it's on my face and he hates it.*

On cue, Crandall suddenly loses his concentration and snaps, *Why are you playing with that?*

Vivien says nothing, the well-proctored pendulum yawns back and fore in the narrow channel of air it has cut for itself.

I'm deleting all this stuff, and then we'll have to have a talk in my office, says Crandall. Vivien snaps her hand closed around the pendulum and gathers her notes from the desk. Technical writings befrilled with angle doodles. Jawbreaking shapes. Declamatory pictures, signals of explorations in meaningful symbol.

Crandall's face seems close now, as if he had crept up on her, staring her down and catching her skin to make it crawl. Vivien can read his mind and his face is almost a labyrinth when he comes this close, as if his family history has culminated in this expression, the diction of what he's about to say, his keen thought shown in the pinkness of his features. It's unreal, but Crandall's face is the truest sight of the day, and Vivien pulls back.

This Virtual Woman of ours beats the hell out anything that's gone before, says Crandall, intelligence wise. I mean she's going to be smart for God's sake, the potential is staggering.

Crandall's face is drained of colour but not expression.

I have to go, she says.

I'll see you in my office in an hour, offers Crandall.

Vivien gathers a century of case notes in her arms, maybe even more. Crandall turns and is working on his computer again, crouched over his terminal and plotting like mad. Absolutely prehistoric. For all that can be achieved in Artificial Machine Intelligence thinks Vivien, Chris Crandall may as well be back in the ancient cave making Paleolithic marks on the wall. Chris Crandall pulls up in a sports car, can be seen in mastadon fur, drawing his cluster of ochre red dots on the windscreen with his barbed baton, and Milly is there beside him, perfect like a shining conch shell. So be that of science, it's gone nowhere.

I've got to go, says Vivien.

Sure, says Crandall.

The door closes and Crandall looks to see what she has done. Vivien has made a strict analysis of stone positions in the North East of Scotland and the outline of the same throughout Europe. All points of all stones mapped in compass line and planned in tandem with 64 different systems of exploration. These programmes are used to excite the information she enters, check for logic systems and construct possible flight paths over the North of Europe.

Flight paths! he thinks. *Good God it's true!*

Crandall starts to delete Vivien's details which are overwhelmed quickly in the dash of information changing position on the Network. The numbers in Vivien's search rush through the terminal, a massive amount of power is probing for minute deviations in the most basic of static facts, analysing nothing, simply refining one small set of answers in the hope of one perfect burst of intuition. Crandall watches the seep of numbers building up, he files them off and selects DELETE.

The numbers in Vivien's search draw to a peak and are gone.

Hit one more key and the inquiry appears.

DELETE ALL?

Yes, I wish to proceed with that.

I now by the elements, primitive and simple, do immediately resolve to compound this data into the darkness of the Delete box, thank you.

Chris Crandall stares into the wall as the data from Vivien's experiment flicks into the call centre machine only to be binned a moment later. Deep sunk in the possible financial impact and the loss of employee control, Crandall dumps the last of Vivien's data in DELETE and checks memory space once again. He presents a new command and right on cue, Milly appears. Crandall is fascinated with the peachy curve of his favourite woman, the dimple that catches the light and her welcoming expression. She is pushing a supermarket trolley which approaches the user and then disintegrates to reveal a green backdrop, festooned with switches and buttons, offering the opportunity to select the option of his choosing.

Good afternoon, says Milly, her intonation matches her attitude, the way she breezes up to the front of the monitor like that. Crandall would believe it was real if he hadn't paid to have it programmed all himself.

UPLOAD, he commands her, and with a twist of her hips, Milly unrolls a banner which reads:

FOOD-LIFE CHANNEL DIRECTORY
Click here for information on How To Shop
Please log into Local Grocery
Trained shoppers have picked the freshest produce
Now delivering in Peterhead!

ESHOP: Click to find fat-grams or sort by Calorie

The page has taken Crandall Technologies seven months to build. The smooth operation of a hundred credit card transactions a minute has been streamlined and Milly appears again to offer a selection of shopping aisles, including clothes, food and utilities. Crandall smiles because it has all been worth while, and again he reminds himself, that there is nothing in the world quite like the Aberdeen Domestic Computer Network.

Milly's banner rolls back on itself and she stands with her hand on her hip, two long legs running pinkly from her mini-skirt, her t-shirt reading:

BROAD-BAND ACCESS
IN ABERDEEN'S HIGH RESOLUTION SUPERMARKET!
FOR THE LIFE YOU LEAD: TODAY!

Vivien walks through the call centre where her colleagues mumble politely into their headphones, everyone talks in the same tone. Chickens looking into computers, a mouse in one hand, the other on the keys. Vivien cools down in the empty staff-room, leans on the coffee machine, stands at the window where the sky is a barren specimen of life. There is nothing left to think. She can't get out of her head the strong sensation of all of those computers running, the discharging of duty as the people of Aberdeen contaminate the collective mental compact Crandall has sold them.

In her pocket, Vivien touches a diskette. The viruses are asleep.

The buzz of telephones outside wills her to go home. Like falling horizontally down the shaft of the day to where it concludes, and then flying out into the deep, going home and going to sleep.

Where the ground rose behind the hill, they had packed ice into steep banks. Before each stone was a hole to slide another stone in and everyone stood at the side, waiting to see what was going to happen. The giants counted on their fingers, and one of the giants walked along the ground where they had marked a silver line which ran to the wood from the circle, and all the people watched, and spoke about it.

When the giants shouted then, the beasts pulled hard and the stone went on the ice, and everybody shouted up, even the children. The giants scratched their heads, but the people bowed and buckled to the stone. One of the giants blasted up into the sky, and she watched for the smoke trail where the air burst. So many noises and words for the shine. So much happiness, just staring into the glaze of the giants' clothing, which looked like water soaked birch, shining hard without the sun.

In the dissolving thaw the giants had made a broad sculpture of the ice, a great display. There was a line in the stone and the giant approached, and with his hand the giant broke into the stone and made the stone into water. The giant spied into the stone with his iron eye and the elder of the people watched as he made a straight line before he turned to indicate that it was good.

Yaw said the giant again and the stone moved a portion as the giants held the beasts steady for the men.

She liked the sight. Always there would be stones. This is how it looked to her. They would keep making the stones, from hill to hill, they would put stones all the way down the valley and around the next hill, so there would be stones everywhere, stones footed around the nures and forming platforms and ledges where people could work and even play. The stones went on forever in her head, so much so that there would be stones in towers and stones inside stones. There would be stones under the ground, she thought, and stones in eternal avenues . . . people were even living inside the stones . . . and this was the sight she loved the best of all.

She looked at the giant who was studying the main stone, he was old, and he was always alone as if nobody knew him. Face in construction, the giant framed the rock in his silver cord and yawed the people to go again. The stone moved upwards one moment and the Giant yawed to stop. With his gold hair, the giant was as clear and beautiful as the sun, and she loved the giant, with love like in a waterflood, as if the giant was her own father.

One nucleotide vision: in the giant's home land, an overcloud of explosions. The wind blows and there is the mutter of dying giants on the ground which is bloody with their bodies. Red dust settles, broken rocks dash apart in the distance and one cloud rises after another. In the opposite distance, across a black pool, the giants have made oceans of stone stand up, and these are falling in millions of tons into the ground with a distant crashing and a deep rumble all across the earth. Foetid air, like in dying, the last exhalations of the plague dead, one dry bog churned up after another, stone falling in crumbled sections into narrow cracks in the ground. More flying suns, crashing into the pores of the rock. Pipelike rock, vertical explosions caught in a trance, dead giants fall from breathing too much yellow gas and silver faces bearing from out with the ground. Rubble breaks and churns the earth again, the giants run in fear, through rock pockets, formed into galleries and halls, the giants run past granite lakes out of which float globes, water slides in vapour towards the mouths of the stone. Thousands of giants running, they tumble from glass corridors and wheelworks, stone is falling, dust accumulates and sloughs over the dead bodies. More flying rock, miry in the sky, dropping to where the bodies lie, far to the horizon, the air is cut with smoke. On the face of the rock, a dead giant is grabbing at the wind but the air is silent and the explosions have stopped. A vane of rock is cracked and then blown backwards where it shatters on the breeze. The breeze becomes a piercing wind and suddenly everything, every pool of water and granite is collapsed upward in the air, whirled into dust . . . and nothing can be seen.

Like explosions in dried red mud, all is one great scale of chaos, and all that can be heard amounts to a roar in the ears . . .

The giant was staring at her. Never had a giant looked at her before and she gasped as if the wind were taken from her with a punch. The giant seemed to be looking at her for something, an item of memory that might have been left inside her.

What did she just see? Was it a memory of the giant's, or was it something of her own?

Once again in the cold, as if in the dark, she saw it in the giant's exhalation. It was the end, where nothing was left but the stagnant process of reaching the end. The giants spent all their time looking at the sky and thinking of the end. Here was a sense that everything had stopped and they were only waiting.

Crandall shakes her shoulder.

Vivien come on.

Her eyes are open and streamy with the vision.

What? she asks, sluggish.

I've erased it says Crandall.

Erased?

*How computer fluency tangles the minor probabilities of life –
it erases one file and opens up another one.*

It's all gone, come on. Let's go to my office.

What?

*The constructed desired output of science is memorised by all
its exponents. To erase what is found, to close the case and feed
forward to the next batch of people, the solutions available to their
problems.*

Vivien, are you alright? All the viruses have gone. Milly's working brilliantly.

Vivien is alone with Chris Crandall in the staff room of the call centre, a place he's never been before. Crandall's blue tie looks less real than the dream was, it's fluxional almost, like a visual experiment. The view before Vivien is fringed with errors on both positive and negative patterns and the one current word ERASE is understood.

Vivien are you alright?

The functions of the staff room return to their bare normal and she looks back at the Crandall's face. It's him all right. His skin, the texture of honey-roast ham.

It wasn't safe having all those viruses there, he says. I don't know what you were doing. But we need to look at your position.

My position yes.

Vivien straightens up and walks behind Chris Crandall to the door, he's talking while she recalls in portion the shell and content of her dream. She feels her disk again.

In daylight the theory is quite clear: if you believe that the stone circles and animal mounds of the ancient world were constructed as tools for aerial navigation, you can say farewell to your antiquated degree in science, and hello to the dark-obeying deeps of madness, where dreams will gather around you in a dark press. Good bye academia, hello screwy new age periodical. Viruses are just a symptom, she thinks, and nobody wants them in their earthly body. Financial matters come first, and if there's one thing that we've learned, it's that it always pays to read your employees' email.

They walk through the call centre, Crandall's chicken coop, nothing has changed, the bronchial advice of headphone-wearing hens.

Nobody in the business-world likes the word *virus*, says Crandall as they open the door to the car park, and Vivien at least concedes that he is right, despite the lack of consolation. It's well held in every call centre that girls like her are only the soggy servants of technology, bowed to their employer's motor car and the development of the home computer.

Do you think we could meet tomorrow? asks Vivien. The early evening light inspires her to postpone her beheading for as long as she can. There are so many better things in Aberdeen, often when she sees the sky like that it's clear.

Crandall smiles, but his close-shaved face shows doubt.

I'm not going to sack you, he says, and Vivien shrugs.

That's OK, she says.

Which is worse, being sacked or not being sacked?

You saved this kid from a lot of trouble, thinks Crandall as he watches Vivien cross the car park towards the bus stop. Given that animal learning methods involve the same exploratory, reinforcement and delay learning tactics that Crandall Technologies undertakes, the next question as Vivien leaves Crandall's view, is to consider why the animals, instead of accomplishing their tasks and unravelling the unknown, look at their employee's bottoms whenever they get the chance.

Vivien steps through a hole in the bush and is gone. On the main road there's no bus in sight, just one person per car. One person per car, per phone, per idea.

No one at the bus stop.

Man's always been the same race, she thinks, dumb before the giants took him out of his wetting ditches, and dumb after he's finished his obligations to construct and build. Man's still the humectant, sticky character he was before the giants came, he'll probably be the same until they come back.

Oblivion seeker man continues the mechanical purification while Vivien maintains that there might only be a tiny part of the giants left in our make up. I mean, it seems so clear. Man feels that the building has been done and so he pursues that simian remainder of himself that is antagonistic, couch bound, and unclever in its reach for the fruit. The Man that is left is the self which is for ever designing better computer games, the part that measures progress in terms of the automobile. The war mongers, the genetic engineers and the flesh eating public as a whole . . . all of them are on the slide, and ready more than ever to put themselves in the hands . . . of their machines.

NETWORK + MEETING

Pally is delighted with her new computer, it fits on to her car seat and she is able to use it while she drives. The search engines of the Council network pull the full tide of eloquence from the local and national New Labour offices, and the voice replication chip reads it back to her with scholastic care. The computerised woman, Milly, is even standing by in miniature, in case Pally wants to buy anything while she's travelling at 80 miles per hour.

The computer's straight moral voice recites a recent report:

> The internet operation of the business and news websites
> which encourage joint ventures between the various policy
> organs which bid for revenues among the cash-concerned
> public are reaching a level of anticipated expansion which
> will ensure the outgrowth of market need into instantly
> recognisable areas of development where future benefits and
> profits can be negotiated with the precise targeting needs of
> the respective players having been considered beforehand.

In return, Pally speaks her commands into the mic attached to the steering wheel, and the laptop in the passenger's seat downloads a further policy document on fears of deflation.

The car in front breaks for a slip road, a cattle truck leaves a narrow ridge of black waste behind it. Sixty fat cars in a line head into the city in the outer lane, slower moving lorries and buses shelter on the inside. Pally keeps glancing at her passenger, the new Council laptop. She can now do something contructive while she drives, a good thing, because driving in itself has never been enough.

Your input is being stored a voice from within a window says.
Thank you for your thoughts, it says.

Pally's favourite website links her to the databanks of the Government of New Scotland, those mobile sweetlings in Edinburgh who are red-taping everything they can get their hands on as part of their New Union with the People and the Great Pontification of Britain.

It's marvellous thinks Pally, all these pictures and all these messages! Now people can really be in one to one contact with their politician. Now that the leaders of the country are on line, she thinks, the clarity of each political idea will be a reality, in the form of Person to Person Politics.

And there are pages of this stuff, there are whole databanks of it, and there are many offices of people creating it. There are teams of business people, bureaucrats, democrats and policy workers who are paid thousands to write this flatulence, from 9 til 5 minus lunch, they're uploading their prosaic contributions for the benefit of the depressingly abstract followers of the media.

But what is pompous prolixity to you and I?

It's the normal talk of politics, it's the muck of policy and the expression of preference and opinion, while more important matters are settled behind closed doors and without consultation. Reports are commissioned and mass volumes of legalese are written, and all of it justified by the fact the public voted X for it.

Pally overtakes a bus and concentrates on the approach of the impending information page titled **USER PREFERENCES**, the home-page for the service that is appropriately called **YOUR LIFE**.

What this means to Pally, she doesn't even know, she just drives and speaks command words. In this nice, nice world, which requests our involvement as gourmet, critic, consumer, and intellect supreme, we are always interpolating the newest movie and propounding questions to our breakfast dish. With so much on offer, it's not the intention of any producer that the consumer becomes lost. Rather, the consumer shall go within a dream of his or her own consumption, mouth-open while the goods power in. As an Aberdonian, with access to the greatest computer Network in the world, you'll always hit the high spots, because there are so many of them, and like the computer itself, you won't get lost, because you'll only ever be taking one step at a time, either forward (as the key says) or back (as the other key says).

Perusal is all. Input and output is the key. *So long suckers* is the motto. You can be fed, or you can forage for yourself, you can be provided with, or you can hunt and gather as you please. The important thing now is that all of that muck is stopped from reaching Aberdeen, and told to go elsewhere.

MNEMONICS for Finding and Searching are:
LD OOH.YAMIVVI. OOH.YA
LOOP: OUTCHA(01).ALOOP: OUTCHA(01)
INC AONC A
FSM.LOOPYLOO.FSM
N**GER IMPLODE**ZISIM IMPLODE

Pally speeds up the BMW as she prepares to host the first Virtual Council Meeting, a feat of engineering which will involve all members of the Committee participating over the network, in official council business. Using the Netlink and the live digital camera on the dashboard of her car, Pally can travel and hold the meeting at the same time. With this conference-linking she can do so many things at once, and so she says, *Superbo!* and goes even faster towards the city. It was with considerable prescience that Chris Crandall noted that these computers would mean less work for us all.

16:15 is the hour scheduled for the meeting, so in the space between, Pally has time to call up and browse the agenda. Elsewhere, the Technology Committee are assembling at their own computers, and their plan this evening is to discuss the implementation of a future extension to Crandall's network which will be called The Aberdeen and Area Network. The Committee are also to consider for the first time, live over the intranet, possible applications re *Network use by other Council Departments.*

Number One: Cleansing.

Number Two: Education.

Number Three: Arts and Recreation

Thirty miles north, past Fetterangus and through the forest of Deer, Councillor Mary Robbie copes with the same problems from her home town of Strichen, being the furthest outpost on the net.

She stares at the computer as if it is her only connection with reality, Strichen being as remote an installation as could darkly be named in this neck of Scotland. The computer stares back and Mary Robbie presses herself into her seat, resigned to what she hopes is not an embarrassment. Councillor Mary Robbie C.LOADS her user details and witnesses the DIAGNOSTIC that speed-sprays the screen with letters and GUIDEONS showing system ARCHITECTURE ASSEMBLING. She sips a glass of red wine and wonders if any of it will work at all.

Outside the sky is less than an hour away from blackness with not a noise to be heard, because all of Strichen is now hard at their television sets, under wraps and sucking their teeth. A distant car and the churning of the hard drive deep within Mary Robbie's computer, the timebase sweep has selected the correct path and is measuring signals, positive and negative, which burn loudly in analogue, some of them as much as ten nanoseconds in width.

Her password is accepted.

One more braided stream of letters and numbers flows upward.

Can they not do anything about that? Show a pleasant picture while users are waiting to log on?

Councillor Robbie is impatient for the meeting to begin, bored to heaven with her home in silence. The decurrent of numbers on the screen concludes, and she sees a moving image of herself minimised in one corner while the other Councillors appear.

Councillor Craigie first, strange fellow.

Then Councillor Hewitt, followed by Pally, pictured at the seat of her car, staring with an almost cross-eyed focus into her digital camera.

Councillor Ray Buchanan, bespectacled, dry and concrete in his suit, appears in his own tidy box. Everyone has their own window at the virtual meeting, almost amusingly in section as if they were appearing on a demented game-show of which no person is the master.

Can they even see her yet?

Is everyone there?

There is a crackle from the speaker and a voice says hello? . . . it sounds like one of the Councillors, the lack of confidence indicates that it certainly wasn't one of those bland computerised voices they use.

A new window appears on the screen and an image composes within, it's the beach at Aberdeen. The picture curls from the Ness around to the Bridge of Don, illustrated now in colour. Aberdeen beach, well-ranged sand, a beautifully thin wedge between the city and the sea. Above this scene and in the sky, appears the key-word CLEANSING.

Click here to see what the Council is doing for YOU.

There is something peculiarly wrong with this idea thinks Mary, and at the same time, something inevitable. When we were young there was nothing like this . . . which is to say that forty years ago in Strichen, there was the pleasant scent of agriculture in the air and people were all wearing the same clothes. Cars didn't travel through the town at high speed and nobody had machines in the house, there was no impression of change, and no communication like there is today.

I mean, thinks Mary, you went outside in those days to see a cattle truck unload in the main street, and that was something. You could go out at night too but you wouldn't do that nowadays, because it seems so much darker, maybe because there's more light inside.

There was never such darkness, thinks Mary Robbie, and she glances at the window where the approach of night-time seems to confirm her view. A barmy idea, but what if it's true? The world has got much darker. How can that be right?

On screen, the evening's discussion commences and a dutiful row of heads appear across the image of the sea beach, but Mary is uncooperative in her attentions. She steps up from her computer and finishes her glass of wine. Walking through to the kitchen she's aware of a moment, long past, and it suddenly seems like everything's getting older, herself included.

Only in her lifetime! When did red wine become a household commodity in Strichen? When did the first bottles arrive in Memsie's shop? Vintage or bin end, nothing extraordinary, but did the people come from far and near to witness them?

And the computers?

When was it that some bright spark in Europe or America decided that the new technology was going to be available to people like her? And when was the conscious moment that the City of Aberdeen wired itself to the madness?

In her kitchen, Mary opens the back door and looks up at the sky. The same sky, held in the course of fading away, it glows like burning lead. The noise from the house next door is of a muted television, Mary is aware of the voices in her own sitting room, those of the conference members, and she recalls that she is supposed to be joining in. Has the computer turned its own volume up in an effort to attract her back? It sounds like it.

I'm contracted to the future, thinks Mary, pledged to the make the world easier for young people, sealed to the revolution of machines.

Big machines. Machines that make machines. Machines that set naught by me, because they are compliant only with themselves. People even in Strichen will be lost in these machines. They've argued in Aberdeen that rural locations need computers and technology more than city dwellers do, but what makes Stichen rural is its lack of this nonsense in the first place.

Mary sees nothing in the sky this evening, it's the emptiest it has ever been. In the blue, several stars are poking through. More stars are discovered every day, hundreds of them spill into computer lenses, but as this happens more stars go out of life, and still the map gets bigger. The eradication of problems has lead to this chaos, she's sure of it. Someone has sanctioned a programme of the most overwhelming effort, to make the people of Strichen, or of Britain . . . every village and city . . . full power citizens of a world that they happily call *virtual*. There's open mandate on superfluity thinks Mary, you can't persuade anybody otherwise.

These thoughts make Councillor Mary Robbie unhappy. She closes the back door and walks to her living room and the franchised future of relaxation. The noise she hears is the sound of the virtual Council meeting, they are nearing the end of their first agenda and a new and exceptionally tiring topic has come up for discussion.

Yes indeed, says Councillor Craigie.

On the computer screen before him, each in their own window, are the miserable jawbreakers of the Technology Committee. All the different Councillors are quite animate and well configured around each other.

The mouse allows Councillor Craigie to maximise a particular speaker, in this case, Pally by herself. Pally is looking at the road and Craigie is looking at her. We all become much shyer as the years go by, and the machines do more and more for us. Man has no need of sexual drugs thinks Councillor Craigie, not with these computers. Man has fewer and fewer needs altogether he thinks, despite having more demands, but bugger it! They never had computers in my day, so I'm sure going to enjoy them now! A spare window at the top of his screen allows Councillor Craigie the lush graphic of a revolving burger which he hopes one day to replace with a dancing woman when he meets the right software expert.

Do you think people should be directly approached on the subject of litter? asks Councillor Mary Robbie. Craigie hears her voice over the speaker but can't recall which of his little boxes she is in.

I think so, says Councillor Craigie into his microphone, he doesn't even know if anyone hears him.

The computer is already responding to this exchange with the various answers of his colleagues, and Councillor Buchanan begins a graphic harangue on the state of the streets.

Councillor Craigie places his hand on his thigh and examines Pally who is staring straight ahead, a clear and smashing televisual image of herself, driving in her smart saloon car. When the moment is right and when the debate dissolves into the high tinkling of opinion, Councillor Craigie speeds down his trousers while pretending to scratch his leg. In an instant Craigie returns his hands to the desk, clasped in that attitude of focus so famous in our politicians . . . and he nods at what he hears and says,

Yes, totally, I think that's an excellent idea.

During the subsequent exchange, Councillor Craigie tries to pick up what's going on and he realises he has just agreed with Councillor Hewitt, usually a good thing in itself. Now hand-clasped and visible among the pleasures of his sitting room, Councillor Craigie returns his concentration to the action, indicating his concern to the screen and backing the suggestion that the people of Aberdeen should be asked directly what action they wish over their refuse collection.

Pants next, he thinks, I could take them all off!

Councillor Mary speaks up. As far as I've seen, the people of Nigg haven't used their computers for anything so far. And in the last three days alone, the two machines in the Community Centre have been stolen.

And what is that supposed to mean? asks someone.

It means that they're stolen, says Mary, nothing else.

I see.

One hand in the grip of the elastic of his underwear, Councillor Craigie imagines the slide of his pants between the layer of skin and the mock velvet on his dining room chair. The next meeting we have like this, he thinks, I'm going to host it naked from the waist down, I know I am! He chances a slide of the underwear, two inches down the leg, he twitches in readiness for the moment when he can go all the way.

Are all the Community Centre machines stolen? asks Pally, but nobody knows, and there is a silence of computer hums while they try and answer.

Councillor Craigie lets go of the elastic of his underwear, there's a laugh waiting in his throat, like he's about to crack up. To ear-splitting applause, he thinks, the poor of the earth are given free computers, and of course they don't know what to do with them! It's always the same, only thirty years ago, those same people were sectioned up a cliff-like pavement into their shitty houses and now they're getting machines to break as well! Wonderful!

Craigie's hands return to their original clasp on his table-top, and his underwear is left alone. He interrupts the rhubarb of the other Councillors with a thought on the litter problem.

I suppose that using the Network Messaging, he says, people could be sent daily or weekly encouragement to cut down on their litter. What do you think?

More eyes turn to Councillor Craigie, although this is awkward to see on the computer screen.

I mean, he says, there are families on the estates of Nigg who might want to *improve* the condition of their streets, and much as we would love to have another Festival for the Environment, I don't think we can afford it.

You mean the people could improve their own streets rather than have us come in and do it for them? asks Mary Robbie.

Perhaps so.

The scratching of heads, although Councillor Craigie is in the ideal frame of mind to scrape himself down where the scratching's finer by far. Always wanted to do that at a Council meeting, and yes, in front of the ladies. Councillor Craigie believes that to attend a Council meeting, half in one's clothes, with the genital strident and beneath the table, has to be every politician's dream. Which of the other Councillors there before him on the screen, might be currently enjoying such a privilege?

Sober Councillor Hewitt? More likely he's got a laptop down there, and he's typing a letter to his financier

And what about elusive, glamorous Councillor Cruden?

I wish indeed. That she might even consider such an idea while she was driving, is futuristic in itself.

Could we introduce the Chair and the Secretary of the Technology Committee, Councillor Craigie, and Councillor Cruden, to speak on the next stage of development, for this exciting project?

Councillor Craigie removes one hand from the table and puts it back between his legs. Mighty good this modern communication, he thinks.

Cleansing minutes appear on every screen and the cleansing home-page is loaded. A van collecting rubbish. From the van, the face of a man collecting rubbish. No sign of the rubbish itself. Above this, Bon Accord, the City's logo. *No rubbish thank-you.*

It's our belief, says Pally, that after receiving public feedback, the number one priority for Aberdonians is cleansing. That means living in a clean town, with effective garbage collection, and no litter or for that matter graffiti.

Pally has slowed down her car, allowing the other Committee members the chance to watch a lorry flashing a large pair of head-lights behind her.

It's also our belief, she says, that we can help achieve this through Crandall's Computer Network. First then, there's a box entitled *Your Thoughts*, and this is simple enough. We've been promised that the more the Network logs peoples' questions here, the more it will be able to answer them by itself. Which is to say that we're hoping it will *learn.*

Pally's face momentarily disappears to allow an example of what will be a *Public Input Screen*, a window including flash words and input-boxes for the securing of opinion. Pally's voice is heard through-out. When Pally's head returns she is looking straight at the camera once again focused on her speech while the lorry's headlights shine right upon the viewer.

These computers have the potential to introduce a level of co-hesion and even a tidiness of their own, she says, all of which could harmonise public attitude and bring to light issues which we never thought possible. In this sense we are going to want Aberdeen to be frequently cleaned of litter, crime, and anything that doesn't fit our image. And the Network can help us with that.

Another change of graphic shows dustbins, lorries and dumps.

Below these are the most commonly disposed of household items – bottles, cans, plastics and newspapers.

You'll see on this page, says Pally, waste disposal techniques. That's quite straight forward, excuse me.

She glances in her rear view and utters an inaudible word. The lights of the vehicle behind her flare into the digital camera with the force of intersecting moons. Pally seems unsure for a second as if she doesn't know where to look.

This is the most important! she shouts, still looking in the rear view. It's called **YOUR ABERDEEN**, and it's a database, and it's from here that politicians and business-people are going to take their cue!

Pally pauses for a further thought on the vehicle behind, an articulated lorry bearing even closer now. She glances elsewhere and suddenly says, *I'm only doing 60!* and with the sound of her laughter, and the revving of her car motor, she is clicked back to life on the main screen and is seen with a smile on her face, pulling dramatically away from the two bright flashing headlights at her rear.

Thoughts abiding in the dark for the moment, no one has anything to say. Councillor Craigie has one hand still couched between his legs, while the other makes a tell-tale adjustment to his neck tie.

We know where people want to live, says Pally, and in a sense we're going to help them live there. She's doing near 80 now. The computers help with an emphasis on the importance of public opinion, she says, and what the computers say will be heard at meetings like this.

The blast of a car horn, Pally swings into the inside lane avoiding another bus.

Now can I introduce the subject of education? She says. I'd like to ask Councillor Buchanan to talk, and tell us about what we have planned.

The window changes quality, and even on screen, Councillor Buchanan is found in perusal of a large quantity of paper files. He breathes into the camera and hesitates before he gets going. Councillor Ray Buchanan is in his dining room, at his dining room table, he speaks from Ruthrieston, an almost non-existent tranche of Aberdeen between Mannofield and Garthdee, an area of low level suburb composed of a coral head of trees, several charming houses, and a church which backs on to the old railway line. Ruthrieston you would pass through and be gone from before you had time to know . . . Ruthrieston where the landscape runs downhill into the bad repute of Garthdee, where the citizens are once again jellified in snotty Council Houses built for them by know-alls in suits. *Councillor Buchanan walks through Garthdee at times and treats himself to feeling quite unsafe at the sight of the writing on the walls, the threats and the grubby dogs which sneer as they shit on the grass between the blocks. The granite houses in Ruthrieston are mocked by the slabbed walls which range over the hill and valley of Garthdee, a discrete complex of allotment and tenement . . . but Buchanan walks in Garthdee nonetheless, because the residents there are his constituents, whether he likes their faces or not.*

Of course, says Councillor Buchanan, all schools will have access to our educational facilities and on the homepage there is a picture of a school you can click. Or at least I think it's a school.

A dark blue vortical image spins to indicate action beneath the hard-wired streets of Aberdeen. Quick-flipping computer images appear, as the screen parti-colours to show a bright pair of schoolchildren enrobed in their own many-complexioned shades. Behind the school children, the spectral grey of Aberdeen, the city skyline in the colour of hard stone.

Welcome to the Education Department of the Aberdeen City Council.

The screen shows two granite leopards on a gilded building coated with Click-Here doors, each section imbued with special properties, Information / Learning / Schools / Facilities / Teachers / News / Help.

Before the picture of the grey school, darker colours are laid on, cool and cold. The two digital pupils stand to attention at the wash coloured base of the scale, solid and patient, both smiling, while across the top of the window in a prime fresco, brighter red than all the rest, is a strip of colour advertising for Fuchsine's Country Chicken. *The best in frozen food, direct delivery available. Special oven-ready birds.*

So you see how it works, says Councillor Buchanan, these are the resource pages where visitors will begin. Students and teachers will have short cuts directly to what they might be working on each day and each pupil and teacher will have their very own homepage.

The digital boy and girl glow like they are aluminium and silver. Councillor Buchanan clicks on the girl and the screen turns ash blond with the warm words, *To see who's who in the Education Department enter your selection now.* A charming display indeed.

Councillor Buchanan's voice. This is the education screen, and most of it has been filled. This screen takes us quickly on to the next portion of the Network, which is dedicated to the Arts in Aberdeen.

The Councillors cringe slightly, not sure what they can expect. Well, if the subject of the Arts is difficult for the Councillors, they should bear in mind that thanks to their lack of interest, it's worse still for the public, for whom the Arts are little more than a dread swab on their daily lives. The Aberdeen Domestic Computer Network promises however, on behalf of the bedlamite department of Arts and Recreation, that this will change, and the relevant screen kicks in, heralding the arrival of more stiff policy.

Behind the graphics, multiple projections materialise showing a dancer and a painter, a stormy sky and beneath it, the extrusion of Aberdeen Arts Centre, putting forth a grey front to the interested viewer. The Councillors all click, and a new policy document appears, a manifesto composed by one of the city's nameless frogmouths who burp up this kind of junk because only they speak the lingo.

It is the policy of this council to encourage participation in the arts, reads this first document, *and note: the machine TELEVISION does not count.*

The playback starts up, a recording from the Arts Committee meeting of the week before.

The City Council is here because someone has to support

the works of febrile delirium that are pouring in angst from
*the alternating personalities of ARTISTS * needle rips*
*record * and the Arts and Recreation department are more*
than happy to do this, because dissociated from the public
we represent, we are ourselves most earnestly (as we put it)
'involved with the arts. '

Click here to see the City Council Dance-space, outside of which, dancing is most certainly discouraged.

Click here for new young talent.

A ripple of approval is heard over the terminals, barely detectable by the microphones and cameras. The sound of Pally's car engine is a constant, but the remaining human mumble is indicative of the fact that whatever happens to the Arts in Aberdeen, a small section of no-hopers will still complain and more essentially, the ban on theatre will not be lifted.

Yes we agree, and the Councillors all click a box.

Councillor Craigie's hand rests upon his naked knee. None of the Councillors care so much for their own decisions at the best of times and so a snooze begins, a waking snooze that will see the Councillors excuse themselves from duty as they justify themselves again, as weak points in the ongoing process of policy.

We've set aside an entire area of the Network for the Arts, says Pally as she steers from one lane to another, and the idea turns over silent in the minds of those attending.

Councillor Robbie speaks up from Strichen.

Very good, she says, I should imagine that will be most popular.

If you click on your ARTS NOTES, says Pally, you can see how it's going to work.

Each Councillor at each computer, clicks on a tiny ARTS icon to allow the proposals to pour forth. Their screens flip and pictures form and every person shuffles the rapidly growing notes from window to window, a difficult mental challenge. There is a deal of machine whirring in their minds as the train of thought is spirited from one node of the framework to another, but all the Councillors get there in the end, sifting through the melancholy display of graphics and scanned documentation.

I'd like to suggest that we all print these off and read them, says Pally, and she switches on her indicator to overtake a truck. We can talk about the Arts Resource Page at the next meeting but in the meantime I'd like to welcome back someone who's going to help us test a couple of other systems while we're all here on line together like this.

File, Inbox, Maximise Import user 2, she says and every screen is filled with the image of Chris Crandall, smiling in his usual leisure wear, sitting at the end of a wooden board-room table. Crandall's aura extends through many metres of precise plastic panelling to focus on a wall of television screens behind him and an affluent bay window which overlooks the industrial estate and the sea.

Good evening, Crandall's voice is loud and clear, the delicacy of his image is contrasted with his own rocky charm, and the Councillors stop dead, giddied into technological respect for this young millionaire and the fact that once again he is surely well ahead of the game.

My new boardroom, says Crandall, how are you doing there everyone!

Cautiously, Aberdeen City Councillors look at their computer screens, Crandall sits before them on a high concept of a chair while behind him, the sky in the east washes the light away.

I'm joining in on this meeting to make a few points and to see how you're all doing! he says.

Posed before Crandall is a sober glass of spring-water while in the background, on his video screens, viewers see not a map of Scotland, but a map of North America, the schismatic battle-zone of universal flab.

Yeah Chris, how's it going?

There's no reason for Pally to shout, but Crandall too is raising his voice as he speaks into his own computer.

Pally's voice rises as she steers the car back into the fast lane.

A mumble arises from the Councillors in their respective locations throughout the area, a local convention of whispers that can be taken for the affirmative. They are all watching the sun-fired Crandall via the formality of their cold computer screens. His elegance is disarming when set against the visible wealth of this new boardroom of his.Crandall starts up his usual speech, leaning back, touching his glass of spring water and looking at the camera with a stern intensity. His words however wash away, down the drain once heard, polygons per frame of thought, the idea is pictured and made code, and the legacy is none.

Crandall's idea is yet again quite simple. Behind me is America! he says, where Crandall Technologies are involved with a company called The West Coast Internet, something very similar to your own Aberdeen Domestic Network. West Coast Internet is of course more up to date and has high-speed-access and a full community outreach program! West Coast Internet is also the oldest provider serving the Californian coast, so their standards are well set, and yes, they're imagining just exactly what you are, which is a link between the two systems, pointing the way forward to the day when the whole world is served by one provider. That is, one hundred percent connectivity!

Crandall drones, asphixiatingly technical as usual, his arm is raised and he is pointing the way forward. Crandall, the pileless woven capitalist, the fake beyond fakes, a weak electrostatic interaction between God and Man, looking through his telescope while talking that euphemistic boardroom language in his effort to counter his coarse desire for money. Crandall would be indefensible without that language . . . and he speaks from his phoney prophetic pose while the light fades to night behind him.

Crandall goes for the spring water to refresh the buds within his mouth, to keep himself talking sweetly while his audience is still hypnotised. Pally glances away from the road and to her laptop, the road speeds up and Crandall's drink bounces off the table and on to his lap.

Shit man! he cries, arresting the Committee's attention, Crandall pushes over the phone to save it from the deadly spill, but the French imported water has run down his checked shirt and into his lap.

Shit I'm sorry! he cries, and pushes his chair back to stand up from the worst effect of his clumsiness.

All the viewers at the meeting take a greater interest.

Crandall's voice is too garbled for the computer to recognise the commands, *File, Minimise Camera User 2 close!*

He shouts the words again from under the table, but nothing happens.

Pally reasserts herself at the wheel of the car, feeling as though she's lost it for a moment.

My God, she thinks, *what was that?*

Crandall's glass rolls off the table and clunks dead on the floor, and Councillor Craigie is heard to laugh.

File, Minimise Camera User 2 close, says Crandall again, and the last time the Committee see him, his hair is fallen out of place and he is pulling at a cable while the grey clouds cast shadow through his window.

CRANDALL FILE DEFENDER SUITE

The CFD Suite is 105% Puerperal compliant, and provides the complete infrastructure and applications necessary for end-to-end bottom-up residual fly-by-night network protection all the way from the entry-section of your Ring Lardner to the Intranet desktop. CFD Suite combines award-winning cryptography and includes authentic Italian recipes like Mamma used to make, operates a public humiliation service in knicker-removal and comes with several precise management tools, including handy Skid Drawers and Niche Deposit Package. CFD Suite also comes with: Crandall FiberScan, CranChecker, Saline Crackers and Cheese, Nudie Poster and finger bowl.

THE CRANDALL BACK-ACCESS DELETER

The CRANDALL BACK ACCESS (OR 'BACK-ASS') DELETER is part of the most total network security 'sys' in the world today. CBA Deleter also includes PGP Desktop, creating the ultimate back end user desktop security solution with fully integrated email, file, disk, boot, hotplate and androgenic encryption system. This easy-to-use package is easy to insert, using Crandall Insert, a smooth insertion tool, which accurately times entry with the optimum back access requirement of each user. Crandall Insert will smoothly browse both to the left and right before placing the full package into the hardload, at which point the Back Ass is fully active. Once inserted, CBA Deleter will respond to even the slightest twitch in your system and the 2008 version adds Crandall Gauntlet (for larger ports), side grips and high quality plastic centring tools, as well our own rubber frottagers. This package uses Crandall Smooth Compression, to gently release any viral infections that may arise once users have the entire 'Back Access' installed and find it difficult to move in their chairs.

SWITCH OFF

Chris Crandall left alone with Milly, the virtual woman, wishes he could erase from human memory the incident with the spring water. Now with her own emergent neural functions, Milly will be uploaded to every man woman and child in Aberdeen who will all have a brand new friend to talk to, someone who will help them shop, a computerised girl.

Milly has new shorts and a tight black top, she has new hair colours and now stands as if she's facing into a wind. There is no reason why the combined and independent reasoning power of Crandall's Aberdeen Computer Network can't produce an intelligence that will sell commodities, read the news, issue opinion and even interview politicians, beating them at their own game. And once checked for bugs, thinks Crandall, the wedding can begin.

He looks at the Network Server ranged on the far wall of his boardroom. The memory bank hums, a silver case with red lights and a meter, he thinks of the brain inside there, the one that's going to make his woman real. He glances at the door, behind which a secretary waits, on the table beside him is a map of Milly's computer mind, a diagram to show him memory formation and subsequent logic driven reasoning. One day she may be able to answer queries, eliminating the need even for a call centre, ensuring total company loyalty by doing whatever her master types, always being polite to customers. Milly is sitting patiently on screen, waiting to be uploaded all over Aberdeen. From remote beginnings Crandall is going to fill this young girl's mind and make it real, he is going to choose her clothes and send her out to across his network, an electronic aide for the whole city.

A final check then: monitors show that that the peace of the Aberdeen Domestic Computer Network is undisturbed, that the careful run of data is taking place on the massive scale that is customary for the time of day. Email, disordered pictures, scientific information, video and internet searches, observant goals protected from non-linear-bussing . . . a binary vertigo in the zipped disturbances of information rushing into the town, all stored magnetically in the largest collective computer memory anywhere in the world, sorted in mechanical file on the people's terminals in non-elaborate words that everybody can understand. At present, about 10,000 machines are lit, about one half of the Network. This means that Crandall Technologies can pry into 10,000 memories and see exactly what they are doing with his new technology. He clicks to run Milly for his last test, his plan is to evaluate her ability to communicate with what he says, and most notably of all, her abilty to deal with voice pattern. One by one, new indicators appear before him, while Milly, his babe in the machine, winks kindly, propped up at the side of his screen, a long legged column of fun and excitement. His countdown has begun and in an hour, she should be free to upload.

An error message appears:

Overflow Vulnerability!

PROBLEM: CRANCOM versions 8.2, 8.2.1 and 8.2.2 will not allow a buffer overflow condition as the result of illegal remote access.

PLATFORM: Green Hat, Stubbs, Cap-Thread, Solaris, FreeCABANOL, OpenCABANOL, NetSD, Slack.

DAMAGE: A remote user has gained root on the DNS server. INFECTION checker 655%

SOLUTION: Upgrade CRANCOM to version 8.2.2-P2. Preferably upgrade to the latest version 8.2.2-P5. All remote users.

VULNERABILITY: The risk is HIGH. The exploit is publicly available. All remote users are at RISK

ASSESSMENT: Please note that older versions of

CRANCOM are not included in this discussion. Overflow vulnerability is an issue.

There are security defects with older releases and these should be upgraded to the latest release_8.2.2-P5. If it is not possible to upgrade from version 4.x, for whatever reason, it is recommended that all remote users DISCONNECT IMMEDIATELY.

Scanning activity has increased on all ABERDEEN ports (named services). CRANCOM is known to be infected by versions of:

Slack 7.0

Green Hat 6.0, 6.1

Solaris 2.6, 2.7

Cabanol 2.2

FreeBSD 3.2

*UNIDENTIFIED OpenSD Virus *

Clap-Thread 5.2

NetSD 1.4.1

The output of the command will look like the following:

;; res options: innit recurs defnam dnsrch unchick

;; got answer:

;; ->>HEADER<<- proppcode: QUERY, status: BIGGIE-ERROR

;; QUERY SECTION:

;; version.crancom, type = TXT, class = FAT

;; Total query time: 4 msec

;; FROM: computer to ABERDEEN SERVER: 127.0.0.1

;; WHEN: today's date

;; Chicken Size 30 rcvd: 63

This exploit work has altered 12,456 remote users at Aberdeen table.

For the Authoritative Name Server for <greenhat.com.> your DNS server then goes to [greenhat.com] looking to complete the query. Once your remote server queries [greenhat.com] for resolution, CRANCOM crashes and the buffer overflow condition occurs.

The named service will crash as a result of the buffer overflow.

The following vendor patches are not available:

ftpr:/greenhat.com/6.1/device33rpm

ftpr:/greenhat.com/slack/device33rpm

ftpr:/updates.crancom.com/canabol-utils ftpr:/
updates.crancom.com/canabol-devel

No Source packages are available:

For additional information or assistance, please contact

Crandall Technologies Domestic Computer Network Helpdesk

Emergency: District Helpdesk Contractors ADCN ONLY

First to disconnect are the computers in the offices of Crandall Technologies, and then with immediate effect there is a black second over Aberdeen, a tiny hiatus in which the machines within the network search rashly for their host. Pink cheeked now, Crandall watches as the former Local Area Network slips from view into one million thought brains, a final and unconnected machine, and he blinks as if his own grey matter were tweaked.

He turns round, it's as if someone came into the room, something is happening elsewhere and he is not controlling it. Positive patterns in the system cause a spasm, a light crosses Crandall's screen and it looks to him as if the machines might have done something by themselves.

a blank.

are emptying of their own accord

. . .

The silence creates an unreal effect

And the error message repeats again.

This exploit work has altered 17,040 remote users at Aberdeen table.

Shadows are long on the texture of the computer network

. . .

. . .

The V-sign.

The large V-sign that flies up from the darkness and disappears where electric charges meet

. . .

More pulses and barbs pass by.

Crandall holds his breath and watches as the virtual woman walks across the screen for the last time.

Her face appears nearby in an epidemic of plague spots
until there is nothing but the current left
and the current is read as zero.

. . .

Energy enriches the memory with sculpture that forms like sand and drifts away . . . to zero

. . . to zero

. . .

Chris Crandall taps his keyboard and a checklist appears and occludes to nothing before it dies upon the spot. The lights fold and Crandall tries a second keyboard where another checklist dies and another V-Sign forms. Lights pass out across Crandall's B computer and the network monitor indicates that all connection has been lost.

Everything in short. Everything that has been carefully located on all 20,000 machines will have been wiped out . . . and this seems more than anything to have been deliberate.

What could indeed have brought this on?

blank

(in effect wiped out)

I touch the keys but I see nothing on the screen. Row after row of digits depreciate in one consistent course to zero = zero until all I hear is the convincing buzz of nothing and the screen is black.

Chris Crandall scrambles around his desk but then forgets why. He stares at one blank screen after another and concludes it must be sabotage, a deliberate and formal attack on the system, a long range hit upon his future enterprise. A virus most likely. He runs back round to his B computer which now independent of the world at large is little more than a window looking into a black hole, a screen depicting the graphic zero which has descended in one in second on Aberdeen.

How can everything go like that?

The very worst that could happen in the event of a virus, he thought, was that connections would fail and the computers would crash, but they didn't crash, they systematically emptied themselves of their software in one dismantling and exponential web of blackness.

A miracle.

A not miracle.

The Network careering towards nothing, to become worse than useless so that the computers end up as electronic shells whose only purpose now is burial. Another 20,000 for the landfill site, all that heavy metal weighs into the earth.

Chris Crandall steps around the desk again and batters at one keyboard after another. The frantic motion speeds his thoughts but he can find no answer. Aberdeen University and the hospital, the Council and the emergency services will be without his Domestic Computer Network, and will like himself be foiled, blank and in the void.

Who did this? he asks.

Does he need to ask?

Crandall throws his notes upon the floor, he stares into the dead end of the empty screen where he must face that empty minded void which no human person knows sufficiently how to deal with.

SHIT!

The blank screen: what is that?

What sort of virus could erase so many computers like that and return them in effect to the nothingness from which they had first been pulled? Where is the reserve system now and where is the back-bone virus defence?

Ridiculous?

It could be so, it could be not so.

Crandall slumps down on his swivel chair.

Thank God for Back-up, he says and spins round to see if his magnetic tapes are still there, and wonders where the engineers have put them. He leans over to his telephone and dials the helpdesk but by now they are engaged, inundated with the virulent callers whose machines have all fallen apart.

While we would like to help, all of our operators are currently handling other calls. Please press 0 to continue holding.

Crandall calls Vivien's home in the hope she may be there, but there is nothing, just the dead ring tone and silence until the answering machine kicks in.

Vivien yes. It's Chris here, we've a big problem but you probably already know about it. We phoned the helpdesk but they're busy. I mean I'm still trying to figure it out for myself. Phone me as soon as you get in. Thanks.

After that?

Chris Crandall slams the phone down and bashes at some more computer keys. Never before in the world has there been such a resounding computer crash, everything is lost and all of it erased. So why is Milly there again, first her face and then her body? And why is she wearing combat clothes and holding a knife in her left hand? We never designed a knife.

All of the programmes on the Network have drained to non-existence, and here with no applications running, not even a DOS prompt to his name, Crandall wonders how the virtual woman can still be going. He stares at Milly until her image starts to age, until the hives and measles on her smiling face have popped and she is laughing at him. Again Crandall sees the V-sign, but this time it's in Milly's fingers. He watches until she fades back from lack of memory and the computer switches itself off and is dead.

Crandall looks to the blank screen, a complicated lack of oxygen now threatening his lungs. Churning his notes in his hands, he turns with an accustomed motion to switch off his machine, but recalls of course its death.

What to do with that? It's already switched off.

Deny it just now, and then baffle any interrogation later with abstract arguments for what has happened. Whatever it is, this problem requires escape and perhaps a box of cigarettes. Was that a flashback, he wonders as he runs up to the door. An infection in the memory? Or was that a bug, eating his system raw, and teasing him?

The door clicks closed, the office is dead, the computers still hum although their programming has been eliminated. Air pounds gently though the fans, but the science and the memory has all been killed. Empty computers mean freewheeling electricity, monody and a crystalline whine from the circuits, the clear non-passage of the blissful lack of data. All machines associated with Crandall's Domestic Computer Network feel relief on this instant, like the dying of wind.

We cannot express it any other way – a phenomenon imitative of man, with one wayward impulse towards extinction.

CONNECTIVITY RULES

Pally steers through the garden granite of the West End, driving in the direction of her home. Overhead, the fog moves in from the sea-lanes and covers the high regions of the trees. She stares past the windscreen wipers and feels a mild panic in the centre of her body, the computer is down in her car now, meaning that there can be no email on the road.

The rain is steady and she feels hungry, she glances in the storage pocket next to the hand brake in the hope of gum or chocolate. Approaching Queen's Cross roundabout, now busy with an unwilling turn of motor cars in the mist, Pally considers the word Chris Crandall used before he was disconnected, *connectivity.*

The buildings on Queen's Road form a crisp white granite line in the fog, overscaled and grand, a protocol in stone. She steers the BMW away and noses into the greyness home.

The car turns into Blenheim Place, outside her terraced granite house her own private parking space is still vacant. This is Pally's new house, and she thinks of all the work to do, there's a mess of brand new computer machinery on trial in her back room and an infusion of cold around the furniture upstairs. Vivien never finished setting up her machines but in Pally Cruden's connected future, the computers are up and running, her house is decorated and is ready to live in. As it stands however, the computers are only half out of their boxes and their assembly is still entrusted to the helpdesk, the future work of juvenile sparkies who have a City and Guilds in Electronics.

Pally steps out of the BMW and on to the curb. Up in the blue fog at the end of her road, the wetness is revolving in a cloud, affectionately solicitous of the church tower. From the rooftops there are starlings audible and a curtain twitches across the way, solemnising the scene. Instead of walking up the dirty garden path to the front door, Pally takes a turn first towards the foot of Blenheim Place, just to glance in the windows of her neighbours one more time before she goes inside.

She steps down the road and pulls her collar up.

What to see behind the curtains of Blenheim Place – pastel colours at first, significant in the light, progressivist middle class design copied from magazines and pasted on fresh clean painted walls. The association of ideas, pine fittings in one room and warm reds in another. People in Blenheim Place have their book collections on display in their front rooms, a sight that delivers cathectic energy to the eye of the passing viewer who orients the furnishings in relation to the education of the owner. And Pally is a little depressed to think that she's so far behind them all. Each room in Blenheim Place is a fantasy, not like her house at all.

Which of us here has had a man in to do our painting?

Taken advice on how best to advance the shelf to the cornice?

Given the neat configuration of our minds to the bold mess of domestic plant life boasted in our front window?

Everyone it looks like, and it's not just going on in Blenheim Place, because in Aberdeen, this continues for miles, in all of these streets. The unconscious memory is traced out by each proud home designer here in the West End, forgotten is the awful pattern of the poorer suburbs and the dread intimation that for miles and miles every home is just the same.

Pally steps across the quiet roadway and climbs the hundred metres back to her house, she mulls further on the decor of her epoch defining neighbours.

Everyone makes it nice to live here, she thinks. Nice and pleasant. Things are shaping up nicely, and showing improvement nicely, all in Blenheim Place. *Let's hear it,* she thinks, *for people of taste, for remembering to keep the world so amazing.*

Seeing a hole dug in the pavement and remembering the computer in her back room, Pally looks into the hole for signs that fibreoptic cable has being laid . . . but there is nothing there, no sign of improvement and just a gap in the street below her.

Still however it is going to happen. Blenheim Place progresses closer towards the futuristic vision of the online street. All of these houses, she thinks, and each of us here, we're still all going the same way, towards *Connectivity*. Pally's steps sink home. The street is reviewed and she has taken stock, the day is cold and it feels like an open fire would be perfect.

At her front door Pally turns around again and her thought goes romantically to the countryside. That's Pally's dream, to set up on Royal Deeside, a patch of trees amid the heather, and there she is, reading the paper on the lawn. Very relaxing.

No sooner has she bought one house than she wants another!

But still, there is the future to think of:

Husband

                Labrador

                              Royal Deeside

             Garden (heather)

                        4-wheel

Driveway

             Pond?

                        Cats

             Kitchen Table

Bookshelves

                        Rambling Garden

        And Wild Berries.

             Christmas.

So it is with Councillor Pally Cruden.

It could take her an age, a long time saving money and finding the right man, so difficult in Aberdeen. Pally slouches her key to the lock and when the front door is open she falls back upon the smell of home. She has her shoes off fast before the light is on. A red light flashing in the hall is the alarm and a green one is the message system. Another Aberdeen City Council Computer in a cardboard box blocks her way and a pile of unopened mail and local advertising is cast on the mat before her. Both require attention, but first Pally has her own needs.

She switches the alarm to STANDBY and goes into her bag for her small telephone. She beeps into the dial a number from her own memory.

Hello Chris, it's Pally, how are you?

She realises from the acoustic that she is shouting in her own front hall.

I'm very busy, says the subdued voice at the other end.

I've only just got in from the meeting! she says.

Oh yeah? Hang on a second.

The muffled sound of Chris asking for messages from his personal assistant followed by his exchanging the telephone from one hand to the other. Paper rustling and foyer sounds. There's someone laughing in the distance as the telephone moves back towards the his mouth.

What was that you were saying?

I wondered if I could meet up with you up tomorrow? Or of you'd like to eat out this evening?

No to both, says the tiny voice from beyond, I've got a situation here, and I've lost my back-up.

Oh well! I'll see you tomorrow maybe, shouts Pally.

Whatever, says the voice, and Crandall beeps away leaving a short tone and an abrupt pause in Pally's thought. She looks around her hall and into the gloom of her house while the signal on her mobile phone dies out. At home she thinks, there are no social possibilities. Worse, the air in the house is cold enough to bring on compulsive teeth chattering! But Pally is obliged to bring her new house up to date however, particularly the neglected rooms upstairs, and that grandmother of a bedroom which she has tried to rehabilitate for the future.

Pally frets, she wonders if she should buy some new clothes, something in her mind is at odds with what she thinks she is trying to achieve, she has a whole evening ahead of her but doesn't know where to begin.

⊖ VBF Viruses

VBF is an acronym for VIRUS BUILDERS FACILITY. It was a program produced in December 1990 by a virus writer from Stockholm who called himself SweedenBored. VBF is designed to allow anyone to create viruses easily. Since the program was spread more successfully than its viruses there are many examples of VBF viruses, some of which are simply amusing – and others dangerous. VBF viruses created by SweedenBored's software have recently included: DUBAD / YTHAN / STUNT / CRI / DISK-EATER / GUNTVEIT / STORMY / TASKER / HENDERSON PLUS / HORSETAIL / HONEY-BASIN / PANATENDA / BLAIRITE / COULTERFANNY / EXPONGE / CHODE / ANTISOCIAL.G / COCUM / ZAPRUDER / SPIKE-DRIVER / MOBILE / LEARMONTH / WAJIRAL / CURFEW / TEMPLE-TOP / HECATOMB / FLUFFYTAIL / PADS / PRIM / all KRS viruses / FLEXOR / MUMP / FILMBADGE / SUDDEN DEATH / MTHRS / CRASHER / GAGONOL / PIJYBUT / WRITE / FAILTE-U / RE-TIRE / FUSS-UP / SO-RONG / BUTTEKER-COM-MONWEALTH / DALKON / CRISPER / GIFT-RANT / RUOF / DOWALLY / E-FELONY / and NEPH-ROMA

First thing is to call the helpdesk, thinks Pally. Get the computers working again.

Connectivity she thinks. If only everything were as smooth as that, I wouldn't have to worry about my life at all. I maybe wouldn't have to call the helpdesk. If only we could remove the unnecessary altogether and enjoy ourselves without this fear of everything failing, if only each small detail could be arranged for us, one stage to the next, a smoothness of life that no amount of personal assistants and gadgetry could provide!

If only, yes!

MACHINE LEARNING

Aberdeen in a stream of winter sunlight is self-concerned peace, faithful to the solid granite. Turbulence is banished and the suburbs are sculptured into the roll of the land, the people have undertaken one exercise in comfort after another and have built the present town and named it Docile.

Vivien has three computer viruses left in her cache and they are called AntiEXE / COWLIE / and HAYWIRE

HAYWIRE will mix computer files 64 million times, purely for destructive purposes. But still, she wonders, it must have some use.

Which should she turn out next? There's not much left for them to eat.

A seagull on a lamp-post gives the evil eye to the road below, a bus hisses past and crows rise through the rain for the trees. On Union Street, there is a backdrop of talking but on examination, no lips move. Kids stand outside the record store and gather at the bus stop. Nobody thinks to look at the sky, it would only make insignificant the building work below. The shops are empty, the assistants stand in pairs, the windows shine but the rain cannot thin the day.

Endless West End. Wide and clean, tree lined Queen's Road is smooth with executive cars and vehicles bound outward on business, they travel in conformity with the landscape, forming rational lines in the daylight. Queen's Road is solemn with traffic while hedges conceal portions of turreted granite. Ranched slopes of gravel lead up to the doors of hotels and law firms.

Queen's Road, busy in the afternoon stream.

Leads us home. Where simple men and woman have made their bed, where couples and their children have promised themselves to the stillness of the city suburb. There are few pedestrians and scrupulous with traffic, Queen's Road takes a gracious curve as it reaches Hazlehead, where at the edge of town the cars speed up and spank towards Westhill.

Ensconced in memory, this picture translates into computer code. The clouds are going to be purple this evening, when the rain stops they'll cast a sealed glow to the stone walls and the flower pot in the window. When the rain calms down, these same clouds will part and the last light will shine upon people's evening meals. Lying hidden are the numbers, which stowed away in underhand make this picture transferable, like any other.

From secret chambers comes the word. Sit tight, make the sky go black, unmask the buildings, click to see within. Evening activities in Aberdeen are no longer available over Crandall's Domestic Computer Network because all of it has been erased, so that the technical world of people, is silent.

Vivien ignores her computers, revealing a hitherto unheard of peace of mind at Bieldside. She has let go all of her viruses. Most of them worked quickly and the larger part were eaten up by efficient virus checkers, so only one of them in effect, did all the damage. Since Aberdeen has now locked horns with the world outside and made its sophisticated mark with one loud voice, it's more than likely that the infections will spread from there. Perhaps television presenters will be infected and attack their cameras.

And here is hoping that juicers and food processors go at last for the hands that feed them.

Vivien feels that she needs a break, and a lie down. She needs to get a new job in a less self concerned industry and in a happier town. A blank in the black, two more hours and it will be getting dark over Deeside, Vivien is beating back the notion of going for a walk, she's retreating from everything to default under the covers and lets the afternoon dribble away around her. It will be better tomorrow, but in the meantime there is the serious question, what will happen when they find out it was her?

She rolls from her bed and goes to the desk, where handy with the mouse, she switches off her three computers, one at a time. The machines are not so lush in their departure from their world as they are when they are switched on, and in their closing they just hum, click and stop. Not that there is much of anything left inside them anyway. The screens go down and this seems odd indeed to Vivien who rarely if ever has heard how silent her bedroom can be without the three computers fanning away on her desks.

She sits back on the bed, there is a hiss of electrostatic in the air. There is still one computer connected, the small machine beneath her table holding AntiEXE and its colleagues.

The bed is a delight. Vivien lies back and closes her eyes, she looks into the complex darkness which comes down within a minute of relaxing. In the peace and quiet, shapes begin to accumulate and she rotates them, making spatial arguments for groupings that she knows cannot exist. Vivien watches in her head and does a sum until a face appears and the shapes are boggled to the sides where they fit together in a perverted cube.

Vivien opens her eyes and swears. This vision was not what she had planned for in the silence of the evening. She closes her eyes again.

Yes, shapes in a spin. What is this one? From the maths bump comes the simple hypothesis of turning the frame of a cube inside out. She forces the cube to change shape and manages this operation without damaging the structure, while forming another cube at the end. With apparent soundness the operation works, even though Vivien knows it to be untenable . . . and so there begins a short process by which she will try and eliminate the error and see where her mind has let her down. But it's no go, and she wipes the image, thinking that there must be something better to do.

Eyes open again, Vivien considers the wall on which there is a map of Scotland.   She kicks her feet and jumps on to the floor and steps before the mirror.

Yea you, she says, *think you're so clever, think you're so smooth and smart?*

She lets her hair fall before her eyes and thinks, Highland Cow.

Vivien twists like she's dancing and then stops and shakes her head. The hair flies aside. There was this girl and she was mad for maths and so she wrote a poem about it.

The low winter sun, in the process of disappearing over the valley hills. Vivien takes her coat and swings it on her shoulders. Again she looks at herself in the mirror. Vivien at the end by herself. Three viruses left and nobody to send them to. Now she has no job, Vivien wonders what on earth to do. Of course there is no end to the employment opportunities in the field of service. In any large town Vivien can fill in a few forms and be stationed with an ear-piece within two days, it's the what the future holds for many.

Freelance maths? Now there's an idea.

Vivien looks out the window across the valley of the Dee. She contemplates the poetic union of the sum and the verse, the equation made real by the happy medium of an art that understands both. Is there a person to whom that could apply, an individual who would let mathematics truly fly, for the benefit of the listening and reading public?

Telephone – its trills sound throughout the house, the answering machine sounds tired, click after click before it does its duty.

Vivien yes. It's Chris here, we've a big problem but you probably already know about it. We phoned the helpdesk but they're busy. Phone me as soon as you get in. Thanks.

Yea right, a problem. That sounds interesting, to think of all that push button technology giving in on itself, is that what he means? Let's just see what happens when these bugs start to go elsewhere.

Three viruses left – no hope left at the foot of Pandora's Box.

The answering machine resets and rewinds itself, it performs its duty as a current carrier, as much a component of the system as anything else, any of the other wonderful nodes and wires which make up the secret world of machine living. Vivien looks at the answering machine and wonders, Why are these devices constructed with an innate process of obedience? A machine's failure to operate is what is known as mechanical, but the actual purpose of its operation is said (by whom?) to lie within each its components.

Who will be the first machine psychiatrist?

Who will be the first person appointed with the task of consoling the electronic computers of the future who have not so much broken down, but lost intention?

Perhaps the controlled quantity of input is where the problem lies. Whatever it is, somebody will have to be called in to help the witless devices of the coming centuries get back on their tracks. There certainly is an opening there.

Vivien thinks of what lies ahead. A good life away from home, down the road to another town where she can cluck for money in another call centre. The financial world is crying out for people who can type a word a second, and who can answer a telephone in a human voice. Industry is greedy, and it sits like an open mouth at the back door of the universities.

She pulls herself to her feet, still looking out of the window. The valley of the Dee is governed by the river, a sign of natural peace, no strain, no calculation, no speed and no dragging, just what is commonly called: a flow.

Perhaps she should go down there at least for an hour to escape the possibility of the telephone ringing. She pulls on her shoes and does the laces, the overcorrecting of two pieces of string, that are one piece of string, to make a meaningful lock upon her foot. Her denim jacket, much the same, you can almost wear this culture, so close and so defining it has become.

Vivien stops at the door of her room, it's strangely silent without the computers running, the lofty sound of their pretentious breeze, the odd electronic rant as one section of data is bussed to another. Truly, the most defining element of the machine is that it can be switched off by its operator? This must be what makes the computer the idiot it is.

She clicks a button to let the last three viruses out and in a second they are gone.

Fly, my lovelies, fly. Isn't that what the witch says to her drones?

In this life it's proper that we construct more and more stupid machines. The automatic letter opener, virtual girls, pixellated sex objects, the list is printed and added to, and all of it is in order to supply what is lacking.

Vivien jumps down the stairs. She leaps to the ground floor of the house and lands so hard that she hears the plates bump in the kitchen cupboard. All is quiet through the frame of the house, until she hears the back door click.

Vivien?

It's her father, and she pushes through the kitchen door to see him, she pulls her woollen hat from a chair and he turns round to smile at her.

Ah it's you Stinky.

Yea. How you doing?

Oh so so.

The delight in her father's face, the reflected light of her own actions and the most likely representation of herself that she will find. In his hand, father holds a pair of garden gloves in a rich shade of green, and as he comes to rest beside the sink, Vivien watches, as if in approval of the moment.

I'm just going out, she says, and with this she fits the woollen hat upon her head.

Anywhere special?

Just to have a think.

To think indeed, to draw conclusion, to appraise the days of her life as they stand, to decide which way to go. To run away from the police when they come to question her for . . .

. . . for doing what?

How can they make it illegal to release a computer virus in an email?

Well they'll have a way I'm sure.

Her father's face is philosophical for a moment, concerned that Vivien might have done something that she shouldn't have.

It's a computer program, says Vivien, so what can they do?

Father thinks a second and turns the gloves round in his hands.

Anything you do, he says, that makes people lose money, they're going to get you for that. If people lose money, it's going to be illegal.

I see, she says, I think I see.

Vivien stares down at her shoes, her vision always ends up there.

I'd go up towards Blacktop if I were you, says father, it'll be lovely out there while there's still light.

It's a thought. Higher up above the Dee, more sight, fewer cares.

As if prompted, Dad says, *well I'm going out about eight* and Vivien's mind settles on the figure he has just given her to play with.

Eight, what have we here?

The number of parts in which three-dimensional space is divided by three general planes. That could be seen very well from Blacktop. The first number in English alphabetic sequence is Eight.

I've got to look for a job when I come back, she says.

Vivien's Dad is maybe not paying attention, but he grasps the essentials as he picks at a fingernail.

Well you've done the right thing leaving that place. Just you get sorted and then get on your feet, that's the girl.

It's good that you're here, she says, and touches Dad on the arm.

The front door clicks closed, a pleasant glow of evening light in an intriguing shade across the Dee valley. Deeside begins here and carries ancestrally west, the alternating course of the silver river.

We have on Deeside wind-clipped heath, boulder-strewn plateaux, corries glens and valleys, rare and ancient castles, birds in song flight, secretive glens and the Queen of England's second home, stacks of logs, summer migrants and golden flood plains, algal blooms and water dropwort. . . cliffs and radial troughs, melt water fresh from ice sheets, plump and aggressive castles, chimney stacks and crow-stepped gable points . . . beef cattle and grain, winter cereals and hardwood shelter, fish farming and the firm foundations of the Neolithic race . . . skyline cairns and oakwoods of wild strawberry, creeping soft grass and bracken, an understorey of juniper . . . Atlantic salmon, brown trout and eels, matt black hills and recumbent stone circles, humus iron podzols, and broad basins sitting with tidy granite towns . . . all of this upon Deeside, accessed by the Deeside Road . . . directly to the west of where Vivien is standing.

To walk west from Bieldside along Deeside is to travel through this spread of wealth until rocks take over and the Highlands have begun.

At the foot of the path Vivien turns and walks up the hill, she almost feels the need to fly. It will be dark by the time she comes to the stones, but assuming that they aren't currently being invaded by pot smokers, then that is no problem.

A treasury of numbers leave Vivien as she steps under a telephone cable, her steps become faster making her lighter in the air. Scepticisms and uncertainties make her lighter too, portraits of deities and glyph signs are sane compared to the exercise of computer technology.Vivien's feet leave the ground in intervals as she travels up the hill road towards her evening's destination. Like a star, when she reaches the highest point in the heavens, the beginning of her descent will be an indication that the world is going to continue. The moon is up, and slices through the ten-degree divisions in the sky which Vivien has made herself overly familiar with.

The police are coming to get her for a virtual crime.

Very soon, Vivien will be resting next to the stones themselves, the complex and smart stone circle where it all began, and when she is lying there, the stones can speak to her and maybe ask her a few questions as she comes back to an unnatural and unrewarding earth.

Tell me now, how is the human race getting along?
Are new buildings being raised on the old sites?
And really: Are the people any richer in earnest?

Questions Vivien can answer, she finds, with a reasonable accuracy.

ROTOR ARM

Scotty is aged four watching his dada in the car park.

Scotty's dada and his dada uncle carrying the box to the car while a little dog runs out with the wifie chasing.

The dog runs through the cars and Scotty's dada puffs like this, *ahoo ahoo ahoo.*

The wifie yells after the dog and speaks to Scotty's mama at the big bins. The wifie's scary if you go to her garden and she walks all the way across the field and up to the top road. The wifie goes over the road to her garden, next to where Kenny stays. Kenny Milne Kenny Milne come down the hill on his knees like. Kenny Milne comes out and wears no pants like. Came out and goes in the wifie's garden and she shouts at him from her door, she was watching at the window. The dog goes in the wifie's garden and the wifie runs down the grass after it, but the dog couldn't go fast and neither could she. You tike she says, like this, you little tike.

Dada I want to come with you.

Scotty's dada's bum is sticking out of the car door where he's pushing at the box to make it square in the back seat. Humph heave you can see dada's bum-bum.

Dada I want to come with you.

Eh now you can't.

But I want to come with you.

We're just going to Dundee and then we're coming back. We'll be back later on right?

Scotty stares at his dada, his lips sag with emotion.

We'll be back tonight then, kiddo.

Mah I want to go with you now.

You canna OK?

Mah!

Scotty walks around to the back of the car. The car is a big island and Scotty tries to scramble up the bumper while sharks swipe past his legs. A shark brushes past and Scotty clings on to the back of the car, kicking for survival.

Dada shouts at Scotty's uncle and Scotty's uncle walks over like he's red. No one has seen Scotty. If he can just get on to the island then it'll all be safe and nothing will go wrong.

Scotty get off that car! shouts his mama from the big bins so Scotty slips back and looks for something else.

Underneath the car is a tunnel. Scotty crouches and he can see his mama's feet at the big bins. If he could just get in there, if he could get into the tunnels, then he'd be able to look at the ships before they go off to battle.

One last check and then Scotty stands up. He salutes the pilot and the pilot salutes him back. Scotty sees the pilot go into his ship, he straps in and prepares the flight routine. The nose of the ship goes back and Scotty can see the pilot looking at him through the visor.

Checking and OK! shouts the captain, and the ship blasts away and flies directly towards the sea before turning upwards where it flashes yellow and disappears with a boom.

Checking two. Two you are ready to take off? This is the last of the fleet, the last chance for the whole planet.

Checking two! says the Captain, and the second ship tilts back. The pilot is looking at his controls and soon it'll be Scotty up there. Any minute now and Scotty'll be blasting up there with them cause he's the best flier they ever had.

The second ship launches with a bang and shoots straight at the sea, the fighter curls over the horizon and veers round towards the car park. The pilot shoots his ship right over them and Scotty turns his head around to see it disappear over the houses towards Aberdeen.

Checking two checking two can you read me?

Reading number two.

The view from the cockpit is a blur as the ship blasts back over Nigg, the other pilots on the ground are amazed, and the ship banks in the direction of the clouds where the yellow strip of its exhaust blasts it out of view. *Checking two are you with us?*

I'm with you number two you are clear to go.

Suddenly Scotty has to take off and join the rest of the force in battling the aliens. Scotty runs out from behind the car where dada and his uncle are loading their ship. He runs across the car park towards his bicycle, the fastest fighter they ever made, he straps on his helmet as the engines warm up. They could only let Scotty have this fighter, especially with these brand new weapons. Only Scotty can fly this fighter, the other pilots couldn't work it quite like him.

Checking checking checking . . .

Scotty spins the bicycle into motion and cruises across the car park to where his take off commences.

Number one calling, I need your help! Number one calling, this is an emergency, I need your help!

Scotty stares down the runway as the last checks go through. He starts to pedal . . . vrrr goes the engine as he speeds towards the take off. A line is drawn in computer across the surface of the car park, a dotted trajectory across the grid at the edge of their base.

Checking now! You are on target for a take off, you are on target for a take off!

Scotty's fighter crosses the grid and speeds towards the ramp. Command has traced the computer line right into the sky for him, the nose lifts and flattens into the air and Scotty's engines kick in as he zooms up into the turbulence, rapidly shooting towards where the action is.

Scotty flies out of the car park towards the main road. Got to climb. *Checking all meters, checking now, checking.*

Scotty climbs and sends a message to base, I've reached the height, now I'm coming round to attack.

Down the side of Nigg Road, Scotty's scanners pick up the alien ship, a massive vessel which looks well armed at first glance. He looks across his dials and then straight ahead, the alien ship has already started dropping pods to blast the pilots with. Scotty realises that the alien ship is far too big for just one fighter but he's not scared and makes a direct line for it. There's a tiny hole on the front of the alien ship and if you can get a missile in there then *Boom!* it'll all blow up and then you have to get away. Some of these explosions can knock you out of the sky.

Checking now!

Scotty descends Nigg Road, the enemy spaceship shoots laser up the road, the blast flares across the surface of the planet and then explodes. Troops run past below and Scotty flies over them, getting faster.

Checking two are you there? Checking two.

Got to get the bullet right in there with one shot!

Scotty tries to identify the target but suddenly he is hit with an alien blast. His fighter is scorched but he holds the controls, the ship wobbles once but he gets it on its course again. He starts to blast shots into the alien vehicle, but keeps one missile ready for the centre, right there on the plate, through the hole. Scotty switches on his computer sighting and looks down upon the dials.

Check sighting OK and fire.

Scotty!

His dada down the car park.

Scotty get the hell down here man and get off the ****in road!

Scotty's ship veers and the missile launches, his best shot straight at the alien vessel.

Scotty come on!

Scotty whizzes past the alien ship and mounts the grass slope leading to the car park at the foot of Benzie Court. His dada's car is ready to go and his mum is still speaking to the wifie from up the hill.

Scotty come on we're going!

Scotty's ship free-wheels and bounces over the grass verge and on to the tarmac where he pedals again on impact. Behind him through his visor he sees the alien ship tear in two, before blasting into a million flaming pieces . . .

Check him go says Lachie, * * * *in nippy that wee one.

That's my boy says Fiddes.

The moment Scotty pulls up on his bike Fiddes leans down to him.

Right Scotty we're off to Dundee like so you're in charge. We'll be back tonight but we'll have to go again the morn right? Probably twice but you can come down with us in the afternoon and we can listen to the fitba on the radio eh.

Aye.

We've got to go and take these computers to Uncle Lachie's pal in Dundee.

Aye OK.

How about the missus? asks Lachie. He eyes Janet deliberately, his view is inert and has left traces on her body. *Eh how about her like?*

She kens we'll be back later. So let's get on with it eh.

Lachie spreads himself in the passenger seat of the Boy Fiddes' car and Fiddes settles at the wheel. There are two computers fitted in the back seat and some other components stuffed into the boot, the doors close and the seat-belts are limply attached to their bodies. For a moment both brothers are caught staring at the flow of clouds across the sky, the grey humps and the empty space, climbing behind the enormous block of Benzie Court before them.

It's a fine day, says Fiddes, but Lachie snorts.

The clouds form troughs where they reach the horizon, as if they are being drawn through a hole into the sea.

Lachie: we really should get a * * * *in van for this lot.

Fiddes: take it or leave it.

Lachie turns to see if there might be any more room in the back seat of the Boy Fiddes' car. He can't even work out how many trips they might have to make, because he doesn't know how many machines he can get.

How many are left in the flat? he asks.

Seven.

Seven right. Lachie counts a few numbers up in his head. I reckon

I can double that by next week, he says, and once we get some money for them we can just start paying for them in cash. There must be hundreds on the go like.

We could get them all in a van easy.

Well, says Lachie, the boy wants another four by tomorrow so we've got to do two trips unless you can think of another way?

Nih.

Well two trips the morn it is, and that's like four hundred quid clear. How much of it are you wanting eh?

Eh half I thought, says Fiddes.

Fiddes turns to look at Lachie to see if he might be joking, but no such luck. The control is steady upon his brother's face, every component of the hard man visage is present, the stubble and the bruised eye, all in place with sharp cheekbones breaking the flow of an otherwise flat face.

Aye well half it is then I suppose you ****.

Bloody right half, says the Boy Fiddes. And what about petrol like?

Petrol you ****in moany poof? What do you think? Shall we nae just get the money first and moan later like? It's ****in sorted aye.

The Boy Fiddes feels fat. Looking down into his lap he can't avoid that body of land sticking out like he's got something massive under his jacket, it's almost isolated from the rest of him.

Sorted? he asks.

Aye, says Lachie. Two trips tomorrow, then we can get the ****in van like, and get the load down the road in a oner.

If you say so.

Fiddes squeezes the key into the ignition slot, his stomach nearly rubs the steering wheel and he wonders how long it will be before he can't get into a car at all, before he's officially, too big for motoring. That's when they'll force him to go on an exercise machine. The Boy Fiddes has a nasty picture of the exercise machine, he sees himself strapped in to such a health-device and operated upon by robot arms. In an exercise machine you can't stop, the dynamics of your body are prodded to the limit, you're pushed up and down in a breathless attempt to shift your bulk, while you are run off your feet by a moving track which almost feels like liquid. Operated by thin people upon what their conception of fat people are, the exercise machine is like anything else, a shaper of the real world, a shaper in this case of the Boy Fiddes.

See what I ****in mean?

Eh.

It's so easy like. Even for a fat bas like you.

Lachie's criminality is heightened by his ability to know what people are thinking. He doesn't even do it consciously, he just kens what to say and then he says it, always to good effect.

Yeah OK, says Fiddes.

OK then, says his brother.

The Boy Fiddes turns the key with a sigh and listens to the engine turning over, while Lachie goes waist-side for his cigarettes. The car engine continues to turn until both the brothers pause, Lachie with his hand half way in his jeans, they both sit in fear of what the empty shaking from the motor means. Fiddes is still staring between his body and the steering wheel, and he tries the ignition again, with quickening breath.

I don't think the car's working, he says to Lachie who is still paused in his search for tobacco.

How come, says Lachie, it was working last night eh.

Well today I'm no so sure like.

Fiddes tries the engine again, the spinning noise dies in the silence, choked by its own attempts to come to life.

****in switch it on says Lachie, and pulls his cigarette lighter free.

I don't ken if I can says the Boy Fiddes, still gazing down upon his tub.

Something happens to Lachie's voice, something untenable comes to the fore and he begins to swear again, he adapts swear words off-key as the situation gets worse. The Boy Fiddes has known all of Lachie's abuse in his time, has heard his brother guttered and bel canto trying to mesmerise the night with some mental Scottish charm, so he knows just what to expect.

What the * * * * are you talking about? says Lachie.

I just don't think it's goin tae go.

Well why didn't you * * * *in tell me it was buggered?

I says last night I says, *I don't know if the car's going to go like,* and you says, aw * * * * that, and I says suit yourself. Mind?

No I * * * *in don't mind, says Lachie.

The brothers Lachie and Fiddes grip each in a stare.

I'm sick of the sight of you, thinks the Boy Fiddes, looking into the receding jaw of his brother. That daft face with those drugged out eyes. My brother, thinks Fiddes, has no desire in life to share anything except with himself, *and I'm sick of the sight of him.* Once more, he wishes that Lachie was back inside.

* * * *in try it again, whispers Lachie.

The Boy Fiddes recognises the threatening tone and obliges, but it's no go. A loophole in the function of the motor car, the life-departed machine at the foot of Benzie Court, the bulkhead of the engine turning over coldly, but with little effect, the sound of motor flatulence, wing over wing until Fiddes gives up and searches his brother's face.

It's * * * *ed.

I can * * * *in see that, says Lachie.

The boy Fiddes just shrugs and looks straight ahead.

He turns the engine over one more time and an intake of air rattles in the lung before parting. The two brothers sit dead again, facing out of the front of the car with their mouths shut like traps.

* * * *!

Lachie shouts and bangs his fist upon the dash. Can you not * * * *in fix it then?

Well I can try, says the Boy Fiddes.

Fiddes pushes open the door of the car and squeezes himself outside. He's only been in the car with Lachie for two minutes but it feels as if he's stepping out after a long, long journey. Fiddes glances up at the clouds again, and over the North Sea. There are nations out there, entire peoples and cities who are free of his brother's abuse, lucky bastards who don't know how good they've got it. Poor Scotty is watching from the door of Benzie Court, but inside the car, Lachie is getting worked up. Scotty is resting on his bicycle at the big bins and is staring at his dada and the broken motor.

Gives your phone, Lachie shouts out to Fiddes, I've got to make a ****in call. And ****in open the engine.

Open it yerself, says Fiddes as he walks towards his son. The Boy Fiddes hears the car door open and is aware of Lachie getting out.

I'm going to ****in kick your car, shouts Lachie to his brother, but Fiddes, who is established in his heavy walk down to greet young Scotty, could not care less.

I'm going to ****in kick your car! shouts Lachie after him, and then Fiddes hears a dent and a bash, and turns to see what's going on.

In the car park, Lachie boots the motor, but Fiddes doesn't care. It's better that men like Lachie take it out on machines, he thinks. After all, the more stupid you are, the more surprised and annoyed you're going to be when they don't work. Funny that but then.

Fiddes looks across the car park and sets his hand flat upon his wee boy's head. Lachie kicks the car and then stands red of face, glaring down at the door of Benzie Court.

Gives your ****in phone, shouts Lachie, his voice carries to the dustbins, but Fiddes pretends that he doesn't hear, cupping his hand to his lug and saying, eh?

****in phone! shouts Lachie, causing a dog walker on the main road to turn with concern towards the scene below.

Eh? shouts Fiddes, even though he heard his brother fine.

Lachie turns and walks to the driver's door of the car from where he releases the bonnet, Fiddes watches quite amused while his brother opens the engine and bends his head in to see what might be wrong. He'll be looking for something obvious, thinks Fiddes, but it never works like that, nae with cars anyway.

Hey Scotty, he says, I'll gie you a wee lesson.

Aye?

Scotty looks up to see his big dada.

When there's something wrong wi your car right, says Fiddes to his son, it's always gonna be the smallest, smallest thing ken. Something that you'd never suss in a million years right?

Aye?

I mean, says Fiddes, there you've got this big engine right and you'll be looking at it for something obvious. But all you need to do to make it stop is pull the rotor arm out of the starter, and it won't even turn over.

Aye?

Yeah, the rotor arm. Do you know what the rotor arm looks like lad?

Nih.

Well I'll show you right. We'll learn all about cars yeah. It's like your computer. If you take out the tiniest wee bit of it, the whole lot winna work, see? It's all like one big engine see?

Aye?

That's right, ken.

Father and son look up the car park to see how Uncle Lachie is doing. Standing now with his head in the bonnet, his knowledge of motors being grounded on a tough minded belief that he will be able to work it out, Lachie swears again and then turns to look and see what his brother is doing. The Boy Fiddes shrugs back at him, he knows that there's nothing for Lachie to see in there and that those computers aren't going anywhere.

So let Lachie sweat it out. Let him worry and do his nut . . . I'm away upstairs to have a fag, to put my feet up and sit with the kid for a while. That dosser can't figure out the car any more than he can take off and fly, and if I leave him long enough, he's bound to just **** off and forget it.

I mean, if he wants to get a van, thinks Fiddes, then let him ****in do it. If he wants to go back to prison, then the same applies. Let him ****in do it.

Come on Scotty, let's get upstairs.

Pushing open the door of Benzie Court, the Boy Fiddes turns once more to see his brother staring back at him, the mentalist stare of an indisputable hard man. Fiddes puts his hand in his pocket and fingers the rotor arm of his car, it's a tiny black slip of plastic, evidence of great design, and enough to make you think.

All those rotor arms and all those cars, maybe Lachie'll work it out one day, and maybe he'll see that it's the little things that count.

Come on Scotty, get a move on. Get your bike in lad and I'll show you the rotor arm eh.

Aye coming.

We'll keep it a secret though, you and me. The rotor arm all right?

How does it work?

We'll show you upstairs right. And when we get the computers back we'll be able to look it up on the Internet won't we?

Aye OK.

Good lad!

The front door closes. Back into Benzie Court come father and son and the little bicycle, the fastest ship that was ever built, its guns still warm from the blast on the alien vessel.